HUNTER'S HEART SERIES BOOK ONE
REDEMPTION'S
CURE

Upcoming Novels

Hunter's Heart Series Book Two
Redemption's Curse

Upcoming Series

The CD Chronicles

Thank you for buying this book, I sincerely hope you enjoy the world of Ecalardia.

Like all authors, I would love to get an honest review, they are the golden coins of our trade. If you don't feel that my book deserves a five-star rating, then an honest, civil, and thoughtful review can help make sure I improve so that you and other readers may enjoy future novels. If you love my book and believe that it deserves a five-star rating, then that can help other readers know that it is a good read.

So please consider whether you would feel comfortable leaving a review after you read the book. Once again, thank you for buying this book.

TAUNIA NEILSON

HUNTER'S HEART SERIES BOOK ONE
REDEMPTION'S
CURE

Celestial
House
Publishing

Publisher's Cataloging-in-Publication Data

Names: Neilson, Taunia, author.
Title: Redemption's cure / Taunia Neilson.
Series: Hunter's Heart
Description: Centerville, UT: Celestial House Publishing, 2018. | Summary: Tiel Lambrie is blamed for starting an apocalyptic prophecy. Now, she must save those she loves from its dangers while deciding what is the truth.
Identifiers: LCCN 2018908849 | ISBN 978-1-7321365-4-0 (Hardcover) | 978-1-7321365-1-9 (pbk.) | 978-1-7321365-5-7 (kdp pbk.) | 978-1-7321365-0-2 (ebook) | 978-1-7321365-3-3 (audio CD) | 978-1-7321365-6-4 (audio file) | 978-1-7321365-2-6 (online resource)
Subjects: LCSH Human-animal relationships--Fiction. | Bounty hunters--Fiction. | Ghosts--Fiction. | Prophecies--Fiction. | Dystopias. | Fantasy fiction. | BISAC YOUNG ADULT FICTION / Science Fiction / Apocalyptic & Post-Apocalyptic | YOUNG ADULT FICTION / Fantasy / Epic
Classification: LCC PZ7.1 N41 Re 2018 (print) | PZ7.1 N41 (ebook) | DDC [Fic]--dc23

Printed in the USA
First Printing December 2018
ISBN: 978-1-7321365-1-9
LCCN: 2018908849

Celestial House Publishing
P.O. Box 16
Centerville, UT 84010

15 14 13 12 11 10/10 9 8 7 6 5 4 3 2 1

Book Editors/Photograph: Raquel Jones & Valerie Bybee
Book Cover created by ebooklaunch.com

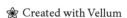 Created with Vellum

There have been many people who have helped with this project. They have all left their marks in some small way, of which I am eternally grateful.

But there is only one person who stayed by my side, and never gave up on me. He stayed through all the frustrating lessons, the ups and downs, the enumerable changes, and always believed I had what it took to be an author.

That person is my eternal lover, personal confident, best friend forever, my husband Joe. It is to him I dedicate this book.
Thank you love

GLOSSARY

Acodoe – *Ah-coo-doe* – A clan of large serpents that are sentient. They are an ancient clan that are an omen to the beginning of the Day of Renewal.

Badoe – *Bah-doe* – A large creature that is carnivorous and looks likes a hairy form of the earth elephant. The southern merchants have herded and domesticated these animals for generations.

Bamboodii – *Bam-booh-dee* – a golden straw that turns as strong as stone after it's harvested. It is the main source for constructing homes.

Coulliou – *Cool-lee-oh* – The main god that is worshipped on Ecalardia.

Ecalardia – *Ek-ah-lard-ee-ah* – The world on which the characters live.

Jainu – *Jah-new* – Aven and Tiel's initiate (apprentice).

Jonaxx – *Joan-ax* – The King of the Acodoe and pure black.

Laisen – *Lay-zeen* – Two of the hunter clan leaders. Mistress Laisen (Lidena – *Lah-deen-ah*) and Master Laisen (Radames – *Rah-dam-eez*).

Larquetz – *Lar-cet-z (hard k)* – it is the Hunter Clan's form of a trial.

Luhitzu – *Lou-hit-zoo* – According to the Hunter Clan, it is a hunter that has been ostracized due to the hunter continually breaking their laws or committing a serious crime.

Oljnen – *Say 'old' with a hard 'j' sound then add an 'nen' sound* – A diamondback rattlesnake acodoe who is a gem guardian.

Rutzix – *Rut-zix* – A box of energy that Tiel puts her soul current into. The soul current represents the form of her telepathy, and when it is in the rutzix she is safe from the thoughts and emotions of others.

Sendenia – *Sen-den-ee-ah* – The Queen of the Acodoe. She is a green diamondback cobra and wears a diamond gem stone, in the form of an octave star, below her right hood.

Staged – When someone tries to take something away from another, or does something sneaky or underhanded to get their way. Usually by using treachery or a grand scheme.

Watosh – *Wah-toosh* – A watosh is a tree that makes up the Watosh forest which is also known as just 'the Watosh'. It is strong as stone and the forest large enough to hide gigantic predators.

PROLOGUE

LUHITZU'S HYMN

I cannot see you. I can only remember.
You, who are spineless, brainless, and insignificant. You, who arise, walk and sleep.
You, who experience sorrow, anger, and hate.
You do not see nor remember what these gifts are for.
The Gods, they claim to know what they see in their eternal scope.
They sit in their celestial citadels taking innocence in exchange for eternal suffering.
They are blind to everything but their own desires which chain our souls to their lofty dreams.
We will arise from our slumber and bind, intertwining our hearts, bodies, and souls.
We will see and remember how to use our sorrow, anger, and hate, reclaiming what was stolen.
We will march, trampling all who oppose us, crushing the holy sanctuaries beneath our feet, shouting for joy when the smoke ascends to the citadels on high.
Time is of no essence. I am here. I am waiting.

Tome 3 - Luhitzus - Author Unknown

CHAPTER 1

STAGED BOUNTY

Several dark streaks of blood covered the green leaves of the plant that the huntress was studying. She stroked the plant's limb with the blade of her Hunter's Heart as the plant wrapped its limb around her gloved hand. The whip-like branch tightened for a moment and then went limp and fell away, unable to sense any exposed skin. The huntress turned and observed the surrounding lower forest. She spotted more than a few plants with blood reflecting off their motionless branches.

"Where are you, Maestro?" she yelled into the depths of the Watosh Forest, an entity said to be aged past the memories of men. The forest was quiet now though the blood testified that the lower forest had been active earlier. However, the massive watosh trees showed no sign of activity. They rarely did even though she had heard them groan or seen them shudder before. The huntress turned away from the forest to a pair of footprints in front of her and sunk her Hunter's Heart into the surrounding soil.

Its translucent hollow blade with inward-curved teeth tore into the soil testing the sponginess of the forest floor. The rolling waves of the blue crystal handle fit perfectly in her hand. Its pleasant warm heat matched the day's weather. The poisonous liquid inside the blade splashed with her movements.

She dragged the knife's teeth along her skin, depositing soil samples onto her tan arm. The soil easily parted underneath the pressure of her fingers. Turning back to the bushes of the lower forest, she rubbed her chin for a moment, then stood.

"I need a report from you, Maestro!" she yelled again. She let out a deep sigh and leaned against a tree trunk while fondling the crystal clasp attached to her shirt collar. She let her fingers bounce over the intricate pattern of a grown watosh tree.

The upper foliage moved in a wave, indicating a traveler among the intertwining branches above. Tiel stood and banged her Hunter's Heart against the tree, and the clanging sound of crystal against stone reverberated through the clearing. The wave movement progressed closer while a deep rumble sounded.

"What took you so long?" She moved a strand of russet-gray-streaked hair out of her face. "Shea, the sun, is faster than you are today. She is already peeking over the horizon as she begins her second path."

"Tiel, being seventeen and a member of your species has given you a huge lack of patience," a deep voice resonated from within the foliage. "It's a pity. I found a badoe, and it is hunting."

"That is noteworthy," Tiel acknowledged. She took a piece of leather cloth out from a shirt pocket and tied up her hair to keep another wayward strand from tickling her cheek. "Is there anything else that is noteworthy?"

"Yes, the badoe's scent was from the stables." An oversized panther leaped out of the watosh trees. The feline stood for a moment, studying Tiel. Its twitching tail matched the mischief in its light blue eyes. The panther's powerful muscles rippled underneath white fur with blue tufts as it walked up to her.

"Right again, old friend. It's not tax time. So, a stable owner wouldn't need to release his merchandise to avoid taxes."

"You've never told me about the job," the animal purred as he stopped eye-to-eye with the huntress. His lips and gritted teeth formed a teasing snarl. Tiel smiled and playfully shoved Maestro's face aside.

"Did you expect me to tell you with the gossips' orbs around?" She elbowed Maestro in the stomach. As usual, he refused to flinch.

"How much is the bounty?" Maestro looked back at her.

"Enough to give a boost to our abode savings."

"Boring." Maestro spun around on his hind legs, landed, and walked away. "de Menzaile will be ecstatic."

"Hegert is involved," Tiel smirked when Maestro turned back. "Could you tell what scent the badoe followed?"

"No, I only found its scent, and I found no footprints. I thought you said you received a messenger's note?"

"I did. Telepathically, Hegert's stench was all over it."

"So, what do we have?" Maestro prompted her.

"Well, the note said we were to go find someone who 'wandered' into the Watosh Forest and bring them back alive. Also, we were not to let any forest predators leave. But these prints show…"

"Two of the prints are from acodoe warriors." Maestro bellowed out a yawn as he stretched. "They carried something heavy, dropped it here, and left. Then a third set of prints wander into the forest."

"Now who's impatient?" Tiel chuckled.

"You have that lopsided smile that signals you want to drag things out," Maestro answered. "I thought you were in a hurry."

Tiel raised her eyebrows and squatted down pointing her Hunter's Heart at the footprints, its jagged teeth gleaming in Shea's light. "The footprints do have the acodoe warrior serpent mark." She turned to the forest behind her and pointed the Hunter's Heart at the bushes. "Yet, if you look closer, you will find that there is blood on the leaves and stems of the lower forest plants. We both know the lower forest loves to harass uncovered appendages, which short hems and sleeves are traits for an acodoe warrior's ceremonial garb."

"True." Maestro shrugged and looked at her.

"Think, my dear friend." She banged the Hunter's Heart against her low-heeled, knee-high, brown leather boots, then waved her arms down showing the brown outfit that framed her curved, athletic body. As she stood once more, a light leather tunic dropped below her hipline. Leather pants stayed tucked inside the boots, and the tunic sleeves covered the tops of the elbow-high gloves. She watched Maestro's eyes widen with under-standing.

"Of course," he grumbled in embarrassment, "what fully trained acodoe warrior would go into the Watosh wearing only his ceremonial garb?"

"So, there were henchmen sent to carry someone out of a village," Tiel explained as she parted a slit in her pant legs. Then she parted two folds within her leg underneath and deposited the Hunter's Heart into a skin pocket lined with steel gray biometal. "More than likely the Bamboodii Harvest Festival…"

"Because that is where acodoe warriors garbed in ceremonial robes would be at," Maestro growled in a low tone. "My brain is too slow today."

"No, more than likely my young age trumpets your age, old cat," Tiel boasted as he chuckled. "So, we have an abduction and dumping in the Watosh Forest, a carnivorous predator loosed from the stables, and an anonymous note."

"Yes, Hegert's stench is all over this. She's trying to set you up for failure."

"Yes, she's trying to stage me." Tiel sat down and rested her arms on her crossed legs. "You expect something more?"

"So, who does the High Councilwoman Hegert want dead," Maestro mused, "besides you?"

"That is why we are out here. If we must fight a badoe, I may double the bounty. I will need to see if the badoe is interested in our lost wanderer. No sense in chasing it if it isn't."

"Go ahead. I'm the cat, not the telepath." Maestro rested his head on his paws. "By the way, how are your mind and body?"

"The forest's electrical field is light. So, my biometal won't be too heavy for a while." She took a deep breath and exhaled. "The field has also released the voices. My mind is free."

"You'll be able to take the time needed to do a thorough search?"

"Why do you harass me? You know I like to conserve my strength for any little surprises." Tiel smirked.

"If you'd take the time needed, there would be fewer surprises, which means I would have fewer battle scars."

"Shh, as you already admitted, I am the telepath." Tiel continued to leer in his direction. "Since it has been calculated that telepaths encompass less than a quarter of one percent of the population, that means that as one of these few, I would be the one who knows how to use my abilities." She giggled as Maestro gave a deep sigh. "Besides, this little talk wastes time, and you get a thrill from the excitement."

Tiel closed her eyes and exhaled, ignoring Maestro's grumbling. Directing her mind inward, she prepared herself then sent a current of energy, called a soul current, toward the direction Maestro had indicated. She searched and swept through each life-form, clinching as she felt their intake of air, the coolness of the shade, the heaviness of the humidity, or the cold drip of water upon the life-form's outer shell. She progressed past every life-form except for the defiant watosh trees. Their frames stood firm against her energy current, which caused her to encircle the trees by splitting the wave in two.

The soul current pulsated toward two moving entities that projected heightened emotions. Her muscles instinctively tightened as the current passed through a badoe. Matted blue hair stretched and pulled at the thick skin, which caused several areas on its round-barreled body to itch. The beast's belly churned with emptiness. Thick streams of slick saliva tickled as it dripped down the sides of a large mouth with ivory tusks under a long trunk. Hot, scratchy air rasped in its swollen throat. Large clipped ears flopped around while its heavy legs ached and burned.

Then Tiel pushed the soul current through the badoe to a man farther in the forest. His skin prickled with bumps as his frame shivered. Sweat stung his eyes and cracked lips. His breath imploded inside him as he gasped for air. He twitched around as his sanity melted away. An array of imaginary fears, doubts, and enemies taunted him every moment.

Air whooshed out of her mouth, scratching her throat, as the current pulled at Tiel's chest. She stopped her search and pulled back, leaving each life-form alone. The brief connection left a memory that would gratefully disappear with time.

"Already finished?" Maestro's voice boomed as she returned the soul current to her own consciousness.

"It's Fallon Hanover." Tiel stood and marched forward. "Playtime is over."

"Makes sense, Hegert hates Fallon more than you." Maestro climbed a tree once more. "She's just meticulous."

SHEA WAS STILL FAR from reaching high arch by the time Tiel found herself behind a thick wall of unruly bushes. She could hear the badoe as it snacked on the other side. Previous tracks showed that the badoe had trampled over a fox. A quick glimpse at the beast proved that the fox was now the badoe's snack.

Tiel glanced back as some chirping sounded behind her. A small, purple and green lizard bounded up to her while holding a little thin bronze box in its mouth.

"Lizard! I haven't seen you in a while." Tiel let a soft, telepathic current drift down to the animal. Lizard's pleated skin hood opened behind her head. A patchwork of green and purple vibrated as she shook. *"I see you've kept track of your master."* She put out her left hand and Lizard climbed up her arm. A voiceless current of worry and nervousness drifted from the animal as she scanned the bushes. *"Don't worry. As soon as Maestro gets back, we'll figure out what to do."*

As she petted the animal trying to calm it, Maestro appeared to her left. Tiel sent out a small soul current, sharpened it to create a blunt edge, and used it to tap him above the eyes. Maestro relaxed. His mind opened allowing his soul current to spill out. She wrapped her current around his and intertwined them together. Little, jagged, white, beads of thought traveled from Maestro along the soul current and into her mind. *"The badoe is too concerned with Fallon to pay attention to anything else."*

"I know. I tried to put it to sleep. It's too excited. I couldn't get into its mind." A soft electrical string traveled from Tiel to Maestro as she petted Lizard. *"Although, I thought I sensed a cliff on the other side of the log Fallon is in."*

"That would be right." Maestro lay down and let his tail tap on the ground.

"I found that first. The drop dragged almost all the energy out of me. How big is the clearing?"

"Small, but we can move a little."

Tiel peered over the bushes again. This badoe didn't even span a quarter of the width of a watosh, so it was still young. It bore the ear clippings and golden earrings of a merchant. The remains of the fox sat in between its feet while the animal used its trunk to twist off body parts and put the food in its triangular lower lip. Resting had cooled it down; although it's breathing still had a dry, raspy sound.

"It's a southern herd animal. There are no chains, so its owners have set it free." Tiel observed the badoe as she let her thoughts permeate the area. *"Can't see its ribs yet; so, it was just released. However, it's starving which will make it near impossible to get it off Fallon's scent."*

"Any ideas?" Maestro licked his paws. Lizard rotated the bronze clasp in her mouth. *"I take contacting Fallon telepathically is not an option?"*

"No, he's not used to it; and his brain is in a weakened and frenzied state. Too dangerous." Tiel took hold of the small, slim box and examined it.

"Lizard does your master's camera clasp still work?" she asked. She pushed the crystal button which produced the click of a mechanism and a bright flash. Tiel peeked at the badoe. It had seen nothing.

"Good, we need to make the badoe interested in us by making it mad at us. We must attack." Maestro growled as he listened to Tiel. *"We'll lead it to the other side of the Watosh Forest until it tires. That will be soon. It's overheated already. From there, it will find its way home."*

"Again, how much is the bounty?" Maestro growled at her.

"One hundred fifty gigots." Tiel looked at him.

"What if it rampages?" Maestro thumped his tail on the ground.

"We have to kill it." She moved Lizard off her shoulder and patted the animal's head.

"I take it the laser pistol isn't working?"

"No, not under the forest's electrical field. All we've got is firepower and my Hunter's Heart." Tiel pulled out her knife and waved it around.

Maestro waited a moment, then nodded in agreement while rolling his eyes.

"Hey little lady, you think you can use the camera to get your master's attention?" She petted the animal once more. Understanding flowed from the animal which made Tiel smile.

"You are a brave, smart little lady. Go with Maestro. Use the flash to get your master's attention, then lead him back toward the village. Do you understand?" Lizard jumped up and flicked her tongue on Tiel's cheek. An intense feeling of comprehension emanated from the animal.

"I have seen Lizard use the camera before," Tiel remarked to Maestro. *"She's smart, and it's one of her favorite toys."* Lizard jumped on Maestro's head. *"We don't want her to get trampled. Put her on the far edge of the clearing. She should be able to do the rest."*

Maestro spun around and walked away while Lizard chirped on his head.

"And Maestro," Tiel called as she moved in the opposite direction, *"don't hold back on the firepower."*

"I won't."

Some clomping sounds signaled that the badoe was moving. She looked over and watched the badoe amble across the clearing to the log its victim hid in. Fox hair and matter dripped from the beast's mouth as it became absorbed in its attack on the log. The wood groaned and cracked from the badoe's sheer weight. She heard Lizard's hiss followed by a flash of light.

"Fallon is lucky to have that little lizard," she thought to herself. The badoe kept up the rhythm of the attack. Fallon stayed quiet. Lizard hissed, and light erupted once again. A groan came from inside the log.

Finding an opening, she crept forward behind the badoe; its small tail swung in time with its attack. The log shuddered as a crack formed down the side. She lifted her Hunter's Heart and aimed it at the badoe. The badoe pushed forward as it slackened its attack. Tiel nodded to Maestro who appeared to her right, his tail twitching in anticipation. He opened his mouth and roared.

A blue tunnel of flame erupted from Maestro's mouth, striking the side of the badoe. The badoe jerked back and trumpeted in anger. Finding the source of the pain, it turned and charged straight at Maestro.

"I better get something out of this bounty!" Maestro's voice roared as he scrambled up a nearby watosh sapling overlooking the cliff.

"I'll get you some tall scratching posts," Tiel shot back as she ran along the opposite side and sliced the badoe. The badoe screamed and turned its full attention to her. She backed away as Maestro leaped from the tree, roaring as he spat a short burst of flame in mid-arch, then landed on the badoe's back. The badoe screamed once more, and Tiel watched Fallon scramble out of the log. He looked only once as the badoe shook its body and then he fled the clearing.

"Time to get out of here." She looked up to find Maestro attached by his teeth to the badoe's neck. His body jerked back and forth with the badoe's shaking.

"Sure, just one moment," he growled between clamped teeth. Tiel rushed forward as the badoe reared up on its hind legs; its tortured calls blasted through the forest. The badoe crashed into the watosh sapling, causing it to shudder and groan. Maestro's figure flew up and plummeted over the cliff.

"Maestro!"

The badoe landed on all fours to crush Tiel under its feet. She dove and rolled away as the ground trembled. Looking at the badoe, she watched singed, blue hair fall from a large red welt. The badoe turned and rushed her straight on. She rose and ran in the only direction open to her, toward the cliff.

The badoe continued its rush. Its eyes glared as red as the blister on its side. Tiel peeked over the edge, located a few protruding roots and jumped. She caught a root thicker than her arm and held on. Clods of dirt stung her head and arms as the badoe trumpeted in anger once more. Tiel listened to it grunt above her for a few moments. Then everything became quiet.

"Surprise!" Tiel jerked at Maestro's voice. She looked to her right to discover the feline attached to a web of roots. A breath of relief whooshed out of her giving her the strength to look up.

"I was expecting it to go over the edge." She wrapped her legs around the root and relaxed a little.

"So was I. It's smarter than we thought." Maestro scanned the cliff's edge as he sniffed the roots. "Maybe we can find the mythical acodoe to help us out?"

"Oh, yes! Let's depend on a giant snake that eats badoes and found in a child's bedtime story." Tiel laughed as she climbed. "Let's not depend on Fallon's agility too much, shall we?"

"Agreed." The cat passed her by as she climbed hand over hand. When she reached the top, the watosh sapling shuddered. Its upper boughs jerked as some bark fell. Tiel put a hand on the bark and rubbed her hand along the various interlacing shades of gray.

"Sorry, young one, we will tell Lord Del of your pain and suffering. You deserve a proper explanation of our presence here today."

"We need to hurry! The badoe hasn't given up on Fallon. It's heading straight for the village," Maestro said turning to her.

"You want me to ride on your back?" Tiel asked.

"We'll make better time taking the paths in the upper forest." Maestro pointed his nose at the lower forest. The vegetation's branches jerked around where there was no wind to move them. "The badoe's pursuit of Fallon has injured and angered some lower plants."

"Perhaps you're right." Tiel climbed onto his back, tightened her knees against his sides, and wrapped both arms around his thick neck. This kept her prone on Maestro's back and her head positioned under his ear away from any passing foliage.

Maestro's movements were so smooth she barely felt the surging action beneath her. After he climbed a watosh, he navigated the thick limbs that connected with each other. She watched the forest floor pass by through gaps, spying trembling lower plants, some of which lay crushed beyond recognition.

"The only reason the forest hasn't trapped Fallon is because of its promise to Lord Del," Tiel telepathically called to Maestro. A few moments later, they passed over the rampaging beast. Its bony spine ran straight up its back and connected to its head that just missed the branches on which they were traveling.

"I have seen no sign of Fallon," Tiel called to Maestro. In response, he ran faster, and she looked under the badoe's trunk.

"He isn't dangling from its mouth. He must be up ahead." The feline sped up, and the gaps passed by even faster. *"Mount the badoe. We've got to stop it."*

Maestro jumped, legs outstretched, and landed on the badoe's head. Tiel jumped off Maestro's back, pulled out her knife and jabbed it into the spine as Maestro bit into the neck. The badoe screeched in pain and reared up on its hind legs. Swinging from side to side, she clutched at the handle of her knife as the badoe plummeted back down, forcing Tiel's body to stretch upward.

The badoe hit the ground, and Tiel's insides rattled as gravity pushed her into matted hair that stunk of dung. While forcing her head up to breathe, she pushed a button on the end of her Hunter's Heart, releasing the clear liquid inside.

Maestro roared next to her as he lost his hold and fell off. The badoe reared up, lost its balance, and toppled over sideways. Tiel jumped off and rolled away only to have shockwaves vibrate through her body as the ground trembled beneath.

CHAPTER 2

PROPHECY AWAKENED

The badoe refused to move, rasping its last breath as its sides rose and fell with pain. Tiel climbed over the heaving beast and gripped her embedded knife. The badoe wrenched one last time as she pulled it out. She watched its eyes glaze over and dim while blood spilled onto the ground.

"The unwarranted death of one so young has done nothing but stained Shea's paths for me today," Tiel lamented aloud while wiping her knife on her pants. "I will make sure it also stains Shea's paths for Hegert." Maestro groaned, and she turned as he slowly rose, sniffed his entire body, then bounced as if testing his legs.

"Yes! Everything is still working!" He sat down and cleaned his paws. "What's next?"

"Back to the village to get our pay." Tiel worked her way over the badoe's sticky side, slipping occasionally. Laughter and cheers broke through the stillness bringing Tiel's attention to the forest's edge.

"Looks like the Bamboodii harvest is at its high arch," Tiel sighed while taking out a leather cloth and the watosh crystal clasp from a large pocket in her pant leg. She put the fabric around her neck and attached the clasp to both ends. She pulled it up to the middle of her chest, bringing the cloth ends together. Maestro walked up next to her while sniffing the ground.

"Fallon was here just a few moments ago," he rumbled at Tiel. "Looks like the newlyweds are out in force this harvest. That will leave few bamboodii stalks for the merchants to harvest." More cheering broke through the forest edge. Tiel used energy waves around her and formed a box she called a rutzix. While gathering her soul current into this box, she placed it at the back of her mind and sealed it. She only opened it when there wasn't a barrage of currents from an emotional multitude such as the one she was about to enter.

"Perhaps we will stay and join in the many wedding festivities, watching people build abodes." Tiel shook her head due to a rising static inside her mind. "I know where there are bookings if you want to bet a few sigots and guess on a couple's stability," she said with a laugh.

"I take it that the last comment was sarcastic."

"Of course, why do you think I took my stellove oaths in private?" Tiel shook her head again. The buzz inside only grew louder. "It irritates me that people think it is okay to make money on how long a couple's marriage lasts."

"I thought it was to keep it exciting by seeing how long you can keep your union from the Drakners." Maestro yawned and sat down.

"We will tell them soon." Tiel stopped and watched the forest scene bounce between fuzzy and bright as the static grew worse affecting her vision.

"Your eyes are wild again. Is the 'buzz' back?" Maestro's tail switched in front of her vision bringing Tiel's attention back to him.

"Yeah, the 'buzz' is back," she admitted as she shook her head again.

"I know that I've asked this before," Maestro said letting out a deep sigh, "but, is it due to your telepathy?"

"No, as I have said before, I can't control this. It has nothing to do with my telepathy." Tiel searched the area. "I have boxed my soul current. Why do you keep asking?"

"Because it is like working with someone with two different personalities," Maestro growled.

"Help me find clues to where these voices come from." Tiel stared past the forest's edge. "I hate hearing the old man's voice. It's like having someone constantly attached to me."

They strode forward as the increasing buzz drowned out the cheers and joy from the celebration. Tiel took a moment at the forest's edge to survey the scene, and search for a cause to the static.

She shifted her gaze to the harvest floor littered with remnants of straw crackling under the newlywed's white boots. Their bulky, white, sweat-soaked suits stretched as the newlyweds severed the golden straw with curved blades. Cloths covering their noses bulged in and out with their breaths. Creaking carts bounced around as the newlywed's families dropped heavy sheaves of bamboodii straws onto their wooden backs. Tiel's gaze followed the stronger members of the families as they leaned on cart handles, grunting while they pulled burdened carts through open bamboodii gates. They disappeared under the arch of the massive stone bridge where they would build the newlyweds' hut.

Her gaze reached the top of the arch that supported throngs of villagers. Some villagers crowded the ledge laughing and throwing flower petals over the harvesters. Others mingled around the various food huts while chugging frothy ales or downing sweet pastries. The voices of different children mixed as some danced, others jumped, and even a few cried around adults that seemed to be in charge. Different musicians strove to rise above the noise as they played conflicting music that still blended in a chorus of merriment.

A coughing fit brought her attention back to the harvest floor. The sound came from the acodoe warriors to her left. She examined their leather foot wrappings and legs. None exhibited signs of having traversed the Watosh earlier. Unscathed hands held small bamboodii straws and stayed at their sides. The straws emitted a high airy sound, like a serpent hiss. It usually scared away any wild badoe wanting a human snack. Every-thing about them confirmed what Tiel knew. Councilwoman Hegert had staged the whole affair. Tiel vowed to more than double the bounty.

More cheers erupted as a pair of newlyweds raised their sickles into the air. Tiel caressed the watosh clasp as an older man in the tan robes of an architect bowed to the pair. A strip of tan cloth dangled from his neck. Unlike the fabric clasped around her neck, known as a maicalla, the archi-tect's maicalla had colorful ancestral stripes at each end. His ancestral stripes were eight hues of blue on the left, representing his father's ancestry and eight different colors on the right, representing his mother's ancestry.

The pair of harvesters bowed to the architect and gave him their sickles.

Tiel smiled as she mused how most of the harvesters' maicallas had the same ancestral strips. Her clasp being in line with the middle of her chest signaled to all she was open for a business conversation without unnecessary chit-chat. The newlyweds, their families, and all others on the floor had their maicallas closer to the navel point, signifying they were open for most communication. The acodoe warriors' maicallas were pinned up to the neck or closed to all conversation, which matched their stiff, upright postures.

No matter what Tiel saw, she knew their search would be futile. She would not find the source to the noise in her head. The static always sounded like a room full of muttering people.

"Do you see anything unusual?" Tiel whispered as the last sliver of hope died when Maestro shook his head.

"Do you hear the voices yet?"

"Just the usual background hum of busy people."

"I'll go when you're ready," Maestro's voice rumbled.

Tiel studied everything once more, letting the air whoosh out of her. She hoped that the old man wouldn't be paying attention. She hated it when he talked about her.

"Well, let's see what is on Shea's paths now." Tiel's leg quivered over the border for a split moment. Then, she completed the motion and emerged from the forest.

"Here they come." Tiel forced her hand to stay at her side, resisting the urge to squeeze out the high-pitched female voice booming in her head.

"Is the cat still there?" the old man's voice sounded distinct.

"Yes, Master, standing right next to her as usual," the female voice confirmed.

"What do you hear?" Maestro interrupted her thoughts.

"We are being watched." With her hands shaking, Tiel managed to loosen her hair and use the cloth to clean her Hunter's Heart.

"That is not unusual." Maestro's head jerked around as he growled. People jumped out of the pair's way as they walked. Tiel could see the fear in their eyes, wondering if the knife or Maestro's teeth would tear them apart.

"Look at the power in his muscles. He must be royalty. I know it with that stance." The old man's breath sounded as if it were right over her shoulder. "Have we found what his subspecies is yet, boy?" There was a pause with the usual static. Tiel scanned the multitudes before her, and, once again, located no one who paid undue attention to her.

"The old man is looking for your subspecies," Tiel announced.

"Good. Tell them to let me know when they find out," Maestro's voice echoed behind her. "Of course, we need to know who *they* are first."

A sudden bump brought Tiel back to the harvest floor. A young man stood gaping at her as his camera clattered to the ground. The flash erupted into the air as he scrambled back into the arms of loved ones.

"You bounty hunters think you own everything!" an older woman yelled, her gray hair swirling around her contorted, snarling lips. "We are here enjoying a wedding, something I know you don't care about." She stepped forward as the young man disappeared into the crowd. "Go. Be with your dung heap, bounty hunter. Leave good people who fear Coulliou to their ways." She shooed Tiel away with her hands.

"TEAR HER UP, TEAR HER FLESH FROM HER BONES." Tiel froze as the old man's voice echoed in her brain. The old woman's gray hair still danced in the breeze, her face firm.

"I'LL BET YOU FIVE SIGOTS SHE WON'T DO ANYTHING," the female voice challenged.

"AH, I'LL TAKE YOU UP ON THAT. I JUST WISH I COULD GET HER, CONTROL HER. SHE'D DO IT WITHOUT THINKING."

Tiel searched each face around the area. Some villagers watched her. Others went about their business. *"They're betting on me?"* her thoughts chimed in among the background ruckus. *"They're betting on me!"* She felt a growl escape her lips. With any move she made, someone would win. There was no out, and her next move would give someone power over her. She opened her rutzix, forgetting about the possible mental overload from the densely populated area.

A strong push on her back moved her past the woman and towards the crowd under the bridge. She spun around and found Maestro's face dominating her vision.

"GET THAT CAT OUT OF THERE!" the old man's voice commanded. The young woman's voice sighed in disappointment. "CURSE THE GODS FOR THEIR INTRUSIONS. I HATE IT WHEN A BET TURNS INTO A DRAW," the old man lamented.

"It may be a good idea to put your Hunter's Heart away," Maestro suggested, his voice soft. Tiel felt herself relax. Realization dawned as she felt the tension in her raised arm and the strain of tight fingers holding the knife in striking position. She let her arm drop, the weight crashing against her leg. Her fingers relaxed, and her Hunter's Heart dangled in her hand.

She quickly gathered up her chaotic soul current around her and closed it back in the rutzix.

"You saved me once again, old friend," she whispered. With nothing more than a flick of her wrist, she sheathed her Hunter's Heart while rubbing Maestro's head with her free hand. Maestro rammed his head into her chest turning it from side to side.

"MEETING EVERYONE." The old man's voice faded away until a familiar click left her mind temporarily free.

THERE WOULD BE no medics to help him today. Fallon knew that. The blood, bruises and torn clothing were a testament to that fact. He ran his hand through his hair and brought back a dusty clump of light brown hair that looked dark against his white skin.

I am supposed to be dead. His whole body trembled as he shifted himself on the stone bench atop the bridge. The smell of the bar and food huts made his stomach lurch as he tried to control his breathing. The sounds of annoying children passing by rang in his ears.

Whoever had set up his little foray into the Watosh would wait to hear news of his demise. He knew the one waiting would be Councilwoman Hegert. The Bounty Huntress could confirm his suspicions. She was contracted to bring him in.

Gazing over the side, he spied Tiel walking under the bridge with that cat next to her. He contemplated how sometimes she had a murderous look about her. Just as it happened moments before, something would click, and her eyes would almost gleam again. It was the same with her rival, de Menzaile. He patted Lizard on the head as he mused over the similarities between the two different bounty hunters.

"What in Shea's path have you been up to?"

Fallon turned then sucked in gasps of air as pain racked his body, causing the trembling to increase. A nobleman with black hair dressed in a black robe with gold trim stood just beyond him. Fallon snorted and gingerly turned back again. As far as Fallon was concerned, this specimen was a child who gorged off his parents 'zahule', an idea that encompassed the well-being of someone's soul. In the past, Ecalardians took pride in flogging young men who lived off their parents' zahule. Sometimes, society forced these same young men to work as servants for seven octaves. Now? No one cared.

"Xeth, what brings you to my realm?" Fallon kept his back to the noble.

"I was the one who placed you in this quadrant. Now, I have to answer for your blatant disregard of the council." Fallon, from the corner of his eye, saw Xeth's fingers reach out. Lizard's hood vibrated as she hissed at the intrusion, the fingers disappeared.

"Touch me again, and that's the last time you'll use that appendage." Fallon readjusted himself on the seat and spied a small woman with red hair up in a bun. She wore a thin, orange gown and held a handbag that matched. "So, I see the real reason you're angry. Hegert's intentions interrupted your plans with Jenn. May I offer my apologies?" Fallon managed a grin as he leaned for support on the bench's back. "I suppose that's the price you pay as somebody's errand boy."

"I make my own decisions." Xeth gritted his teeth.

"If you were your own man, I would be on Ecalardia's tech side. Then you and Jenn would be..." Fallon thought a moment. ".... enjoying your time together."

Jenn pursed her lips and moved her hands toward the maicalla wrapped around her neck. With a snarl and glaring eyes, she moved a silver bird clasp up her maicalla to her neck. Fallon smirked at the apparent rejection.

"Do you want to be considered an outcast?" Xeth eyed Fallon and pointed to his maicalla clasped at the usual respectable length.

"I'd think as a noble, you'd be more concerned with the well-being of an injured man, than whether he wore his maicalla. Besides, I prefer the solitude."

"I'll see what I can do," Xeth whispered glancing around.

"I won't wait too long. Hegert wants me dead." Fallon chuckled again. "Hegert doesn't let her boys do anything without permission. She'll take her time getting me medical attention."

Xeth gritted his teeth; veins bulged in his fists. Jenn reached out and placed her hand on Xeth's arm.

"Yes, Jenn, take your little plaything along with you. I am sure you can siphon enough of his family's zahule to last for octaves. Shea's light knows Xeth has none to give." Fallon closed his eyes and grimaced as he held his side. He remembered a time when he had anticipated having her at his side.

"Come on, Xeth, we have endured enough of his slander." Fallon winced upon hearing Jenn's soft pleading. It dug at the longing he had for their old friendship. After a moment of silence, Fallon opened his eyes to see the couple returning to Xeth's hovercraft.

The hovercraft's black metal shone under Shea's light. Its long, rounded design complimented the dark-tinted windows. Below it, two oblong power crystals tapered to a point at each end. The hum of the engine was nonexistent as the craft floated in the air. Jenn silently let Xeth direct her into his hovercraft.

Fallon took out a silver ball from a tattered pocket and threw it into the air, all the while marveling over the miracle that he still had the ball. Lizard fixed her gaze on the toy. Jenn slid over to let Xeth in as she pulled out a bright red shade of lipstick from her handbag. Fallon threw the ball up once, twice. Lizard pounced, her tongue flickering in anticipation with every toss. Xeth sat down across from Jenn and Fallon threw the ball over the door. Lizard arched with the ball, disappearing into the hovercraft.

Jenn screamed. Xeth cursed. Glasses clanged as a red liquid poured out of the door, followed by bits of bouncing cheese and mashed fruit that stuck to the vehicle's rim. More screams and the hovercraft jerked, followed by more cursing. Fallon leaned over while holding onto the bench. Lizard hissed, and the hovercraft shook as its door swung open. He could see Lizard as she slid across the table inside, following her ball, batting it back and forth as she tore into the plates of food. A frosted cake splattered on Jenn's lap and wine surged into Xeth's jacket.

The door closed once again, the hovercraft jerked followed by more screams and cursing, then the ball bounced out the door in Fallon's direction. He stopped the toy with his foot watching a dessert-covered Lizard exit the hovercraft, carrying Jenn's pink maicalla in her mouth.

"My maicalla," Jenn's voice cried from the hovercraft as Lizard jumped into his lap, dropping her prize in his hand. The door opened once again as

Fallon took in the cloth's aroma. Long walks, soft laughter, and deep soul talks all mingled into his memory. He peered at Jenn over the maicalla. She pursed her lips, and little wrinkles formed around her narrowing eyes. Fallon threw the maicalla in Jenn's face and slammed the door shut with his leg.

THE MERCHANTS' voices collided with each other as they called out to the crowd of people. Wares from badoe-hide tents to blue-clay pottery and plates were on display. On her right were scores of villagers in various stages of building bamboodii huts. Laughter filled the air, and children ran around the adults. However, there was no food or drink vendors. They were on top of the bridge. Tiel promised herself to visit a bar hut and secure a mug of sweet ale.

She scanned the moving throng for Chief Del. Hegert's note had mentioned he would meet her here. A crash sounded, and Tiel turned to find some broken plates on the stone floor. A merchant shoved a small girl out of the way while he scolded her. Maestro sat up, his bath interrupted.

"Bounty Huntress," a high male voice summoned from behind.

"Chief Del." Tiel turned. She and the acodoe warrior bowed to each other. "I believe I have met my bounty contract. Where is the payment you promised?" The warrior scratched his hardened suntanned face.

"What was the agreement?" he requested. His red braids covered his shoulders. A bronze headband with a coiled hooded serpent rested on his brow.

Tiel produced a thick, decorative, tan piece of paper and handed it to him.

"What did Hegert say to you about this?" Tiel probed.

"I got a note like this one. Its instructions were for me to meet you here. What makes you think it involves Hegert?"

"Let's just say there are things no one wants to know about a telepath."

"Fair enough," Chief Del rasped out as he surveyed the note.

"How do you prefer to pay?" Tiel asked noticing a few hanging rugs bumping into each other as some bamboodii straw farther down plummeted to the floor. She scratched at a jolt of itchy energy that traveled up her legs. Maestro's attention stayed on the harvest floor, his tail twitching.

"By holo image." Chief Del held out a small thin silver tube.

"I see you do not hate the technics of Ecalardia." Tiel smiled as she glanced in Maestro's direction. His muzzle moved up and down as he sniffed the air. She kept her eye on him and hurried to complete the transaction. With her palm toward the ground, she opened a slit on the top of her glove. A shimmering, thin piece of metal glimmered in the light. She pressed it with her finger, and a small white square appeared with even smaller colored squares positioned on top.

"I may like the privacy of the villages, but I do not agree with a lot of the villager's inclinations." Chief Del waved the fingers of his right hand over his tube producing the same holo image. He moved his fingers over the image, finished and pocketed his device. Tiel waved her fingers across her holo screen, and it disappeared into the back of her hand.

"Thank you for the business." She thanked the chief as Maestro ran towards the opening. The sound of breaking merchandise rebounded throughout the room as merchants scattered to save their wares. Abodes fell apart, their bamboodii straw rods collapsing upon each other. The ground quaked under her feet, and Tiel turned to follow Maestro out to the harvest floor.

A loud trumpeting sounded. Screams erupted from the harvest floor as the harvesters and their families rushed under the bridge. Tiel pushed her way through the onslaught of bodies.

The acodoe warriors craned their necks upwards and blew through the straws creating a loud ear-splitting hiss. Turning to her left, Tiel watched a badoe stomp out of the forest, shaking its head that held two, long, ivory tusks on either side of its mouth. Bronze rings in its clipped ears clanged against each other as the badoe trumpeted its anger. Its feet trampled the cracking bamboodii straw.

Tiel unsheathed her Hunter's Heart feeling her heartbeat in her palm as she held it tight.

"I don't like this surprise," Maestro roared out above the commotion. "You can't hold enough poison in that blade for something this big. Didn't you sense it while we were in the forest?" Maestro steadied himself as he stared at her.

Tiel shook her head.

"How about putting it to sleep?"

"Too much anger, too large, and its mental power would overtake me." The clank of metal brought Tiel's attention down to the ground. An iron shackle, clasped around the beast's foot, dragged an iron chain behind it.

"I thought the southern merchants had control over their herds!" she yelled at Chief Del as he appeared at her side.

"They usually do, however, see this one's nipples?" Chief Del pointed at the underside of the beast. Two swollen nipples jingled from the underbelly of the badoe. "That means this one is a nursing mother. You didn't hurt a young badoe did you? That is the only reason this one would break its chain."

"Shea's light," Tiel cursed under her breath. Wiggling its trunk around, the badoe sniffed the area, then it bent its head and glowered at Tiel and Maestro.

"You killed its calf, why?" Chief Del questioned.

"Ask Hegert!" she yelled back.

A rumble escaped the badoe's throat as it chewed the inside of its cheek, lifted its trunk and knocked on the nearest watosh three times. The loud thuds vibrated through the harvest floor as the badoe bent towards the ground, letting another rumble escape.

A huge wave of emotion broke upon Tiel shoving her backward. The badoe's hatred enveloped her, breaking open her rutzix. She stared at the badoe's eyes, its anger boiled inside her at the loss of a loved one, and a mother's revenge tore at her heart.

"I really don't like this surprise," Maestro's voice echoed outside her consciousness.

"Let's see what happens when it can't walk on one leg," Tiel growled low as she steadied herself. The badoe's emotions consumed her, wiping away all thought but the beast's own desire to stomp out this intruder.

"What? No!" Maestro's objections faded as she sprinted towards the bellowing tower of meat. The badoe stomped towards her. Tiel rushed the badoe, stopped to where she stood just under its knee and shoved her Hunter's Heart in deep. Trumpeting in pain, the badoe lifted its foot. The knife's serrated edge caught on the skin keeping Tiel from pulling it out. She hung on while a cold current of air rushed past her and chilled her face.

A low growl escaped her lips as the badoe dropped its leg and Tiel watched the ground rush up to her, the immediate danger causing the artificial anger to dissipate. With her head clear, she turned the knife, dislodged it and jumped right before the badoe's foot hit the ground. Crushed bamboodii straw crackled as her back hit the ground. The straw tore and stung her skin while ground tremors bounced her body along the harvest floor.

Tiel slowed her breathing and struggled to push her telepathy back into the weakened rutzix. She would not stare the beast in the eyes again. The badoe's feet moved towards her and she, and she rolled out of the way, staying under the beast's belly.

"Stand up!" She heard Maestro roar.

The badoe shifted its direction. Tiel rolled onto her feet and once again balanced herself despite the jarring vibrations beneath her.

"Move right," Maestro's blurry form yelled beyond her. Tiel complied as she bounced with the tremors until the badoe stopped.

"Move! Move! Move!" Maestro roared. Tiel kept his blurry form in front of her. Her jelly legs moved as fast as they could. She ducked as she ran from the badoe's shadow, expecting the swaying trunk to throw her across the field, and blessed Coulliou when it didn't happen. She continued to run until she fell into the soft fur of Maestro's neck.

"You will get a lot of soft cushions from our bounty today," she laughed. "What made it stop?"

The badoe's high-pitched scream answered her question as a huge shadow chilled the air. She plugged her ears until the badoe took a breath leaving only the sound of screaming villagers. The ground shook again as Tiel forced herself to turn and survey the scene. The badoe had changed course to go back into the Watosh, trying to circumvent the largest serpent Tiel had ever seen.

"Your contract is void, Bounty Huntress," Chief Del screamed. "This is why we didn't want a forest badoe to come. You have brought out an acodoe."

"It is a herd beast, not a forest beast!" Tiel screamed back. "I hold you to your contract."

"The council will decide." Chief Del looked back towards the edge of the harvest floor.

The acodoe's girth spanned half the trunk size of one watosh as its hood blocked Shea's warmth. The badoe's screams pierced the air once again, unable to drown out the rising cries from the onlookers beyond the harvest floor.

Something hit her body, and she looked to find Maestro turning towards the bridge. "Being under the bridge may have merit," Maestro roared out to her, keeping his voice above the ruckus. Tiel retreated and followed him passing the warriors intent on closing the bamboodii gates in the bridge opening.

The acodoe glared and brought its head parallel to the ground. Its black pupils were pinpricks inside the white eyeballs. Its prey shrieked again and ran the opposite direction. The acodoe's burnt brown underbelly scratched along the ground as it shifted its head from side to side, scales of sapphire on top of its trunk waved in rhythm to its motion. Its body curved and rippled causing the bamboodii to crackle under its weight as it impeded the badoe's path. The acodoe kept moving its head back and forth, exposing two great pits on either side of its face. Flicking its tongue, it slithered towards the badoe.

The shrieking badoe changed direction and ran for the gate. The acodoe raised its head, exposed its fangs, and spit a white liquid toward the badoe, hitting one eye. Its prey stumbled, regained its footing, and rammed the bamboodii gate causing it to shudder and groan. A bolt from one hinge shot out and hit an acodoe warrior, collapsing him.

The badoe rammed the gate again. Screams echoed as villagers ran in all directions. The acodoe reared hissing and spread its hood as the badoe shrieked and rammed the gate again. A young woman ran, smacking Tiel in the shoulder as she screamed. "The prophecies are alive! They're alive!"

The badoe rammed the gate once more as the acodoe lunged, jaws wide, clamping onto the badoe with its ridged teeth. A rank smell permeated the air as the acodoe breathed out, creating an echo of coughing and gagging sounds from everyone under the arch.

The lower jaw clamped on the meal as the badoe wrapped its trunk around the bamboodii gate still shrieking. The gate groaned, two bolts dislodged and ricocheted around the interior. Tiel dove to the floor covering her head to escape the flying projectiles. Chief Del and Maestro flattened themselves next to her.

The acodoe's swollen right jaw moved forward, the small teeth on the upper jaw held the shrieking badoe. The left jaw moved forward, and the right moved backward as the badoe slid towards its grave, still holding onto the gate. Tiel jerked as the voices boomed inside her head once more.

"WHAT'S AN ACODOE DOING OUT THERE?" the old man's voice yelled above the commotion.

"I DON'T KNOW, MASTER. A BADOE APPEARED AND THEN THE ACODOE," the young woman answered.

"COULLIOU SHOULD BE BURNED IN HIS CITADEL FOR THIS. IT'S NOT TIME, NOT YET," the old man cursed as his voice diminished.

The badoe shuddered as its blood gushed down its side. The acodoe's fangs worked their way into the bars of the gate as the badoe slid down the now swelling throat of the acodoe. Cheers from the crowd on top wafted down through the entrance.

The acodoe finished and attempted to back away from the gate as more metal projectiles launched into the air and Chief Del's body jerked causing him to yowl in pain. It closed its mouth with the gate securely attached to its fangs, and the metal lock screeched as it bent in two. The acodoe righted itself, pupils widened, and it looked cross-eyed at the object in its mouth. It shook its head, its hood waving around as it backed up.

The clap, clap, clap of the beating sides of the gate rang out as the acodoe opened and closed its jaw. It looked cross-eyed once more, the pupils even wider. It breathed a little, rotated its head sideways and slammed the edge of the gate onto the ground. The gate splintered in a few places but held firm. The acodoe raised its head once more and slammed hard sending tremors through the ground. Bamboodii shafts flew in every direction as the gate shattered.

Tiel covered her head as the hollow sound of straws whistled around her, jerking as a few rods stung her back. When the noise stopped, she opened her eyes to glimpse the acodoe's tail as it disappeared into the Watosh Forest.

"The prophecies are alive! We are all dead!" several onlookers wailed in remorse while they fell to the ground. Other cries echoed the same anxieties as medics entered the scene. Crowds of people ran out onto the top of the bridge. Some had fainted or lay injured from the debris. Others blessed Coulliou for showing them the 'Day of Renewal'. Some cheers still resounded from above among the abandoned shops. The whirlwind of papers, flying in all directions, matched the hectic surge of fear, joy, anger, sorrow, and excitement which almost destroyed the last of the energy in her telepathic box.

The inward strength to stand came slow, but when it did, Tiel took a mental inventory of her body and realized she could still move with little difficulty. Maestro himself was sniffing at several areas of his own body.

Turning her attention to the ramp, she walked up to the top and Maestro followed. She searched the crowd of crazed villagers and found Fallon. She smiled, walked over, and put her hand on the writer's shoulder interrupting his picture-taking.

"Nice to see you haven't lost your passion as one of Ecalardia's most famous reporters." Tiel smiled. "Let's get you some medical attention. Also, I am interested in what you know about Hegert."

CHAPTER 3

RIGHTEOUS AMBITION

*T*hree **wooden mugs** missed the faded target turning the cave wall a deep red. Cheers and jeers from the surrounding mockers resounded off the walls and mixed in with snores that came from three other tables.

A bar made of bamboodii stood in the back. A tall, stout, old man with thinning gray hair worked behind it balancing a wood mug on his round stomach. Several other mugs lined the counter. All needed repair.

Straight sweet malt that would not drown out Tiel's common sense filled a mug to her left. She sat at a table and looked past the cave's opening. Dry brown dirt, with a few tall trees, stretched out to a paved stone highway. Now and then a hovercraft zoomed by.

The Hunter Caverns edged the Watosh Forest allowing the residue of the forest's field to soften the voices in Tiel's head, without the heaviness to her body. The farther in she went, the quieter her mind. In the Front Caverns, the inner static was constant, and so she preferred the noise the 'mockers' gave her.

The mockers' ruckus calmed down allowing Tiel to study the group of hunter hopefuls. These hunters were dirty, disheveled, and sucked off the Hunter Clan's zahule. Yet, the ritualed hunters used them to their advantage.

The next mug she threw hit the target dead center. Cheers and laughter once again picked up to a healthy roar. Tiel wished that her expected visitors would show. She looked back at the holo screen above the barkeeper. Images of earlier events played in fifteen-minute intervals. Sometimes it showed the acodoe eating the badoe. Other times, like now, it showed Tiel as she attacked the badoe. The gossips of Ecalardia enjoyed showing the small scratch her knife had inflicted on the animal. She had rammed her Hunter's Heart in deep, but in the end, her attempt had been futile. Her antics were now the 'dim act of the season'.

Comments flew in from all over Ecalardia. People cried or shouted for joy in other scenes. Many had quit their occupations and roamed the streets. Some families had packed up to leave although Tiel did not know why. There would be nowhere to go. 'The Day of Renewal' was supposed to end with a desolate and torn planet heaving out fire and ash from within its core to be reborn.

"Huntress, here are the other mugs you ordered." Tiel looked up to find a small boy with sandy blond hair beside her. He wore plain, tan, woolen clothing and held a tray with two mugs. "Jacquard says it is a good thing you have good credit here, or he'd take the cost of all the mugs you broke out of your hide."

Tiel grunted and motioned for the boy to put the drinks down on her table.

The boy bent down to her ear. "Are you waiting for someone?" His emotions of extreme curiosity and sincere concern for her teased at her feeble telepathic border. She had tried to form her rutzix, but the encounter with the badoe had destroyed any hope of success. It made putting up with her young initiate's concerns necessary to get rid of him as gently as possible.

"What do you think the answer to that question is?"

"I think you are waiting for some members of the council to show." The boy bit his lower lip in anticipation as he tried to hide an almost girlish smile.

"See, Jainu, you're smarter than those mockers over there." Tiel picked up a mug and threw it, missing the target on purpose. Cheers and laughter erupted again followed by sarcastic jibes.

"When you're finished with the council, Jacquard says I have finished my work for the day." Jainu bobbed his head toward the barkeep. "Meet you in the back caverns?"

"I'll be there," Tiel said as she lifted the mug.

"Seems you have gained a little notoriety." The slow, deliberate voice behind her produced needle-like soul currents of accusation that jabbed at her border. She had hoped to get some rest from any strong emotions. The mockers drunken soul currents were not a threat since they hit the floor like rocks.

Tiel turned to discover a man in a long brown robe approach, a tattoo of a coiled serpent decorated his tan bald head. Tiel had little respect for this man and was always tempted to call him by his name, Sethrich. However, he was her superior, so she called him by his title out of respect for his position.

"Elder Hunter." Tiel nodded at Sethrich.

"Ecalardians are despairing." Sethrich sat down and waved Jainu off. "It is the name of The Bounty Huntress they curse."

"Yet, others are praising my name." Tiel put down her mug and snarled. "It is all just a nuisance. Soon, they will travel on Shea's lighted paths and get back to normal lives."

"You do not believe the prophecy?" Sethrich asked, his waves needling her harder.

"Which one?" Tiel asked.

"I see." Sethrich squinted his eyes. "You also don't believe in the old ways that founded this Hunter Clan you take for granted. You don't believe our interactions with Ecalardia should be a secret." His constant accusations made the wave even sharper causing her to wince a little. "You could have easily gotten your pay later and kept the Hunter Clan out of this fiasco."

"We have moved beyond the 'old ways', Elder Hunter." Tiel let out a feral growl from deep within. The man drew back. His waves swirled protectively around him. She laughed and stared him down. "Some say you have become too hard in your ways to be of use to the clan anymore."

"I have not heard that." Sethrich defended himself and stood. "Anyhow, do not forget. No matter what others may or may not say, I am still your inner clan leader and head of the Winged Court. I am the one that ultimately decides what you may do *within the Hunter Clan*. That means your union with de Menzaile is not yet formalized *by the Hunter Clan.*" His voice took on a definite menacing tone at the last.

"What?" Tiel rose, almost turning over the table. "You are not the only one that can formalize our union."

"You are right. Although de Menzaile's ways have made convincing a certain other party of your union's legitimacy… problematic." Sethrich ran his hand down the back of her hair. His waves formed a soft, loving flow as one would love a pet. Tiel's stomach lurched, forcing her to suppress a gag as she punched his hand away. Sethrich just chuckled.

"Don't worry. I'm sure the clan will formalize your union. It's a tradition from the old days." He furrowed his brow and his emotional waves took on the form of a striking serpent. "Maybe you are right though. Maybe we should rethink some of the 'old ways'." The waves struck and the energy in her border dissipated a little. A draining weakness depleted the energy from her body. Sethrich turned to leave.

"Don't you dare go anywhere!" Tiel's growled. Sethrich's waves wrapped themselves around his body. She continued, "I am not some toy for you to play with. I know my rights and the laws. The only reason I haven't attacked you is because you are my inner clan leader." Tiel leaned on the chair to support her weakened frame but she continued. "But there are other ways… legal ways to protect myself and my interests."

"May your travels on Shea's paths be filled with light." Sethrich's voice suggested a hint of fear, and his waves tightened around him as he walked away.

"Two messages came for you." Jainu appeared at her side. "Are you okay?" His currents swirled in a jumble around her; his emotions and thoughts of concern strong. Tiel moved away and signaled for him to stay.

"I'll be fine," she said while reading the messages. "It figures. Hegert is stalling, no doubt trying to get out of paying."

"You expect better?" Jainu asked.

"No." Tiel laughed at his remark. "Go get Vengeance and tell him to meet me in the east parking lot. Looks like I'll have time for some needed rest."

TIEL FOUND a quiet place in the Back Caverns to eat and get the rest she craved. This helped her to restore a light version of the rutzix and research the day's events. It didn't take long to find plenty of proof concerning Hegert's part in the whole 'acodoe affair'. She sent a message which included the evidence, informing Hegert that she would share the findings with the High Council and Fallon if she didn't receive a triple bounty.

After that, she proceeded to the East Caverns where she could view the Watosh Forest. Two large square hovercrafts with no windows floated near the entrance. The metallic shells changed colors with the surroundings. As of this moment, they were different shades of green which were easily seen against the orange and red of the caverns.

A man about her height with a slight belly stood in front of the hover-crafts. He was older with streaks of silver in his trim, brown hair that framed his olive complexion. His brown eyes studied her as he adjusted a blue maicalla, using a bronze soldier button for his clasp. A rainbow of stripes adorned both sides. He wore the uniform of a peace enforcer general; which was black pants, a black coat with a gold embroidered eight-pointed octave star on the left sleeve, brass buttons down the middle front, and a red sash tied around his waist.

"General ManCane, it has been a while." Tiel turned as a clean version of the mockers walked up beside her. "Here is your lost agent."

"Agent Raul." ManCane bowed in his direction. "I take it, like the others sent here, that you have nothing new to give us?"

"No, general," Raul answered, "I have no new information. But, thanks to your words of guidance, I am coming out of here intact."

ManCane gestured at the vehicles and the back portion of the first vehicle melted away showing comfortable seating.

"As you requested, agent, your family is already relocated." ManCane stepped away as Raul came closer. "You will get a shower first and then attend a debriefing before your reunion."

Raul bowed again and entered the vehicle. Its side materialized and the vehicle left.

"Why do the Peace Enforcers keep sending agents among us?" Tiel questioned. "He almost got knifed in the back."

"That is for another time," ManCane whispered. Tiel thought she saw a tear. "There will be no more agents assigned to this place," he promised. "I need to talk to you about other things."

Tiel raised her eyebrows but stayed silent.

"Do you realize that there is a..." ManCane screwed up his face which made his eyes almost squint shut. "There is an epidemic of child abductions?"

"There are always child abductions. Some of the best hunters are victims themselves." She looked at him with one corner of her mouth raised in a smile.

"Yes, yes, I know. But these are different. Usually, the abductions happen in the middle of a crowded street or while the child's parents aren't looking. Now, they happen in the middle of night while the children are at home." Tiel backed up a step as ManCane continued. "It is more common now that the children get taken out of the arms of their screaming parents. To make things worse, the abductions happen in clusters. Have you learned of anything?" His eyes moved as he searched her face. She just shook her head.

"I don't just mean from the other hunters." ManCane tapped his forehead. "I mean from inside?"

"No, nothing." Tiel touched his shoulder. "I'll keep my ears and mind open for any news though. I'll tell you if I hear anything." She looked at him and then continued. "If you want, in the next larquetz, I'll take The Block and explain things. That way the other hunters will keep watch."

"You think they'll help?" ManCane smiled, letting his eyes open. Tiel smiled in return and nodded in an affirmative response.

"Thanks." ManCane sighed. "That leads us to the next subject. Do you know about the Peace Talks?"

"Yes, between the merchants. The enforcers invited some of the more prominent hunters as honorary bodyguards, me included but..."

"But," he interrupted, "they suspended all the hunters' invitations upon the request of a certain officer in charge." He rubbed his chin with his thumb. "I believe that is Lieutenant Jerome Orton." Tiel let a small smile appear on her face. "I secured one of your empty cavern rooms." She shifted her gaze to where he pointed. "I need you to read his mind."

"Why?" Tiel's smile disappeared. "You know I hate doing that. Besides, I am a little weak after my earlier trials with the badoe."

"Yes, yes." ManCane waved his hand. "You're weak and it's easy to feel their souls. A scary business in some cases. However, I do not ask this favor lightly. Someone abducted the delegates' children."

"What?" Tiel exclaimed and followed the man towards the cavern room.

"With the way he's been acting, I would stake my career on the fact that Orton had something to do with it." ManCane turned to her. "And, I know he has information about the other abductions. The peace talks are suspended until someone solves this problem."

"I will need time to prepare, so I do not lose myself." Tiel's heavy sigh echoed in her ears.

Before ManCane could answer, a peace enforcer in a cadet's plain, blue uniform ran out of the cavern, his face pale from fright.

"It... it... it just appeared!" the man's voice wavered. "It just appeared!"

"What do you mean?" ManCane turned towards the room.

"An orb appeared out of thin air and attached itself to Orton's chest." The cadet's face went pale. "There was nothing we could do. You'll see."

"Get the medics and technics," ManCane ordered the soldier. Tiel ran towards the cave.

A cold chill caught Tiel's spine as she entered. Lieutenant Orton sat slumped on a wood chair dressed in blue uniform pants and a brown sleeveless top. He gasped his last few breaths of air through his marbled gray face. Purplish veins stuck out like ribbons that crisscrossed his bare skin. A gray metallic orb with a silhouette of a badoe on top cleaved to his chest. A faint glow pulsated along with Orton's beating heart.

"Get that thing off him, quick!" ManCane pushed Tiel aside as he screamed out his orders.

"NO!" Tiel barred some arriving technics with her arms. "it has an explosive device attached to the bottom." She pointed below the badoe on the orb. A small red plastic tube taunted them from the underside.

"That could blow up an entire third of the Hunters' caverns," Tiel warned. The technics backed up and Tiel followed, leaving ManCane.

"No answers for you." Orton rasped a few bars of malicious laughter. A jagged, corrupt soul current emanating from Orton seized Tiel's soul in an icy grip, stopping her in her retreat. Tiel groaned and clasped her hands to her head. "Hearing voices, are we? They will find out," Orton gasped. A hollow screech escaped from his lips, his head fell on his chest, and eyes became vacant. The orb disappeared into thin air as Tiel growled.

"DEATH! DEATH FOR FAILURE." Laughter echoed inside Tiel's head as she pressed her back against the cavern wall. "REMEMBER, MY CHILDREN, DO NOT FAIL ME."

"Tiel?" ManCane's voice echoed from a distance. The cavern room turned hazy while a low scream rose in a spiraling crescendo and drowned out the voice inside Tiel's head. Tiel stumbled as her vision faded in and out. The scream intensified into a hollow moan that grabbed at Tiel's bowels; her midsection tightened into a hard ball. The moan disappeared leaving an eternal moment filled with weeping. Finally, the weeping faded away and the constant internal buzz of other voices dominated her consciousness. Her vision faded as the last of her rutzix shattered. She embraced the darkness descending onto her; knowing it was the only way she would find peace.

CHAPTER 4

THE INITIATE

iel? Tiel?" Maestro's deep baritone voice penetrated her thoughts. Tiel reached out and located a moist muzzle. "Are you all right?" he asked, his voice soft with concern.

"When did you get back from hunting?" Tiel croaked as she stroked Maestro. The rumble of his purr beneath her fingertips chased away the dark soul currents that lingered around her. As her mind cleared, she found herself on the stone floor, the cold chilling the sweat on her body. She slowly opened her eyes only to see Maestro and General ManCane's concerned faces peering down at her.

"What are you two so interested in?" she croaked again. Maestro knew enough to keep his emotions in check. The general, however, did not realize how his soul current blasted into her psyche.

"I take it the voice was too painful." ManCane rubbed his temple. "What was it saying?"

"Nothing much, just happy about Orton's death." Tiel looked over at the body slumped in the chair. Orton's lifeless eyes were open with a final grimace of false triumph chiseled into his face. "We hunters don't like dead bodies in our caverns." She got up from the floor and shook herself. "Get him out of here before Maestro digs Orton a grave."

"Go rest," ManCane suggested. "I may have to ask for further assistance later."

"Depends on the price and how I feel." Tiel started for the door. The entrance teetered and swayed in her vision. She lunged towards Maestro and grabbed onto his back for support. "Right now, I need to get rid of the buzz and to repair my telepathic control. You'll find me at the Drakners."

They exited the room and turned right. Tiel crept towards the Rear Caverns where the daily life of the ritualed hunters took place.

"You were in the room when he died." Maestro kept pace with Tiel as she fought the urge to grab onto the walls. "There was screaming again, wasn't there?"

"Yes." Tiel nodded as she straightened herself and entered the hunters' courtyard. "Orton's screams were there."

As Tiel surveyed the surrounding area, she saw the various hunters in their chosen attire. All outfits were as colorful as their owners' personalities and absent the traditional maicallas.

The caverns themselves were a product of the hunters' ingenuity. Tall lanterns glowed with red crystals in the courtyard. Other crystals of different hues gave needed light to the wide variety of flora in pots from the luscious green bushes to the dainty, colorful flowers.

Their homes and shops were bamboodii hut fronts with windows, doors, and sides on either end, leaving the back open. Welders wrapped steel sheets around the ends of the frames and welded these into the rock walls in front of upper and lower caves. Some owners accessed the upper caves with the use of bamboodii ladders. The avid owner would take months or octaves to carve out stairs and make the caves more like actual rooms. Above these buildings, a carved balcony made more room for a second tier of homes and shops.

Water and drainage pipes, also welded onto the walls, surrounded the buildings. These they decorated with hanging flora or colorful art. Pipes ran into the homes and shops to bring in life-sustaining resources or to empty the waste outside. Some pipes vented the smoke from the stone fireplaces inside. This smoke would ascend to the top of the cavern where other openings in the cavern ceiling circulated incoming air from the Watosh.

The cavern resonated with the constant howl of the outside air currents which was never enough to drown out the ever-present voices of the hunters. Their voices softened into a whisper of gossip as Tiel walked into the hunters' square. A severe headache replaced the buzz in her head as she passed the first huts. She diverted her eyes to the floor to block the glare of the lamp lights.

Jainu sat at one table that stood under the lamps with a holo stick in his hands. His shouts of glee reached her ears, and his jumping threatened to make the scene before her spin. She raised her hand, then lowered it. He returned to his seat, and his smile faded as she walked up to the table.

"What happened?" he whispered while he looked around. "You okay?"

"Let's just say you're lucky that you were in here and not out there with me." Tiel sat on the chair next to him. "You know how we handle the voices. Let's concentrate on other things."

Jainu sat down and gazed at the holo screen as his fingers drummed on the table. His soul currents of concern swirled around her, causing a deep ache.

"What is it?" Tiel held her head in her hands and watched Maestro clean his fur.

"The acodoe appeared just like it said in the prophecies." His voice faded as he glanced from side to side. "They say it is your fault the end of Ecalardia has come." Jainu shrugged his shoulders. "Everyone says it's your fault."

"Look, I don't care what the other hunters or everyone else on this forsaken planet say!" She cradled her head again. "There are too many prophecies. All are different somehow and none agree with each other. It depends on what religion one gets stuck with."

Tiel took a deep breath. The energy it took to speak overwhelmed her. It made the blood in her head pound more fervently each time she mumbled something.

"We can talk about this later." She watched the worried youth. "As far as I know, there is no huge rift in the floor that can devour us. Therefore, I choose to go on with life as normal. Let all the hysterical idiots sort themselves out." She put her hand on Jainu's hand. "Let's enjoy life. If it happens, we will take care of ourselves the best we can. Okay?"

Jainu studied her and then smiled. "I like that. It's more positive."

"Yeah, it is!" She ruffled his hair. "We like to be positive, don't we?"

Jainu gave Tiel a toothy grin. "There is good news."

Tiel didn't answer hoping that her silence would signal Jainu to be quiet. It didn't work.

"I heard on the news that the master scientists can prove that the acodoe reappearing isn't bringing the prophecies to light. They say Shea the sun needs to weep red tears before the Day of Renewal comes. They say they have studied the sun for decades with the telescopes and there isn't any proof that Shea would produce anything like red tears."

"Jainu, my head is pounding, so this will be the last statement I clarify. All the master priests and master scientists have two things in common. One is they both rely on faith. The master priests accept that fact while the master scientists deny it. Second, they put the fulfillment of their predictions of faith into the future. The priests, however, say it can happen anytime, just keep yourself in Coulliou's good graces in case it is not soon.

"However, the funny thing about the scientists and their predictions of faith is that they set their timetables hundreds, thousands, and even tens of thousands of octaves into the future.

"It's interesting that both the master priests and scientists say their predictions won't happen until after their deaths. It's convenient for them, I think. That leaves them enough time to make themselves famous."

"So, who do you agree with?"

"Enough!" Tiel slammed her hand on the table, making Jainu's soul currents harden against her flimsy border causing her body the flinch in pain. "Go get me an herb elixir so I can pay attention to your lessons without my head exploding." Jainu disappeared and Tiel let her border relax. Maestro growled from his prone position on the floor whenever other hunters got too close.

Cutting through the distant firestorm of jagged points of soul currents came a soft array of soul currents which encircled her. Tiel didn't need to search for the source. She knew the currents came from a group of young children, around five octaves old. It was only a few seconds later that the group arrived with their teacher and stood looking at a gigantic, eight-sided, crystal star hanging from the ceiling not too far from her. Most of the children whispered in wonder at the bright, colorful prisms the star created on nearby walls.

"Now, children, our forefathers found this in our knowledge repository. One of seven in all of Ecalardia that we know of." The teacher calmly taught the fidgeting children. Tiel sat back. The elementary lesson was helping her clear her mind, which relaxed her, so she let the lesson permeate her thoughts.

Their teacher explained amid giggles and often extreme silliness how the eight arms kept time. First, there was the calendar that measured Ecalardia's orbit around Shea the sun by lighting up red notches along the edges of the star's arms. There were forty-seven notches on the long arms and forty-three notches on the short arms. A complete orbit was an octave, with three hundred sixty days in an octave divided into forty-five weeks, eight days in a week and twenty-four arms in a day. At the base of each arm was a small silver notch that would light up for each day of the week. In the middle of the star were forty-five golden notches for each week of the octave. The first-week notch was lit at the base of the northern arm.

It was at this point that the teacher brought out snacks, asked the children to sit down, and continued with the lesson by having them answer each question. Tiel smiled at the children still squirming in their seated positions as they learned that there were sixty minutes per arm and that an arm of time was from one tip of an arm to the next arm tip, which kept the measurements equal. A golden line made three complete rotations throughout the day called paths or Shea's paths. It would light up white notches on the top spine of each arm that represented minutes. There were forty notches on the long arm and twenty on the short arm. Each path lasted eight arms. During Shea's first path which started at midnight, the star was a dark purple. By the time Shea peeked over the horizon, the star turned light blue for the next eight arms or Shea's second path. Shea's third path turned the star green and started just before last meal ending at midnight.

Tiel's stomach rumbled as she noticed the golden line just passing the star's tail, which was blue. It was noon, time for second meal. The teacher ended the lesson with the fact that the God Coulliou himself created the octave star. She pointed to the longer northern tip, with the carving of the acodoe at its base. A lighted red notch on the head's spine revealed that it was the third day of the first week of a new octave.

"Children, the reason the acodoe's appearance scares people is that the prophecies state that an acodoe is to appear during the first week of a new octave." This produced a lot of oohs and ah's, amid more squirming. Tiel couldn't help noticing the teacher's glance in her direction.

"They will make themselves look like fools. It's just an animal that has stayed hidden for a long time in a dense forest," Tiel murmured as a strong soul current wrapped around her refusing to let any other current pierce her telepathy. When she realized what it meant she looked up, unable to control her excitement as she gasped in wonder.

"Aven!" she yelled, then regretted her mistake as the sound pummeled her head.

"De Menzaile," Maestro acknowledged as he laid his head on his paws.

"You need food and some rest." The hunter whispered as he gently kissed her ear, his blond hair tickling her chin. His steel-blue eyes viewed her with gentleness. "Everything else can wait. I'll take care of Jainu's lessons. Now, let's go." Aven didn't give her time to answer. He bent down, put his arm around her waist, and pulled her up into his embrace. Her headache softened as they touched noses for a moment.

"I have missed you," she whispered just as he bent to kiss her.

IT WASN'T until the next morning that she woke with a clear head which allowed her to form a strong rutzix. The morning messages had confirmed that Councilwoman Hegert had paid the amount Tiel asked, which made her smile.

"Yeah, Hegert will make sure I pay for my actions," she laughed to herself. She returned to the cavern square to find Jainu talking with a few boys his age. Aven was drinking a strong malt from a mug with a large plate of food in front of him.

She walked over and hugged Aven around the neck. "Hello." Aven turned to her and nibbled her hand.

"Hello," Maestro growled, shifting his weight as he lay on the cobblestone floor. Aven glanced his direction and smirked. "What happened yesterday?"

"I was in the room when a man died. He was not in favor with Coulliou." Tiel took a deep breath.

"Was the weeping too loud again?"

"Weeping?" Maestro lifted his head. "I knew about the screams, you never told me about any weeping."

"It was all too intense." Tiel shivered. Aven watched her. "I had no control over my abilities." She eyed the plate and tore off a piece of the meat. Aven did nothing and she put the flavorful morsel in her mouth. He intrigued her. She should have sensed his soul current. However, she had never discerned Aven's thoughts. She had been united with him for six months, and still his moods were a mystery to her.

"Give me some sign of how you're feeling, will you?" She hit him on the shoulder.

"I am waiting for you to finish your explanation. You may have all of my meal if you like." Aven kept staring at her. "How weak were you?"

"I had no rutzix." Tiel sat down and held his hand. "However, I am now healed. Did you hear the old man? He ranted when the death happened."

"Yes, I heard him." Aven shifted his legs as if trying to locate a comfortable position. "He sounded too happy for my liking."

"It's good we have each other. I wish Jainu could get rid of the old man's voice as easily." Tiel laughed a little. "Sometimes I am too scared." Aven's gaze searched her up and down. "Sometimes..." Tiel took time before continuing, "Sometimes I think the only reason we are stelloves is because the voices go away when we're together." Tiel's hand quivered while she looked at Aven. "There's also the fact that I find you to be a shield from the soul currents of others. That isn't the only reason we love each other, is it?

"You know there is more." Aven touched her cheek with his fingers. "The voices didn't disappear when we first met. We weren't close enough for it to happen. And I was no shield to you. The first thing I saw was you helping twins find their grandmother. That's when I first saw your beauty."

"Yes, and you stood there, cheeks turning red with a pathetic grin plastered on your face," Tiel agreed and let her fears slip away. "You couldn't look me in the eye. It was cute. You're right. It was then I knew I loved you. Have you heard any news of the upcoming larquetz?"

"What larquetz?" Jainu's voice startled Tiel. Aven turned to face the boy behind him.

"Sit, boy!" Aven commanded and Jainu did. Aven turned back to Tiel. "Mistress Laisen tried to get it for yesterday. Master Laisen thwarted her efforts."

"There is not much we can do. We just have to worry about Sethrich."

Aven shifted his weight at this. "Is it that bad?"

"He confronted me yesterday." Tiel grimaced at the thought. "From what I can get, he is more than likely to side with Mistress Laisen if she refuses our union."

"We'll deal with that if and when the time comes," Aven said. "The interesting news is that Mistress Laisen is using the basic Hunter Codes for your trial."

Tiel cocked her head to the side upon hearing the news.

"What is going on?" Jainu interrupted.

"You will get to see an actual larquetz today. One in which a hunter will need to defend their actions," Aven announced as Jainu looked between the two.

"There are concerns about my actions yesterday. I have possibly broken two hunter codes," Tiel explained. Jainu stared at the table's surface. Aven ate his sandwich and let Tiel continue. "Since our esteemed mistress sees no reason to use the higher laws, why don't we use this as an opportunity to instruct Jainu?"

Aven nodded his consent as he chewed his food.

"Tell me which two hunter laws I could have broken."

"What?" Jainu raised his head.

"Go ahead, look up the laws. You know enough to figure out which ones." Tiel smiled at Aven. He returned the gesture as Jainu turned on a halo screen.

"Well, it's not the Prime Code."

"Which is?" Aven prompted the boy.

"Always protect the innocent and those unable to protect themselves." Jainu recited. "Tiel was doing everything to protect the innocent, especially Fallon Hanover."

"So, which ones did I break?"

"The Hunter's Wisdom is measured by what oaths they bind themselves to?" Jainu probed while biting his lip.

"I told you to tell me, not ask me."

"That is one. The Winged Court can say you should have thought twice before dealing with Hegert."

"Correct!" Aven patted Jainu's back. "But what could have happened?"

"She could have been guilty of breaking the Prime Code. It would have taken time to get answers, and Fallon could have died."

"Well, you're learning. Fantastic!" Tiel ruffled Jainu's hair. "I will bring up that fact in the larquetz. Now, tell me the other law I may have broken."

The screen obscured part of Jainu's features as he studied the image.

"It will be hard, just think about it," Tiel said as she leaned back.

"He'll get it. He's smart," Aven chuckled.

"The third! The third!" Jainu jumped up and smiled.

"Why the third?" Aven tested Jainu.

"Because the third is 'The Hunter is loyal first to their stellove, next to their family, then all others'. Loyal means to be true to someone. When you attacked the badoe, it left Maestro in danger because he could have put himself in danger to save you. You were not loyal to him, and that was very important since none of your family or Aven were around."

"I told you he would get it." Aven winked at Tiel.

"But how do you debate that?" Jainu's eyes switched between the two hunters.

"Jainu, the clan obeys the prime code, no matter what." Tiel ruffled the boy's hair as he squinted at her.

"And since Mistress Laisen didn't base her grievances on the higher laws, Tiel should have an easy time defending herself using the basic codes." Aven smiled at her. "So, how do you plan to defend yourself?"

Tiel poised herself to answer when the clang of several bells echoed through the caverns. She shrugged her shoulders as they left the tables.

As they walked, Aven nudged her and asked once again how she planned to defend herself. She giggled and explained Hegert's business in the whole affair. Jainu behaved like a normal boy of ten octaves as he zoomed around the bodies of hunters that filled the cavern halls. Aven chuckled at Tiel's account of the day's events.

They passed houses and shops that lined the cavern walls. Jainu often squatted and hid behind barrels or plants along the hall, jumping out at what he thought to be opportune times. Tiel and Aven feigned slight surprise or ignored him. Maestro walked alongside yawning. Inside, lights dimmed as hunters emerged from the caverns. It wasn't long before the halls became crowded. After Tiel finished her story, Aven seized Jainu as he jumped out from behind a potted bush and turned him upside down. He held the boy by the legs as Jainu hollered for help between squeals of laughter. Tiel was about to tickle the boy's ribs as Jainu's shirt slid down and covered his face when eight hunters appeared.

These hunters dressed in black and had long, dyed, black hair. Four males and four females paired off and approached Aven. The lead male's body matched Aven's in stature. The female alongside him stood shorter than Tiel. Light blue and white daggers lay painted along their left cheekbones; the only part of their faces not covered in black.

Aven righted Jainu and placed him on his feet causing Jainu to teeter from the sudden change in direction. The lead male waited while Aven steadied Jainu, the lines in his face showing concern and empathy.

"It is not good news," the hunter stated. "Mistress Laisen is vehement about this larquetz. She won't even council with Master Laisen about it. He wants to see both of you in his chambers immediately."

"Anised, your sister's paths are still dark concerning our previous relationship I see," Aven grumbled.

"It is what it is." Anised shrugged his shoulders.

"Anised," Tiel said stepping forward, "She won't even council with you on the matter?"

"No." Anised's dark hair swayed with the shaking of his head. "My clan and I will escort."

"That is unneeded," Aven protested, but Anised held up his hand.

"It is the Elder Hunter that requested we escort Tiel to her larquetz."

"Like a common criminal?" Tiel growled, "My zahule is clean enough for me to make it to my larquetz."

"I am sorry. He wanted me to do this yesterday, but I refused." Anised looked at her. "But today he got Mistress Laisen's permission, so I must. Follow me please."

"Maybe Master Laisen can enlighten Shea's paths for us." Aven admitted. "Let's get this taken care of as fast as possible."

LIKE ALL DEEP caverns Tiel had been in, the lower caverns were cold, uneven, musty, and dark. Sporadic wall crystals lighted their way. However, there were lapses in the coverage which kept most corners and hallways dark. Anised and his stellove walked behind Tiel, Aven and Jainu. Maestro had elected to take up the rear behind the other six Dark Sentinels.

"Having me escorted is a way for the Elder Hunter to show that he controls my destiny," Tiel murmured in frustration.

"Are you sure the Elder Hunter is oblivious to our investigation?" Anised's stellove asked looking at both Aven and Tiel.

"Yes, Shaine, he's more concerned about how our union affects his plans to control *me*," Tiel answered. "Trust me, he thinks of me as a pet, not a real threat. Aven is only a clog in his plans."

"Sounds like the Elder Hunter only sees what he wants to see on his paths," Anised mused out loud after a period of silence. "He is clouding his vision with his arrogance."

The group progressed along the corridor, Tiel in her own thoughts until the scent of heavy perfumes and incense assailed her nose. Heat surged through ducts in the ceiling. The sudden warmth chased away the chill and pricked at Tiel's skin. She paid attention to the scene that materialized around her as large crystal lights now chased the shadows away. Elaborate rooms with lights on each side of the entryway lined the hall as the narrow walls gave way to wider hallways. Tiel raised her hand to shade her eyes until they adjusted to the new glare. The uneven, cold floor gave way to plush, heated carpets; the warmth penetrated Tiel's boots.

"Wow!" Jainu whispered, "You're taking me through the Laisen's chambers."

"Of course," Anised said laughing along with everyone else, "how else do you expect to get to Master Laisen himself?"

Tiel watched as Jainu's head swung from side to side as he gazed at the opulence before him. Mistress Laisen's favorite color of red dominated the rooms on the left. Tall, bald, muscular men dressed in red pants that flared out at the thighs and cupped tight around the ankles moved barefoot among the rooms. The tails of gold sashes that wrapped around their waists below their bare chests trailed behind them.

Master Laisen's favorite color of purple permeated the rooms on the right. Long-haired women moved or lounged about in these rooms. Their clothes were the same fashion as the men except for purple and they wore a broad band around their chests. A golden sash wound around a flowing ponytail on the back of their heads.

Luxuriant furniture adorned the rooms. Deep mahogany wood cabinets stood along the walls. Thick cushions and pillows lay on couches and chairs. In the middle of the hallway were two large rooms. Each room had a large bed in the center. Soon after, Anised motioned for the group to go right and they turned into a large room with more plush couches and a deep mahogany round table in the middle. A tall hunter, of normal build and black hair, dressed all in white, filled glasses with water.

"You have arrived." The young man looked up and smiled. "Good, good, we need to talk." He motioned for the group to sit down. Anised bowed and waved his clan out of the room. Shaine stayed at his side.

"I am sure you already know about the details of the larquetz. May I offer advice?" Master Laisen brought the glasses of water to his guests after they sat. Maestro lounged next to the couch. "Would you like a bowl of water, Maestro?"

"Yes, please. Thank you." Maestro purred.

Master Laisen placed an already filled bowl in front of Maestro, then turned and looked at Tiel, saying nothing.

"I would love advice, Radames," Tiel sputtered after she realized he wanted an answer. "I assumed you wouldn't have any since Mistress Laisen wasn't open with her plans."

"It may be good or horrible advice. I will let you choose." Radames leaned against the table. "And thanks for using my name, cousin. I don't hear it enough." He sighed and then continued. "Lidena, Mistress Laisen, is focusing only on her pain. For some odd reason, the Elder Hunter is more than willing to help her with her plans. My advice is not to start by defending yourself." Tiel felt her breathing pause but let Radames continue. "I know it may appear weak. But don't assume you know what she will do. She is committed, and she has proven herself to be cunning before if you will remember how she attained her position."

Tiel remembered. Lidena had been patient, then struck ferociously at the opportune moment, surprising the whole clan. She had been so effective that the previous huntress chosen to be Mistress Laisen left the clan with a battered zahule and no kindred to look after her. Master Laisen had made friends with all of his opponents, then offered them leadership positions. The two leaders handled things differently, yet Lidena often listened to Radames.

"Lidena won't listen to anyone else," Radames continued after taking a drink, "which means she is on a warpath. Your best hope is letting her cloud her own paths. I can calm down the clan after she makes her case. However, if you want, defend yourself."

"Is she asking me to put my Heart on The Block?" Tiel asked.

"Yes," Radames whispered after a pause. The room fell quiet until Jainu raised his hand.

"What is it, young one?" Radames smiled at Jainu.

"What has Tiel done that requires her to be killed?" Jainu asked with tears starting. Tiel felt confused until she realized what Jainu must be thinking. She pulled out her Hunter's Heart and showed it to the distraught youth.

"Jainu, what is this?" She asked the boy.

"Your Hunter's Heart."

"This goes on The Block." Tiel gave him a moment. She continued after Jainu allowed himself to sink into the couch cushions and relax. "When I defend myself, I push the button on top and throw my knife onto The Block. After the knife hits The Block, the poison will seep inside The Block. Octaves of poison seeping into the wood caused the dark red hue on The Block. Apparently, you have been listening to a few horror stories about hunters being killed on The Block."

Jainu nodded fervently. "The Elder Hunter told me those stories when I was getting him ale at Jacquard's."

"Shea's light, that man won't let up." Tiel's breath seethed between her teeth. Then she turned back to the youth. "There is no proof of anything like that happening. The clan will cast me out if I am found guilty. They will know me as a cursed one, or Luhitzu." Jainu just looked confused. "I'll explain later."

"Are you sure he doesn't know we're investigating him?" Radames asked.

"No. He's just mad that I am not his adoring pet," Tiel sneered. "He will not attempt to protect my interests during the larquetz. I assure you, I am on my own."

"No, you're not," Aven and Radames both insisted. The whole group snickered at this.

"There is something else I need to discuss." Radames filled his glass again. "There is a reason I sent Aven on some errands."

"What reason?" Aven leaned forward.

"We have noticed that you and Tiel were quite… unrestrained when chasing a bounty." Radames took a drink and thought. "That is until you two were united. The rest of Ecalardia doesn't know you love each other, but I suggest you let that come to light as soon as possible. I believe there will be less trouble if you do. However, is there anything, medical or psychological, that I need to know?"

Tiel felt her stomach tighten. Aven didn't look in her direction. After a few minutes of silence, Radames let out a heavy sigh.

"You have a little time. I can only help if you let me."

"How long?" Aven asked, his voice sounding tight.

"Until someone who wants to get rid of you finds out your little secrets, then enlightens the rest of the clan of your situation. It will go much easier if you come forward. The clan would help then."

"We will think about it," Tiel whispered.

"Think hard, cousin." Radames lifted his glass and took a drink. "Now, I have a favor to ask. I believe Jilandro is using his telepathy to soften my mind. I need you to confirm this for me, Tiel. Can you?"

"Yes," Tiel answered. "Jilandro is loyal to the Elder Hunter. So, it makes sense that Sethrich would use Jilandro's telepathy to his advantage."

"Can you shield me, Aven, if I need it?" Radames asked.

"Of course, let Tiel examine the situation first," Aven agreed. "If Jilandro is causing problems, she can give me a signal, and I'll move in."

One of Radames maids entered the room. "It is time," the young lady announced. Radames nodded his understanding.

"Would you like to join me for a meal after the larquetz?" Radames offered.

"I am expected at Ma's, cousin." Tiel smiled. "Unless I can use you as an excuse for not…" Tiel stopped as Radames shook his head.

"I will not get in Aunt Emiline's way." Radames backed up at the thought. "We will meet later. Give her my love. Aven, you and Jainu are with me." Radames hurried out of the room. Aven followed, his brows furrowed in confusion.

Tiel just laughed to herself.

CHAPTER 5

LARQUETZ

*T*wo large stone doors opened as six muscled servants pulled on brass rings welded into the doors at the height of a man. Debris from the ceiling dusted the group as the doors scraped along the cavern ceiling.

Tiel was alone with the Dark Sentinels who surrounded her. *"At least I am not chained up,"* she thought to herself while opening her rutzix a little, allowing herself to see the soul currents that flowed around the pit.

A roar erupted from a circular pit beyond the entrance. A host of bounty hunters bellowed out screams and stomped their feet in anticipation as they stood on stone tiers that cascaded down from the top of the pit. Three sets of stone stairs broke the tiers into four sections which allowed movement from the bottom of the pit to the top. The smooth floor before her held an ancient carving of an octave star within a circle that bordered the stone tiers and alcove beyond the entranceway. The west, south, and east arms of the star pointed to the stairs. Its north arm pointed to the alcove in which Tiel stood.

Tiel contemplated the dome ceiling above her. Anciently carved leaves attempted to imitate the ambiance of a watosh. Tiel often mused about what would be tall enough to stand from the floor of the pit to the ceiling. Now that she had her latest adventure behind her, she imagined that an acodoe could even though its head might disappear inside the dome. She chuckled to herself. A creature that large couldn't enter the caverns.

She studied the scene before her as she walked through the raw soul currents of emotions that haphazardly collided into each other. This action caused the currents to weaken so that when they hit, they ricocheted off her or dissipated altogether. Tiel was more worried about the two hunters in the second row of the stone benches in long black robes. Sethrich sat next to the middle staircase and sitting next to him was Jilandro, who was wrapping his soul current around Radames. The effect weighed down Radames' soul current causing it to hit the floor and disappear. Radames stood slouching to the right of a huge wooden block, eyes just about glazed over.

Lidena, Mistress Laisen, stood to the left of the wooden block with her right hand resting on top. A white dress left her tan shoulders bare and was at a length that reached matching slippers. A white scarf tied her long blond hair. Tiel sensed a strong soul current that surged from Lidena beyond The Block towards Aven. He stood in front of the tiered seats with his arms folded and his face stern as he watched the mistress. Behind him, Jainu sat on the first tier of the pit with a somber face. Maestro lay on the floor.

Tiel rubbed her chin and looked at Aven. He moved in between Jilandro and Radames, his presence acting like a knife slicing through Jilandro's soul current. Jilandro looked toward Sethrich but said nothing. Radames stood straight as if coming out of a dream and shook his head.

As Tiel drew nearer to The Block, the room filled with the yells of the hunters from all but the second tier. The second-tier of hunters and huntresses, the Winged Court, sat silently in long black robes. Tiel looked down at The Block, its shape ragged with notches from hunter knives. The four sides revealed shadows of ancient carvings that bordered the bottom. Ages of poison from the hunters' hearts tainted the sides and sunk into the pores on top, defiling the light-yellow wood with a russet stain. Two hunters' knives stood embedded on the top of the wooden block, a third of each blade hidden in the wood. The deep yellow of the crystal lamps positioned around the pit shown through the heart of the knives which seemed to ignite the crystal inside with a bright flame.

"Why is Aven moody and solemn, Mistress Laisen?" Tiel asked in a soft voice.

"I just explained things to him," Lidena smirked. "How did you get someone so... devoted?" Her eyes danced with the flames of the crystal light as she poured her thoughts in Aven's direction. Tiel fought the urge to search them.

"Perhaps you lacked devotion." Tiel waved at the crowd which brought on some cheers. "More than likely, that is why he didn't stay with you."

Lidena hissed as she pushed a hidden button under her hand. Narrow slits of white light burst out of The Block's sides which signaled the start of the larquetz. She raised her hands, and the noise in the pit stopped. Every hunter sat down. Lidena spoke, and her voice carried to the top tier of the pit.

"One of our clan members has informed us, the Laisen, that one of the Winged Court has brought great shame on her zahule, her stellove's zahule, and the Winged Court's zahule. For this, she stands before The Block to have her heart judged. Judged whether her heart is true to the oaths she has taken or false, thus turned to ash and forgotten. The huntress we speak of is the Winged Court's very own Bounty Huntress." At this, the mistress pointed at Tiel and the hunters roared with contempt.

Tiel raised her own Hunter's Heart, a signal of her confidence. Cheers burst through the contempt.

"Is there anyone who stands with this huntress?" Lidena called out. The hunters quieted down and watched as Aven's determined footsteps resounded across the pit. Lidena's soul currents solidified. Concrete visions of her comforting Aven and his eventual declaration of love proved she had molded these dreams into a treasured alternate reality.

"What is this, an adolescent fantasy?" Tiel hid her contempt as her own thoughts raced around in her head. Lidena shaking her head in warning towards Aven made Tiel feel a little nauseous and furious. *"All that is amiss in this fraudulent trial are giggles from a cluster of fidgeting girls whispering in the back."*

"I will stand beside my stellove. Her heart is true." Aven's voice rang out.

"If you stand with her and her heart goes on The Block, the clan will cast you out. You'll be a Luhitzu. The hunted not the hunter." Lidena tried to warn him, her voice still carrying to the farthest ears.

"My heart is with my stellove and I will share in the same fate." Gasps sounded throughout the pit. Aven snarled at Lidena as her gaze hit the floor.

"Our hearts are true and will not be on The Block this day. Especially with unscrupulous charges that involve Hegert!"

"Hegert?" Lidena laughed as her eyes met Aven's once again. "My dear de Menzaile, those are not the charges. Councilwoman Hegert soiled her own zahule so much that its yellow color has long molded and sprouted bugs of its own." That remark brought on cheers from the whole assembly. "Since you are not clear what the charges are, I will offer you another chance."

"What are the charges, Mistress Laisen?" Tiel hissed at her while sending a separate thought current to the mistress. *"And cool your tone and thoughts with my stellove. I consider your manner to be too fresh for my taste."*

Lidena took a step back, a normal reaction to a telepathic penetration, and her thoughts vanished. Her upper lip trembled. She focused on the crowd and raised her arms once more.

"The charges are simply breaking the Prime Code." Lidena half smiled, half snarled at Tiel. "That of protecting the innocent." She turned back to the hunters among shouts of astonishment. "The Bounty Huntress did not keep focus on those entities around her. We all know she is a strong telepath. Therefore, it is easy for her to keep focus. But, through her failure, she brought out the acodoe, which brought to pass the prophecy. The citizens of Ecalardia are in deep turmoil. This broke her oath to protect the innocent, for no one else is guilty of the calamity that has come. The Bounty Huntress is a member of the Hunter Clan, which brings the blame for Ecalardia's end upon us. She has laid this blame at our door and therefore soiled her, de Menzaile's, and the Winged Court's zahule."

"What calamities do you speak of?" Sethrich's voice carried over the commotion. A white embroidered wing donned each shoulder of his black robe. "These calamities should be connected to yesterday's events."

"Have you seen the news, Elder Hunter?" Lidena strode forward to answer him. "Families have packed their belongings; citizens everywhere have quit their jobs. Others just sit on the walkways, already dead within themselves. What calamities? Look around you. This is because The Bounty Huntress led an acodoe out of the Watosh." Sethrich bowed his head in acknowledgment, the striking tattooed serpent seemed to hiss in fury as he sat back down.

Lidena pointed her long forefinger at Tiel, a smile twitched on her lips. "I have brought my case before the court. What say you, Bounty Huntress?"

Tiel threw her Hunter's Heart. It landed on The Block in front of the other two knives. Gasps sounded from the crowd as whispers echoed all around.

"I deny the charges and will prove that it is your own zahule you soil." Tiel glimpsed at Radames. He stood with his arms folded, eyebrows arched.

"And perhaps after I do, I will bring charges of my own." She directed her thoughts to Mistress Laisen who stood among imbalanced currents of confusion.

"Bounty Huntress, do you wish to confer with a counselor before you begin your defense?" the Elder Hunter called out to her.

"Thank you for the kind offer, but no. I am fine, Elder Hunter." Gasps and roars of excitement thundered through the pit.

"What are you doing?" Aven mouthed amid a cacophony of threats and cheers.

"Follow my lead," Tiel mouthed back. Aven tilted his head and smiled. She kissed the air in his direction and walked towards the tiers.

"My kin of the Winged Court and honored ritualed hunters, I have but one question to ask of you." Tiel smiled at Lidena, then faced the second row as they stood to face her. All the second-row hunters and huntresses stood with their arms folded in front while their right hands held crystal hunter knives filled with liquid. The knives rested against their left arms with the blade down. They bowed their heads in acknowledgment as the pit once again quieted down.

"My kin, Mistress Laisen says I am guilty of bringing to pass the acodoe prophecy and the calamities that destroy Ecalardia along with it. I humbly ask, which prophecy does she speak of?" The air from the tunnels whispered with tentative shrills that pierced the silence. Everyone concentrated on Tiel. "Which prophecy does she speak of? Does she speak of the prophecy that claims the acodoe will come before the calamities begin? On the other hand, does she speak about the calamities which have already begun?"

Aven called out with his knife in the air, "Or, does she speak of the prophecy in which the acodoe will bring the deathly wind that will steal the flesh of Ecalardians?" The hunters cheered and hooted. When it died down again, Aven continued, "How about the prophecy in which the acodoe will come as Ecalardia bleeds from her pores?"

"Or, is it the prophecy where the acodoe will bring in a season of peace and prosperity?" Tiel called out. "Apparently, not that one, with all the current calamities Mistress Laisen has cited." A few chuckles echoed from the crowd. "Or, how about the one where a great king will come to his own mind, able to do his own will and save the citizens of Ecalardia?"

"What great king would that be?" a male voice taunted as the laughter rose in volume.

"We don't have one, much less one that has the zahule to come to his own mind!" A female voice brought more laughter from the crowd. Tiel winked at Jainu whose face beamed at the turn of events.

"Or, is it the prophecy that tells us that the Blessed of Coulliou himself, the one who shall release the acodoe, will be the one to fulfill his will?" Aven yelled out. The laughter stopped, the pit echoed a thoughtful silence. Tiel peered at Lidena. Her cheeks looked hollow. Her eyes stared down while her hands lay clasped in front of her. Tiel smiled and focused on the crowd.

"There is even a prophecy which declares that Ecalardia will split open and swallow whole bodies of waters, devour mountains, valleys will turn into mountains, and deserts turn into seas when the acodoe appears. Ecalardia herself will heave flames and ash from her pores. I ask, am I so great I can control the very planet we live on? Am I to become a god? If so, how can a god be judged by mere mortals?" A few bursts of laughter resonated at Tiel's question. "Let me assure you, my kin, I am no god. Since I am a mere mortal, there is no way I could have held back an acodoe much less control the endeavors of a whole planet.

"Councilwoman Hegert herself blackmailed a badoe herdsman to release a calf for her own purpose. The beasts or conditions of the Watosh would have killed the calf. The mother would have sensed this and stampeded in anger and grief straight into the largest food source it could find." Tiel paused a moment and allowed the hunters time to think. "The largest food source was the innocent citizens who attended the bamboodii harvest. What we thought to be ancient myths record that an angry badoe attracts an acodoe. How am I supposed to watch for a myth?"

"Tell me, who of you could have held back the response of the citizens of Ecalardia due to this event?" Aven raised his voice once more. The crowd turned their attention to him. "Mistress Laisen has only given you the information she wanted. While some cursed the acodoe's appearance, others hailed its appearance. They rejoiced and celebrated. Then they brought good news to the depressed and lifted hearts. Soon, this will all be forgotten and the citizens of Ecalardia will once again return to their normal lives."

"Everyone knows there is no way a case with Hegert involved will win. So, I ask each of you, why would Mistress Laisen seek with great diligence a case against me?" Intakes of air hissed through the pit as cries of disgust filled the air at Tiel's insinuation.

"I would be careful before bringing suspicion upon the Laisen, Bounty Huntress, especially since you are still an accused," Sethrich warned.

"Allow *me* to pose a question." Aven stepped towards him. "Why give a devoted stellove a second chance to change his alliance?" The crowd hissed even louder, then quieted and looked past the pair.

Tiel turned to see Lidena with both her arms raised, holding her Hunter's Heart. "I will answer those questions. Even though I am a leader, I am not above my hunter oaths." After a momentary pause, she lowered her knife.

Radames observed this scene, his eyes narrowed. Mistress Laisen took a deep breath, then sheathed her knife on her right thigh under a slit in her dress. She peered at Radames out of the corner of her eye. He took a moment while rubbing his thumb against his lips, then he pulled the other knife out of The Block and sheathed it in a large pant pocket on his right thigh. The pit stayed silent as Mistress Laisen focused on Tiel and Aven.

"As Laisen, we are responsible for the zahule of the Hunter Clan." Mistress Laisen directed her comments at Tiel. Tiel sealed her rutzix against feelings of anger, envy, and resentment. "When we see havoc brought about because of the possible ignorance of one of its sisters, the clan must have the chance to decide that hunter's heart. We did not look for a case. We saw what happened and interpreted the information."

She took a deep breath and directed the next set of comments to Aven. "In our position as Laisen, we studied the past and found destroyed lives when their stellove's heart was put on The Block. These hunters need nurture and care. Such a thing has driven hunters mad, which could happen to you since you both have proven your devotion to each other. As an outcast, the support you need would not be available. And what of Jainu? We needed to consider and protect his interests."

Mistress Laisen again directed her comments to the Hunter Clan. "However, since de Menzaile and Tiel presented some concerns, I did not carry the Laisens zahule well and have soiled it. I ask the clan, the Winged Court, de Menzaile, and The Bounty Huntress to give me their forgiveness that I may use it to cleanse the Laisen's precious zahule, so it is white once more." She stood with her head bowed.

The crowd roared with acceptance as Tiel watched the Winged Court, one by one, sheave their knives until Sethrich was the only one with his knife still unsheathed.

"What is your decision, Elder Hunter?" Radames demanded.

"The Bounty Huntress needs to repair the damage she has done to the Laisen. She is not guiltless yet." He glared at Tiel and held his head aloft.

"That may be true," Radames spoke in a slow and deliberate tone. "However, she is not the only one who damaged someone's zahule. Is that right, Mistress?"

"What shall I give the great Bounty Huntress to amend my wrongs?" Lidena inquired.

"I would like to take The Block this moment to speak to the clan," Tiel answered as she forced her voice to be steady.

"What say you, Elder Hunter?" Mistress Laisen asked.

"I say The Bounty Huntress should take The Block if she seeks to help repair the Laisen zahule." He raised his black eyebrows and stared at her.

"Of course, I will follow the wisdom of my elder kin." At Tiel's response, Sethrich stared a moment, sheathed his Hunter's Heart, and sat down.

"I shall also follow his advice. Take The Block, my dear Bounty Huntress." The Laisens bowed and stepped back from The Block. The hunters stamped their feet and roared their enthusiastic consent of the past events. Jainu jumped and cheered as Maestro laid his head on his paws. Tiel took her position behind The Block. Aven followed, throwing his knife behind hers. The crowd fell silent, and all took their seats.

"As Mistress Laisen has brought to our attention this day, this clan has taken an oath to protect the innocent. General ManCane has alerted me to a grievous exploitation of the most innocent people of Ecalardia. How does the clan view General ManCane's zahule?"

"White, his zahule is white," several voices yelled out as cheers backed up the opinion.

Tiel raised her hands, and the hunters quieted. "I am glad to hear this, for he has saved several of us from the soiled zahule of those under his station."

Murmurs of agreement echoed as Tiel continued, "He has always respected our ways and has never sought to soil our zahule."

Tiel let the murmurs subside. "Yet, my brothers and sisters, his heart is heavy this day. His duty is hard to bear in the current events that over-shadow his travels on Shea's paths. We all know of the frequent abductions. Some of us are victims ourselves, the knowledge of our parents' identities lost." Hunters' heads nodded as murmurs started once more. "It is worse, my kin. Mass neighborhood abductions are now common. They snatch chil-dren out of their weeping parents' arms as they sit in their homes." The hunters' voices rose in shock and anguish; many squirmed in their seats. "The general has requested our help, so my brothers and sisters, do we protect the innocent as our great Mistress Laisen has reminded us this day?"

The hunters rose as one force. Their voices roared the loudest of the whole event. They pounded their feet and waved their knives in the air. Tiel raised her hands into the air and the commotion stopped, but all stood erect.

"Then protect these small innocents. Watch the neighborhoods, find out any information you can, and bring it to us." Tiel turned to Aven, and he bowed his consent. She returned her attention to the hunters. "If you see an abduction in progress, save the innocent and bring the perpetrators to the Peace Enforcers in ManCane's name. Will you do this?" The hunters stood still, their gaze beyond Tiel.

Radames had moved forward and now raised his Hunter's Heart into the air. "My honored kin, can you believe there is a question about the recogni-tion of these hunters' union by the clan?"

Whispers filled the room as Tiel turned to Radames. She didn't realize that there was even a hint of doubt to their union though Sethrich had hinted at the possibility. She made a mental note to ask Radames about this later.

"Mistress Laisen herself recognized the love these two share in her explanation of the day's events." Tiel looked to Lidena. She stood, a seething glare directed at Radames. He ignored her and kept speaking. "And have not their actions proven their devotion? I move that this assembly accept their union and officially recognize them as stelloves."

The hunters roared and stamped their approval. Tiel turned to the crowd to find Sethrich missing.

"HAVE you learned anything I taught you?" Sethrich's voice boomed through the closed cave that sixteen of the Winged Court stood in. They bowed their heads, and the black hoods of the robes covered their faces. These were his prodigy, the ones he devoted his teachings to. The ones whom he molded into the images of the hunters of old when the laws of the clan were absolute.

His best prodigy, his telepath Jilandro, stood next to him. He was of a normal height with thick, black hair and a cropped beard. If Sethrich couldn't perform his duties, Jilandro would be the one to represent the Winged Court. However, the youth made his mistakes. The room vibrated with telepathic interference which shouldn't be happening since Sethrich hadn't ordered Jilandro to use his talents. He would discipline the youth later. Sethrich turned his attention back to his pupils.

"She is not one of us. She relishes in studying from the corrupted tomes of the Laisen's Repository!" he yelled and picked up a wooden chair, slamming it on the ground, feeling a little satisfaction as two legs splintered. He picked it up, slamming the chair again until only a cracked seat lay on the ground. When he looked up, his students stood huddled in the corner, some averting their heads.

"Look at you, cowards in a corner." He pointed at them. "I should have seen this. You lack the courage to condemn her, just as you lack the courage to stand up to me. ME, an old, useless man."

He observed them for a few moments, "WHY, WHY?!" The hunters before him averted their eyes. "WELL?!"

A young girl of about eighteen octaves stepped forward. "She and Aven proved that she was innocent."

"AVEN, AVEN!" He threw the seat of the chair against the wall and reveled in the sharp crack as it split apart. "Aven is a love-struck simpleton. He'll let Tiel lead him by the nose, laughing with a twinkle in his eyes while she does it."

He took another seat and sat down at the table. With his eyes closed, he breathed, willing his heart to slow and his temple to stop pulsating. When he opened his eyes, he studied his students.

"Her defense was that she was not a god." His slow, deliberate speech sent the group backing up against the wall. Jilandro shied away from him also, head bowed. "Come here, come here." He wiggled his fingers and let his soft voice coach them closer. "She spoke the truth as she sees it. As a telepath, she should have looked for danger before leaving the Watosh Forest. She lost control of her anger, almost stabbing an old woman to death. Plus, her actions allowed a huntress to fight seen in front of the gossips' orbs." His voice raised a little, causing the others to shuffle.

"That is not the least of her offenses. She brought in a gossip herself to have him mended and is now using the clan to fulfill the wishes of a peace enforcer!" His voice rose again as he slammed the table with his fist. "A GENERAL IN THE PEACE ENFORCERS!"

"There are no laws forbidding kindness to others." A hunter spoke from the back. "In fact, we are to uphold the Prime Objective, protect the innocent."

"Ah ha, yes, yes." Sethrich pointed at the young man, his voice a whisper. "But you didn't disagree with me about her temper or fighting in the open in view of the gossips' orbs."

The hunter bowed his head. "And as for protecting the innocent," He said as the spit shot out of his mouth, "THE HUNTER CLAN IS THE INNO-CENT!" He stood up again and advanced on the group waving his hands in front of him. "Forget the mistress's pathetic little problems. Tiel Lambrie, The Bounty Huntress," he spat out the name, "has soiled the Hunter Clan's zahule. And de Menzaile relished in it. He protected her. Both deserved to have their bowels removed with their own Hunter's Hearts."

"We should have thought of that," the first huntress admitted. "Sorry, Elder Hunter."

"No, no," he whispered letting the crowd shrivel in the silence. "No, you should have paid attention to your studies that I graciously gave you. The ones that instruct you about the Hunter Clan's Golden Age. You would have known everything she did should have been unseen. All anyone should have known was that someone performed a gracious, pious act.

You would have known the laws allow only the ritualed in the back caverns, or their problems brought in front of the clan on The Block. But most of all, you should have watched me. I knew this all along. My Hunter's Heart never left my arm, so your Hunters' Hearts should not have left your arms. I would have brought all this up. She and Aven would have lost, and the general's problem would not be eroding Shea's paths before us." He beheld the bowed heads of his students.

"Do not worry. It is all part of your training." He waved his hand and slumped in a chair. "Just remember today so you do not disappoint me on another of Shea's paths. Next time, I will bring the accusations. I will tell you how to judge beforehand."

He sighed and lowered his voice. "We are the judges, the body that upholds the laws. It is our sacred duty to purify the Hunter Codes and Laws once more, along with those that take solemn oaths to uphold them."

The silence permeated the room and Sethrich laid his head in his hands. "Go. Go," he whispered. A heavy silence followed the shuffling of feet and closing of the bamboodii door.

"Jilandro." Sethrich lifted his head. The telepathic currents dissipated. "What am I to do?"

"You have taught us all well. They have learned much today." Sethrich felt his pupil's hand on his shoulder.

"You comfort me, my boy, when you feel it is in your best interest." Sethrich's voice turned threatening.

"What, Elder Hunter?"

Sethrich elbowed his pupil in the chest. As the youth bent down trying to breathe, Sethrich slammed Jilandro's face on the table. "Do not use your telepathy again unless I tell you to," Sethrich instructed.

"Yes, Elder Hunter," Jilandro coughed out.

CHAPTER 6

INTRODUCTIONS

*A*ven's arms felt warm and secure around Tiel's waist as the group made their way from the pit. She breathed deeply, taking in the outdoor woodsy scent that always permeated his person. His heartbeat was strong under her cheek. Jainu jumped up and down ahead of her, ramming his fists into the air while yelling in excitement. Maestro walked alongside, avoiding Jainu. Lights from the various shops and abodes brightened as the crystals warmed up from their nap. She heard the casual conversations and jubilant laughter coming from all around her.

"Are you sure he's a wave-seer?" Aven asked, his soft voice booming through his skin.

"Yes, that is the only way to know when a telepath is active," Tiel answered. "My only saving grace was that he thought it was Jilandro who was using his telepathy. Jilandro took a beating and said nothing."

"That could benefit us. Perhaps I will go visit him in the medic's cavern before leaving." Aven's arm embraced her tighter as he looked towards the entrance.

"If you say so. It scares me that I haven't realized it before. I must be careful if only for Jilandro's sake." Both hunters fell silent for a few moments as they took in the elated atmosphere around them.

"There's no time. We'll be late for last meal." Maestro's white hair tickled her face and cheek as he pushed his way in between them. "It's about time you came with us." He stared at Aven.

"It is long past time." Aven let his chest deflate. "But I have to acquaint myself to a new hunt. My patrons promised a lot of sigots for its completion."

"Well, don't forget to look at our account. Hegert helped our savings for an abode," Tiel said while rubbing her face and nose vigorously. "Maestro, you want to wrestle."

"Yes!" Maestro roared as he moved forward. "This fleshpot is the only human that can give me a good workout."

"If you continue to interrupt, I will let Ma know it's your fault we're late." Tiel glared at Maestro who stopped and sat.

"Come on. When are we going?" Jainu yelled.

"I'll give you two time to say your 'see you laters'." Maestro crouched and made his way towards the boy letting a deep growl escape his chest. Jainu jerked around at the sound; and, seeing Maestro slinking around the tables in the courtyard, squealed in laughter and ran to the right.

Aven pulled her body into his. He bent down close to her face and she felt his breath warm her cheek. She gazed into his eyes as he took his plain maicalla out of his back pants pocket and took off a clasp made from a brass soldier's flat coin. The back had an octave star obscured by the welding of the clasp onto the metal. The front had a soldier with a sword and flag criss-crossed behind him.

Aven gave the clasp to Tiel. The coin's weight rested in her hand as she studied it. They had exchanged maicalla clasps as a sign of their union. It would be best for the Drakners to learn about their marriage from them and not from recognizing that Tiel wore a different maicalla clasp.

"Don't worry. If I can make it, I will." Aven smiled as he lifted Tiel's chin. "I know we wanted to wait until we had time to spend with them. But, Maestro is right. It is time. We can get to know them later."

Tiel returned the smile and caressed his cheek with the back of her fingers. She pulled out the crystal watosh clasp and handed it to Aven who tossed it in his hand. She locked eyes with him, feeling secure in his presence.

"Is Emiline Drakner really that tough?" Aven asked her as he turned to watch Maestro play with a giggling Jainu.

"Let's just say she has a way to make you feel her disappointment deep down in the soul. She does this in such a way as to keep one guilt-ridden for a score of days." Aven leaned back at this. "We need to get a family outing together quickly."

Jainu's squeals of laughter rang out among the tables as Maestro's deep rumbles persisted.

"I am taking Jainu with me. Ma is the one who helped me deal with the voices inside my head. I am hoping she can help Jainu. He needs the practice."

Aven pulled her in as close as possible, both arms firmly around her waist. She closed her eyes as his face drew near and she felt his nose nuzzle her cheek for a moment. Tiel caressed his cheek with her lips. He drew back as she opened her eyes and they both simultaneously mouthed 'I miss you'. He moved in for a kiss, and Tiel's lips met his in a lingering, impassioned embrace.

LIDENA SLUMPED on a couch in her lounge room. It was too large to fill with furniture. What furniture she seized from the Laisen's storage room stank of old age. No matter how expensive the deep mahogany tables, cabinets, and shelves appeared, she knew they represented a duty that echoed of failures.

"I remember when that pout could get a man to do anything, Lidena."

She looked and found Anised leaning against the entrance way. His painted face somber, his black eyes danced with a capped fury.

"My dear big brother, there is only one man I want that to work on." She stood and went to the table sitting behind the couch. "And you are right. It worked well on him... once."

"That man united with another." Anised stepped forward and took the bright orange drink offered to him by a servant.

"What does she have that I don't?" Lidena grabbed a glass from the table and threw in some ice from a crystal bowl.

"It doesn't matter. He has chosen," Anised restated. "Your outright stunt soaked your zahule with the darkest of dung. Consider other men before it is your heart on The Block." Anised gritted his teeth.

"Anised!" Lidena hissed. "It is not your place to put..."

"To put you in your place?" Anised questioned. "It is everyone's place, get over it. Find someone else."

Lidena cursed Coulliou as she slammed the glass on the table and walked out.

"BE CAREFUL SITTING THERE, JAINU," warned the female artificial intelligence as the vehicle's gray sides melted away.

"What are you talking about, Sarje?" Jainu asked while looking down into the interior. "Oh, Aven left you something, Tiel."

Tiel leaned in the vehicle and retrieved a bouquet of flora wrapped in a clear package, sitting on Sarje's passenger seat. A giggle escaped Tiel's lips before she realized what had happened. The different shades of the blue flora smelled wonderful. She breathed in the scent which brought to her mind clear crystal lakes and waterfalls. After a few moments, she put it between the seats. Soon they were on their way with Maestro lounging in the backseat, his tail thumping against the window.

During the ride over to Daton, Tiel decided to use Aven's gift as an introduction to her union. She didn't think Aven's first introduction to Ma should be Ma's sad gray eyes combined with a heartbroken look. This way Ma would be excited and would even put together one of her famous meals. She spent at least half an arm chiding herself for not thinking of this earlier.

They left Sarje parked outside the village as were all the other personal vehicles. Maestro rushed Jainu along the walkways, chiding him for not going faster. Tiel shushed him up by smacking Maestro on the nose, then pointing to her head. The static was lower than usual but Jainu wasn't used to it, so his attention was on trying to ignore the intrusion in his brain.

The journey was as expected. The other villagers they encountered were dressed in an array of colorful outfits from the drunk villager sitting on the side of the walk to the best-dressed lady or lord meandering around trying to look important. She used her telepathy to avoid the areas where angry villagers gathered.

They passed shops and abodes that held manicured lawns, enclosed in with bamboodii fences painted various colors that matched the abodes. An abundance of flora grew everywhere giving charm and elegance to the large village. Crystal shafts jutted out from the tops of each abode and shop, supplying the needed power for the villagers inside. Street corner crystal lamps held smaller versions of octave stars so that everyone would know the time. These stars showed that the golden line had moved just beyond the northeastern point of the now green stars.

"We will get a scolding from Ma," Tiel warned as they opened the front gate to the abode.

"In that case, it's time to go hunting." Maestro peered around the edge of the abode to the Watosh Forest behind the long backyard.

"You know both Ma and Pa want you to say hi before you go hunting beyond their backyard." Tiel pushed the door open ignoring Maestro's growl of irritation. The front entrance held a small parlor for guests and their families. Two small bamboodii couches lined the walls on the right with an oval table sitting in front. A colorful, handmade, throw-rug, showing a vista of the Watosh Forest, lay on the floor in front of the table. Several pictures of past orphans that the Drakners had taken under their wing hung above the couches. To the left stood a thin, tall, bamboodii table with two drawers under the lip. Above that was the family octave star. Tiel pushed Jainu in front of her and placed the bouquet in his hands.

"Give it to Ma. It can be a shield," Tiel whispered as she pushed the boy forward and boxed her soul current. The group's feet made clomping sounds as they crossed the light amber wood floor. Maestro pushed on Tiel's back as he walked in the doorway.

"Thanks for making me the sacrifice," Jainu complained. Suddenly he stopped and gazed around the room as mouthwatering aromas wafted out of the kitchen. Tiel smiled at Jainu's open mouth as he inched toward the kitchen.

"Ma, Pa, I know you're here," Tiel shouted which caused Jainu to jump. He turned around and stuck his tongue out. Tiel adjusted the clasp on her maicalla, so it lay opened to her mid-section, perfect for family mealtimes. "The hut smells wonderful."

"Boy, does it ever!" Jainu exclaimed. He wore no maicalla due to his age. "What scent candles have you been using?" Tiel gritted her teeth and dug her fingers into the boy's shoulder. Jainu winced at the pain. Maestro grumbled and Tiel could feel him slouching behind her.

"A hut should always welcome someone home with the aromas of a hot meal," Emiline said as she appeared in the doorway. Emiline was a small, slightly plump woman. She wore a full white apron that folded over at the waist so as not to drown her short frame. Her pink floral shirt and pants matched the bright pink maicalla with both sides of ancestral stripes done in shades of light to medium brown. Her marriage clasp, a crystal sun representing Shea, hung at the same point of her body as Tiel's clasp did. A solid thick bun sat on top of her blond hair with not a strand falling around her face. Her gray eyes studied Jainu. "I *do not use* flavor additives or scent candles, dear boy. *That* is real food aroma coming from the kitchen."

"Wow!" Jainu's eyes grew big as he reverently whispered the proper praise for the occasion. Tiel let go of the boy's shoulder and she could sense Maestro standing up straight once more. "It never smells like this when Tiel or Aven cooks." Tiel grabbed the boy's shoulder again as Maestro chuckled. Jainu shrugged her off and moved forward.

"This is for you." He handed the flowers to Emiline. "You deserve them for making food that smells delicious." Jainu's grin was wide as he gazed up into Emiline's eyes.

"Well, thank you. You bought these for today?" Emiline questioned Tiel.

"No," Tiel said as Emiline's eyebrows furrowed, "but you deserve them."

Emiline shook her head, recovered herself, and then smiled down at Jainu. "Well, what a sweet boy. Let's find a vase. We'll put them on the table outside, so we can enjoy their beauty while we are eating." She led Jainu down the hall.

Tiel made her way into a larger, oblong room that served as the kitchen and dining area. She spied an older gentleman and chuckled. Emery Drakner wiped his hands on his white full-length apron that covered his plain, gray shirt and pants. His white complexion smiled down on Tiel as he peered at her from over his glasses. Black hair with silver edges framed his ears and his Shea clasp held his jade-green maicalla at his breastbone. It had ancestral stripes on the right in brown and on the left in various bright colors.

"It has been a long time, young lady." He winked as he worked at the grill encased in a rock island. The starched vegetables he tossed were toasted in a generous amount of fat that was bubbling on the solid steel grill surface.

"Way too long," Tiel agreed. "I haven't had a decent meal in ages."

"Now, whose fault is that?" Emery tried to sound serious, but the twinkle in his eyes gave him away.

The smells from the kitchen and octaves of experience told Tiel that a pink roast beast was in the black pot hanging over a fire in a large rock fireplace behind Emery. Emiline had often told Tiel that she could never understand why anyone would want the cold, silver, modern appliances. The fireplace and grill worked well and cooked things evenly every time. It took time to make the hut smell good enough, so guests felt comfortable to sit, eat, and enjoy a good conversation. The only modern appliance that Emiline embraced was a sink and a chill box nestled in between two rock walls.

Tiel focused her attention on the dining area. On a wooden table, the corners of a golden basket extended from under a quilted towel. The thick, hot aroma of fresh bread tempted Tiel.

She leaned back to look down the hall. Maestro sat in front of the first room entryway moving his head from side to side keeping watch. Tiel chuckled again as she gave in to the temptation, grabbed the towel and lifted it only to pull her hand away from Emiline's stinging slap.

"Ma, if you want no one to sneak at your food, you shouldn't make it so good." Tiel glared at Maestro wondering why he let the woman get past him without warning. He averted his gaze.

"Don't you dare try to scold me, young lady! And Maestro has better manners than to warn you about me coming when you're up to something." Jainu laughed behind Emiline as Tiel stood up straight with her hands behind her back.

"I took you in as a little lost soul at eight, right after we found you beaten and battered by your kidnappers. And you don't have the decency to say hi and give a hug before you barrel into someone's carefully prepared homemade meal?!" Emiline's eyes smoldered as Tiel bent down to wrap her arms around her.

"I love you and thanks for having me around, as usual." Emiline relaxed and returned the hug.

"Well, that's better. We are always happy to have you home. Now, this boy tells me he hears the same voices you do?"

Tiel nodded which caused Emiline to draw in a gasp of air. Emiline's eyes shifted between the two as she listened to Tiel. "I was hoping you could help him as you helped me."

"Do you have the authority to grant his medical care to me?"

"Yes." Tiel looked her in the eye.

"Well then…" Emiline studied the boy. "At first we should give you some medium doses of chems for your size. We will teach you some coping techniques later. It will take time, but we can accomplish it."

"He needs to stay here," she informed Tiel.

"I see no harm in it as long as you know he will need to go on training with me." Tiel saw the gentle smile on Emiline's lips and moved over to the fireplace. She used a nearby thick glove to lift the pot lid. The dark pink beast released a sweet honey scent that drew Tiel in closer only to get her hand slapped again with a wooden spoon. She let the lid drop while shaking her hand and mouthing the word "ow".

Tiel turned to tease Emiline but saw a face set in defiance. Her eyes way beyond smoldering, now bursting into flames.

"What am I being accused of now?"

Emiline frowned at Tiel. "Is de Menzaile coming?"

Tiel cocked an eyebrow at the woman.

"I have seen how you two put on a show when the gossips' eyes are on you. Oh, you fight each other when the gossips' eyes are present. But neither of you have even broken an appendage. I will bet my cooking talent on the fact you two are more than friends." Emery held up his hand in protest but put it back down when Emiline glared at him. "So, his real name is Aven. How long have you two been married or united?"

Emiline's presence dogged Tiel as she moved over to the table. "Well, am I right?" The woman's voice rang in her ears. "Are you married to the young man!?"

"Yes." Tiel spun around and faced Emiline. "We wanted to wait to tell you when we were both here together. Besides, what will your religious clan think when they find out I got married without Pa performing the ceremony? They already think I am undisciplined, what will they think when I haven't 'officially' invited Coulliou and his beloved into my union. Won't the gossips just love that I have stained your zahule?"

"Since when have I worried about the loose tongues of the lofty headed?" Tiel stared back at Emiline's question. Tiel watched Emery walk towards Emiline, his hands poised to grab her around the shoulders. "You are so level-headed and mature, you already have a career, despite your hot temper. You're not like the girls your age at our religious meeting. Why they constantly quibble about who is wearing the right clothes, has the right hairstyle, and which boy is their boyfriend for the week." Emiline nodded her head as if to prove herself right. "Your honesty and integrity in the matter have done nothing but brighten our zahule. I hope you are using your head concerning this young man." Emery put his hands on Emiline's shoulder and pointed her towards the kitchen.

"How's the beast doing?" At Emery's question, Emiline threw her hands up in the air, ran to the fireplace, and fussed over the beast. Emery winked at Tiel and she leaned on the table breathing a sigh of relief. Jainu rubbed her back smiling just as a knock sounded.

"Ah, that would be General ManCane."

"ManCane?"

"Yes, he has a job for you. When you told him you were coming here, he couldn't pass up one of Emiline's meals." Emery disappeared.

"Why do you think you didn't get scolded for being late?" Emiline put the lid on the pot. "We were waiting for other guests. We also expect warrior Cadune and Lady Angela Lavonne." She brushed her apron and winked at Jainu. "So, is Aven coming?"

"He said he would try to make it if he could. He's securing a bounty."

"Well, let's hope it doesn't take as long to meet him as it did for us to find out about your marriage." She walked over to Jainu and placed her hands on his shoulder. "Let's get you some help for those voices. At first, you will be a little sleepy, but that will wear off as you get used to the chems, okay?"

Jainu shifted his gaze between both women.

"It is okay. She's experienced. It is what helped me."

"Yes, now she only needs them when they get really obnoxious." Emiline looked at Tiel with a smirk on her face. "She hasn't been here for chems in a long time, a little over half an octave I believe. Now, what would that reason be?"

Tiel felt her face flush as she averted Emiline's gaze. Both Maestro and Jainu laughed.

"Enough, let's get you some help." Emiline led Jainu past the kitchen table only to stop at the entryway into the front. "It's nice to have you here, Jack. Last meal will start as soon as the others arrive." Emiline led the boy down the hallway.

General Jack ManCane tromped into the kitchen area. He wore his maicalla at the same point as everyone else. His jacket was off, the sleeves on his brown shirt were rolled up, and the side buttons on his pants loosened.

"Any news on the children?" Tiel watched the general as his chest heaved from aromas coming out of the area.

"Yes, and it is not good news." He unconsciously toyed with his shirt sleeves. "I would like to wait till everyone is here. You know how I hate telling things twice."

"It wastes time that you could spend doing other things." Tiel smiled. "Like enjoying Ma's cooking."

"Exactly!" The general grinned and raised his eyebrows. "Is de Menzaile coming?"

Tiel sighed in exasperation.

"Should we expect Fallon Hanover?" Emery asked the general.

"He's still recuperating from his wounds. However, he will show up tomorrow. We need him to keep the enforcer's zahule brilliantly white."

Another knock sounded as Tiel snarled at the news. She avoided any more questions by answering the door and shaking her head as the buzz quieted down.

"I have already filled him in." She heard ManCane continue.

Tiel opened the door and saw a woman and a man standing there. Both had deep brown complexions with black hair. The woman stood just above Tiel's height, her long hair reaching the middle of her back. She wore a simple, cream-colored, knitted form-fitting shirt paired with lighter-cream pants. Her jade-green maicalla hung down with yellow and purple stripes on the left side, and brown stripes down the right. Her marble clasp, in the shape of a sand croc, was halfway down her chest.

The man was slightly taller with short black hair. He balanced himself on light brown wooden crutches. He wore the acodoe warrior tunic with a brown maicalla. His marble maicalla clasp, in the shape of the badoe, was also halfway down his chest right above his ancestral stripes which were shades of red to rust on either side.

"Lady Angela Lavonne and Warrior Cadune, welcome to this humble abode." Tiel felt her voice echo inside and the static grew even quieter. She rubbed the back of her head trying to ease the echo.

"Thank you, Huntress." Lady Lavonne's soft reassuring voice answered back. "I hope you don't mind. I took Emiline's suggestion."

"And that was...?" Tiel backed against the wall to open the door wider. Her eyes followed the pair as they walked in. The echo in her mind diminished, and the static died out. Her vision glazed over for a few moments. *"Why is the static disappearing rather than shutting off? The only time it disappears is when...?"*

"That was to have another Bounty Hunter on this job, for Cadune's sake." Tiel blinked her eyes as understanding dawned. "After she explained things, I knew you wouldn't object."

A shadow materialized on the door. Tiel turned and gasped when she saw Aven's frame filling the doorway, his maicalla at the expected level.

"Ma!" Tiel hissed under her breath.

"Aven!" Emiline's voice sang out. "It is nice to finally meet you. You are larger and more handsome than what the holo tube shows. No wonder Tiel likes you so much."

Tiel caught Aven looking at her out of the corner of his eyes.

"We're being staged. We waited too long," Tiel mumbled as she hung her head while rubbing her forehead with her left hand.

Everyone's footfalls echoed on the wood floor as they positioned themselves around the room and in the kitchen doorway. Emiline strode right up to Aven.

"So, Aven, have you eaten?" Emiline's eyes gleamed with anticipation.

"I always eat before I discuss a potential job." Tiel smacked her face with her right hand letting the door hit Aven in the side. He twisted and caught the door handle among snickering from the audience.

"You have eaten?" Emiline's voice turned soft as her lips quivered.

"Not that much." Aven shook his head but Emiline's eyes smoldered once again.

"Do not lie, young man." Tiel held the door open once again as Emiline marched closer to him, hands on her hips, craning her neck back to look straight up at him. "You have eaten something, a fine thing to do before you come to someone's house for a meal. Out with it! What was it and when!?"

"Two triple black beast sandwiches with soda and starches on the side, two arms ago, ma'am." Tiel stared at him. She knew Emiline and Emery's presence demanded respect from anyone. But it was a shock to hear *ma'am* come out of Aven's mouth.

"That's all and two arms ago? That is hardly a snack for a young man your size." Aven shifted his weight and folded his arms while leaning away from the door. "You will need to build up your strength for a job, won't you?" Emiline queried while squinting her eyes.

"Yes, ma'am."

"Oh, quit with the ma'am business. I'm not an old woman you know." Tiel heard Aven sigh in relief as she watched Emiline turn and prance back toward the kitchen.

"Good thing you came over. I will make sure you are ready with all the food you need," Emiline sang while Maestro laughed as he approached the back doors. Emery and ManCane parted to let Emiline through. Tiel caught Aven inching his way back towards the front door and grabbed his shirt, turning him back towards the kitchen where Emery awaited his arrival.

"Come on in, young man, and make yourself comfortable at our table." Emery smiled at Aven, then turned to his other guests. "We will eat out in the backyard today." Tiel watched Maestro through the glass rear door as he trotted around the table and vaulted the bushes that lined the back property. Within moments, his white shape vanished into the dark interior of the Watosh. "It is time for last meal. No sense in keeping our stomachs waiting any longer."

Everyone voiced their affirmations as Tiel swung the door shut.

"*Ma'am?* You called her ma'am? A little scared, are we?" Tiel peered up at Aven who was busy rubbing his arm where the door had hit it.

"No, with the way that woman expertly staged us, I am completely terrified."

CHAPTER 7

LAST MEAL

*T*iel could tell that, as usual, Emery tried to keep the yard manicured to his inclinations. A small, fat watosh branch that had fallen off a forest tree daunted his efforts. Emery had looped a thick leather cord through a hole hoping to drag the stone log. She'd have to get Aven to move the log. He would have no trouble.

Flora of various shades of red, pink, purple, and white filled gardens along the sides of the yard and complimented the expert placement of bushes. Plush green grass carpeted the rest of the backyard ending at a line of bushes that created a natural living fence. Several birds sang to each other from the Watosh Forest.

The table sat in the back closer to the Watosh. Emery sat down on the edge nearest the shed. Everyone took a seat with Jack sitting across from Emery. Tiel relaxed, preparing herself for the expected feasting that a last meal by Emiline required.

Emiline placed the meal on the middle of the table around a clear crystal vase filled with Tiel's bouquet. The guests around the table awarded her efforts with gratified whispers and the bubbly ooh's and ah's. A harmony of mouthwatering aromas filled the air around the dishes, making Tiel's stomach rumble.

The roast beast came first. Next came the grilled starched vegetables, sweet onions, a huge bowl of greens, jellies, butter, and fruit salad with cream. Jainu's eyes grew wider with each dish. Everyone moved their plates and silver utensils out of the way. Aven stared at the food, gawked at Emiline, and then stared at the food again.

"There is nothing special about *this* day!" Aven raised his eyebrows at Tiel who just grinned while everyone else chuckled.

"Every meal is important. Therefore, every meal needs the upmost attention." Emiline took a moment to pat Aven on the shoulder.

Next, came the fresh bread, a medium creamer filled with thick dark golden honey gravy for the beast, small fried fish, and a sweet-smelling cobbler.

She stopped and examined Aven. "I better see you eat at least three plates full. Young people don't eat enough these days, all skin and bones. Why, a good wind would blow them away. I would put four plates in front of you, but you already showed no sense by eating before you came. If you and Tiel had visited earlier, you would have already known better." Emiline glared at Tiel who put her hands up in defeat. Jainu giggled, and Emiline turned to him. "Well, with your frame you will probably get in only one plate but make sure it is a full plate. I don't need you to faint on us. We will also test you on the first law." Aven looked between both women, down at the food, and then back again at Tiel.

"Don't look at that girl. She must eat at least two plates herself." Emiline sat down and filled Aven's plate.

"Emery, you fill Jainu's plate to make sure he gets enough," Emiline instructed as Aven tried to reach out for a spoon.

"Everyone, help yourselves!" Emery only had to give permission once. Utensils clanged against dishes as the guests filled their plates. Aven moved his hand back when Emiline swatted him with the fruit's serving spoon. He let her load his plate which elicited more laughter from Jainu. It was clear that Emiline meant three overflowing plates of food. Tiel just grinned as she loaded her own plate.

"Now, Jack, why don't you tell us about the children?" Emery invited while he sliced the beast.

"I was hoping not to ruin everyone's meal," ManCane answered while Tiel took the first piece of the beast that Emery carved.

"Oh, please, let us wait for a little while," Lady Lavonne begged. "As I understand it, we can do nothing till well into Shea's next travels. I would like to get acquainted with the hunters."

"Excellent idea," ManCane replied while he filled his plate. "If we could do something, we wouldn't be here loosening up our pants. Sorry, ladies." A few chuckles echoed around the table.

"Give him two huge slices, dear. He needs the protein." Emery obeyed and placed Aven's beast slices on a different plate.

Aven's laughter at Emiline and her joyful attention to his plate almost escaped Tiel's notice as she engrossed herself in the coveted piece of bread she had snagged. She bit into it, savoring the moment. The warm inside was firm and melted in her mouth along with the spiced butter.

"Tiel and Aven," Lady Lavonne started, "how is it that you two chose your hunter's names? The talk is that they are rather plain."

"Mine is simple. I wanted the Avenger, and found the eastern sea tongue version was available," Aven answered first. "de Menzaile doesn't have flair, but it has worked well for me. Those who complain about 'plain names' usually dress in bright colors and end up looking like strutting birds."

"Hum, you hunters have to go through a process to get those names, don't you?" Lady Lavonne asked. Tiel nodded as she watched Aven look at Emiline, his plate crammed with food, and back at her. Emiline hit him in the shoulder and motioned for him to eat.

Tiel watched Aven carefully pick up the onions with his fork. He smelled them, raised his eyebrows, and put them in his mouth. His eyes shifted back and forth, and he swallowed. Next, he tried the fruit salad, scooping it up on the fork, and put it in his mouth. He chewed slowly first and then examined the plate to his right that held the meat. Emery lifted the creamer with honey gravy. Aven accepted the offer and poured the light golden liquid over the beast. Tiel watched juices cascade down his chin as he chewed. His eyebrows went up, and he grunted with pleasure. He leaned over his plate, used his left arm to protect it, and dug in. He glanced up at Tiel a few times as he ate but his left arm always guarded the plate. Emery laughed to himself.

"My story is that I was so busy completing my tasks for my Ritual Oath Ceremony, that I forgot to pick a name," Tiel explained between mouthfuls. "It can take arms or days to make sure no one alive has already chosen the same name. So, I chose The Bounty Huntress, expecting it to be taken already. They approved my name in under half an arm. Everyone is so interested in names like Purple Rose, Crimson Seas, or whatever that nobody thought about The Bounty Huntress. I realized it was the perfect name. I was *The Bounty Huntress*.

"What kind of special apparel does one get for a name like Purple Rose?" Cadune inquired as everyone settled in. Jainu scraped up his food and looked around. Emery signaled for him to dish himself up some more, which he did with zeal.

"One that retires a hunter early in life," Tiel answered. "Purple Rose is now a teacher. You only get one chance at a name. Parading around in purple made her a target. Even with dramatic names most of the best hunters never wear ostentatious clothes. So, that tells you something about Purple Rose."

"You two are quite open," Cadune stated.

"Every hunter will tell you about their hunter name. It's their selling point," Tiel explained. "We won't tell you about the ritual though."

"What about Maestro? Is his fire-breathing technique a secret?" Lady Lavonne asked.

"Ecalardians know about it," Tiel answered. "We just don't advertise how it happens. The question is, do Ma and Pa think you are trustworthy?"

"Considering we five are the only ones who knew about the acodoe before yesterday," Emery announced, "I think they are very trustworthy."

"Wait! What?!" Tiel's eyes darted back and forth between the Drakners.

"Well, that's not true. There are two others," Emery continued, "Chief Del and a chief in another little village who has a rather pressing badoe problem."

"We've kept the secret because long ago people hunted the acodoe for sport," Cadune interrupted.

Tiel shook her head and let out an exasperated breath.

"Would you tell us about Maestro?" Lady Lavonne asked. "Do you know where he's from?"

"No. He doesn't know where he is from." Tiel answered the question. "However, I can get him to remember some things when he is in a *pre-dream* state. Finding out where he is from, well…" Tiel bobbed her head from side to side. "… he can't tell me. There's a mental block placed around that memory.

"He can remember swatches of his previous life, but not names, parents, or anything else. Every time I ask, he almost goes into seizures until he wakes up, and then has migraines afterward." Everyone looked at her. "Try to live with him while he feels that way. I no longer ask those questions." The yard filled with chuckles. Light crystals hidden within the flora shone as Shea began her travels around the other side of Ecalardia. The day birds quieted down while the night insects warmed up their legs to begin their serenade.

"He also let me take med scans of him," Tiel continued. "He has a third lung. Many cubs born with this lung die before they get to their second octave of life. A thick mucus lines the lung. His body produces that mucus to line the esophagus and mouth when he gets ready to breathe fire.

"It is fascinating to see his body at work when he is in a med scan. It all happens within microseconds. He decides to breathe fire and his body produces the mucus. This mucus forms a membrane that covers the organs, then the lung opens and releases acid. The acid combines with oxygen from his other lungs and he breathes fire.

"Those that live through the *learning stage* get a higher social standing. One more thing, the female cubs do not breathe fire, they breathe ice." Tiel shrugged her shoulders and sat back.

The night air turned crisp as everyone sat back from the table one by one. Shea's fading light illuminated a storm with a blue tinge off in the distance over the Watosh. The stars were bright and clear.

"Now we need to learn about the job." Aven directed his attention to ManCane.

"Yes, it is past time." ManCane joined Aven in a complimentary belch, to which Emiline smiled. "Tyne is the one that holds the children hostage." Tiel snapped to attention and glared at ManCane; a low growl emanating from her chest and her fingers drumming on the table. "He called in his demands not long after I left you at the caves."

"You know you should have told me earlier than this," Tiel snapped. "We have wasted time."

"Wait to hear the rest." ManCane held up his hand. "You will understand there is nothing we can do at this moment."

"Who is Tyne?" Warrior Cadune inquired right before he dipped a spoon into the fruit salad.

"Tiel, why don't you answer the question," ManCane offered. Tiel glared at the older man before she answered.

"My third capture two octaves ago was Tyne Baritone." Tiel leaned forward. "He kidnapped a young kerlar under Ma's supervision. Held her in a hut with a laser pistol pointed at her head. It was a low-powered laser which had just enough power to knock someone unconscious."

Emiline stacked the empty plates as Tiel continued. "However, he used it to torture and destroy the cells of her body. She has dents in her arms, legs, and she has missing fingertips." Lady Lavonne choked back tears. Tiel continued. "Anyway, he tortured her for over two days. In that time, he taught her a little song. He promised he would allow a rescue to succeed. However, he also promised that if she stopped singing that song, he would know, hunt her down, and kill her cell by cell. She believed him. Does she still sing that song today, Ma?"

"Not for a long time," Emiline replied as she watched Jainu's head droop under the weight of sleep. "However, you know I will have her secluded from the holo images for at least three days. I need not hear that song again."

"If that wasn't bad enough," ManCane continued, "he has the children in the Acodoe Queen's cave."

"Where is Sendenia?" Emery asked.

"Angela!" Emiline's motherly voice interrupted the conversation as she pondered her guest's state of mind. Lady Lavonne sat with lips pursed, staring at nothing. "Angela!" Emiline repeated. Cadune shook her arm and Lady Lavonne came out of her troubled thoughts.

"I am sorry. This disturbs me." Lady Lavonne shook herself awake. "Sometimes I wonder when all the hate will stop."

"My dear, trials are what strengthens us. It will end when the Day of Renewal comes," Emery said and smiled as they all laughed at his comment. "That could be closer than we think."

"Back to the problem at hand," ManCane asserted. Lady Lavonne took a deep slow breath. "Sendenia and the rest of her clan are out in the Blood Rain. She has not been near the cave for the past two days."

"Blood rain?" Tiel queried. She looked at Aven. He looked back at her and signaled that he was listening. Then he picked at some food from the middle of the table.

"Yes, what do you know about the Blood Rain?" ManCane stated.

"It happens when the humidity in the forest draws out the oils from the plants and then mixes those oils with any passing storms," Tiel confirmed. "It is toxic and has put many hunters in the medic clinic."

Emery nodded his head at Tiel's understanding. "The acodoe love to lie out in the Blood Rain. This moisture softens their scales and protects their skin at the same time. However, animals become drunk from it whereas the rain kills humans."

"I take it Sendenia's cave is somewhere behind us?" Tiel questioned. "That is the only storm over the Watosh."

"That would be correct," ManCane answered. "Tyne not only has the children in the cave, but, he has also told them that Sendenia's eggs are just rocks. And, to keep them entertained, he lets them carve into the eggs."

"That will kill Sendenia's unborn," Lady Lavonne croaked, tears streaming down her cheeks.

"Yes, unless we get people out there soon after Shea rises above the horizon tomorrow. The Blood Rain should be beyond her cave by then. Would you two be ready to leave?"

"What if Sendenia comes back?" Tiel questioned ManCane. "Last thing I want to do is fight an angry - possibly drunk - acodoe." Aven grunted his agreement at this.

"I also wanted to send an emissary to the queen and her clan," ManCane announced, "but that emissary has already disappeared into the forest. It could be late before he comes back."

"Will the forest let us in? After we angered the forest yesterday, I doubt we can get through," Tiel warned. "I have never had a problem but..."

ManCane raised his hand and shook his head. "Chief Del has already spoken to the forest on your behalf. He has learned that the forest blames Hegert. It knows what happened with the badoe. It will let you pass."

Aven and Tiel glanced at each other. They smiled at each other and Tiel raised her hands. "Yes, but I expect the payload to be big for this one."

"The first half is already in your holding account," ManCane replied smiling. "I believe it is large enough to help a pair of newlyweds with the purchase of a possible new abode." He raised his eyebrows a couple of times. "We still need Maestro. He needs to hear Cadune's story."

"Cadune's story?" Aven asked.

"Yes," Cadune replied. "Lady Lavonne has convinced me to tell you my story. It should give the party information about the cave's location and the surrounding danger." He shifted his weight. "Or I could just lead you there. However, I remember little since it was so long ago."

"Cadune is coming as another emissary to the queen in case Maestro fails." ManCane sat back and loosened the side buttons on his pants another notch. "Plus, he's good with children. He'll be able to entertain on the way back."

"I am sorry, I don't think it's a good idea." Tiel examined Cadune once more. His legs caved in where his muscle had been destroyed. "Cadune, you will need a litter and more than one person to carry it. It's too dangerous for you and the party."

"We have no choice," ManCane interrupted. "As you pointed out earlier, you may come up against an angry, drunk acodoe or Sendenia herself. Cadune has developed a deep relationship with her. She is more apt to listen to someone she recognizes."

"I would like the story," Tiel requested. "With your permission, I would also like to use my telepathy as you tell the story."

"How does that work?" Lady Lavonne queried, her voice full of concern.

"Well, I am a high telepath. This means I can search his mind for details I think I need. The problem is it could cause minimal to severe damage." Tiel took a drink of her punch. "But, as he relives the story through telling it, he will experience *wandering memories*.

"The mind records everything. The person just can't see all that the mind remembers. However, as he remembers the memories, I can see what he saw. The wandering memories act as a path enabling me to search the deeper memories." Tiel turned to Cadune. "I may see terrain and landmarks. It will exhaust you but that should be all." Cadune raised his eyebrows and waved his hand in consent.

"Now, if only Maestro will show up," ManCane reminded her.

"I know right about where he is at. He doesn't stay quiet as he eats." Aven stood and went over to the log. He pulled on the cord and the log moved easily as Aven walked back to the forest, leaving a trail of pressed grass. Soft black dirt remained where the log once was.

"I have tried for a month to get enough people over to move that log." Emery stared at the spectacle. Tiel hadn't seen his mouth drop open that far in a long time.

Aven continued to the forest and stopped just by the bushes. They waved their branches in the air, blocking the entrance. Aven bent over, put his hand in the hole, and picked up the log. The log reached Aven's waist as he balanced it on the ground.

"Hey, fur-ball!" Aven yelled, his voice echoing through the trees. "Heads up!" With that, Aven bellowed as he lifted the log and threw it into the forest.

A roar sounded as a flash of blue light pierced the darkness.

"Go back to sleep, you lazy hut-fed cat," Aven yelled out. Sticks and brush snapped as something dashed through the forest with incredible speed.

"You're too fat to accept a real hunt," Aven taunted as he backed up, then stood firm, his torso leaning forward.

With a roar, Maestro leaped out of the forest and cleared the bushes. Aven's laughter thundered as he ran forward; with his arms opened wide, he met Maestro as the feline completed his arc. Aven stood firm as the onslaught of fur and muscle hit him square in the chest. The two teetered on their feet for a moment, locked in a comical dance. Aven heaved, letting out another bellow as Maestro landed flat on his back. Jainu whooped with excitement as the adults sat frozen in their chairs.

"They've wanted to do this for a long time," Tiel sighed in exasperation.

"Well, it's good to see the boys get along." Tiel heard Emiline get up from her chair. "I'll go get some more punch while they work out their extra energy.

Tiel watched the bundle of blond hair and white fur roll around on the ground.

MAESTRO PANTED as he lay next to Emery, a smile spread across his face. Aven leaned on the table, taking in deep breaths. The other guests judged the wrestling match as a tie which wasn't unusual.

Tiel sipped the sweet punch and got comfortable as she watched Emiline put four full pitchers of punch on the table before she sat down. Chairs squeaked as everybody shifted in their seats and settled in. Aven breathed in and gave her a nod. He had once stated that when she went beyond his border, he often felt a heavy strain on his chest. His nod had reassured Tiel that he would be comfortable, and it was best to do it while no one else's thought currents would compete for attention. She let her telepathy open Aven's shield around her and concentrated on Cadune's story. Aven gave no inclination something was happening.

"It was over ten octaves ago," Cadune began, "and I longed for riches. I wanted to go into the forest and find a Golden Branch. The Golden Branch is a dangerous plant. Some say the acodoe plant them to guard their cave entrances.

"No matter how it got there, the plant grows deep in the forest. Its leaves are of the purest gold. No one could dig into the planet and find gold so rare. Yet, it is carnivorous. If one looks close enough, they will find dead bodies of animals intertwined in its wooden appendages as the plant slowly devours its prey. Because it is so difficult to get and so pure, one leaf from the plant would make a man rich beyond his dreams.

"Nevertheless, one day I decided to find a Golden Branch. I had enough supplies for a few day's journey including a tinderbox for fires. I had not gone fifty yards when I encountered another danger from the forest. The plants themselves crept upon me and obstructed my path, teasing and taunting me. I whacked at their branches only to come back empty handed. Again, I attacked. Again, I came up empty-handed. I turned back only to discover that I was almost in the tentacles of other plants. I readied myself to attack when an idea came.

"I calmed the plants with a promise of fresh meat, opened my bag and brought out my tinderbox. I showed it to the nearest plant which ran its branches along the tinderbox. I opened it, brought out a match, and lit it. Then I threw it at the plant and watched as it burst into flames. The other plants trembled in fear as their comrade withered in agony and then slumped onto the ground dead. I pulled out another match but the path both behind me and in front of me became clear.

"'I now believe you plants are intelligent,' I called out. 'All it takes is one attack and I light this match and throw it.' The plants shook in fright. 'Excellent!' I continued. 'Now for my generosity of sparing all of your lives, you will show me where I may find a Golden Branch. Now!' I demanded.

"Upon my demand, the plants parted and stayed still, but did not obey my wishes. I took this as a good sign and continued forward. It was late in

Shea's second path when I saw a golden glimmer above the other vegetation.

"As I drew closer, the glorious leaves spread out for all to see. Its luster made my mouth water. My head spun with images of wealth and glory. Houses and servants galore danced in and out of my thoughts. Fine foods and wines reeled around in a magnificent bounty. Rich, luxurious robes adorned my body as I sat on fine plush furniture.

"So engrossed was I with my dreams that I never thought once to consider the plant's frame. I crept forward. The leaves of the plant lulled me closer as they danced in the breeze. My eyes focused on the luster of the gold that mesmerized me.

"I reached out for one leaf. All I needed was one leaf. I felt a sharp jolt in the lower part of my leg. Looking down, I saw that one branch had jabbed a needle through my leg. I remember hearing myself scream in terror as I turned to run, but the plant pulled on my leg and I fell flat on my face. I scrambled to get up. More pain erupted in my other leg and in my left arm as the plant thrust more needles inside my body. I reached for my blade, but the plant cracked another branch in the air and caught my right arm. I felt three stabs of pain in my back as my screams intensified. My jaw was next as I fought to regain control. The plant dragged me closer; the lower part opened to devour its long-awaited meal.

"Just as I was witnessing my feet entering the open grave, the needles jerked out of my body. The pain was so great I could no longer scream. However, I found I still had the strength to move backward. As I did so, my head bumped into something solid and I looked up, into the face of an acodoe.

"'All is well,' I heard it say. 'You will still live, but how is up to you. Just remember your hate only produced more hate.' The acodoe pushed towards me with its tail the plant I had burned earlier. It pointed towards the Golden Branch. 'And remember still your greed only produced more greed.' I still remember the lesson taught that day.

"I was a guest of the acodoe for a time, its cave just beyond the Golden Branch. My hero brought in a doctor to help me. I had problems with my memory for a while. My body suffered the most."

The thoughtful silence after the story gave Tiel the chance to memorize the images from Cadune's thoughts. The yard stayed quiet for a few moments. Aven let a breath of wonder escape, bringing Tiel back to the present.

"The plant did this to you?" Aven questioned pointing to Cadune's legs. Tiel now noticed two round, light scars on Cadune's left cheek.

Cadune nodded his head. "It took weeks for my body to fight the poison the plant had injected into my system. The poison destroyed muscles and caused permanent nerve damage in my legs."

"Why are you going back?" Tiel questioned.

"To repay a kind deed done. It was the queen who saved my life."

ManCane cleared his throat. "How fast can you get going, Maestro?"

Maestro stood and stretched. "Immediately. Anything else you want to tell me?"

ManCane shook his head, at which Maestro leaped back into the forest. Jainu lay asleep on the table. Lady Lavonne stared into the forest, lost in thought.

"We should get going soon after Shea shows herself over the horizon." Tiel suggested.

"Should be no problem, just give the crowds plenty to cheer about, will you?" ManCane asked.

"Crowds?" Both Tiel and Aven asked in unison.

"Compliments of High Councilwoman Hegert," the General explained. "You have irritated her. She was talking to the news masters today, unfolding a dire tale in which you would lose your temper and leave someone dead in the Watosh."

Tiel sighed in frustration. Hegert was living up to her reputation for revenge.

"Tyne likes to torture his victims. They will need good help." Lady Lavonne changed the conversation. "Do you think you would clear your appointments for a little while, Kerlar?"

"I was already considering it." Emiline smiled at the young lady. Lady Lavonne sat back in her chair and took a deep breath as Emiline continued. "You make sure that the general has his best kitchens available."

"Yes, yes," Lady Lavonne giggled. "I remember your fiendish ways. I have heard you may have even used the soldiers under you for tasters when you were working on new recipes."

"And none of them dared to complain." Emery broke in. He expertly took a slap on the arm from Emiline with a large grin. Everyone else at the table laughed.

"How is Tyne torturing his victims this time?" Lady Lavonne's voice became serious once more.

"He is teasing the parents," Tiel replied. "This is slow, and it helps him to feel powerful."

ManCane sighed aloud.

"Jack, what is it?" Emery's voice tensed. Tiel glanced over at the general to find his face drained of color.

"Tyne didn't call the children by their names." ManCane let out a loud breath, and he gazed up at the heavens. "I only wish we could get there sooner."

"What did he call them, Jack?" Emery asked.

"He referred to them as the queen's sacrifice." ManCane's voice broke as everyone gasped. "He said it over and over. I think he plans to feed the children to the queen. If the queen is angry and drunk, it may just happen that Tyne gets his wish."

"No!" Lady Lavonne cried out in shock. "Sendenia will be in torment forever. She'll never forgive herself."

"And there is your reason." Tiel got up from the table. "He plans to control the queen through guilt. A nasty weapon indeed."

CHAPTER 8

TO THE RESCUE

The next morning brought the sound of the floating media eyes which caused a thread of pain to travel up Tiel's spine. It ended in her head and added to the irritation she was feeling from the static. Tiel winced as the whirling noises and static mixed in her head and pounded in her ears. The gossips' chattering reached her as she waved their orbs away. She wondered how many communications jammed the airways with the gossips talking to their respective news masters.

She already knew what was behind her. First would be a line of cadet enforcers, laser pistols at their sides, maicallas cinched up to their neck. Emery, Emiline, and Jainu would be at the front of the crowd, showing support for their family members. The media would be behind them. Farther up the hill would be throngs of Ecalardians with drawn faces. Some held signs on sticks. The words condemned her for their current problems.

She let out a heavy sigh as the glint of orbs announced their owners were undaunted. Realizing that part of her pain stemmed from her clenched teeth, she concentrated on slow, controlled breaths, unfolded her tensed arms, and looked towards the Watosh.

Two people stood in front of the Watosh. Aven paced behind Chief Del, both were facing the forest. Tiel gazed at her stellove's muscular body. It was perfect, not skinny as a skeleton nor burdened with knots of muscles.

His smooth complexion masked the real reason for his strength. Aven's robotics were not like Tiel's. She had thick strands of metal replacing skeletal and muscle parts, especially in her legs which helped her to have more speed than the normal human. However, his biometal wove and interconnected with his muscles and skeleton, giving him his uncanny strength. Tiel smirked at the cliché. And yet, unlike the crowd ready to riot behind her, she realized the futility of changing the past.

Tiel let a small soul current out of her rutzix and sent it over to Aven. Usually, she would have knocked on a person's head right above the eyes. However, a telepathic wall surrounded his body which her soul current traveled along allowing her to sense its strength. She used the stream to tap the wall, and it softened, a small soul current drifted out. The entwining was easy as Aven's soul current interwove with her soul current, leaving little for Tiel to do. Small, round, smooth beads traveled up the current and combined with Tiel's beads. It had only taken a couple of months for Aven to become a 'working participant' rather than just a 'willing participant' like Maestro.

"Is there any news from Cadune or Fallon yet?" Tiel asked, her impatience showed as her thought beads became rough.

"No. Getting distressed won't help. We'll leave when we are able." She sensed several thoughts moving around in Aven's consciousness but, as usual, she never pried. It could damage a participant. After a few moments, he called to her again. *"Do you trust General ManCane?"*

"General ManCane is not the problem." Tiel answered back. *"We could almost be there by now. I don't know if Cadune or Fallon understand this. The more time we wait, the more danger the children are in."*

"Not necessarily, stellove," Aven answered back. *"You're anxious because of the gossip orbs behind you."*

"Yes, you are right," Tiel admitted. *"The noise is giving me a headache. If I move, they will follow. Care to help with this problem?"*

"Not at all. Address the little gossips. We can scare them off."

Tiel let the connections go and both soul currents dissipated.

"Care to tell Ecalardia why you feel it necessary to clean your zahule this way?" The orb's mechanical voice carried its owner's question from the crowd, bringing Tiel back to the problem at hand. She turned and searched the crowded media line. No one tried to show themselves. The orb's whirring in her ear amplified the inner static.

The orb pushed against her shoulder. Tiel felt her Hunter's Heart in her hand within a moment. Sparks flew from the orb's molten eye as she pierced her knife into it. The next moment a slim figure slunk away from the crowd. She pulled the knife out letting the orb drop on the ground sputtering, which only intensified the static inside.

A couple of enforcers parted as she stepped over the orb and up to the line of reporters. Just as she expected, the reporters with clear floating orbs behind them ran up to her, their maicalla clasps positioned above the breast. Tiel adjusted her maicalla clasp to their level.

They all spoke at once, yelling out their questions. She waved them off. "One at a time or you will get no answers." The commotion died down, and Tiel pointed to a blond in the second line. The older woman came forward and announced her name. "I don't care about your name, give me your question."

"How do you feel about the upheaval you caused?" The blond woman attempted to interrogate her.

"I caused no upheaval. If I could, I would march all of you, this mountain of dung heaps, in front of a looking glass so you could see the problem. Then I would get rid of the stench by shoving you gossips down a crevice, so that we can breathe clean air." Tiel saw the reporters' scowls and smiled. She raised her head glaring straight into the orbs above her. "Since time began, the council has spoiled their zahule by lying to you. This petty society of gossips has no problem spreading the droppings of those lies." Tiel waved her arms around pointing at the media. "Go to your councils, demand the truth. Demand to know why they hid the acodoe. Was it to make part of a prophecy true? One of their own sent out an innocent man to die in the Watosh. To cover the stench of her zahule, she brought me in to rescue someone she had already deemed unworthy to live." Tiel saw Emiline look at Emery out of the corner of her eye. Neither seemed happy.

She focused her attention on the orbs again. "Now we see the reason. It has only been one day and already a known criminal has taken innocent children into the Watosh. All just to soil the Acodoe Clan's zahule, putting them in danger of retaliation." She looked at the Drakners once again. Their bodies appeared more relaxed.

"So, what does this tell you about the validity of any prophecy? Even if it was valid, how could I stop a God? Isn't it supposed to be Coulliou's prophecy?" A few signs disappeared, and the chattering subsided, too late to ease Tiel's headache. "Get up and quit waiting for a doom's crevice to swallow you whole. Get back to your lives. If the prophecies are true, soon it won't matter. If not, you'll all still have happy, fulfilling lives." She smiled in disgust at the floating orbs and returned her gaze to the media line.

"Why are you willing to go on a job with de Menzaile?" a dark-haired man called from behind.

"There are innocent children in danger." Tiel twirled her Hunter's Heart in her hand. Everyone's eyes watched in anticipation. "Tell me your zahules are clean enough to understand that concept?"

"Bounty Huntress!" Tiel turned to see Aven standing behind her. "Do you love the gossips so much that you have to bathe in their stench?"

"Get back in your place," Tiel roared raising her hunter's knife. The enforcers hesitantly raised their laser pistols, looking at both hunters, not daring to move.

"If you would stop touting your own zahule, I would have a place to stand in." He pointed at Chief Del. "He needs answers and I am not the one leading this rescue party, that is unless you want to step down."

Tiel threw the knife. It appeared in Aven's right hand a moment later causing gasps to erupt from the crowd. He sneered and threw it back. It landed at her feet without her flinching. Aven backed away. Tiel picked up her knife and followed him.

"Good show, stellove," Tiel complimented Aven when they were far enough away.

"It is just as I thought." He smiled as Tiel sheathed her knife. "Nobody wants to get between two fighting hunters." Aven trotted for the tree line.

"Anything new from Maestro?" she inquired when she got close to Chief Del. He had already aligned his maicalla clasp at the appropriate position. Aven leaned against a tree near enough to hear. She had heard Maestro's reports up to a few arms ago.

"Nothing yet. He said he would send a message as soon as he found the queen and knew about her situation and temperament."

"Is there any reason the Watosh is unwilling to help more?"

Chief Del smiled. "I wondered when you would ask that question. The

Watosh worries about the queen. It knows what the risks are and wants no harm coming to her, especially in the form of bad press. It does not trust the humans and their gossip." Chief Del frowned. "It believes you hunters are putting more than enough humans in harm's way and if someone gets hurt, it could mean hard times for the acodoe."

"But doesn't it understand that if the children get hurt…" Tiel questioned the Chief as he raised his hand.

"Yes, now it does, and it has decided to trust us. It hopes you succeed, and that Tyne will be the only one punished." Chief Del stopped and scratched his head.

"What?" Tiel and Aven asked.

"It would like for you to make some promises, Bounty Huntress. The Watosh wants no one to hurt any forest life while on this mission."

"Well, at least I know it's still wary of me after my last visit," Tiel mumbled to herself.

MAESTRO HAD SPENT most of the past arm cleaning his fur and dealing with the drowsiness without success. He let out a low growl as he rolled in the dirt and checked his fur once more with his nose. A few drops of smooth, clear oil dropped off. The scent caused his eyes to ache. Maestro wiped it off with his paw. He roared in frustration and lay still.

The clouds had not moved away which was why Maestro had skirted the storm's outer edges. It hadn't worked. The storm shifted, and he was caught in it. He had traveled in a brilliant oily haze with his senses becoming cloudy, his vision turning blurry, and the Blood Rain's scent drowning out all other smells. It had taken at least two arms before he found a rotted out watosh log and had waited for the Blood Rain to stop.

When the rain had passed, he had ventured out again, but his fur was thick with oil and the woodsy scent had made him even more groggy. He couldn't remember how he made it to the waterfall, but he had taken a bath. The bath did little to clear his head and only matted his fur.

Now he lay in dry dirt thinking. Rainbow prisms danced before his eyes, circling the watosh trees and curling around the plants on the ground. He hated the sensation and needed his mind clear for his audience with the queen. He didn't need to be lost in a drunken stupor.

A small rat appeared next to his head. It smelled deliciously clean and Maestro growled out a question. The rat squeaked and ran off straight ahead. He thought he felt his feet slip under him as he rose. Weaving, he followed the small rat. Bright blue birds that would normally stay high above his head when he hunted teased him, sensing his vulnerability. He snatched at the ones that flew in front of his face, missing each time. They squawked their challenges above him as he continued to move forward. An ache grew, and pressure rose in his stomach as he felt a painful burn cascade down his throat and mix with his stomach's juices.

Maestro looked around as his stomach rumbled. His feet took on a life of their own as they lifted to a strained rhythm. The rumble mixed with the heat and traveled past his stomach, burning his insides. He ignored the birds that now nipped at his ears and bits of his tail. He continued to dance and look around as the rumble passed through his body, a burning pain traveling down to his hind end.

The rat peeked back at him and scampered off. Maestro grimaced while a hot flame shot out behind him. Birds squawked and the sound of retreating wings escaping through the upper foliage echoed far above him. Maestro peered behind him hoping to find nothing. Instead, beyond the singed fur of his tail, he found two blackened bodies on the ground and bushes frantically bashing burning limbs. The birds' necks were twisted while their beaks formed a fatal grimace with eyes wide open. Maestro bowed his head as the rat chattered excitedly from a distance.

THE PLANTS RUSTLED with their news as Chief Del translated for Tiel. The latest report hadn't come from Maestro but the Watosh after it sensed Tiel's worry. Lizard now danced along Lady Lavonne's arm, tickling her ear.

"I will take care of this precious creature for you." Lady Lavonne laughed as Lizard curled up on her shoulder underneath her hair.

"Thank you. I appreciate the help." Fallon breathed a sigh of relief. "No telling what predator would hunt her down."

"He's doing what?" Tiel questioned Chief Del, confusion in her voice.

"The Watosh doesn't quite know how to explain. But he needed to take about three sulfur mud baths." Chief Del shrugged and listened as the plants in the Watosh rustled. He turned to Tiel

"Your Maestro got caught in the edge of the Blood Rain." Chief Del narrowed his eyes, the shrubs shook with impatience.

"The Blood Rain," Aven and Tiel repeated. Fallon mumbled from behind.

"Maestro tried to skirt the storm's edge, but he still got caught in the Blood Rain. The forest says he was walking funny."

Tiel backed up and contemplated, "Did Maestro become drunk?"

Chief Del nodded. "The Watosh sent a rat to lead him to sulfur mud and water." The forest rustled again. "But not before…" The Chief listened with a look of confusion. "It says fire came out from him, in the back. Two large birds died from it." Tiel sighed and dropped her head. Aven appeared confused, then understanding dawned, and he howled with laughter.

Chief Del furrowed his brows at Aven.

"Bad gas," Tiel spoke, covering her eyes. When Chief Del still seemed confused Tiel continued, "When he has bad gas, his 'fire' travels through his stomach and he passes a 'gas fire' out his hind end. Trust me. He sleeps outside when he has bad gas." Aven roared even louder as the rest of the company laughed along.

Chief Del continued with a smile. "The mud takes away the funny walk and strange things in the eyes and only a small scent of the Blood Rain remains."

"Is there a way to get sulfur mud to the acodoe?" Tiel rubbed her chin with her thumb.

"Not mud, but the trees have pools of water in their upper branches. It is a byproduct of the Blood Rain. They save it to sober up a drunk acodoe."

"Excellent! I have an idea." Tiel explained the idea with Aven listening. Soon Chief Del was conversing excitedly with the Watosh.

"Have you heard from Cadune?" Tiel inquired while looking at Lady Lavonne. "He's wasting time, how long will he be?"

In answer to her question, a cot carried by eight large men came into view. They balanced the cot between them while moving forward at a good pace. They were prison inmates called robies, working off their sentences. They wore only tunics around their waists and flat sandals. Cadune lay propped on some pillows as he waved to the party.

"Shea's light! What were you doing? Did you have tea with the warden?" Tiel yelled. There was a murmur in the crowd as orbs flew around Cadune. Cadune just smiled at Tiel as the robies approached. "Never mind, no explanations necessary. Whatever it was, it wasted almost two arms."

She turned back to Chief Del, ignoring Cadune while he greeted the party.

"Chief Del, please ask the lower forest to not snack on any party members in return for its promised safety," Tiel said with a sigh. "The robies don't need to come out with bits and pieces of flesh missing," she explained looking at the media line. Hegert had been busy all morning with the news masters indulging them with gossip about Tiel's rumored bad temper. Her outburst at Cadune only excited the media line. She didn't need to come back with injured robies.

"Let's go, no time for formalities." Tiel picked up a pack from among a pile that lay against a watosh. "All of you have already wasted enough precious time. Shea is far above the horizon, which means it will get hot." Without waiting for an answer, she started into the forest with Aven following close behind.

MAESTRO SHOOK the sulfur water off his fur. The wave cascaded from his head, through his body to his tail, spraying the surrounding plants. The woodsy fragrance that had saturated his fur was barely noticeable.

He considered the state of the surrounding plants. They appeared exhausted, their leaves drooped with a hint of paleness. The branches and trunks seemed to stoop. Yet the forest's fragrance was alive and new. The rat waited, hidden under the brush to his right. Maestro growled. The rat squeaked, and Maestro nodded. The rat turned and ran off.

Maestro sniffed the air once more and proceeded. Before the Blood Rain, he had been following a trail that led to a small outcropping of rock. He found that same landmark and continued. He was enjoying the cleanliness of the forest when a new scent hit him as wrong. A large, brown creature moved in front of him, at which Maestro snapped up in an instant, thinking while he was eating. At first, his appetite had been small, but now as the oil effects wore off, he was getting hungry; hungrier than usual as if his body was making up for the lost nutrients from before.

The previous scent hung in the air. Among a thousand other aromas that were clean, vibrant, and full of life, this one reeked of rot and sickness. A search brought up nothing that would explain the unpleasant odor. He finished the meal and moved on. For the next arm, everything smelled right.

Shea was just reaching her zenith when the rotted scent surfaced once more. He looked up and studied the upper forest. The watosh around him stood strong while the lower plants still appeared exhausted but alive. The woodsy aroma still clung in the air but now made his stomach turn as it mixed in with the stink of decay. Maestro circled the trees but discovered nothing. He sniffed up and down but couldn't place it until he entered a small clearing, the stench hit him as a current of air assailed him. Maestro almost buckled underneath its force.

Looking up once again, he found healthy trees scarred with bits of dried, black, blood-smeared flesh. Climbing up, he noticed the flesh had scales laying over each other in a row, like a snake's outer layer that had shed. Underneath were rotten patches of a yellowish stinky crust. On the trunks of the trees were large smudges of blood as if a huge creature had stayed and used the trunks as scratching posts. After satisfying his curiosity, and seeing no trace of the creature, Maestro climbed down and made his way to the rock outcropping, losing the nauseating odor after a full arm's travel.

Two arms later, Maestro lay on the shelf above a clearing filled with acodoe bodies. Each acodoe imitated a giant log on the forest floor below. Their bodies crushed the high growing grass in several directions. The watosh trees stood tall around the clearing, right up to the rock cliff where Maestro lounged. He could hear the acodoe hiss air between their snouts as they slept, their breath was almost as fresh as the forest. A tail here and there would pick up and crash down sending leaves and sticks flying. Some acodoe had a gem attached to their foreheads. One jade colored acodoe had what looked like a white gem in the shape of an eight-pointed star next to the back of the left jaw. Maestro kept his eyes on the other side.

Shea now traveled just past the third arm of her second path. Her rays worked their way through Maestro's tired muscles, warming them, working out the knots. Shea's warmth also heightened the rancid scent coming from where Maestro was keeping watch to his right. He had circled the clearing several times and stopped when his nerves and heartbeat picked up from sensing danger.

Every so often, a twig would snap. At other times, the deafening thud of a falling tree would send forest animals and birds scurrying. Sometimes he thought he had heard a hiss right before a foul wind would rush through the clearing, causing a few acodoe to sneeze and turn their snouts away. Maestro could sense a host of other animals, all of them still, not wanting to disturb whatever was out there. The Watosh kept the mystery hidden behind its foliage.

He finally sent word through the forest. As he did, he thought he heard another laugh as the rancid wind intensified causing Maestro to sneeze. His raised his ears. There was rustling to his right and back by the ledge. He gathered his haunches together, ready to sprint away.

A weak sapling rocked forward and straightened itself. Maestro rose and watched the tree. After nothing happened, he eased back down. The tree moved once more, and he was up on all fours. The tree swayed, this time farther. Maestro shifted to the left. The acodoe just under the tree hissed in his sleep. The tree rocked farther, teetering for a moment and swung back the other way only to stop in mid-swing, hold for a moment, then plummet back the opposite way on top of the sleeping acodoe; its roots splintering as dozens of birds rose squawking into the sky.

The acodoe hissed in pain as it writhed out from under the tree. It shook itself and surveyed the surrounding area while weaving back and forth. "Infected one," it cursed through its snout as it wound around the roots of the tree. Maestro ran up to the top of the cliff and observed the forest beyond. Watosh trees parted to either side as a path opened and closed. It snaked around the clearing and disappeared farther out into the Watosh Forest.

A sweet wind blew across Maestro's back, ruffling his fur and scooting him to the backside of the cliff. He dodged to the side, twisted in midair and landed on all fours, facing two acodoe.

"Issss thisss the one?" The acodoe to the right questioned, its hissing pronounced due to its intoxicated state.

"No, too ssssssmall," the other one hissed, "pretty kitty needssss to change his color. Pink fur not look good on kitty." The acodoe flicked its tongue.

"Kitty sssmellsss good." Maestro sniffed his fur and detected a whiff of the Blood Rain while looking back at the acodoe before him. "Kitty sssmellsss good. Can I keep you? Purple and orange fur, I like thosssse colorssss."

"I believe I do not have the time to consider your proposal this day." Maestro paced back and forth, standing on his hind legs and sniffing, deciding whether it was safe to stay. The acodoe in front of him were weaving, bumping into each other, sinking, and then catching themselves and straightening up again. He decided he could run far enough away before he became somebody's doll. "Is the queen awake?"

"Queen, queen, queenie, boo, boo, diddy, do," one acodoe sang as it turned around. Maestro went cross-eyed and suppressed a laugh. The acodoe with the star gem weaved up between the other two, knocking the one on the right. The scales on the back were a dark jade as they cascaded down to her tail with a soft cream lining a diamond pattern. Her belly was the same soft cream as the outline of the diamonds, with two red stripes running the full length of her body. Her eyes were an emerald green and her pupils dilated in and out.

"I am the queen," she said as she squinted her eyes and steadied herself for a moment. "You look sssomewhat familiar. Why do you have sssso many horns? No creature ssshould have ssso many hornssss." The acodoe turned to leave and Maestro stepped forward. "Time to head towardssss my cave," she called out to the rest of the acodoe. The acodoe weaved as they rose. Loud clunks sounded as some acodoe bumped into each other. The ground vibrated beneath Maestro as others fell back into their previous beds. He shook his head at the dizzying sight in front of him. The queen turned to leave the field.

Maestro roared twice. The acodoe hissed in pain. One acodoe near him tried to push him off the edge but he easily dodged the weaving tipsy serpent. "Please Your Majesty, if you will listen, things have happen...."

"Do not do that again!" The queen shook her head, returning to the cliff. "Thisss isss not a good time. The Blood Rain messsessss with our ssssensssesss," she explained, her hissing more pronounced than the rest. She turned back to the field.

"I realize that. Therefore, I would not bother you if it wasn't a state of emergency. Please, I have been sent as an emissary by Lady Lavonne, Lord Cadune, the Drakners, and General ManCane."

She zigzagged up to him and tried to focus on him. "Lucky for you I am familiar with thossse namessss. I will lisssten for a little while. Prove it isss asss bad asss you sssay or I leave for my cave and a meal."

"When you leave, I implore you, take me with you, Your Majesty."

"You would like to be in my ssserviccce? I already have ssservantsss," she replied. The other acodoe lay down for a while. "You ssstill have too many hornsssss."

"I am sorry for that, Your Majesty. And no, I am already in the service of another, which is why I am here."

"Ssspeak the reassson you are here or jump on. You are boring me. I go sssoon before I become famissshed." The wind coming from the queen's mouth rushed around Maestro. It smelled as if it came from an empty pit. "But firssst, which horn are you using?" She inquired.

"I will speak from whichever horn you desire, Your Majesty," Maestro answered smiling.

CHAPTER 9

APPETITES

*E*verything was quiet. Not a bird chirped, not a mouse scurried through the underbrush, and the forest plants didn't rustle their limbs in response to anything. Tiel surveyed the cave from the ledge they stood on which was overlooking a dry clearing. The ledge's banks were at an angle that would allow the party to descend. The gray ledge and cavern stood across from each other. Dirt clung to their sides as the previous rain had washed down debris from the tops. The clearing was big enough to hold three or four acodoe. It was empty except for the dry brush scattered across the ground and a plant lining almost the exact center from one side to the other. It faced the party like a wall guarding the cave across from them. Its golden leaves captured Shea's rays using them to dazzle the onlookers above.

"No one can blame you for trying to go for that prize," Fallon whistled, "I would have gone for it myself if I was interested in quick riches." Cadune just grunted at his remark. Aven kept quiet as he chewed on a harmless green weed he had harvested earlier, its sweet mint aroma wafted in on a cool breeze. The robies sat panting from the trek. Tiel had kept up a fast pace, and the robies had kept pace with her, but now they were paying the price. Their bodies glistened with sweat, and their breaths came in labored spurts while they sat and drank from some canteens.

"You should have gone slower, Bounty Huntress," Cadune commented from his position on the cot. "Robies are treated badly as it is. They kept up for fear of gaining time to their sentences. It was rude..."

"It was rude for you to keep us waiting," Tiel growled in his direction. "You should have done what was necessary to arrive on time."

"I attended to formalities which took time," Cadune explained.

"There are innocent children in danger," Tiel rebutted. "Any formalities concerning the robies are just things to keep the robies in check, to let them know they are slaves. Plenty of people pick up robies in five minutes. Anything you thought was necessary for your own ego's sake put innocent lives in danger."

Tiel turned back to the clearing and let an uneasy silence fill the area.

"Looks like I need to find a path around that thing." Aven broke the silence as he descended from the ledge. "The rest of you stay up here."

Tiel watched Aven enter the clearing. He kept an eye on the Golden Plant and moved towards the forest, keeping far away from the dazzling predator. She heard Fallon's camera click behind her while he laughed a little.

"What is it?" Tiel asked him.

"You let him stage you," Fallon laughed. Aven found a hole in the forest and climbed through as a few plants rustled after him. "First time I've seen that happen."

Tiel gritted her teeth. Her back went rigid at the statement.

"You two are close. I can see it, no matter what kind of show you put on in public. Are you two what they call stelloves?" Fallon ventured. Tiel sighed remembering Radames words as Aven disappeared into the forest. Perhaps it would be best to let Ecalardia in on their real relationship. She wasn't ready, but she also knew missing an opportunity to mold public opinion could be problematic. Maybe the Elder Hunter was right. Anonymity had its merits.

"Are you forgetting my kindness to you?" Tiel tried to get Fallon off his line of questioning.

"You mean your charitable gift of medical attention?" Fallon asked. "Was that charity, or did you do it to get information about Hegert?"

"Yes, we are stelloves," Tiel answered the first question, then added a warning. "However, that is all you will get. You are not here to get a personal interview from me. You're here to report the events of this rescue to appease the public. Stick to your contract with ManCane."

"All right," Fallon conceded, "that is all I needed anyway. You know I do what it takes to get what I need."

"Yes, experience proves that is obvious," Tiel agreed. "But, also know I will do what it takes to protect my interests and the interests of those who are my responsibility." Tiel turned and glared at Fallon. "Your ego and ambitions have gotten in my way before, remember? You didn't come out on the winning end of our clashes." She saw Fallon gulp as he nodded.

Tiel turned back around and checked her rutzix as Aven exited the forest on the other side of the clearing. She had kept her rutzix closed while traveling, and she had no desire to have it open now. If the acodoe appeared angry and drunk, there would be too many erratic soul currents swirling around. A situation like that could incapacitate her. She found the rutzix to be secure.

"Cadune, what do you want to do?" Tiel inquired. Aven was now climbing up to the cavern entrance. He would look inside soon.

"I would like to be near the cave. I am an emissary in case the queen shows."

"Good enough," she agreed as the rested robies stood up to carry Cadune's cot once more. "Let's move out. Fallon, stay up here. You'll get better pictures."

Tiel followed the trail Aven had made. Soon she was next to his side as he leaned near the cavern opening.

"Did you see anyone inside?" Tiel queried. Aven nodded and continued chewing on his mint leaf. "Fallon asked if we were stelloves. I took Radames suggestion." Tiel looked at the ledge. Fallon was busy taking more pictures.

Aven responded. "Perhaps it is time. I think you made an excellent decision." Tiel looked up at him. He winked at her and smiled. A snort from inside the cave brought them back to their surroundings.

"What did you see inside?" Tiel asked.

"Everyone is asleep," Aven reported. "That's why I knew it was safe to relax a little. You've been too high strung during this hunt."

"The trip has taken too long. I wanted to home by now." She moved around and peered inside. Sleeping bodies lay motionless as their chests rose and fell. Their once beautiful pristine clothes hung on their dirty bodies. Tiel could see what resembled five pinkish boulders inside the cave with deep grooves carved into their shells.

"Are those the queen's eggs?" Tiel heard Aven grunt in reply. "I would have just thought they were pink boulders if I didn't know better."

"It looks like they will need new maicallas." Aven kicked one in front of her. "How will we know if the acodoe are coming?"

"If Maestro gets to come with them," Tiel replied, "he will send out a warning, three roars about every 50 feet."

"Nothing like good old basics." Cadune's voice broke the tedium. "Trying to get over that last stretch can kill someone." Tiel peered beyond Aven to see Cadune's cot on the ground inside the forest.

"Here goes nothing. Let's hope the kids will listen." Tiel turned to go inside the cave when three roars sounded from afar.

"Already!?" Aven straightened up. Tiel shook her head and put her fingers to her lips. They listened. After a few more moments, three more roars sounded closer.

"Hey, everybody up! Big snakes are on their way!" Tiel yelled as she ran into the cave. The kids jolted awake but didn't move. Aven ran past her, scooped up two children, and ran back outside. Tiel grabbed two others and headed out of the cave. Three more roars sounded again closer. Tiel ran towards Aven who was returning and handed the children to him. Tyne came out with a smile.

"So, are you taking away my family already, Bounty Huntress?" Tyne exhaled the last word as spit sputtered between his clenched teeth. His brown eyes opened wide, their dark circles growing bigger with the effort. His uneven, dark, matted hair pressed against his stretched tan skin. Mud caked his yellow prisoner's suit.

The kids struggled and broke free, scampering behind Tyne. Sounds of crunching brush signaled that more than one acodoe was approaching.

"We don't want to go with you!" a plump dark-haired boy yelled. Tyne's smile grew bigger, showing brown chipped teeth. Three more roars sounded.

"Trust me, your parents won't turn you into snake food," Aven yelled as he came up and grabbed the kids.

"Is mommy here?" a little redhead asked as she walked out of the cave, her pink dress dry and somewhat clean which showed that she hadn't played with the children. Two girls poked their dirt-encrusted heads out of the cavern. "I want my mommy." Three more roars rang out. This time it caught the kids' attention as the tops of the watosh in the distance swayed.

"We want to take you to your mommy, dear." Tiel smiled and observed the other kids. Two girls and two boys huddled together leaning towards Tyne, gazing at him for support. The younger redhead hugged the cavern walls. Aven appeared at her side once again. "Look, you need to trust me if you don't want to become food for the acodoe." Tiel kept her voice calm as she squatted to look the children in the eye. More watosh closer to the cave swayed. Tyne giggled at the imminent danger.

"Those rocks inside, the ones you have been carving into, are acodoe eggs." The roars burst into the clearing, echoing off the trees. Tyne laughed, raising his arms above his head. The watosh shook as a sweet woodsy wind filled the empty air of the clearing. The forest brush trembled.

"What are you laughing at?" a boy with dark hair asked Tyne.

"We have to go." Aven's intense tone broke through. Roars echoed as the front watosh parted to the side. "We go, NOW!" Aven called and grabbed the two boys. Tiel pushed the girls out of the cave.

Three acodoe emerged from the forest. The queen was in the middle with Maestro on top. She shook her head, and Maestro tumbled off, landing on his feet on the cave's roof. A brown acodoe with half circles decorating its back was on the queen's left. A mute-yellow diamondback acodoe was on her right, close to the cave. The mute-yellow careened and hit the cave, sending rocks and dirt tumbling down onto the spectators. Fallon's camera clasp blinked continuously as he took pictures.

The children screamed under the shadow of the large serpents. The young redhead hid behind the eggs wailing at the top of her voice. The other girls ran away only to be checked by the brown acodoe. It swayed and hit watosh trees sending a shower of needles and branches. A full bough crashed down behind Cadune, sending splinters. The robies backed farther into the forest.

Tyne grabbed one girl and positioned her in front of him. "Here they are, My Queen, your treasure, your strength. Take them, take them!" Tyne screamed with glee. Tiel hit him on the back of the head, loosening his hold long enough for the girl to escape, wailing as she backed up against the cave.

The queen rocked side to side taking in the scene. Seven children were now next to a watosh, screaming. The queen slumped a little and shook her head hissing.

Tiel looked at the belly of the mute-yellow acodoe. It bent down, its pupils almost nonexistent. She grabbed the girl as its head swung, nearly missing everyone as Tiel hopped off the ledge with the girl. She ran to the edge of the forest, placing the girl next to Cadune while escaping being crushed by falling rocks.

Tiel spun back around only to realize that the mute-yellow was lunging at her, but Maestro jumped in the way and let out a volley of white fire, catching the acodoe on the snout. The acodoe shrieked and retreated.

"Maestro, the last girl!" Tiel pointed at the cave. The mute-yellow still shook its snout. Maestro spun around and ran into the cave.

"Your Majesty, take your presents over there!" Tyne screamed again, his arms lifted to her. "Take them! I have brought them here as the proof of my loyalty to you."

"Quiet!" the queen demanded of Tyne, who obeyed and watched the commotion.

"Why are you here?" the queen asked a tall, blond, gangly boy who squeaked out sobs as he hugged a watosh. The queen's pupils shrunk, leaving only the whites of her eyes. Her breathing grew strong and unsteady. Her tail slithered around, coiling itself. Tiel ran up next to Aven as they put themselves in between the children and the queen.

"Didn't Maestro tell you what was happening?" Tiel asked the queen.

"I understood some of what he said," the queen answered Tiel's question. "I want to hear it from this one's lips here." The queen pointed to the blond. "He looks to be the oldest. I want answers from him." She swayed, knocking a branch off a watosh. It bounced off her snout and landed in front of the party. The queen hissed in pain as she shook her head once again, hood outstretched. Tiel saw Cadune wave his arms from his cot.

"Why did you come?" the queen hissed at the boy. He peered at her sniffling while rubbing his nose and eyes. Tiel heard a thud behind her. She turned to see Cadune using his arms to propel his body toward the commotion. Fear and a determination formed the grimace on his face. The brown acodoe teetered into the trees which caused debris to fall, some of it landing on Cadune and sticking in his back. Cadune yelped in pain, yet he kept moving his arms one by one, forcing his body across the ground. The queen hissed and Tiel turned back to her.

"Isn't it obvious?" Tiel asked the queen. "They're here as a sacrifice to you. Tyne wants you to get angry." The flash from Fallon's camera clicked in the queen's eyes causing her to hiss in irritation.

"He has sssucceeded. Now quiet! I did not asssk you!" the queen hissed, her breath coming in torrents, pushing the party against the tree. "Why did you come, boy?!" she hissed again.

"To have fun with the rocks. Tyne said we could have fun with the rocks!" The queen reared back and screamed. The children howled in return. Tiel picked up a log and handed it to Aven. Aven used it to hit the queen on the snout as she lunged forward. He connected, the force propelling him backward. The queen arched back in pain, water welling from her eyes. Aven appeared next to Tiel again.

"You all will pay for this. You are not to be here." The queen weaved and lunged. Tiel pushed three of the children towards the forest. Aven pushed four more behind her. The other children ran around her to get into the forest. Tiel glanced back to discover the queen's maw opened, ivory fangs lining a dark abyss.

Cadune dove in front of the party. "OBEY YOUR OWN LAWS!" he yelled. The queen closed her maw and squinted at Cadune; her coils tightened as she hissed in furry. "OBEY YOUR OWN LAWS!" Cadune yelled once more while pointing at the queen. Fallon's camera clicked furiously. His smile displayed his enthusiasm in capturing the mayhem before him. "OBEY YOUR OWN LAWS!" The queen considered Cadune's words and breathed in. Cadune continued. "You once told me that hate produces hate and greed produces greed. Look about you. These are the Delegate's children." She looked around at the screaming children.

"WHAT HAVE YOU BEEN WAITING FOR?!" Tiel yelled at the canopy above her. "DO IT NOW!"

The queen narrowed her eyes at Tiel. A moment later a waterfall from the tops of the watosh trees flowed down and bathed all three acodoe, the queen getting the full force as she toppled under the weight, her coils becoming loose and falling over each other. A wave of cold, putrid water cascaded over Tiel. She lost her balance and ended up on the ground as Cadune's body rolled over her. Splinters in his back scratched her face, causing burning pain to erupt in her cheek. As quickly as the wave had ascended, it dissipated, leaving Tiel dry heaving on the ground from the foul, slick taste caking her mouth. Her back arched, sending a wave of pain up her neck and around her lungs.

After she had regained her composure, Tiel surveyed the surrounding area. The acodoe were on the ground breathing hard. Aven and the children were to her right coughing and gasping. Cadune lay motionless behind her, blood seeping down his back. One robie lay under a huge log. The other robies were gone. Tiel stood and turned back to the acodoe, looking at the cave entrance. Maestro stood there, behind a confused Tyne, not a wet spot on them. Fallon's camera still flashed from the other side of the clearing. Tiel walked up to the queen.

"Did not Maestro tell you Tyne kidnapped and brainwashed these children?" Tiel asked the queen. The queen, with her eyes closed, breathed slower. "They didn't know what they were doing. We all came to rescue them and your unborn. We learned last night you could be drunk from the Blood Rain. Quite a good opportunity for someone to cause problems with the Acodoe Clan, don't you think?" At this, the queen opened her eyes, the pupils larger. She hissed a little as she surveyed the area. Tyne looked on in confusion, shaking his head. Fallon's camera flashed. Tiel could hear Aven console the crying children.

"Your Majesty, these are yours. Why don't you take them?" Tyne cried out, looking at her. The queen shook her head as the ground rumbled from where she came. Yelps sounded in the distance. A small rat came out, chattered at Maestro and then disappeared. Maestro turned and ran into the cave. The bushes shook, the rumbling grew stronger as the children's cries intensified. Three small badoe burst into the clearing with wild dogs barking and nipping at their feet. The dogs disappeared back into the forest leaving the intended meals to realize their situation. But the queen was quick.

"Eat!" she commanded the other acodoe, and the badoe disappeared in a matter of moments, little time given for them to thrash or squeal. The pupils of the acodoe enlarged and their breathing slowed.

"Why, Your Majesty? The children were here for you!" Tyne cried once more. The children's sobs softened. The queen eyed Tyne for a moment and slithered closer to him. The other two acodoe coiled their bodies, staying out of the way. Dying badoe shrieked inside each acodoe.

"What have you done?" the queen hissed at Tyne. She shifted her head side to side while flicking her tongue. Tyne backed towards the entrance, shaking his head, fear replacing confusion. "WHAT HAVE YOU DONE?!" The queen's hiss echoed through the clearing, her body coiled tight as Tyne bent down, putting his arms up in defense. The queen's tongue flickered, her coils becoming tighter as she moved her head forward. She snatched Tyne up as he shrieked, his body squirming in fear. The queen threw Tyne across the clearing. Tiel followed the path his body made in the air. Tyne's shrieking stopped as he hit a watosh behind Fallon, his limp body falling behind some shrubbery.

"Explain to the children the situation the best you can. Tell them we are sorry." The Queen's now sober voice echoed in the clearing.

Tiel wiped at the cuts on her upper right cheek, rubbing in sulfur water that dripped from her hair. The water stung, sending pain through to her cheekbone, causing Tiel to grind her teeth. The queen's head came closer, her body uncoiled. Tiel stood firm as the queen flicked her tongue. "Tell them...I am sorry." The queen nodded her head and slithered inside the cave. A high-pitched scream erupted after which Maestro sprinted out with the last child riding him.

Tiel relaxed as brush crunched behind her. She saw seven robies putting the lifeless bodies of Cadune and their companion on the soaked cot. Six of them picked up the cot, a seventh stood at the head and looked at Tiel. Tiel waved for them to move towards the ledge. The robies started along the path they had come through earlier.

"Wait!" the brown acodoe called. The acodoe flicked his tail and the Golden Branch opened a path in the middle. "This will be faster."

Tiel thanked the acodoe and turned back to Aven. He already had most of the children standing. She guided the children toward the opened pathway. When she peered at the Golden Plant, the robies had already cleared the opening and were heading for the ledge. Tiel continued to guide the children towards the clearing as both the mute-yellow and brown acodoe disappeared back into the forest. Upon seeing the clearing empty, the children ran through the opening, weeping hysterically. Tiel followed and scanned the ledge to see the robies on top placing the cot on the ground.

They came back to the crying children and helped them up as Fallon kept taking pictures. Tiel growled in her throat. *"The least Fallon could do is help the children."* Maestro passed her with the girl still on his back.

"Where's Aven?" Tiel asked herself as she twirled around. He stood next to the Golden Branch. Several of its limbs snaked around him, long thin black needles aimed at his torso. Aven reached out for a leaf, his hand shaking.

"Aven!" Tiel called out. As Aven's hand reached closer, the Golden Branch's limbs shook with anticipation. "Aven, what are you doing?!" Tiel yelled. Aven shook his head and looked around. He pulled back from the leaf he was aiming for a moment earlier.

One limb shot out and speared a needle through his lower right leg. As Aven screamed in pain, the plant pulled on his leg, toppling him over. Tiel ran for Aven.

"No, keep your promise!" Aven screamed at her, pointing her back towards the ledge. "Keep the children safe," Aven directed. Another needle speared him through his outstretched arm and he cried out in pain once again. Tiel rushed towards him once more. He looked up at her and his soul current broke through her rutzix. A surging river of fear for her enveloped her, its horrific power seized her and drove her back. She cried out in anguish as the fear stole her courage.

"DO NOT SOIL OUR ZAHULE!" he yelled, his face set in a defiant stare as the plant pulled him closer to its lower branches. Tiel turned and ran up the ledge. She grabbed Fallon by the arm as he continued to take pictures and pulled him along. Tiel left the clearing, Aven's continuous screams echoing in her mind.

CHAPTER 10

RESPITE

*T*he huntress brushed a tickling strand of hair out of her face and scratched her nose. She shivered from the sudden chill of the night air and turned back to caressing the soldier's maicalla clasp. The unevenness of the design interrupted the coin's smoothness. Everyone's currents were lethargic with no edge, except for Fallon's. His currents were swirling at a rapid pace, colliding with everything.

Tiel sighed. She tried to form a strong rutzix, but Aven's fear still lingered in her soul. Its dark stream prevented her from gathering a strong enough current, and it filled her mind with an angst of its own. After a few minutes, she formed a flimsy rutzix and stored her soul current in it.

The thundering sound of an adjacent waterfall filled the campsite despite Maestro's heavy breathing and digging. Dirt flew under the silvery light of Dommo, the moon, as his front paws tirelessly moved back and forth. Six of the robies finished piling two mounds of iron ore rock. The robies' dead companion lay by the almost-dug out grave site, wrapped in red blankets head to foot. The last robie sat next to Cadune, tending to his every need.

"You needed to keep your promise to the forest," Cadune said, "Aven understood...."

"Understands!" Tiel said between her gritted teeth. The sting of her cuts gone long ago, she sat by the hole, arms resting on her knees, not facing anyone. She could hear Fallon playing with his camera. The children were quiet as they slept by the campfire.

"He understands that," Cadune whispered. "The Golden Plant tricked him. The fight and the frenzied feasting of the acodoe drove it mad. Sendenia will punish it."

"An unneeded gesture," Tiel growled. "If you two dung heaps had gotten to the Watosh early, we would be far from here, with Aven." The day animals were bedded down for the night. Occasionally, a wild dog's yowl would pierce the air as it bayed at Dommo. Sometimes, the song of a night bird among the incessant chirping of crickets would attempt to calm the tense mood. The campfire infused the air with smoke and the aroma of burnt wood.

"What would make you outwit an acodoe, even the queen herself?" Fallon's chuckle echoed around Tiel.

"It doesn't matter. It would take an act of the whole High Council to make that tradition a reality," Cadune countered while moving on his pillows. His body was a patchwork of bandages covering his main scrapes. Underneath the bandages were bruises of different varying colors of red and purple. His breath came in short gasps as he fought to get comfortable.

"What tradition? You mean the one where you become Emperor after offering your life to an angry and hungry acodoe to rescue others?" Fallon taunted Cadune. "I want to know how it feels to be the next Emperor of Ecalardia?"

Cadune lay quiet for a little while, his labored breath fast and shallow. The sweet breeze curdled for a moment. Tiel raised her head as Maestro stopped digging and focused on the forest beyond the children, his tail twitching back and forth.

"I do not wish to be an emperor," Cadune whispered. "It will only harm Ecalardia."

"What? And break Cong's own rules?" Fallon laughed in mock disappointment at Cadune. "What will the Head Chiefs or the High Council say when you refuse the crown? That would cause another war. The crown would be up for grabs." Tiel tilted her head towards the conversation.

"There is no crown." Cadune's voice rose with earnest. "There was no

REDEMPTION'S CURE   111

rule, just a moment when someone was offered a position. I will just educate people on a possible new voting system."

"You already do, yet it still isn't working. You know the people want an emperor. Give it up. A voting system will fail." Fallon smiled and aimed his maicalla clasp at Cadune. "Your first thoughts, Emperor."

"My thoughts are there should be no emperor. I do not want to follow in Cong's footsteps. That type of power corrupts. I want nothing to do with it." Cadune spat out the last sentence as he coughed, his body overtaken with his emotions.

"Are you sure?" Fallon pushed, "I know of several Chiefs who would take the crown. You at least have a chance of teaching the people about the vote, ease them into it." Cadune shook his head violently at Fallon's words. Fallon laughed and turned his attention to Tiel.

"What do you think, Bounty Huntress?"

"Are you going to report everything?" Tiel rotated the rest of her body towards the party. The air became rancid. Maestro sniffed at it and crawled out of the grave site.

"I am just here to make an honest report." Fallon lay back down in between his blankets. Tiel caressed the watosh clasp once again as the air became sweet.

"You never make an honest report," Tiel challenged letting a small soul current out of her rutzix. She let it swirl in Fallon's direction. "You always taint the story somehow to take care of your interests. So, what are your interests?"

"None of your business," Fallon mumbled as he fought to get comfortable.

"Wrong, this whole rescue is my business. That makes what you're planning my business. So, what are your interests? Most people would stay home after what you've been through."

"I am here for the Peace Enforcers." Fallon waived his finger as Tiel approached. "And if you value Aven's and your zahule, you'll let me make my report."

"Don't speak to me about zahule," Tiel snarled. "When it comes to your interests, you have very little. I have kept my promise to the forest and rescued the children. My and Aven's zahule is just fine." Tiel drew closer.

"Put your companion's body into the pit," Maestro ordered. The robies complied. Afterward, they fell onto their knees while raising their heads to the heavens. Tiel used her soul current to feel around Fallon's now erratic currents and retrieved her answer.

"Hegert scared you," she said, her lips quivering in anger. "You're hoping to get Hegert off your back by publishing something about me!" She felt herself growl as she moved closer. "And Aven's disappearance works right in with your plans. Do you realize what could happen? You could put the acodoe in danger."

"Don't speak about danger," Fallon yelled. "I report one silly little thing about that woman, and she tries to kill me. I will report the truth; it is convenient enough. The acodoe attacked the party, wanting to eat the children." Fallon fluffed up his pillow.

"They were drunk and protecting the queen's eggs," Tiel countered.

"I will include all the facts, but the attack will sell better. And you left your stellove to be devoured by the Golden Plant."

"We already covered that. It was to keep our zahule clean." Tiel's voice resonated with indignation.

"Perhaps the public will see it that way, perhaps not." Fallon sat up as Tiel moved towards him in a crouched position. "Besides, you also have the Peace Enforcers' zahule to consider." He waved his finger at her, and she stopped, narrowing her eyes. After a few moments she sat back down, and he lay down once again, grunting to himself.

"I have everything stored up here." Fallon yawned as he closed his eyes. "I have you backed against a wall. There's nothing you can do this time. A good tale never hurt anyone, in the long run, that is." Tiel grimaced at his smile as he fell asleep.

Maestro shoved dirt back into the pit, enough to cover the body. "Fill the grave with the iron ore," he commanded. Tiel watched the robies toss the heavy rocks into the pit. The ore clattered against each other and a dust cloud formed over the grave. Soon, Maestro and the robies were sneezing.

"Prisoners don't get proper burials. They know this is the only chance to give their companion one," Cadune whispered. Tiel turned and observed Cadune when she heard the tightness in his voice. The robie next to him held up a wool satchel and put it in front of his face.

Cadune shook his head and averted his face as he had done all night. "How will these events affect you? Fallon will look after his interests."

Tiel turned, took a deep breath, and let it rush out of her. "That would be my business," Tiel answered while deliberating the answer herself. Cadune moaned again.

"You'll need the herbs. That is the only way you will get some comfortable sleep," Tiel called out to Cadune as he rejected another offer from the robie, "and it is the only way I can get rid of your soiled pathetic excuses. You already caused enough harm today. I will need you at your best tomorrow."

Cadune took more labored breaths, then gave up and nodded.

The constant clattering of rocks brought Tiel's attention back to the grave. When all the rocks lay in the pit, Maestro inhaled deeply and opened his mouth letting out a spiraling cone of blue fire. Tiel, along with the robies, scooted back from the heat. Maestro stopped, inhaled a little and let out another blast.

"Does he do this often?" Cadune's voice was relaxing.

"Every time someone may not get a burial." Tiel put her maicalla back in her pocket. Maestro was breathing deep once again. "Never seen him run out of firepower though. Those rocks will melt, eventually."

"I ammm sorry, sometimes I get too buurdeened with traaditions." Cadune's words became elongated as his eyelids closed. The robie arranged pillows and blankets around him. Tiel ignored his apology as she gazed at the grave. Fallon's breaths were deep and rhythmic, yet his thought currents were still active.

"What are you going to do, Fallon?" Tiel mumbled as she watched Maestro work. Fallon could be brutal in his reports. If he represented the acodoe as bloodthirsty monsters, it would mark their clan for retribution. General ManCane oversaw the rescue attempt. A negative report could diminish the public's trust in the Peace Enforcers. If he represented her as an uncaring, opportunistic hunter that left her stellove to be devoured... she exhaled forcefully focusing her attention on Fallon.

"That is an unforgivable sin as far as it concerns the clan. Especially after he stood beside me at the larquetz. The hunter extremists would be ruthless in their hunt for me," she murmured, then surveyed the surrounding group to see if anyone was listening. No one indicated they heard anything.

"If I made it to another larquetz before getting killed, they could put me in seclusion, under my inner clan leader for retraining." She shivered hard at the thought. The Elder Hunter's 'retraining' would include making her his pet telepath. Her head swam with the possibilities, and another blue funnel flared, bringing her attention back to Maestro. "At least he's taking action." Those last words jolted her awake. She slowly bobbed her head as understanding enlightened her mind.

"Shea's light! The acodoe are the real victims here. The Peace Enforcers are doing everything to keep the peace, and I will not be somebody's puppet." She whispered.

Tiel crept over to Fallon. Excitement filled Fallon's swarming soul currents. She could tell he had been counting gigots from the published story.

"And you would soil everyone's zahule just for a few gigots," Tiel thought as Fallon's mouth formed a soft satisfied grin, making the small wrinkles around his eyes more pronounced. She touched his face. It was cool and a little rough from the growing stubble. She waited a moment more than grabbed Fallon under the chin with her right hand.

Fallon's eyes opened and stared into hers. For a few moments, he lay still. His body jerked, but she held his face firm. Tiel could sense everything Fallon's body was doing while she used a thin, sharp current to delve into his memories, manipulating it to bring out his thoughts and emotions. Scenes from his previous life mingled inside her mind. She searched for the perfect substitutes for perception and emotion.

Fallon's arms trembled, and his breathing quickened while Tiel spread her current out into a flat blade with several protruding appendages. She took memories from one part of his life and weaved it into the memories from earlier that day.

Tears flowed out of Fallon's eyes as his feet writhed in agony, scraping the ground underneath. Tiel used previous emotions of disappointment and frustration to conceal his excitement. She made this new memory fallible, allowing it to disintegrate over time.

A foul odor permeated the air as a hiss of laughter escaped from the forest. Fallon's body slumped and lay still as she put her telepathy back in the rutzix. His eyes rolled into his eyelids. After a few moments, his eyelids closed, and his breathing slowed. Tiel released her grip and caressed Fallon's cheek with her thumb. She turned around and saw Maestro glaring at her.

"What have you done?" he asked. A foul odor blew through the campsite again.

"What needs to be done." Tiel stood and went over to her backpack. The robies stood staring at her. She pulled out her bedding and arranged it next to the fire.

"Someone is happy about what you did tonight," Maestro announced sniffing the air. "Although, I don't particularly like..." A crash resounded through the forest, and a line of watosh collided into each other. Screams erupted from the trees followed by hissing as a putrid wind rushed through the camp. The ground thundered with hostility, knocking over all who were standing.

Tiel and Maestro crawled as low to the ground as their bodies would permit while still being able to move towards the children. The quakes in the ground intensified as the sharp cracking of splintering logs filled the night. Tiel made it to three of the screaming children and laid them down as she put her body over them. Maestro made it soon after and covered five others. The last one held onto Maestro. Tiel watched the sky for flying debris. She moved the children when one large log crashed near them, sending splinters careening in all directions.

Hissing resounded through the clearing causing Tiel and the children to cover their ears. She watched boughs and splinters spray into the air again. Forest animals skittered over them to cross the clearing. Watosh continued to collide with each other as a gargled scream spewed out. The ground tremors escalated and then stopped with the last explosion of shattered tree limbs and boughs spraying into the sky.

Quiet fell on the region. Tiel covered her head as she cuddled up to the children while the last of the debris fell. She looked up to find that three of the robies had covered the sleeping forms of Fallon and Cadune with their bodies, the other four lay sprawled close to the grave.

"What happened?" Tiel questioned Maestro who only shook his head. "Did we leave Tyne near that commotion?"

"I believe we did," Maestro answered. "You weren't able to telepathically sense anything?"

"Too much going on," Tiel said while shaking her head. "I wasn't able to concentrate. Go look. I'll stay with the children," she said as Maestro sniffed the air and growled. He trotted over to the tree line.

Tiel took her time in getting the children calmed down. She dried their tears, gave drinks of water, and tucked everyone in. When they finally fell asleep, almost a full arm had elapsed. The robies were waiting by the grave with no sign of Maestro.

Tiel motioned to the robies to stand by the children. Two obeyed. She made her way to where they had left Tyne.

A few minutes later she found Maestro laying down facing the forest, his tail twitching back and forth. Broken branches mixed with strands of rope littered the area around the small tree. A fetid smell in the air almost caused Tiel to lose the contents of her stomach. Maestro growled and pointed his muzzle up at the lower branches of the watosh neighboring the small tree. A chunk of raw, black, bloodstained skin with a thick, yellow crust lay on the branch below blood spatters.

TIEL SPLASHED cold water on her face from the pool. Shea's morning rays shimmered off the surface, causing Tiel to face the cliff. The waterfall's roar could not drown out the emptiness that clenched at her insides, attempting to tear apart her resolve to stay calm and collected. The water trickled down her hair and brought Tiel back to her unwanted reality. She peered down at her reflection in the water distorted by the lapping waves. Fallon's reflection stood behind her wavering image.

"That could have been some nasty business yesterday." Fallon stood with his arms folded. "I was hoping for at least a little drama. The whole affair was too calm to get a good story."

Tiel breathed in and kept looking into the pool, preferring the altered images it offered.

"Well, sometimes it goes that way. When are we heading out?" Fallon's image disappeared as he spoke.

"As soon as first meal is over." Maestro's voice came from behind. Tiel could see Fallon's hand wave in the air in acknowledgment. Maestro's image appeared on the pool's surface. "Mark my words, last night's deed will come back at you tenfold." Tiel refused to look at what she knew would be Maestro's glare. After a long moment of silence, Tiel looked back finding Maestro gone.

She peered into the pool again. Its surface shimmered and danced in Shea's first rays. She could hear the children's cries for their parents as they woke up. Cadune moaned a little but stated that it was easier to move, the herbs having staved off an infection.

Tiel splashed her hand in the water. Her fingers tingled as the cold liquid swirled in between them. She hummed as she drew shapes on the water's surface. As she was drawing a large square, her fingers brushed against the rough surface of a tiny piece of cement. She plunged her hand into the water to pick it up only to fall backward as the object's weight held it firm in the muck. Tiel returned to the pool's edge and put both arms in the water above her elbows. She plowed through the stinging coldness and removed the muck from the cement. The cement transformed into a tablet with figures carved into its surface.

"What have you found?" Maestro's voice caused her to jump. "Part of a storyboard?"

Tiel nodded her head and continued working. Maestro dug next to her, moving the muck even faster. The water reached halfway up his legs.

"You are not angry?" Tiel didn't look at him as she kept digging.

"No." Maestro stopped and looked at her. "I understand. However, I fear you will have consequences for your actions." He cautioned and plowed into the muck once more.

"Do not worry. It will last only about a week." Tiel pulled on the cement tablet that was emerging. As it moved, pockets of muck sank, emitting a stink that made Tiel cough and exposed corners of another tablet. Tiel turned her head from the smell and waited.

When the muck had settled, she pulled the rest of the tablet out. The smooth, thick stone was a light cream color. The sides had two sets of grooves with thin, silver metal lines inside. A chiseled surface had runes etched on the top. The muck had protected the tablet which meant it would take little effort to clean. Tiel held the tablet up and gaped.

Standing on the cliff to the left of the waterfall was a figure. It had the curves of a woman, dressed in a plain, brown robe with a hood. A wild dog stood next to the figure, and a falcon rested on its shoulder.

"Think you could get up there to find out who that is?" Tiel asked Maestro.

"No!" Maestro had stopped digging to study the figure. "Too steep for me to climb."

Tiel observed the figure. It stayed a few more moments and then walked out of sight.

"A piece of forgotten history," Cadune's bass voice boomed from behind. "This would be the Prophet Drakner's specialty." Tiel turned back to see Cadune sitting behind them. He wore a clean tunic covering the bandages.

"Why? Because you consider him to be a 'prophet'?" Tiel asked.

Cadune shook his head. "No. I know that his specialty was archeology even though he is known for his raids on the master merchants long before we knew him as a prophet."

"Why don't we try to get the other one?" Maestro suggested still watching the cliff. Tiel tried to pull another tablet out, only to find it connected to a whole line of tablets.

"It should take an arm or two to get the children ready. That should give you two plenty of time," Cadune announced. "By the way, what is wrong with Fallon's memory?"

"Awake," Diandra called to the emptiness in her mind. She waited a few moments. Four other girls shared the room with her. They were still, eyes open, looking around. The thin board that was her bed caused her back to stiffen.

"Awake," Diandra called again. She kept her focus on her bright red, long hair which rested on the smudged pillow under her head. She had to pee, and if she didn't get an answer soon, she might wet the thin, ragged blankets under her. Then, she would be picked for sure.

"Awake," Diandra called to the silence of her mind again. Her body shook with fear, and her belly ached from the effort of holding her bladder's desires at bay. She was about to announce herself again when a slight click sounded at the back of her brain.

"All right, my little cards, I hear you." Lady's voice chuckled. "Get up. You cards have a long day ahead. There is plenty of food to prepare." The girls rose, and Diandra rushed to the water closet. "Oh, and Diandra, meet me in my office. The master has a special job for you

TODAY." The click sounded again, and the other girls smirked as Diandra's spirit fell. Working for the master meant that Lady didn't want her. It was the first step to 'being picked.'

She dressed in plain, blue trousers, a pink shirt, and a pair of strap sandals. Nobody in the party zone wore maicallas. She left the room before the other girls had finished dressing. The empty halls of stark white walls and cold floor tiles flew by as she rounded the corner to the stairs and bumped into a floating pile of plush, colorful blankets.

"Watch where you're going." Rheswyn peered around the towels she was carrying. As usual her smile drooped. In fact, Diandra noticed these days that everything about Rheswyn drooped; her smile, her shoulders, her hair, her eyes… everything drooped. Rheswyn used to be one of Lady's best girls. Now she was twenty-four, which was too old for Lady. Rheswyn was the call girl to her previous subordinates.

"Maybe I'll see you in the pick," Diandra thought as she scooted around the older girl and up the stairs. She ran up three flights and opened a door.

Diandra turned left into a plush hallway and ran towards the end. A thick warm red carpet covered the floor. Petal-shaped crystal lamps hung on the walls painted with vibrant colors of soft off-white mixed with rust. Sturdy wood tables and chairs with soft cushions lined the hallway.

Diandra passed several wood doors on either side until she reached her destination. Two large wooden doors stood before her. Their swirled pattern matched the motif of the round golden doorknobs.

"I'M HERE." Diandra mentally reported. She stood straight with her hands behind her back. There was no reason to look like Rheswyn. Diandra still believed she could avoid being picked.

The door opened and a tall, blond girl two octaves her senior stood before her.

"Lady has already given you to the master." The girl shuffled through some papers in her hand that concealed her pink outfit. "You are to be at the exit site in one arm, on the north side of Daton. You will receive your instructions when the master is ready." The girl shut the door.

Diandra heard a chuckle as she slumped against the wall.

"Lady won't even see you." Rheswyn snickered. "Looks like you and I will be picked next."

Diandra ran towards the girl with her arms outstretched and knocked the carefully piled blankets out of her hands. She turned back once to see Rheswyn kneeling on the ground piling up the blankets. She felt sorry for just a minute but dismissed the emotion as she ran back down to the basement.

Voices of girls her age bounced off the walls as she neared the kitchen. Clangs of pots and pans followed as she opened the door. Warm air from the three large, crackling fireplaces enveloped her when she stepped through. Girls worked furiously to scrub the dishes piled high in the sinks on the right. Some heads had disappeared inside pots that bobbed up and down with the girls' scrubbing efforts. Long wooden tables with benches filled the middle of the kitchen. The sound of wooden knives hitting chopping blocks drummed in time with movements of arms and wrists. Bland cooking aromas wafted in from the pots in the fireplaces.

Diandra stepped into the pantry farther in the rear. She checked the scene and decided the girls were too busy with their chores to notice her. The pantry had several shelves that lined the walls up to the ceiling and a steel door that lead to the outside. She ignored the food on the shelves. Anyone would be a fool to steal the food. Lady ordered her bosses to count the food stocks three times, sometimes more, each day. However, the currency cards were never counted.

A steel shelf stood just inside the doorway. She opened a box and flipped through the cards. Lady liked being a big spender. However, it wasn't wise to pick a card that had an unlimited amount of currency. Old scars on her back attested to previous errors in choosing the wrong card. She picked one with a mediocre sum available and put the box back. One quick check of the kitchen affirmed that no one was paying attention. Diandra opened the steel door and stepped into the back garden.

She breathed deep. The bouquet of the flora rejuvenated her mind and spirits. She put the card in her back pocket and walked into Shea's rays. It had been too long since she felt the warmth of a bright clear day. She let her body stretch, enjoying the moment. After her futile attempt at being normal was over, she ran to the back of the gardens. She hurried past the colorful flora, pristine white benches, stone paths, and past the man-made waterfall to the stone wall. Once there, she made her way to a black iron gate and stepped through to enter the alleyway.

CHAPTER 11

AFTERMATH

Scores of villagers wearing an array of colorful maicallas, their clasps at varying lengths as they talked and laughed, filled Daton's busy cobblestone walkways. Round, wooden tables sat in the middle of the walkways with chairs positioned around them. Some even had people sitting while drinking or eating the food from the Bamboodii huts that lined the streets. All the huts had counters with stools on the front. Behind the counters were the wares that each shopkeeper sold, the shopkeepers dressed in bright-colored outfits. Sometimes Diandra wondered if there were contests for which shopkeeper wore the most outrageous outfit. She chuckled as she saw some possible winners.

Diandra inspected each shop as she made her way to the exit point. There were some new, brightly colored clothes in one shop and different shapes of shoes in another. The aroma of fresh, sweet-nut bread from a bakery made her stomach grumble in anticipation. She'd come back to that hut. She made her way through the walkways as the shop huts gave way to living abodes. Most had nice looking lawns with some floral arrangements. Diandra kept walking until she reached the north entrance of Daton. Beyond, the Watosh Forest dominated the landscape. As she drew closer, the crowds became thicker and noisier. Babies cried, children laughed as they danced alongside their parents, crowds of drinkers cheered and wrestled each other, and reporters staked out a piece of the lawn with the floating orbs. Most maicalla clasps were at the mid-chest point or lower. Some of the rowdier villagers' maicallas were opened with no clasp. All the commotion kept the line of Peace Enforcers on edge. Their eyes darting around the scene betrayed their anxiety hidden beneath the straight uniforms and maicalla clasps cinched up to their neck.

Diandra searched and located a spot where she could sit on the grass and wait. She rubbed her hand in the soft, cool gentleness of the lawn. Her stomach growled again just as she heard the familiar click in the back of her mind.

"ALL RIGHT, THE MASTER HAS ME WATCHING YOU THIS DAY, PUP" a young male chortled as Diandra slumped just a little. "I EXPECT THE PARTY TO RETURN SOON, SO LOOK NORMAL." Diandra stood up and looked around. The crowd was getting worse, and a few playful children now started to whine. She moved toward a group of children her age. "NO, NOT THAT TYPE OF NORMAL. FOR SHEA'S SAKE, USE YOUR BRAIN. I KNOW YOU HAVE ONE, I AM TALKING TO IT."

"Fresh bread, sweet-nut bread, rolls, cakes all right here." Diandra looked for the voice and found the owner of the bakery holding out a basket of goodies. The smell of spices assailed her nose, and Diandra swallowed the extra saliva that collected in her mouth. "Where are your parents, little one?"

"Mom wants something for the babies, twins, and they get really hungry." Diandra smiled as she handed him the card.

"Now, isn't that sweet." The man took it and pulled out a small light pen from his front apron pocket. He tapped the pen, and a small red light turned on, after which he scanned the card and handed it back.

"What will it be, little one?" He tipped the basket towards her. Diandra picked two loaves of sweet-nut bread and ran off.

"I DIDN'T REALIZE LADY TWIBETT LET YOU HAVE A CARD. OKAY, I GUESS A KID EATING WILL LOOK MORE NORMAL THAN JUST STANDING AROUND." Diandra smiled and tried to work her way to the front, but the crowds were too thick. "DO NOT MESS THIS UP FOR ME. GET TO WHERE YOU CAN SEE." The demanding tone made her nerves twitch. She scanned the area, some kids her age were sitting on top of the wall separating Daton from the forest. Diandra made her way over.

"I will let you have some if you can help me up." Diandra ducked her head to avoid their swinging feet as she showed them her loaves. The children shrugged their shoulders and reached down. Soon Diandra was on top of the wall overlooking the scene.

The exit from the forest was a bowl-shaped clearing. Reporters mingled with the crowds but stayed away from the column of Peace Enforcers. Diandra could see a band to her left, their various instruments ready for when the party emerged.

She had finished with the first loaf, wishing she had thought of buying something to drink when cheers rose from the crowd. Diandra stood to see over the raised arms. The Bounty Huntress led a small group out of the forest. Her cat kept watch behind the party. Reporters swamped The Bounty Huntress; she merely pulled out her maicalla and pushed up the clasp to her neck, her lips curled into a snarl. The reporters halted. The crowds cheered the move.

Diandra gaze turned to the rest of the party. Robies labored under the weight of the large warrior with three kids. Six other older kids trudged along carrying backpacks. De Menzaile was nowhere. Diandra smiled. The Bounty Huntress was prime. That other Hunter messed with her, and she had gotten her way. Why people tried to stage her, Diandra didn't know. She knew The Bounty Huntress could take on anything, even a big, dead-brained fool like de Menzaile.

"Watch her! the master wants to know where she's going." Diandra kept her eyes on the group. She saw the children being led somewhere else as The Bounty Huntress took their packs. The large warrior grimaced as he held his bandaged chest while several medics rushed to his aid.

"Get down! Get down! They are getting away." Diandra looked around. There was no place to land. "Get down off that wall now, girl or I will whip you myself." Diandra jumped and landed on the backs of three boys, losing her sweet bread.

"Watch where you're going!" A tall woman came over, grabbed her ear, and led her over to the wall. "Wait right there until everybody has left." The woman turned and helped the boys.

The voice inside her head laughed. "That was fun, let's do something else. Kick the dung heap and follow The Bounty Huntress. She's headed to the western lot." Diandra followed orders. The woman screamed as Diandra exited the crowd. "Don't get caught by the enforcers or I'll turn you off now." Diandra didn't look back. She kept her eyes on where she thought Daton's lot would be. The voice inside her head chuckled as she weaved around bodies, tripping over a few feet. Within minutes, she was panting beside a hovercraft in Daton's parking lot. The voice was now laughing. "Find her. See what she is doing."

Hovercrafts filled the lot. She saw enforcers keeping the vehicles safe, but other than that, she couldn't find any evidence of pursuit.

"Let's leave before the reporters find us." The Bounty Huntress' voice came from Diandra's left. She crouched and peered over the end of a blue vehicle. The long, muscular body of Maestro appeared through the window, his tail flicking back and forth. Diandra passed an opening between the blue vehicle and a green vehicle without being spotted, then stopped to calm her heart.

"Trying to sneak around now, are we? This ought to be fun to watch!" the voice inside her head snickered.

"I'm with you. Too tired to even stand." The cat's deep voice boomed. Diandra peeked around the green hovercraft. The Bounty Huntress was placing the backpacks in the trunk of her vehicle. Maestro was climbing in the back.

"You know I must stay hidden from other hunters for a while." The Bounty Huntress finished placing the backpacks in the trunk and stretched her lower back. "Next time I take a bounty like this, remind me of the past three days."

"You will remind yourself." Maestro's voice sounded low, almost as if he was choking. The hovercraft's side slid shut, and The Bounty Huntress walked over to the driver's side. Diandra crouched once again. The Bounty Huntress's hovercraft started with a soft whine and moved out of the stall.

"Well, you pulled it off. I'll keep you for when I'm bored," the voice chuckled again. "The reports show that her hovercraft is usually here. Plus, she likes Daton's shops in the southern square, so she should be there in the morning. You will meet her there, watch her, and find out everything about her. Where she stays in Daton, who she has ties with, everything. One word of warning, if I check back in and find you are in anything that may look like an enforcer's cell, I will shut you off. With the commotion you caused, they are still looking for you. Best sleep outside tonight, so I don't get confused." Diandra heard several voices laughing, and then a click sounded in the back of her mind. She huddled next to the hovercraft with her arms hugging her legs.

Emery opened the door to his hut and walked in carrying a limp Jainu. Emiline followed, carrying a bag of leftovers from the day's counseling session. Emery had packed it knowing Emiline would be too tired to cook, and that he would be too tired to clean up. They had finally left Enforcer Headquarters giving the Delegates and their children precious family time.

Emery looked at the star crystal. It was too late to be just getting home. The dark purple light cast bright shadows on the walls, showing that Shea's first path of a new day had started.

"Put the lad in the guest bedroom for tonight." Emiline removed Emery's and Jainu's maicallas. Emery chuckled at the memory of Jainu's excitement when they had lent him the extra maicalla.

"I don't expect Tiel and Aven will be back for a couple of days," Emery commented as Emiline removed her maicalla. "Wish I hadn't been too busy to miss the reports on the holo screen. I am interested in how everything went."

"I'll open the back curtains. Tonight will be a good night to enjoy our backyard," Emiline stated as Emery navigated through the darkened rooms, having no energy to pay attention to anything. He took off the boy's sandals and tucked him under the homemade quilts.

Emery could hear Emiline in the kitchen as she yawned. He didn't think they would even eat tonight. They had all done too much kitchen work at the enforcer's headquarters. Emiline's counseling techniques and good food had worked. The delegates and their children had mended their relationships. Emery ruffled the sleeping lad's hair. He hoped that Jainu would allow them to sleep late.

Emery heard Emiline gasp from the kitchen. She then called his name. Emery checked Jainu to make sure he was still sleeping. The boy didn't move. He hurried to the kitchen to find Emiline standing next to the back door staring at the floor while holding the bag.

There was enough light from the outside yard lights to show two broken table legs and the table surface scattered in three pieces. One leg lay under the icebox. Emery was looking for the other one when Emiline gasped again. He followed her gaze past the glass back door.

In the back, Tiel sat on the lawn with her head in her hands. Maestro lay next to her, his head butting against her midsection. Halfway between her and the abode was the other table leg. A large hole dominated the back door, and broken glass littered the lawn outside.

"Where... where is Aven?" Emiline asked, placing her hand over her mouth. She looked at Emery.

"Emiline, get your sleep chems!" Emery hurried to the back door while navigating the broken table. "Get them right now. She is in danger." He looked at his wife. She disappeared into the hut, turning on a lamp in the water closet.

Emery opened the door. Tiel and Maestro didn't stir at the sound of tinkling glass. He could hear her sobs as he made his way towards her. Her maicalla lay discarded a few lengths from her.

"Tiel, what happened?" The girl didn't move. Maestro glanced up at Emery and shook his head in despair. "Tiel, talk to me."

"The voices won't go away, Pa," her voice cracked under strain.

"What happened? Where is Aven?" He sat down next to her. Maestro backed away.

"He had to save our zahule," she sobbed louder, "and the voices won't go away."

"Do you want us to help?" Emery asked. Tiel nodded as she fell against him. Maestro growled at the forest.

"Okay, we'll help." Emery turned back to the hut. Emiline was coming out with a syringe, wiping her eyes with the backs of her hands. "We'll get the whole story from Maestro." His silent tears streamed into Tiel's hair as her mournful howling tore at his insides.

DOMMO SHONE on the leaves of the Golden Branch. Its branches drooped and shivered in the cold breeze. Its whimpering had quieted long ago, leaving the clearing silent. Clear oils from the plant dripped on the ground spreading a rainbow of color into a pool below the cave. The scent of fresh dirt wavered in the air around the withered pieces of the plant that lay strewn over the floor. Five needles, stained with red blood, shimmered in Dommo's light. The Golden Branch shivered again.

"Next time, it will watch what prey it tempts," Sendenia hissed to herself. She had scolded it, leaving no room for doubt that the plant's attack was a crime. That was after the human had already done extensive damage himself. She lay in a tight coil in her cave and watched the night terrain for her guards. "They should be back by now." She flicked her tongue sensing the air around her. "They should have been back two days ago."

"Your Majesty, everything is going along as expected." Sendenia raised her head at the sound of Doctor Russet's voice. Nender, an aged gentleman stood behind him. Both humans had been working long and hard to keep the human named Aven comfortable and well. The plant's poison coursing through his veins produced a high fever and occasional seizures. Doctor Russet showed a strong capability in treating the situation with needed chems and herbs. Sendenia's servant, Nender, had run in and out of the room, getting needed supplies. At this moment, Rachel, Doctor Russet's wife, tended to Aven. She held dry, small cloths in her orange apron that covered her blue plaid dress as she sat by Aven's bed. The sleeves of her dress were pulled up as she dipped a cloth into a basin which sat on a smooth, rock surface to her left. Rachael anchored a wisp of light-auburn hair behind her ear that had escaped the bun sitting on top of her head. Aven moaned at which Rachael put the wet, cool cloth on his head as he murmured in a low voice.

Sendenia had rescued both Doctor Russet and Nender from their separate, previous, greedy interactions with the Golden Branch. Nender was old according to his species' length of life. His brown skin appeared more like the skin of dead beasts that humans preserved through what they called tanning. Yet, unlike the smooth surface of the tanned skins, his skin had layer upon layer of wrinkles, something which was very prominent on his bald head. His plain, brown clothes hid a dent in his leg where the Golden Plant's microbes had digested part of his muscle, causing him to limp. Along with his limp leg, Nender had suffered a severe loss of memory. Sendenia had sent other servants, long since dead, to inquire about his identity. They had located his wife and reunited the two. However, Nender thought Sendenia had merely chosen someone suitable for him. Nender's abject worship of Sendenia was often misguided. It constantly led him to do things against her wishes when he thought it necessary to prove his worthiness. Sendenia often wished him gone, yet he showed usefulness this day.

Doctor Darien Russet was an older man, but younger than Nender. His short, dark hair showed strands of white. He wore casual slacks and a shirt. Attached to the top of his pants was a small white box. This human invention took the air around it and changed it into pure oxygen. The oxygen traveled up a long tube that hooked around his ears and had two tubes that stayed in his nose. The oxygen kept him alive since the plant's poison had attacked and damaged part of his lungs. Doctor Russet's memory came and went without warning. Other servants had also found his wife. However, sometimes he thought he was married to a previous deceased wife. Other times, he recognized Rachel for whom she was. The woman was patient and gentle. She played whatever part he needed.

Aven moaned again and Sendenia looked at him. He had not provoked the plant and might lose everything. Cadune was one of the few to keep his memory.

"How is his memory?" Sendenia asked.

"It is hard to tell at this moment," Doctor Russet answered, looking back at Aven. "Clara says he keeps calling out the name 'Tiel.'"

Sendenia chuckled. Clara was his deceased wife. At least the memory loss didn't affect his skills. "Tiel is his stellove or wife. Keep asking him questions about her. That is the best way to save his memory."

"Clara has already been doing that. I will likewise." Doctor Russet retreated to the backroom. Sendenia watched as he talked with Rachel. She smiled and nodded. Sendenia shook her head.

"Excuse me, Your Majesty." Nender interrupted her thoughts.

"What is it?" Sendenia studied the servant as she flicked her tongue sensing his usefulness was at an end.

"I don't believe that is a good plan." Nender shuffled his feet as he tried to explain his reasoning. "He gave his life for someone who just ran away. There is one worthy of him. Let him forget the one who would let him die."

"NO!" Sendenia hissed. "That is not how it will be. Leave!" Nender watched her for a moment, then bowed and left through a back exit.

Sendenia turned back as her brother slithered into the clearing. He had guarded her for many octavians now, and it unnerved her he would appear without his mate, a yellow acodoe. His mate's wisdom had helped him through his middle octaves. The queen watched as he checked out the scene, moving his head from side to side, flicking his tongue in the air. Deciding everything was all right, he slithered forward, his head hanging. The queen sat upright, her jade skin scratching the wall. *Where was his mate?*

"Sendenia," he called her name. The queen flicked her tongue, moving her head side to side. "Sendenia, come out!" She didn't like it. *Where was his mate?* "Sendenia, I know you are there. I sense you. Come out!"

"Come closer, Tiberus, I am in the cave entrance." Tiberus obeyed. He positioned himself in front of the cave and coiled the lower half of his body. "Where is your mate, little brother?" Sendenia leaned out of the cave.

"First, my report, dear sister." He straightened up and exhaled. "We followed the group as you had asked, they, or rather the one called The Bounty Huntress camped at Jaiden's Wash." Sendenia nodded. She hadn't been too successful in teaching her little brother about duty first. His mate was successful in many things Sendenia had failed at concerning him. He raised his torso straight and tall, his bottom half coiled perfectly as he gave his report. "They tied the trespasser, the adult called Tyne, to a tree on the edge of the forest. They ate what they called last meal. The adult named Cadune, may the new emperor always have Coulliou's and Shea's light to guide him, had his servants put the kids to bed. There was a small amount of conversation. We couldn't hear anything, but the infected one could."

"Jonaxx was there?" Sendenia's pits on her face widened.

"I am sorry, sister, we were so engrossed with watching the party we didn't realize he had come up behind us." This he said in a soft voice, his stature slumping. However, he straightened up again. "We believed, and the infected one was happy about it, that The Bounty Huntress used one of *the ungifts.*" He grew quiet and waited for his sister to reply.

"You are wise to let me ponder that. Which one? Did Jonaxx say which one?" Sendenia asked. Her little brother nodded and waited again.

"Which one?" She asked.

"The Soul Mask." He averted his eyes from her gaze.

"What have my faults caused?" she murmured. Aven moaned again. She looked to discover Aven seizing once more. Doctor Russet and his wife backed away, letting the seizures take their course. Sendenia turned back to her younger brother.

"Tiberus, what happened to your mate?" she asked him.

The acodoe slumped but continued. "The infected one was happy about the use of the ungift. He wanted to speak with The Bounty Huntress. We couldn't allow that. We had to use force to stop him. During the fight, he went for my throat and my mate…" He stopped, swayed, and then continued. "My mate lunged in front and gave her life for me."

"Jonaxx, oh Jonaxx!" Sendenia wailed under her breath. Tiberus swayed, his perfect coils turning limp and spreading over the ground.

"Give me of your wisdom, dear sister." He fell to the floor. "How do I get past this?"

"Dear brother, it is my faults that have caused this," Sendenia whispered, shaking her head. Tiberus sobbed while his body shook. Sendenia slid out of her cave and curled her body in a hug around her brother. She nuzzled his snout, her tears creating rivulets that coursed down his trembling body.

"MISTRESS LAISEN, there is someone here to see you." The servant's voice boomed through the room, exploding inside Lidena's head. "He says he has the answer you are looking for."

"What, is he a telepath?" Lidena used her arm to dry her tears. She had cried since Aven did not return with Tiel from the Watosh three days ago. Her eyes ached, her neck wouldn't move in any direction, and any noise reverberated in her head. She hated waiting for word from Anised. For once, he hadn't argued with her about bringing in The Bounty Huntress. "Trust me. I have no patience for telepaths at this moment." She walked to the table behind the couch and chucked ice into a glass. "I'd have them all butchered for their cowardice."

"Not a telepath," an old voice croaked. The sound grated on her nerves. "Just someone aware of your fondness for the one called de Menzaile."

Lidena turned to see an old, stick-like figure standing in her doorway, his slumped frame shriveled next to the muscular servant standing next to him.

"Nender, you may think you are part of this clan, but I assure you, your presence will only bring trouble to you." Lidena waved the servant off. He bowed and left.

"Even if I know of de Menzaile's present state of health?"

Lidena stopped and looked at the old man. "How do you know about de Menzaile's state of health?"

"I serve Sendenia, Queen of the Acodoe." Nender stepped into the room. His over-sized, light-brown pants and shirt rustled as he shuffled in. "My job was to keep an eye on the Hunter Clan, to make friends here. She never thought I would make it into the inner circle."

"Tell me about de Menzaile, old fool."

"It is simple. The queen is having Doctor Russet nurse him back to health."

"Nurse him back?" Lidena put down her glass and inched closer. "How is he?"

"In a very precarious situation, and we need to hurry back to her cave." Nender touched her hand. "If we don't, it will be too late, and you will be the one he forgets forever."

"Wh- wh- what?" Lidena squinted her eyes.

"Hurry, there is not much time." Nender shuffled back to the entrance. "I will explain on the way."

Nender shuffled out the doorway and vanished to the left.

"Mistress Laisen, may I have a word with you?" The Elder Hunter appeared in her doorway.

Lidena stared at the empty space behind him, then shaking her head she called for her cloak, and without a word to the smiling Elder Hunter, she followed Nender.

THE PHOTOGRAPHS WERE ALL TOO fuzzy. Fallon knew the term wasn't professional, yet he was in his office, and looking at these pictures drained any energy he had. Anyone looking at these would think he was only exploring the craft instead of being a seasoned photographer. Digital tech would only go so far in doctoring and fixing bad photographs.

The wall screen that held the images Fallon was looking at buzzed and popped. Its width spread across the smooth side of the rock wall above a plain, black, stone desk. A small hole below the wall screen held his camera clasp. A bright light glared out as the technology interpreted what was in the camera and produced the results on the screen.

Fallon sat in a soft, black, leather chair that rotated in every direction. He swiveled as he thought about his problem. His gaze barely noticed the bookshelves that lined the other five rock walls. The crystal light above him was bright and wired for cavern homes. It did more than light the current path in which his life traveled. He gave up looking at the photographs and lazily followed the stiff, slanted wire that ran from just above his desk, past the wooden pins that hung on it, and above the door frame where it was attached. There he found Jenn standing in the doorway.

"Fallon?" A female musk permeated the room. It brought back to Fallon's mind nights under the stars.

"Jenn?" he responded. She wore a rust-colored tribal cloak that fit her curves and came just above her knees. Her maicalla opened below the midpoint. Her whole demeanor contrasted his depressed, plain-clothed state of mind. She smiled at him as Lizard entered the room and crawled up the bookshelves next to the door. Fallon scowled. "What are you doing here?"

"Nice to see you too, love." Jenn fussed with her long hair. Fallon remembered the soft silkiness of her hair as she wrapped a strand around her finger. Lizard waited on the top of the bookshelf, her tongue flicking.

"Where's Xeth?" Fallon questioned. He put the clasp on his maicalla just below the neck. Jenn just shrugged her shoulders, ignoring his move.

"Answer the question. Why are you here?" Fallon queried, letting his voice turn soft as he got up from his chair and leaned on the bookshelf. The books rattled while Lizard circled a few times flicking her tongue again.

"Well, our dear editor has solicited my help with this story."

Fallon couldn't help but laugh a little. He leaned over, keeping his eyes on Jenn, and pushed a large pin up the wire.

"And why does he think I need help?" Fallon inquired as he smiled. Jenn's scent glided to his nostrils, bringing in memories of long walks. He left the wooden pin by the door. Lizard pounced up and down and spun three times; the books rattled again. He could see the animal shaking out of the corner of his eye.

"Are you implying that I would…"

"You are in her way." Fallon stepped back.

"What?" Jenn turned just as Lizard leaped onto her head. Lizard spun around once and put her head in front of Jenn's face. The animal's claws caused Jenn's hair to stick out at odd angles.

"AHHHH!" Jenn scrambled to get Lizard off her hair. Fallon smirked. Lizard, finding her perch not so fun, jumped over onto the wire above the doorway. All four claws grabbed the wire as the animal hissed at Jenn, who was busy trying to get her hair back into place. Jenn clenched her teeth, sneering at Fallon.

Lizard left Jenn alone and concentrated on the wooden pin. She stretched and clasped the pin in her mouth. Standing on her hind claws, she tiptoed back dragging the pin on the line with her until she grasped the edge of the door with her hind legs.

"You did that on purpose." Jenn tried to smooth out her roughed-up hair.

"How did you get Gel's permission?" Fallon's tone turned business-like while still waiting for Lizard to finish. Lizard had worked the pin up to the top of the wire. She took a moment, then let go of the door frame. Jenn screamed as Lizard rocketed down the slope of the wire, holding onto the pin with her mouth, her legs and tail wiggling, and her hood waving in the breeze as she did so. Lizard's ride stopped just on the other side of the desk. She continued to wiggle for a little while and then opened her mouth, dropped, ran across the floor, and climbed back up the same bookcase. Jenn glared at Lizard who flicked her tongue at her while sizing Jenn up.

"What do you mean how?" Jenn looked back at Fallon. "It wasn't hard. Your story does not match the story the delegate's children are telling." Fallon once again saw Lizard flick her tongue and shake, this time her hood was out. He stood, keeping Jenn's attention on him. Lizard pounced again, landing on Jenn's head and this time flicking her tongue in the woman's face. Jenn screamed and scurried backward while flailing her arms as Lizard jumped on the bookcase. Fallon roared with laughter.

"You... oh!" Jenn pursed her lips but moved to the center of the room. "I am here to help you." Jenn wailed as she searched for something to help bring her hair back to its normal state.

"Help me?" Fallon let himself laugh. "You mean help you. You're so jealous that I am getting the best stories you had to wriggle your way in."

"Why didn't your last big find sell?"

Fallon stopped laughing and glared at her.

"From what I see from these pictures, the children's stories are correct." Jenn smiled, and Fallon kept his eyes on her as she pranced over to his desk. "I have to admit I was suspicious when the only report from you was about a nice walk in the park." She kept her back to Fallon as she studied the wall screen.

"What are you talking about? That's what it was." Fallon snarled at her as he pushed another pin up the wire. Jenn stared at a picture. Fallon continued with his narrative. "There were giant, gentle creatures accepting whatever fate handed to them. Two bounty hunters staged each other for nothing. Then the robies dumped Cadune out of his cot because of their fear of the acodoe." Jenn stepped back as Lizard slid down again, this time using her body to rock back and forth.

"How boring and so unlike you," she stated. Fallon watched her lean into the picture. "But, you said nothing about The Bounty Huntress' cat shooting off flames."

Fallon walked over and looked. Jenn pointed to the frame she was looking at.

"That is just Shea's rays glaring off the lens of my camera. I couldn't get any good pictures. Everything is out of focus." Fallon winced as his temple pulsed.

"What? Everything is in perfect focus, like always." Jenn stared at the pictures on the screen. Fallon grabbed hold of the desk chair as he felt himself teeter.

"Perhaps we can explain things." A male voice interrupted the conversation. Fallon twirled around to discover four people entering the room. Lizard hissed from the top of his desk.

"The Bounty Huntress did a Mind-Over-Lay on you," the man in front explained. There were two women and two men. Their plain, black shirts and pants contoured their athletic bodies and their boots clomped on the stone floor. Their long black hair swayed with their easy movements.

Fallon scrutinized his new guests. The black clothes, the black paint on their face with a picture of their hunter knives on their left cheeks, the winged tattoos on their right arms, all represented one hunter group.

"Do you recognize us?" one huntress inquired.

"I have heard stories of the Dark Sentinels." Fallon picked up Lizard and backed against the wall.

"Dark Sentinels?" Fallon heard Jenn's wavering voice behind him. "Where are their maicallas?"

"They don't wear maicallas," Fallon whispered back, keeping an eye on his guests. "If you know what is good for you, stay quiet!"

"Do you know of our ritual of honor?" the first sentinel probed. Fallon shook his head.

"May we enter?" the sentinel asked.

"Do I have a choice?" Fallon's back was now against the wall. He could feel Jenn leaning into him on his right.

"We shall leave if you ask, but you will have even less of a memory than you do now."

"What do you want?" Fallon asked as Lizard scrambled down his shirt and entered his pocket. Fallon buttoned the pocket as she squirmed around.

"To know what transpired during your *little outing*." the sentinel stood with his arms folded.

"And what do I get?"

"You get to lose your migraines and clouded vision."

"How do we know we can trust you?" Jenn asked. Fallon elbowed her in the stomach and smirked when she groaned in pain.

"Would you like to know the answer to the little gossip's question?" a female sentinel asked Fallon. He nodded his head.

All four sentinels reached down to leather sheaths strapped to their legs. Golden wings adorned their leather surfaces. The sheaths held blue crystal hunter knives. These they unsheathed and moved over to Fallon's desk. Fallon followed their movements as each one stabbed his desk with their knife.

"This is the Honor Ritual of the Hunters. It signifies that just as our knives' hearts are empty of poison, so are our hearts. We mean you no harm."

"Your knives hold poison?" Fallon repositioned himself. One female stepped in front of him.

"Focus. That is all you and your visitor will find out." She stared into his eyes. Fallon cringed away from her.

"We ask that neither of you publishes what we have shown you." the first sentinel said smiling as he rubbed his chin. "Although it doesn't matter. We can just return and erase that memory later."

"Why don't you do it now?" Jenn asked. Fallon felt her hands bar his elbow.

"Trust me, gossip, one more word out of your mouth and I will make sure you land up in a medic house for many of Shea's paths." The sentinel who had blocked Fallon sneered at Jenn. Fallon glanced back to find Jenn looking down as she melted.

"What's a Mind-Over-Lay," Fallon asked.

The first sentinel waved his male companion forward.

"A Mind-Over-Lay places a false memory over a true memory. I am the telepath of this group. I will remove the false memory. This will take a lot of energy, and I will not be strong enough to erase any other memory." The sentinel stopped and clarified with a smile. "I will not have enough energy today. It will take only a few days to recuperate. I can come back if I need to."

"Are there side effects?" Fallon's voice faltered.

"You may lose some knowledge for a while." The sentinel's smile faded. "However, that returns within a little time."

Fallon waved the sentinel forward. Jenn's shaky hand touched his shoulder. Fallon pushed her off. The sentinel positioned himself in front of Fallon and stared into his eyes.

A DARK CYCLONE of forgetfulness whirled in Aven's mind. Bits and pieces of memory swirled around; churning, bubbling, bobbing, pulling, pushing, and heaving on his sanity, all at the same time. Warm liquids would go down his aching throat relieving it and his stomach. Then the churning would increase and cause his stomach to boil and his body would convulse under the damp chill of sweat caused by the pricks of fire exploding through his skin. He would try to swim out, reaching for memories, grasping at the fleeting images as they spun, taunting him in his futile attempts. He would almost make it out just to have a golden light blind him. His brain would recoil in pain. His stomach would eject any leftover liquids.

A voice continually called to him. "Tell me about her, about Tiel?" Memories coalesced within the whirlwind with each question. Each one he would yank out of the whirlwind; each one he would examine and find the

now all the movement would have helped some to recover. It is unclear how that will affect his state of mind. It may destroy his memories."

"Can anything help?" the queen asked.

Doctor Russet thought for a moment and nodded.

"Only one thing can be done. Help him with his memories. We must start now, but we'll stick to the most recent and go backward. With luck, it will only be simple things that are lost." Doctor Russet returned to Aven's bedside.

"How long will it take?"

"Only a few of Shea's paths," Doctor Russet answered.

Sendenia turned back to Lidena.

"You have caused much damage due to your foolishness and pride, child." Lidena put her tail under the woman's throat and rotated her head. "Look at Nender and remember. Remember that I may defend those in my caves from intruders such as you." Sendenia moved her tail, forcing Lidena to face her once more.

"Remember! For if you do not follow my exact commands, I will have you hunted, and I will punish you." She flicked her tongue in Lidena's face once more. "You owe The Bounty Huntress much, and you will repay it ten times over before I finish with you. Go to her. Tell her the good news that her dear stellove will return."

Sendenia brought Lidena close to her. "I can get into the caves easily, *Mistress Laisen.*" She emphasized the name with a shrill hiss. "I have servants everywhere. Some can hunt you and bind you how I wish. You cannot escape me."

Sendenia removed her tail and let Lidena fall to the ground.

"Get up and go. Do as I command. Let the noble Bounty Huntress know that I take care of her stellove."

Lidena looked up, her shaking legs barely holding her weight.

"GO!" Sendenia sprung forward. Lidena jumped up and ran out the back halls of the cave.

TIEL'S EYES POPPED OPEN. Shea's rays warmed Emiline's homemade quilt that covered her. The soft mattress made it hard to want to get out of bed.

She stared at the bamboodii door across from her as she tried to remember what had happened. Tiel could remember periods of light meals mixed with an ache that caused tears to gush. She took a deep breath and felt her chest tightening from the strain. She relaxed, realizing that days of sobbing had strained her chest muscles and lungs. Fuzzy memories of Emery, Emiline, and Jainu comforting her weaved in and out. Jainu had been emphatic that Aven would return; that he had promises to keep.

The memories of the last hunt flooded her mind. She felt her eyes water but again she took a few deep breaths to calm her anxieties. If Emiline heard her crying, she would come to comfort and cuddle her. Then, when she couldn't handle the pain anymore, there would be more chems. Emiline hadn't kept her chemed up all the time, just when she had growled and threaten to burn down the Watosh Forest. She wanted to figure things out now, so she took slow deep breaths while getting quietly dressed in her freshly pressed and cleaned hunter attire.

Tiel remembered that it had taken all the strength she had to act normal after arriving at Daton. The sudden onslaught of emotions had shattered her rutzix. Then the flood of soul currents had almost caused her knees to buckle. Despite everything, she had held it together until they left the lot in Sarje. After that, she had wandered highways outside the villages for a few arms. Instead of the old man, it had been some witless joker in charge. However, that had given Tiel some information and allowed her to identify the redhead named Diandra. First, they named Lady Twibett as one of the old man's direct underlings. Tiel remembered that the voice had been cruel to Diandra. Tiel was sure the boy just wanted to feel the power of his position. The enforcers hadn't even taken notice of Diandra jumping off the wall.

Upon entering the kitchen, she observed the surrounding scene. The floor no longer held bits and pieces of broken glass and a shattered table. The sound of wood chopping came from the shed in the backyard. A thick quilt hung on the door, hiding the hole in the glass, and laughter rang out above the chopping. Tiel took in a deep breath and then stuck her head through the large hole. The forest beyond the yard stood still; not even a breeze blew through. She listened, laughter boomed from the wall of trees on the right. She could distinguish the peacefulness in their voices as she pulled herself inside.

Tiel rushed past the doorway to the first room and examined the octave star.

"Six days? I've been out for six days?"

"You've been asleep only five and a half days, but who's counting?" Maestro's voice boomed from behind her.

Tiel spun around and glowered at the cat.

"So where are we going?" Maestro lowered his voice.

"Out for some sweet milk."

"Good, I'm ready for some fresh air. Let's hurry before they find out, shall we?"

Almost an arm later, Tiel was sitting near Daton's central town square with her maicalla closed to her neck. Her boots tapped on the cobblestone street underneath her as she read the news from her hand holo device. Shea teased the holo image with her rays that had just cleared the horizon. It made seeing the images difficult.

"Is there a problem?" Maestro queried from his prone position on the cobblestone.

"What do they think they are doing?" Tiel watched as villagers entering the village square sat beneath the huge Octave Star that Emperor Cong had presented to the village's elders long ago. She tried to form her rutzix, but the chems had weakened her so much that she could construct only a weak rutzix.

"Who?" Maestro asked as he lay on the street, his tail twitching. Merchants around the edge of the square called out to the numerous villagers.

"The Dark Sentinels. Fallon has published his story, mentioning that someone helped him to recover his memory." Tiel rapped the stone bench with her fingernails for a moment before the sound got too irritating.

"That could cause damage," Maestro replied.

"It did. His writing doesn't flow as usual. My Mind-Over-Lay would have melted away. Now, who knows if he will regain the abilities he's lost." Tiel explained. "I know Anised and his clan are just hunting for the truth. But Vanqish should know better than to do a second Mind-Over-Lay."

"Did Fallon write anything else?" Maestro grumbled from the pavement.

"Yes, he doesn't mention Aven," Tiel answered, "at least not negatively. He didn't write about Aven's incident with the Golden Plant. The real problem is that there is no mention of Tyne. He needs to be found before he hurts someone else. If someone circulated Tyne's picture for everyone to see, there'd be a chance of him getting spotted." Maestro let out a rumble. Tiel realized that the sound of her foot tapping was unsettling as the arrhythmic sound only made the buzz in her head more pronounced. She stopped it by adjusting herself on the bench.

"Hegert is causing problems also," she announced. Maestro pricked up his ears. "Now I know why she's after me. The badoe merchant admitted that Hegert forced him to release the calf but claimed it was my suggestion that he tell the truth. She's in danger of being bumped to Junior Council. Now she's trying to stain my zahule by claiming Aven's disappearance could only mean I killed him; and claiming it is the reason I erased Fallon's memory." She growled softly causing a few passing villagers to scurry out of the way.

"As I said, you are now reaping the consequences of your actions." Maestro turned to her. "Fallon's whole story may have been a lot better."

"I know," Tiel admitted as she sipped the sweet milk, letting the tangy, smooth liquid run down her throat.

"How is your head?" Maestro asked.

"Buzzing, what else do you expect?" Tiel shrugged her shoulders. She took a deep breath holding back tears and sipped her sweet milk. The milk's tangy, slight bite puckered her cheeks. She surveyed her surroundings looking at the villagers. There was no sign from their lazy soul currents that anyone took Hegert's stories or Aven's disappearance seriously.

What interested Tiel, however, was a small girl entering the square. Diandra's frame was small, and her skin sunk in and stuck to the bones. She wore rumpled, mud-smeared clothes. Her hair needed a good brushing, and the dark circles under her eyes showed a lack of sleep. The buzz in Tiel's head softened as the previous nitwit voice from before talked, although Tiel thought she could hear the old man in the background. She nudged Maestro as Diandra entered. Maestro turned his head in the child's direction.

"YOU SEE HER? SHE IS IN THE CENTER. TAKE A SEAT AND WAIT FOR HER TO MOVE. THEN FOLLOW." Diandra signaled for a waiter, but none would pay attention to an obvious beggar. In fact, Tiel knew the Peace Enforcers would soon escort her out. The truth was, Diandra wouldn't be alive before Shea ended her last path of the day.

"The old man has Diandra following me."

"Are you going to help her?" Maestro asked.

"How? Her psyche is too broken from octaves of abuse," Tiel whispered. Maestro turned his head back and grunted. "She won't listen because of her brainwashing," Tiel admitted and then thought for a moment.

"Waiter!" Tiel called a young man in a multi-colored outfit over. She ordered a light meal and told him to take it over to Diandra and say nothing to her. He nodded his head and left. Diandra still fidgeted, and her eyes jerked as she scanned the area.

"The old man's in charge, and he's not happy about Diandra's condition. In fact, I believe somebody just got selected to die," Tiel announced.

"She's not doing a good job staying inconspicuous," Maestro observed. Tiel shrugged at Maestro's statement while looking at her holo screen but kept an eye on Diandra.

"You know what is even more curious." Tiel smiled at Maestro. "It seems that Diandra can't hear the old man now." Maestro's tail stopped twitching at this news. She thought she saw a slight grin on the panther.

A few minutes later, the waiter brought over the meal and placed it in front of the girl. She stared through him, then looked at the meal. The waiter left, and Diandra searched again, twitching at the laughter of other girls her age. She finally yielded and nibbled at the sandwich while hunched over the table.

"At least she'll get a little something to eat. In for a trek into the Watosh?" Tiel asked. She expected Maestro to refuse. "The old man has nothing new to say. He's only ranting, trying to get something to work."

"I was wondering when you would ask." Maestro stretched and yawned. "Think your disappearance will worry the Drakners?"

"Of course, why do you think Ma kept me chemed up for so long?" Tiel chided herself for doubting her longtime friend.

"DIANDRA, GET BACK TO THE PARTY ZONE!" The old man's voice refused to be ignored. In an instant, the clatter of a chair brought Tiel's attention back to the center. She looked only to find Diandra rushing from the square with several villagers looking on. Her meal lay with the broken plate on the cobblestone.

"Well, that was unexpected," Maestro stated as he watched the girl depart. "I thought she was supposed to be following you?"

"She was." Tiel stared at the empty table shaking her head. "The old man got angry." She moved off in another direction. "Let's hurry. I want to get supplies before we go."

JAINU HAD BEEN SITTING on the workbench, enjoying the company of the Drakners when Tiel had stuck her head out the door. He had excused himself by saying he wanted to watch the holo imager. They let him go with instructions to check on Tiel before getting engrossed in a program. Instead, he went to the house and waited for her to leave the street. Now he watched from behind the bread hut as she drank sweet milk. Jainu would make sure Tiel wouldn't leave the village as Emiline feared.

He scratched at the buzz inside his head but stopped, chiding himself about self-control. Clasping his hands behind his back, he paid attention to everything around him until the buzz softened and a young boy's voice dominated the voices inside his head. A few moments later he noticed an ugly, young girl walk into the village square. She wore dirty rags for clothes that hung on her skeletal frame. Jainu decided it was most definitely a party girl. He also knew it wasn't her fault she appeared in public that dirty.

The girl's name was Diandra according to the voice which she followed to perfection. She entered the village square. The voice inside his head grew softer as she came closer to his position. As she sat down and tried to get a waiter to come over, the voice became softer until it disappeared. Jainu straightened up and shook his head, confused. He searched for an answer. As he backed away onto a cobblestone walkway behind the hut, the voice once again blared into existence.

"WHY IS SHE DRESSED LIKE THAT?" the old man's voice echoed. Jainu breathed easy for a moment, furrowed his brow, and looked at the girl again. "HOW MANY TIMES HAVE I TOLD YOU IDIOTS NOT TO FOOL AROUND WHEN OPERATING THE CARDS? GET OUT! YOU'RE PICKED." Jainu moved closer to the girl once again. The voice diminished in strength before his mind became quiet. Diandra jerked around. She didn't even look at the waiter when he brought her a meal. She accepted it and after a while nibbled on it, but she kept glancing around as if looking for something.

Jainu back up again. The buzz grew in his mind once again. He moved closer to Diandra and heard it fade away.

"Just like Tiel and Aven," Jainu mumbled to himself, looking around. He stared at the girl, enjoying the peace in his mind as he smelled the delicious aroma of bread coming from the hut. A side door opened, banging his head, and throwing him onto his back.

"What are you doing back here?" a stout woman holding a tray of small bread for sandwiches asked.

Jainu stood, wondering how to fix his mistake. He backed up to the pavement behind the house. The old man's voice boomed. "DIANDRA, GET BACK TO THE PARTY ZONE!"

A clatter of dishes made the woman turn around. Diandra was rushing from the table down a cobblestone pavement. Jainu took advantage of the distraction as he banged his hand beside his head. He took a path behind the huts and just about collided with the retreating girl. She ignored him as she ran at full speed down the path. He stood for a moment and surveyed the square through the huts. Tiel and Maestro were leaving. He looked back at the fleeting form of Diandra and took off after her.

It took about a quarter of an arm for Diandra to slow down, another quarter of an arm for her to arrive at a two-story hut. It was Lady Twibett's main party house. Pink clay with bright blue and purple trim covered the outside bamboodii straw so that only a few of the straws would stick out for aesthetic purposes. Ecalardians often quoted that Lady Twibett's business was all about presence. This hut's presence dominated the avenue with its colors, grounds, and loud nightly ruckus from inside. As of now, it was quiet. The buzz was gone, leaving his mind as quiet as the hut.

Jainu followed Diandra to the stone wall behind the hut where she opened a black iron gate. He let it slam shut and waited. The stone wall failed to provide a sense of security as he crept up to the gate, his back sliding along the wall. Gathering his courage, he twisted his body around to look through the bars and gasped at the sight. An empty luscious garden filled with stone statues and fountains adorned the premises.

He tugged at the gate only to find it securely latched. The iron lock was a simple one which Aven had taught him how to open long ago. He pulled out his set of straight bars wrapped in a brown cloth from a skin pocket on his outer left thigh. After a few minutes of feeling around, he set the tumblers inside to where he wanted, and the lock clicked.

A bright thin red light from above turned on. Jainu backed away and watched it. Soon it faded off, and Jainu opened the gate letting it shut behind him. He listened for the click and watched the light. It stayed off.

The garden was huge, and Jainu gaped at everything as he strolled through. Several pools with statues of scantily dressed women stood in several places, water pouring out of various sizes of basins. Each woman wore the wicked smile that Lady Twibett said her girls were famous for wearing. Different colors and sizes of flora grew all around; trimmed to allow room for some stone benches. Birds sang from the treetops, adding to the mood that a sound of a distant waterfall brought. Black stone paved the walkways of the garden leading up to a porch lined with rose bushes which opened into the garden.

Jainu worked his way around the garden until he located a steel back door. The door opened freely, and another red light turned on. Jainu waited until it faded before he entered. He found himself in a storage area where two men, about Aven's age, were there, smiling at him. They both had brown skin, gray beards, shaved heads, and dressed in a simple black uniform.

"Lady Twibett requests your presence," one of them announced, white teeth showing beneath both of their smiles. Jainu tried to run but failed as they grabbed him, ruffling his hair as they both laughed. One tied his arms behind his back with a rope, and they led him out of the room.

Silence filled the journey through white hallways once they left a kitchen. A red stone covered the floor and the lack of smell, combined with the dim light from the few light crystals that were available, gave the corridors an eerie presence. The men pushed him up two flights of stairs and into the back of a large room.

Jainu stepped forward and felt his boots sink into a pink carpet. A fire crackled in the fireplace to the left. Rose plaster decorated the top half of the walls; striped grays decorated the bottom half. Several crystal lanterns lined the upper walls in between expensive portraits of Ecalardia's elite, both male and female. Some portraits were perfect, and others had a large 'x' painted across the surface. Slashes ran across the faces of a few. The only pieces of furniture were a large glass table in the room's middle with an intricately carved glass chair behind it.

Lady Twibett was a tall woman who stood on the opposite side of the table smoking a long, brown-papered weed. She was what Jainu would call the 'head skeleton' in the hut. Her straight, thin, ebony hair hung below her chest. The wrinkles coming out of the side of her eyes and bright red lips made her look like a deformed cat whose whiskers grew in the wrong place. Her long, bright red fingernails clicked against each other which was the only sound in the office beside the crackling fire. The expensive red shirt, pants, and boots did nothing to make her prettier to Jainu.

Diandra stood in front of the glass desk far enough away that Jainu could hear the static when it turned on. She kept her head down and arms to the side. Two male guards who looked exactly like the ones standing next to Jainu stood on either side of Diandra. They cupped their hands around the sharp edges of her shoulders.

"Is that little dung heap of a huntress your friend?" the woman asked. Jainu willed himself to stand still. The buzz in his head grew louder. Diandra shook her head, upon which the left guard slapped her.

"You talk about her all the time. Now tell me the truth." Diandra stood quietly.

"What do you think, trainer?"

"Does it matter, Lady?" the man shrugged.

Lady Twibett smiled and chortled sounding like an injured bird. She sneered at Diandra again and signaled her forward with a move of her index finger. Diandra stepped towards the desk.

"Do you know what this is?" Lady Twibett picked up the only thing on her desk. Jainu squinted to see a white card. A small gray square was in the upper right corner. Diandra's picture was in the bottom left corner.

Diandra stared at the woman and shook her head. Lady Twibett laughed.

"Look at you. You look like a huge fowl ready to be eaten," Lady Twibett sneered and looked at the card. "This is my key to you. I wonder what happens if I destroy it, hum?"

Lady motioned, and a guard brought a pile of cards and laid them on the table.

"Come to the table."

Diandra obeyed.

"In a moment, I will have you pick a card. But first, let me explain things. You have a biothread inserted into your brain. The Master created this little key before you heard the voices inside your head. It is what keeps out the unwanted noise."

She spun her fingers around in the air while looking at the trainers. The one on the left spun Diandra around and pulled her face upward by her hair. Her eyes widened as she saw Jainu standing behind her.

"You see that lost love, my little card?" Lady Twibett bent down and focused on Jainu as she bit down on her forefinger that was between her devious smile. "He hears a type of back noise. Some rescued lost loves have said it sounds like many people talking at the same time. The Accepted don't get that noise. However, soon he will know the peace that comes from hearing the blessed, one-voice of a master." Lady Twibett twirled her fingers again keeping her gaze on Jainu for a moment as they turned Diandra around to face her.

"This card means you have become an 'Accepted.' Do you understand so far, my little card?"

Diandra stood still, Jainu's stomach soured at the sight of Lady Twibett's smile. Her teeth were pure brown. He wondered where the plastic caps were that gave the woman her famous gleaming smile.

"You need to pick a card." Lady Twibett smiled again and pushed the pile forward.

Diandra looked at her and then at the cards.

"You need to pick the next sacrifice." Lady Twibett let out a heavy sigh of disdain. "That is how you were picked. The last sacrifice picked you. It was only a matter of time. You don't expect me to get my hands dirty with keeping track of good cards and bad cards, do you?"

Jainu tried to move forward, but the men beside him held him firm by the shoulders. Diandra put her hand forward.

"Make it interesting. Pick from the middle." Lady Twibett smiled.

Diandra obeyed.

"Good pick. His eyes are too close together," Lady Twibett snickered to herself as she crossed the room to the fireplace. "You never had a chance." She threw Diandra's card into the flames.

Jainu watched the card brown and curl around the edges. The fire crackled and popped as the metal square blew open. Diandra shook her head, her hair whipping back and forth.

"THERE IS NEWS THAT THE HUNTER CLAN HAS BEEN WATCHING FOR ABDUCTIONS. THEY ARE HELPING GENERAL MANCANE." Jainu knew it was just a coincidence that the voices overtook the static just then. At least he thought so until Lady Twibett's smile grew larger.

"Now you hear other voices besides mine or the master, don't you?" Lady Twibett nodded her head as if to answer herself.

"THE MASTER WILL BE MAD. OUR LIVES WOULD BE BETTER IF WE HAD SHEA'S GOLDEN SPIDERS CHASING US," a female voice interrupted. Diandra's body twitched. Jainu could swear he heard her blubber.

"SHEA'S LIGHT! FIND OUT WHY THEY ARE INTRUDING BEFORE THEY PICK US," a male voice erupted. Diandra's body convulsed and fell to the floor screaming in terror.

Lady Twibett laughed as she waved her hands towards the trainers. They picked up Diandra by the upper arms as she banged her open hands against her head. Jainu watched them escort her through a set of double doors on the left.

"What do we have here?" Lady Twibett cooed as she glided forward, her blue eyes glinted as she pursed her blood-red lips into an 'o' shape and kissed Jainu on the forehead. He lunged back, not liking the feel of rough sandpaper.

"Did he get in on his own?" she asked as she threw the weed into the fireplace. She grabbed Jainu by the ears looking him up and down, giggling in satisfaction. Her long fingernails stung like insect bites as they dug into his head. Jainu tried to pull back, but the silent trainers kept him still.

Lady Twibett drew in nearer and took a long deep breath. Her sharp cheekbone hurt as she scratched his cheek with her leathery face. Jainu snarled while she took another deep breath.

"Why you can just smell the freshness of the air on this little card's aura." She leaned back and considered everything about him. Her eyes searched every inch of his face and neck. Jainu's eyes watered from the weed's scent that seeped out of her body. "You can see the free will gleaming in its eyes. Yes, this is a lost love."

The glint in her eyes grew. "Don't worry, my precious card," she cooed, making the lines on her face more pronounced. "We will take care of that free will. You will only harm yourself with it." She turned Jainu to face the single door he had come in. "Don't worry. We will teach you how to act. You need saving to make it past the Day of Renewal." She took one more long breath. Jainu squirmed as her hot breath tickled his neck. She pushed him forward. "Take him down to the basement. I am sure there will be a grand announcement. The master will collect him tomorrow before Shea's second path. I have regained a lost love. That is the best news to turn a good day into a perfect day!"

CHAPTER 13

LIBERATION

Oljnen lay coiled by the edge of the forest as Shea headed towards the western horizon. His insides rumbled with emptiness, and he saw the world around him as a mixture of gray forms filled with heat fires. The bright blue of the forest's heat fires surrounded him. In Aita village, an array of yellow and orange human heat fires traveled the paved walkways of the village. He could barely hear the cries of their babies or the shouting street vendors selling their precious wares. However, this facade of bounty before him wasn't what was turning him blind with hunger. It was the dark-red heat fires of the badoe herd beyond the village.

Oljnen used the rattle on his tail to scratch around the emerald gem attached to the back of his head. The gem's long, triangular edges often caused his skin to itch, especially when he moved his head sideways. However, now the itching became more irritating as he waited for another acodoe to relieve him. Oljnen had waited three days for a replacement to come that could guard the village against strays as he attacked the herd. It was too much to do alone. Strays from his hunt would circle and attack Aita and that was the reason he guarded the village. The expanding air inside him rumbled again, warning him of his need. Soon, it would be too late, and all the heat fires would be just that, heat fires, and he would attack just to satisfy himself.

One bright orange heat fire appeared out of a gray structure just on the village's edge. He knew that one well. Oljnen was young and the size of a normal serpent when he had explored that human abode. The adventure had ended up with the household's small, pet feline waking Oljnen up from his warm nap inside a basket full of clothes. He had tried to swallow the feline whole but ended up in a tug of war with the woman of the house. Part of her hand had disappeared down his throat for a few moments along with the head and neck of the feline. After that experience, he had abandoned his meal and slithered out of the house but failed to duck an airborne glass jar. A long scar had come from a piece of that jar lodging itself into his back. The scar had grown just as his friendship with that woman's son, named Markel, had grown. Markel had calmed down the woman and treated his wound.

The older Markel now had a human family of his own and was Aita's head chief. His wife, never having to experience her hand down Oljnen's throat, was a lot calmer than Markel's mother had been. This made it possible for Oljnen to create a friendship with her as well. Now Markel stood in the back pouring a bucket of old food into a barrel. The man would let the food rot in there, turning it every few days until it would become soil for his garden.

However, Oljnen saw no color from the sprouting flora that announced the beginning of life for the vegetables. Oljnen's senses brought in the aroma of tender meat from the village and the badoe herd. He and Markel had conversed about the situation during the previous day. Markel would shut the gates to that part of the village and evacuate the villagers for safety if Oljnen gave the signal. It was a backup plan that proved successful in the past.

Oljnen slithered forward through the thick forest. The dark wood of the trees matched his brown diamond hide. Moving among the leaves and through the back of the village, he flicked his tail letting the rattle on the tip sound. Markel looked back recognizing the sign.

"Have a good hunting day, my friend," Markel called out. "The wife wishes you well."

"Then, I shall be even more vigilant, my good friends," Oljnen hissed and progressed through the brush. The gray landscape that merged with the blue heat fire before him made it impossible to distinguish landmarks. But, the path he knew well. He had traveled it many times before. It wound under a small bridge, just large enough for him to pass beneath, through trees and shrubs. The red-hot fires of the badoe herd grew larger as he traveled. Oljnen slithered by the downed trees he had used to scratch himself. The sounds of the village softened as the commotions of the grunting badoe herd intensified. Oljnen's insides rumbled in anticipation of finally getting a meal.

He paused for a moment and shifted his gaze sideways to the left. A recent dead log decorated the landscape. It had to be. It was wide enough, long enough with no heat fire. His insides rumbled again, and Oljnen decided to investigate later. He turned his attention back to the bright red fires that loomed even closer to him.

He slithered forward concentrating on the flames. The fires trembled with fear as they sensed Oljnen approaching. His hide scraped against the forest floor as he slithered faster along the path, flicking his tongue to bring in the needed aromas keeping him on his course. The badoe moved away.

Oljnen felt his snout open in a silent cry as pain jammed through his body. Bright jagged streaks outlined in blue passed in front of his vision. Oljnen convulsed as the pain erupted from his middle down both sides, causing his head to feel as if it was bursting into flame. The pain continued as agonizing waves cascaded down his body. Then his insides exploded as he gasped what he knew to be his last breath.

"GOING to bury your stellove's body?" the familiar voice came from a man walking across the grass towards Tiel. He was tall with dark black hair, white skin and dressed in a colorful shirt and pants. However, his familiar soul current flowed straight towards her. Maestro growled deep after catching his scent.

"Elder Hunter," Tiel snarled in his direction.

"That is not the name I am using." He patted a small box attached to his waist. "But the fact I am covered doesn't matter to you."

"That small holo covering is too easy to destroy," Tiel retorted. She had to concentrate on the Elder Hunter's small features to recognize the thin shimmering veil, but it was there all the same. The box was doing its job well. "What do you want?"

"This holo covering is older than you are," he answered with a snarl of his own. "The old things last. What I want is to talk about you. You have stained your zahule. The gossip in the caverns is that hunters are considering Hegert's words. So, I will ask, did you kill your stellove? Especially after he so lovingly stood at your side the other day."

"No," Tiel answered back.

"But you left him in danger."

"I'll explain my story in a larquetz..."

"Two within a month, Huntress. That does not look well."

"It is my right, my legal right..."

"Will Aven be back in time? Or is his body rotting inside a Golden Plant?" the Elder Hunter smiled as Tiel stopped and choked back a sob. "So, you left him screaming as a plant dragged him into its belly. I've seen the reports from the children and Cadune." The Elder Hunter patted the little box again. "I will bring this up at the larquetz. Something tells me Aven won't be able to protect you this time."

Tiel sat on the bench. Her vision turned hazy as the Elder Hunter's soul current caressed her head as he would a pet. "You could forgo the larquetz if you would just ask to be under my protection for retraining."

"That isn't necessary, Elder Hunter." Anised's voice interrupted the conversation.

"Why do you say that?" The Elder Hunter faced the oncoming group.

"You know why," Mistress Laisen answered in a soft, wavering voice. "You were there when I received the message about Aven's condition."

"What?" Tiel asked, shaking her head to dislodge the soul current. "You knew?"

Maestro's roar reverberated through the air, and the Elder Hunter jumped back, his current wrapping around him. Tiel took a moment to let the news sink in while allowing her friend to defend her. She looked up at the man who aimed his Hunter's Heart at Maestro, his hand shaking uncontrollably.

"That knife will never make it, Elder Hunter," Tiel whispered. "He'll fry you before you get close enough. Don't you think I realize what you really want? With or without Aven, I would rather take the larquetz and be judged a Luhitzu rather than be your pet telepath!" As she spat the last few words out, spittle flew in the Elder Hunter's direction.

Anised and his clan circled the threesome. Mistress Laisen stood behind, looking at the ground, her shoulders hunched inward. The Elder Hunter backed away.

"That was your last chance, Huntress!" the man threatened in a raspy voice. He kept his eyes on the advancing panther. "I won't be so pleasant at the larquetz."

Maestro jumped, snarling with his claws extended. The Elder Hunter squeaked in terror and ran away.

Tiel chuckled a little and then stood and studied Mistress Laisen. She rubbed her chin letting her telepathy flow. "What do you mean 'you know'?" Tiel squinted her eyes as the mistress' eyes grew wide and her face turned an ashen color. Her memories rushed out like a river and Tiel growled, feeling her neck muscles tighten.

"You went to see Aven with someone else?" Her voice took on a deep resonating tone. "He is my stellove! You had no right!"

"I know. I know." The mistress averted her eyes. "Please don't look into my mind. You will not like what you find."

"Too late. Your guilt is making your memories a raging flood." Tiel stepped forward with her right hand outstretched, only to have Maestro appear in front of her. "What did you do to Aven?" Tiel growled around Maestro.

"The doctor said he could fix it." The mistress tried to calm Tiel. "I am in your debt. The queen set the amount to ten times."

"Only ten times?" Tiel turned back and stomped. "Only ten times? For trying to take my stellove away from me through treachery? Only ten times?"

"That was the amount set by the queen." The mistress's voice choked. "If you wish, I will go in front of the Winged Court to determine my real debt."

"Tiel, this is good news," Anised said. His current was gentle and did not swirl around Tiel. "Aven is alive, and now he may come back healed. Wait to see before you claim a horrendous debt of the mistress."

"Don't patronize me, Anised." Tiel's roar sounded more feral than she intended. The sound came from deep within. Large currents of air from her lungs pushing through her metal voice box gave her the sound of a real beast. "You and your clan have been investigating me, to see if I have been true to my stellove vows."

"We have to," Anised whispered. "It is done to provide proof of guilt and innocence. We have determined that you are innocent."

"Tiel, this is good news." Maestro's calm voice soothed her nerves as he sat next to her.

"I just wish I had been there with him."

"He will need you when he gets back."

"If he remembers me at all!" she roared again. "Right, Mistress?"

"That is what the doctor and the queen want," the Mistress answered.

Tiel looked beyond the Forest. Shea was close to her zenith, leaving enough time to get to Aven.

"Where is this path you took?" Tiel didn't even try to control the beastliness of her voice. "It will get me there quicker, so I can have more time with my stellove."

"I will show you the path." The mistress choked back her emotions. "You'll be able to get to the cave. Just be quiet and don't disturb him. It may cause more harm."

"As you know all too well..."

"EVERYONE, EVERYONE LISTEN!" the old man's voice boomed as the buzz dissipated. Tiel jerked back at the sudden intrusion. "EVERYONE, THIS IS A DAY OF CELEBRATION, LADY TWIBETT HAS FOUND A LOST LOVE." Tiel sat down on the ground and leaned her arm on a knee. It was best to let the intrusion pass. This was a power show for the old man. It wouldn't last long. He often turned off everything in a fit of joyful sobs which caused Tiel's stomach to turn. But then her mind would be quiet, sometimes longer than a day. She ignored the looks of the Dark Sentinels and the Mistress. Maestro yawned knowing what was going on.

"EVERYONE, I HAVE REGAINED A LOST LOVE. LET'S HEAR HIS VOICE FOR THE FIRST TIME. WHAT DO YOU CALL YOURSELF, MY YOUNG CARD?" There was a scuffle and some laughter. "DON'T BE SHY, YOUNG CARD. TELL US WHAT YOU CALL YOURSELF. THAT IS THE FIRST STEP TO RELEASING YOUR FREE WILL AND COMING INTO OUR FOLD. COME, LET US HEAR YOUR VOICE SO WE CAN WELCOME A LOST LOVE BACK HOME." More of a scuffle sounded. Tiel's teeth clenched as the next voice came through. "JAINU, MY NAME IS JAINU! LET ME

GO. I DON'T WANT TO GO WITH YOU!" Tiel grabbed Maestro's neck and hung on. The old man's sobs of joy made her growl and her stomach churn.

"TO ALL YOU LOST LOVES OUT THERE. KNOW THIS, THAT I, YOUR FATHER, WILL FIND YOU. I WILL, FOR YOU LITTLE CARDS ARE PRECIOUS. YOU WILL SOON KNOW THIS CARD'S, THIS LOST CARD'S, REAL NAME I GAVE HIM. IT WILL TAKE A LONG TIME, FOR HIS WILL IS STRONG, BUT HE IS SAFE AT MY MOST BELOVED SERVANT'S HUT IN DATON, LADY TWIBETT'S HUT. SO, BOW TO HER IN HER DIRECTION FOR THE HONOR SHE HAS GIVEN THIS LOST CARD. HE WILL REJOICE IN OUR FOLD. WE WILL ALL REJOICE TONIGHT. A LOST LOVE HAS RETURNED AND WILL SOON BE IN MY ARMS, HIS FATHER'S ARMS. SO, TO CELEBRATE THIS JOYFUL EVENT, WE WILL INVITE MORE LITTLE CARDS INTO OUR FOLD. WE WILL RESCUE LITTLE ONES FROM THEIR UNDESERVING PARENTS TONIGHT IN LOWER DATON. IT SHOULD BE GLORIOUS! MORE ARE TO BE SAVED! REJOICE TONIGHT, MY BELOVED CARDS, REJOICE!" A few more sobs sounded before the familiar click announced the usual tenuous quiet in her mind.

Tiel looked at Maestro. "Jainu is in trouble. He's imprisoned in Twibett's party zone."

"How did he get there?" Maestro asked as he shook his head. Tiel got the hint and pulled her hand away. A small clump of fur came out. She grimaced in embarrassment.

"I'll find out, but we have to rescue him now." Tiel stood and took a deep breath. "I ask for you to repay a debt now."

"What?" the Mistress raised her head.

"I need the help of Anised and his clan." Anised bowed to the request. "We need to rescue Jainu, and I will need you to take him back to the caverns while I go see Aven."

"As you wish." The Mistress nodded her head as she took off her cloak. Dressed all in black, she unbuttoned the cloak's bottom hem and stuck her hand inside the lining. With one quick move, she pulled it inside out to reveal a black cloak and put it on.

"Why take Jainu to the caves?" Anised asked.

"It won't be just Jainu. Maestro will bring the Drakners also," Tiel answered. "There will be a mass abduction in lower Daton tonight."

Maestro backed up and let a growl escape.

Tiel hugged him. "I am sorry. You know the old man adores you. Get word to ManCane and the hunters about what is happening. Then meet me in lower Daton later."

Maestro grumbled under his breath but then gave her a lick and bounded off.

Tiel turned to the assembled crowd.

"Your telepathy is outstanding," the group's telepath, Vanqish, murmured in awe. Tiel shrugged it off and realized their currents were not strong enough to damage her feeble rutzix.

"Off to save a single renegade, then I will go see my beloved stellove." Tiel ran toward the other end of Daton. "Hopefully, I will have the strength afterward for the hunt tonight." The other hunter's footfalls echoed behind her.

Jainu sat against the cold stone wall with his arms folded. The singing and laughter were irritating, out of tune, and loud. The two guards had dragged him downstairs to the cellar and placed him in front of a wall holo screen. They forced him to listen to the old man's junk thinking and then forced to give his name. Jainu put up what he thought to be the proper amount of fight, and then provided his name, hoping that Tiel would hear. He banged his heel against the floor and yelled in frustration.

"How many times were you taught that a hunter doesn't go out on their own?" Jainu scolded himself. He wished for the safety of the hunter caverns and would gladly accept any punishment Tiel and Aven gave him while hugging them in return. He wiped away more sniffles and tears as he listened to the sound of overblown laughter from the next room.

The room was warm for a stone cellar. The black bars in front held a large bolt lock. With some work, he could open it, but dared not to since he, somehow, had miraculously kept his lock pick set. It was a gift from Aven he wasn't willing to lose. The trainers hadn't searched him, just put him in the cell with a pat on his head. More laughter and the clang of glasses echoed through the basement.

Jainu looked past the black bars into the other room. Two girls lay motionless on the floor. Diandra was one; she moaned a lot. The other was quiet. Jainu watched her for a while and decided he couldn't even see her breathe. Both had blood spilling out of their ears. He believed they had removed the 'biothread' that Lady Twibett had talked about earlier. He assumed this because his mind now quieted down when he got closer to the wall on his left, not when he moved near Diandra. One double window in the girls' room let in the light from halfway above the floor, the lower edge even with the ground outside. That would be his escape if the fate of opportunity presented herself on his clouded paths.

"At least I have a lot of information for ManCane and the hunters." He let his eyes stare at the rock walls and ceiling above him. A small crystal light hung from the ceiling encircled by a chain. There was nothing else in the room. "I hope Tiel heard me," he mumbled and then thought better of it. They could record everything. He smacked his hand against his head.

Suddenly he realized it was silent. The trainers in the next room had stopped singing, laughing, everything. He had noticed no one leaving through the door in front of his cell. Perhaps there was a back door. Jainu stayed in a crouched position as he put his head against the black bars. One trainer sat at the edge of a wood table, slumped over, his breath shallow and quiet.

Jainu backed up and thought as two shadows obstructed the light from the window. He looked up to discover two pairs of legs. His heart thumped against his chest as one person bent down to look through the window. He leaped up and jumped for joy. It was Tiel! She always said it was easy for a telepath to put drunk people to sleep.

He watched the huntress open the window and enter feet first, alighting on the floor. She put her fingers to her lips at which Jainu stood still. Anised entered next. Jainu gawked at the Dark Sentinel. He bowed in return.

Tiel leaned forward and backward as she observed the basement. Then she stood up straight and approached his cell.

"What did you do wrong?" she tested Jainu in a normal volume.

"I went out on my own." Jainu bounced up and down once again. "I'll do any chore you assign me, any punishment. A hunter never works alone, never." Anised laughed at this answer as Tiel smiled. "That is why you brought the Dark Sentinels. I understand." She left Jainu and examined the girls.

"You will leave Jainu there?" Anised inquired.

"He got himself into that cell." Tiel bent down and examined the girls. "He can get himself out."

Jainu smacked his head again as he pulled out his pick locks. "I thought there would be too many for you to put to sleep."

"All the Dark Sentinels are here to help." Anised came over to Jainu's cell as he chose three picks. "We also have a telepath. Everyone is asleep for a long time."

"The older girl is dead," Tiel called out. "However, Diandra is barely hanging on."

"Aven has taught you well." Anised smiled as Jainu worked the tumblers without the slightest sound. "You may need a fourth for that one." Jainu pulled out another pick. He placed the picks between his fingers and worked. As usual, he stuck out his tongue as he concentrated.

"Tell me how and why you ended up here," Tiel called from the other room. She had pulled a pouch out of her backpack and administered to Diandra. Jainu stopped and thought. Anised cocked an eyebrow at him.

"Well, I followed you and Maestro to the village square," he began, pouting as the tumblers moved back to their previous positions. He put down the rods and finished the answer. "I saw Diandra come over and realized it was *quiet* with her around."

Tiel turned back to Jainu as Anised eyed her.

"What does the boy mean by '*quiet*'?"

Tiel held up her hand. When Anised relented, she waved for Jainu to continue.

"I saw that you were safe with Maestro. I wanted to find out why it was quiet. So, I followed her here. I should have run when I saw the red light over the entrance, but I thought nothing of it. I got caught." Jainu tried the lock once again. "The funny thing is that it is no longer quiet near her, but near the wall to my left."

Tiel abandoned the girls and disappeared into the next room.

"Answer no more questions until you have the lock beat. Focus," Anised whispered to Jainu pointing his finger at the lock. Jainu worked the lock again until he heard the longed-for click of the mechanism. The door screeched open provoking a sudden jump from Jainu. Anised laughed, patted his back, and moved aside letting him through.

"Where are the others?" Jainu asked Anised.

"Keeping watch outside and keeping the technology busy with their presence." The sentinel smiled at him. Jainu went around the corner. Tiel stood there studying two tubes that were barely the width of her middle finger and positioned in a steel rack; three of the five holes were vacant. Someone made the tubes from a thin, clear crystal with a dense fog that floated inside. A steel cork stopped the fog from spilling out of the top. Suspended from the middle of the cork was a single, hairs-width strand of metal.

"Is that a strand of copper?" Anised pulled Jainu back and bent down to look closer. "How did they get that blue-green tint in it?"

"I have no idea. Aven needs to look at this," Tiel answered.

"We studied at the hunter's repository together."

"What?" Tiel placed her fingers on the tubes, which she jerked back and examined. "What does that have to do with this?"

"Everything." Jainu wedged himself in between the adults as the two hunters conversed. "For example, what I do know is those tubes are kyro chambers. The smoke keeps the technology inside cold, so it doesn't deteriorate. If it breaks open, it could freeze off an appendage at least. If someone inhales it - a painful quick death." With that information, Tiel grabbed Jainu and yanked him back from the table.

"What I don't know is what the technology is," Anised whispered.

"I suspect Aven, Jainu, and I have plenty of experience with it." Anised cocked an eyebrow at her answer. "I'll explain later. We need to get the one called Diandra out. She is still alive. Emiline Drakner will want to help her. Are we able to bring those tubes along?"

Jainu helped Anised search around the table and detected a steel chest below it with a key dangling inside a lock. He opened it and uncovered three other empty tubes lying in holes of a spongy gray material. A thick gray cloth was folded over two empty holes.

"How will you know which one belongs to Diandra?" Anised asked Tiel.

"I won't." Jainu found comfort in Tiel's gentle squeeze on his shoulders. "Jainu will."

Anised nodded and used the gray cloth to place the tubes into the container. He replaced the cloth, shut the lid, and latched it. After locking the chest, he gave the key to Tiel. "I will get more help. We will need it to carry our packages safely." Leaving the chest, he walked back to the window and crawled out.

"How are you going to punish me?" Jainu asked.

"Do you think I should be the one to punish you?" Tiel bent down and looked Jainu in the eye. He stared at her, confused. "You hurt two very good and honest people today by pulling your stunt. I left you in their care, and you soiled their zahule by dumping on their good intentions for you."

"You are right." He scratched his head with a jittery hand. "It is the Drakners who should punish me."

Her embrace helped sooth his anxiety, and he snuggled in. "To make right what you have wronged, you will accept their punishment as gladly as you would accept it from Aven or I, understand?" Jainu had no problem nodding his consent. A noise from behind alerted him to the fact that Anised was returning. He pulled back and saw one more male Dark Sentinel in the basement.

"This means the clan will think I'm a fool, right?" Jainu mumbled as he gazed at the floor.

"Oh, I think you're safe." Anised's laugh eased Jainu's worries. "How many times were you rescued on your pre-hunter adventures, Bounty Huntress?"

Tiel laughed, which made Jainu look around once more. "I stopped counting." The other Dark Sentinels laughed.

"So did we." Anised laughed alongside the others. "And Aven can say the same thing."

Jainu smirked as he enjoyed Tiel ruffling up his hair.

"We have to hurry. You will go with Mistress Laisen and the Drakners to the caves for safety." Tiel said as she directed Jainu toward the open window. "We have business to attend to. Let's get going."

CHAPTER 14

REUNION

I don't recommend going this soon." Doctor Russet peered over the rims of his glasses at his patient. "You need to learn more basic skills before you're ready to deal with normal life." Aven felt his muscles infuse with energy as he stretched, squatted, and twisted. The queen's cave was cool, dark, and crowded, especially with a giant green snake coiled in front of the entrance.

"Tiel is in danger." Aven decided his body was in working order despite his new scars. He looked at the gap in the Golden Plant and smiled. The day appeared hot and clear. A small chuckle sounded above him, and he raised his head to find the queen flicking her tongue at him.

"You enjoy the idea that you damaged my Golden Plant." A cavernous echo accompanied her soft motherly tone.

"I always do. It's that same fighting spirit that keeps me and those I love alive." Aven put on his pull-over, sleeveless, white undershirt. "I'm sorry, but I need to leave. I've been here too long." He put on his over shirt and brought the sides around to the front.

"Yes, you keep stressing that fact." The queen moved, her upper body forming a small semi-circle around him as she flicked her tongue in the air. Her snout had a darker, raised, green mark with a tinge of purple.

"No need to worry, your stellove is on her way with two other hunters."
She stayed quiet, studying him with her giant green pupil.

"Who are the other hunters?" He felt his muscles turn rigid. "Is there a
bald man with a snake tattoo?"

"The forest does not make those distinctions," the queen laughed.

"The forest?" Aven folded his arms and smirked with a half-smile. "It
could discern Tiel."

"The forest has a long memory. So many ages are gathered in that
memory. So much so that making distinctions about fleeting entities is not
important. However, I am its queen. In helping me, you both have made a
more enduring impression."

"Fine." Aven waved his arm and turned around. "My need is dire, especially if Tiel is with the wrong hunter."

"You have described your Elder Hunter. Is that whom you are worried
about?"

"Yes, I and my hunter brother, Anised, are investigating his zahule." Aven
searched around his bed and retrieved his backpack. "Tiel is acting as our
telepathic spy."

"That could cause problems." The queen moved once again, her scales
rippled past and barred Aven's path to his backpack. She stopped when her
head was above Aven. Aven groaned and paced in the semi-circle she had
trapped him in.

"What do you want?" Aven stared at her. "I won't be staying here." The
queen refused to move, and Aven forced himself to calm down. "Look, your
servants have been very helpful, and I am grateful. But there is nothing
more to be done."

"I will judge that. I find your obstinacy intriguing since she is on
her way."

"I don't trust the Elder Hunter. He can make things more dangerous for
you and your young."

"They are far out still, so give me the chance to see if you are indeed
whole." The queen opened her hood and Aven could swear that if she had
eyebrows, she'd be raising them. "I'd like to make sure that I have paid at
least a small part of the great debt I owe to both of you."

"All right." Aven waved his hand and sat on her body. He'd seen others do this, and she never complained. "Let's get this over. Will the Golden Plant attack me on the way out when I leave?"

In response to his question, the queen rubbed her tail on the wall, and the sound of grating stone reached his ears. A large rectangular stone slid into a hallway beyond leaving a gaping hole.

"Remarkable," Aven stated, "using that could have prevented a lot of trouble."

"What is remarkable is that you claim you are ready. Yet, the doctor had to put your socks and boots on..." The queen studied him with her left eye. "...and you have not buttoned your shirt."

"What are socks and boots?"

"The pieces of clothing on your feet." She tilted her head downward, and Aven's eyes followed. A thick, brown covering with a string that criss-crossed through some holes in the top covered his feet.

"So, that is what feels so heavy."

"Now, that I wouldn't know." The queen kept flicking her tongue at him. "Tiel seems so young to be in such a serious relationship. Does she love you?"

Aven's jaw tightened at her question. "That is our business." Aven's tone became dark. The queen smiled at his response. "I find that she is a more mature woman than some older girls."

"Yes, it is time for you to go." The queen bounced her coil and threw Aven forward. He landed on his feet. She recoiled her body and Aven darted for the backpack.

"Your Majesty, I highly disagree."

"Enough, doctor." Aven heard clinking sounds as the doctor rummaged through his supplies. "Just remember, young one, you are blessed. Your body is whole because of your biometal. The microbes in the poison rejected it..."

"Yes, I know. You have told me this three times already."

"No, I have told you seven times."

"Seven times?" Aven stopped checking the supplies in his backpack and looked up. The queen nodded her head.

"Since you seem to remember so well, tell me the rest of that information."

"The microbes rejected my biometal." Aven took it slow, making sure that he repeated the information exactly. "So, the microbes traveled to my brain but attacked a foreign object embedded there that they were more attracted to. That is why my brain acquired minimal damage."

"Exactly," the queen said and smiled, "and you still refuse to have that foreign object removed?"

"Yes, I have my reasons," Aven replied.

"Well, I shall have my servants keep an eye on you," the queen declared, "to make sure you are truly whole. If ever you're in the forest, it shall be kind to you. You, your stellove, and Adrian are always welcome here as a thank you for saving my unborn."

"One question…" Aven tied up the backpack and put it on. "Why didn't your servants try to get a message to the rescue party?"

The queen tilted her head. Aven followed her gaze to see that Rachael, the doctor's wife was back. The doctor squinted his eyes over an open case as he tried to place one of his instruments into the proper slot. Rachael took his hand and guided it helping the doctor finish his task.

"My servants have a hard time remembering." The queen's voice lowered to a whisper. "They did not have the foresight to do what you suggest. Now, I thought you had to hurry. Please be discreet about whom you relate your experience to, including my cave's location."

"Understood." Aven entered the tunnel, but he turned for a moment. "Thank you for your hospitality." He bowed and then left the cave.

The tunnel was small but level. Aven had no trouble getting to where he could see Shea's rays at the end. *"Who's Adrian?"* Aven mumbled but dismissed even trying to find an answer to that question. It was just another riddle for him to solve.

What concerned him more was the Elder Hunter. Aven inwardly chided himself about using Tiel's telepathy so haphazardly. If the Elder Hunter even suspected, nothing would keep him from hurting Tiel. *"Is he capable of murder?"* He became lost in his thoughts until the full strength of Shea's rays blinded him.

He scanned his surroundings, putting his arm up to shield his eyes. A small, well-worn clear of any plant life stretched out before him. There were very few insects buzzing which left the grunts, calls, whistles, and other noises of animal life to welcome him back to reality. He sucked in a large amount of air. The smell was clean, and the colors of the forest were vibrant.

He started on the path at a moderate pace. As his thoughts returned to the potential of encountering the Elder Hunter, he groaned, and his pace quickened. The forest disappeared as he focused on the path before him.

Tiel's spying had confirmed that the Elder Hunter was mounting a quiet insurrection by using the Winged Court. If the Winged Court was untrained, their appointment to the court was fraudulent. He needed substantial proof to bring it to the Hunter Clan's attention. For now, the Elder Hunter could confront Aven if he became aware of the investigation. Without proof of his suspicions, the Elder Hunter could bring a grievance stating that Aven was the insurrectionist. If they proved his guilt, Aven could be denounced as a Hunter and cast out, deemed as Luhitzu, a corrupted one. Then the Elder Hunter could have Tiel sequestered under his supervision. It would just be a matter of time before the Elder Hunter legally determined that their Stellove Oaths were spurious unless she denounced the Hunter Oaths herself and became Luhitzu. Extremists in the Hunter Clan didn't ignore Luhitzu. They hunted them, and drove most into hiding, lost to everyone.

The queasy uneasiness left, allowing for a bit of fear to fill his stomach as he sprinted down the path. Tiel was smart and her love was strong. Aven just didn't want it tested in this manner. He felt something rubbing his ankles and heels, his throat ached, and sweat dripped down his skin. He ignored it all thinking of only getting to Tiel.

His thoughts continued in this manner, fueling his fears for the next arm until he heard some voices in the distance. He stopped, gulped in some air, and took in deep breaths, trying to calm his nerves. If the Elder Hunter was with her, Aven would need his wits to protect them both. He may not know about Tiel's part in the investigation. Therefore, all would be well.

The voices got closer, and Aven sat down positioning himself on a rock where he could peer through the bushes near the path. Sweat beaded on his face and his wet shirt felt cool against his skin. His breath rasped past a dry throat causing intense pain. His face felt warmer than he wanted, and he found it easier to lean his arms on his shaking legs for support.

"Is my condition due to some basic skills I don't remember? A couple of arms running never affected me this way." He tried to move his swollen tongue only to find a sticky film covering his mouth. *"Tiel will know."*

He contented himself with observing his surroundings as he calmed his breathing. The path made a sharp left turn, and he could see through the bushes that that the path continued until it curved right again. It would take at least fifteen minutes for a group to make the distance before they reached the turn in front of Aven.

The voices got nearer, and the bushes farther up from him shook as a group passed by. A female's voice he did not recognize drifted in. After some silence, Aven took in a sharp breath as Tiel rounded the bend. Her body was whole, but her frame hunched inward as she adjusted her backpack. Her face showed strain in the creases of her forehead, her eyes glazed over. Shea's paths had not been kind to her psyche. He itched to grab her in his arms but held back until the other two hunters appeared. It took just a few seconds until Anised rounded the corner followed by a huntress he did not recognize. The Elder Hunter did not appear.

Aven gave in to his need to cry for joy. His tears trickled down his face, some ending in his mouth which provided a peculiar strong, bitter taste. Anised's calm voice reassuring Tiel allowed Aven to recompose himself. Tiel needed his strength, and they were getting close. That thought gave his body power, enabling him to stand. He wiped his eyes and started down the path, staggering at first until he regained his footing.

The group had almost finished the distance when he rounded the corner. He gazed at his stellove to make sure she was real. He knew she would smell of spices and vanilla and that her body snuggled into his perfectly. Her voice would have a bit of grating from the biometal in her voice box but would still sound wonderful to him.

It took only a few seconds for the group to raise their heads in Aven's direction. Tiel stood, her shoulders rising with her heavy breathing, her face relaxed. Her eyes grew large, and a sob closed the distance between them. She crumpled in front of him and Anised caught her before she hit the ground.

"No! No! No!" Aven forced the wind past his throat as he rushed towards her. Soon she was in his arms, sobbing into his shirt. "What is it, stellove?" Her crying broke his resolve as his tears once again flowed, streaming down onto her upturned face.

At his question, she quieted down. "You remember me then?"

"Remember you," he rasped as he deliberately caressed her forehead with his lips. "Stellove, it is my memories of you that brought me back. That is the only reason I am not a child in a man's body."

"Thanks be to Coulliou and his beloved," she cried into his chest.

"It's okay. It's okay." He said softly as he held her. "Stop crying. You're making me cry."

"You bully." He felt her firm but gentle punches right below his shoulders. "I thought I'd lost you. I get to cry over that." She turned her face up to him. He smiled through the haze of tears. There was only one way to stop her crying. He easily found her lips and poured all of his passion into a kiss. Feeling her body melt into his, he willingly lost himself in the experience.

SNUGGLED UNDER AVEN'S ARM, next to his chest, was where Tiel preferred to be. His heartbeat was strong, and he still had a woodsy scent around him. Even better was the peace his presence brought. She didn't have to worry about her rutzix. She would just let herself heal. After a few arms with Aven, she would be whole again and would be able to control her telepathy.

According to Aven, the poison had tried to do its worst, and it was unclear how that would affect his memory. Yet, some manifestations of a crippled memory were already present. They had to teach him about the necessities of food and water. Luckily, Tiel knew how Aven liked his boots tied. After examining his feet and providing basic aid before any blisters could appear, Tiel put his socks and boots back on and tied the laces securely. She reassured him that he didn't need to button his shirt. Tiel also reminded Aven that his bio-metal grew heavier under the forest's electrical field. He had been moving too fast, and the electric field had hampered his efforts, straining his body. It was then that the group decided they would keep a close watch on Aven to circumvent any additional problems stemming from his memory loss.

What gave Tiel the greatest amusement was what embarrassed Aven the most. Aven had to be reintroduced to the other woman, Shaine, in the party. After Anised reported that Aven had been the first witness to Shaine and Anised's Stellove Oaths, he wouldn't stop apologizing for his lapse of memory. After about the tenth apology, Shaine told him to stop. Aven did so with some soothing kisses that Tiel was more than willing to give.

"What about your fighting and hunting abilities?" Anised asked as they finished a meal in which a lot of Aven's sandwiches ended up on the ground. "You're going to need to work on some hand-eye coordination."

"That I have no problem doing!" Aven emphatically defended. "However, if you like, I will spar with you three. If I don't pass the test, I will stay out of the hunt tonight."

"Your zahule is white on this, brother?" Tiel searched her stellove's face at Anised's insistence.

"Yes, brilliantly white." Tiel heard the two Dark Sentinels let out sighs of relief along with hers at Aven's answer.

"I would like to thank you two for keeping Tiel safe."

"I am afraid that we did not do a good job until recently. She kept herself safe. We investigated your disappearance." Anised peered at Aven with a bowed head. "Lidena was intent on revenge for your possible death."

"Who's Lidena?" Aven asked.

"Apparently, someone who isn't too important." Shaine retorted. Tiel felt her face flush at Shaine's answer and bit her lip to hold back a delighted giggle.

"Well, what did you do when you learned that her zahule was without blemish?"

"We searched for her and encountered her as she was about to enter the Watosh. That is also when she received news from another party of your recovery." Tiel sat up and raised her eyebrows at this. "We helped her with a problem and then escorted her here."

"Well, I still owe you some thanks. You kept your zahules white by finding out the truth and sought to assist Tiel with her troubles." Anised waved off Aven's remarks.

"Now, I am more interested in Sethrich. Has anyone been able to test one of Sethrich's initiates' knowledge?" Aven asked.

"Yes," Shaine answered. "They know nothing. They don't know enough about the repositories, their sizes, or who controls them. They don't even know how the Hunter Clan came into existence, let alone the laws they judge people with."

"And, they don't like it," Tiel interrupted. "From what I got from the last time they met, they are embarrassed and ashamed. The Elder Hunter rules by using terror."

"Should we approach them?" Shaine asked.

"No, let Master Laisen keep watch," Anised answered. "Plus, I hear a few of them have been sneaking into the repositories behind the Elder Hunter's back."

"Interesting." Tiel looked at Aven. "I think it is time to tell Anised and Shaine about the old man, before tonight's hunt," Tiel suggested to Aven. "And Sethrich has approached me; he is intent on making me his pet."

"He said that?" Aven asked.

"No, that is my interpretation of our encounter," Tiel admitted. "But, he has something to blackmail me with, and he is trying to use it."

"What?"

"After we left you that night, it was clear that Fallon would use the events of the day to his advantage. He would have harmed many innocent lives." Aven moaned and rubbed his eyes but stayed silent and let Tiel finish. "So, I did a Mind-Over-Lay that would have only lasted a little while."

"Except that when we were investigating your disappearance," Anised admitted, "we also found Fallon. His reports conflicted with the children, and so I had Vanqish do another Mind-Over-Lay..."

"Which damaged his mind even further..." Tiel interrupted only to be stopped by Aven raising a finger.

"You just said 'even further,'" he commented. "Explain."

"A Mind-Over-Lay isn't a perfect thing. There is always some damage until it disintegrates, and the subject heals. My Mind-Over-Lay should have disintegrated in a few days, leaving Fallon confused for only a little while. But a second one? Few people heal completely after a second."

"That is not what Vanqish told me," Anised commented.

"Vanqish hasn't seen the damage I have," Tiel replied. "And he listens only when he wants to."

"No matter," Aven said stopping the conversation, "damage has been done, and the Elder Hunter will use this to his advantage." Aven kicked at the ground before him. "I don't remember, how much about telepaths do we actually know?"

The group stayed quiet. No one looked Aven in the eye.

"I would like to know the answer to my question. A lot of damage has been done in my name."

"You always say that we know nothing about telepaths," Tiel whispered.

"I wonder, am I right?" Aven questioned. No one answered.

MARKEL STOOD underneath Dommo's night sky. The clear starry night with the tender breeze that encircled him gave him no comfort. The sound of laughter in Anita's enclosed village square gave him no merriment. He gazed out to the fields beyond as he hid in the doorway of an abandoned hut. Three badoe had wandered into Anita's outlying streets, their careless snorts a few lengths behind the hut.

"Oljnen, where are you?" Markel forced a whisper out of his throat. He hoped his old friend would answer his murmured pleas. It hadn't worked so far. He checked around in the gloomy light. No broad looming shadows were apparent, and the snorting badoes had moved farther away.

He proceeded to the area that had concerned him earlier. Ever since the blue streaks of lightning had erupted from the ground, he had watched the area. It had happened too soon after Oljnen left to hunt, and he hadn't heard as much as a slight squeal from the badoe herd. The breeze was blowing in different directions, forcing him to abandon the hope of staying upwind of the badoe. He kept to the doorways of the huts, hoping the smells from inside would mask his odor.

He stopped at his hut and searched the backyard, seeing only the drab blossoms in his garden. Even the night was silent. No birds sang, no night animal stirred, and no cricket chirped. This wasn't the first time badoes entered the village. However, the night sounds grew more frantic at those times. The irrational silence pricked at his skin and turned his knees to mush. He searched again and was unsurprised when nothing materialized.

He entered his backyard and continued toward the forest. The path that Oljnen had taken lay close to his hut. He scanned farther west and saw nothing, just the still night taunting him with no information.

A rough slimy object slid up his back as a loud grunt sounded in his ear. Wet, warm spit spilled down his shoulder as the rough edge of the tongue curled around his face, blocking his vision. Hot breath blasted him from behind. A trunk lay on his head as the scratchy tongue caressed his neck, sending more slime down the back of his shirt. Markel sprinted forward, the tongue held onto his head, lifting him up in the air. Markel's feet wiggled in the air as he grabbed the tongue and yanked on it. The badoe shrieked, impelling Markel to exert more pressure, then the tongue let Markel fall to the ground, jolting his insides.

A soothing hiss sounded behind him, and Markel let himself relax. The badoe screams pierced the silence.

"Oljnen, where have you been?" Markel laughed out loud as he stood. He turned to face his rescuer and stopped. Towering above him, blocking out Dommo's light, was a hooded shadow with an elongated body twice as wide as Oljnen's. The badoe writhed in the acodoe's mouth, and the ground trembled as the other badoe ran for the clearing. The acodoe shook its head and threw the badoe, sending it past the visibility of the lights. Its squeal diminished with distance.

Markel wiped off a thick goo that was splattering around him from above. The sticky substance intertwined between his fingers. The acodoe slithered toward the field letting Dommo's light shed on Markel once more. Markel watched the green-yellow thick goo drip off his hand. A string of goo dripped down in front of his face, onto his lips, and entered his mouth. The putrid taste of rotten eggs covered his tongue as a white maggot fell from his hair. More maggots squirmed from the goo that was plastered up his arm. The breeze assaulted him with a stench that caused the juices in his stomach to churn. Markel backed up, trying to spit out a wiggling object from his mouth. The white form of a maggot fell out with spit and goo. Markel fell to the ground, retching out what was in his stomach.

"Oljnen is dead!" A harsh hiss shattered the still night air. "Oljnen is dead!" Markel looked up and realized that the acodoe was bending over, its snout towards the area where the blue lighting had erupted earlier in the day.

Markel sat down and took a few deep breaths. He could feel the goo hardening on his hand, at which he wiped it off on the grass.

"Bury Oljnen, must bury Oljnen." The hissing continued as Markel got up and staggered into his kitchen. He took a moment to breathe before he stumbled to the kitchen sink and scrubbed off the goo from his hair and hands. By the time he had finished, his hand was raw and bleeding in some places.

He stumbled to his backyard and viewed the scene before him. The acodoe's silhouette blotted out stars from the night sky. Its mouth opened wide as it swallowed a long, cylindrical object.

"What? Oljnen?" Markel heard himself rasp out. "You dung heap, you carnivorous simpleton." Markel stomped around on his porch as he yelled up at the image swallowing his friend. "Your kind doesn't eat their own. I will report this to your queen." The acodoe swallowed the last of Oljnen's tail and bent down for a few moments.

Markel averted his face, hot tears running down. The warm wind blew in, bringing a pungent odor that knocked him to his knees. Yellow goo with more maggots dripped from above. Markel gazed up at the acodoe now coiled in his yard.

The kitchen lights illuminated the largest acodoe Markel had ever seen. Its body spanned almost the width of a watosh. Open, ragged wounds streaked across the acodoe's black, bloodstained hide while yellow pus and wiggling maggots pushed out in time with its breathing. The acodoe dropped an emerald gem on the ground before Markel. Its triangular shape glistened in the faint light.

"When you see Sendenia, give the star's tail gem to her." The acodoe turned towards the forest. "Tell her that Jonaxx buried Oljnen."

Markel raised his eyebrows at this but said nothing as the smell produced more tears. Jonaxx slithered to the forest and stopped. He jerked his head and hissed angrily.

"Get out! Get out of Jonaxx!" The acodoe's tortured scream pierced the air. "OUT! OUT! OUT!" Jonaxx slammed his head and hit it several times against a watosh. A hollow knocking sound accompanied the watosh's stone groan as it swayed in response to the beating. Just as soon as Jonaxx begun ranting, he stopped, shook his body, and slithered into the forest. The watosh slowly stopped swaying, the air became sweet once again, and night birds sang.

Markel crawled towards the gem as a loud crack sounded. He looked up in time to scramble away from a falling watosh branch. It landed with a loud crack, bounced a couple of times and landed on the gem. Markel crawled forward and watched the trees above him. When he decided nothing else would happen, he looked under the branch to find the gem shattered and a light green vapor seeping into the ground.

CHAPTER 15

LUHITZU

*D*ommo and the stars shone bright giving the night birds and insects even more reason to sing with full force. Medium to large living abodes covered the landscape, their yards in perfect condition with trees that towered over Tiel and the hill she stood on overlooking the village. The sound of the waterfalls behind her completed the tranquil atmosphere.

Cool spray from the waterfall tickled Tiel's arms and neck as she stood sending large streams of her soul current toward the left half of the town. She kept her currents from colliding with Vanqish's as he studied the other side. They connected and agreed to move in farther. There was no danger at Lower Daton's entrance. She concentrated and let the current come back to her. At the last second, she whipped Vanqish's wave causing the man to tumble to the ground holding his head.

"*Do not clutter my Mind-Over-Lays again. You have harmed Fallon greatly.*"

"*It will dissipate, along with yours, he will regain all he knows.*" Vanqish nodded at her. "*Besides, I heard you admitted to causing some damage yourself. Aven doesn't look too pleased with you.*"

"*You know Fallon won't necessarily heal. As usual, you only admit and see what you want. Many have not recovered. One is all most people can handle.*" Tiel whipped him once more causing him to grimace. Aven pulled her back as

Anised stood between the two. *"And my relationship is none of your concern. Remember the whip; you know I am stronger than you. Next time I'll hunt you down."*

"Calm yourself, stellove," Aven whispered. "Other things should concern you."

"I know," Tiel agreed. He gripped her shoulders with tenderness, something she didn't think she deserved after admitting to Aven how she had stained their zahule. Maestro had joined the hunt only a few minutes earlier and was now standing next to her, sniffing the surrounding air.

"Can you hear anything else, stellove?" Aven asked.

"No," Tiel said trying to ignore her guilt his love inflamed. "Are you sure your mind is free?"

"I am sure of nothing."

"What are they talking about?" the high-pitched voice of one huntress asked.

"That is none of your concern," Shaine raised her hand. The huntress fell silent. Both Anised and Shaine had taken the news of the strange inner voices well; better than Tiel thought they would.

"Everyone get ready. In half an arm, we'll hit the east entrance of Daton. Make your way west working towards the falls. Watch out for hunters. The orbs are on standby in case they interfere." The old man's voice came without the usual buzz and sounded distant.

"I can see you still hear him, even with me around." Aven's tears pooled in his eyes. "I am so sorry."

Tiel nodded and gazed into nothing.

Aven continued. "The plant's poison destroyed what was letting in the voices. Is there any relief?"

"There is no buzz, and the old man sounds distant," Tiel croaked out.

Aven scowled at the scene in front of him with his arms folded.

"Let's use what we have." Tiel took in a deep breath while she drew closer to Aven, his solidarity shielded her telepathy as before. "The voices could give us knowledge during the hunt. We will consider what to do about them later. The old man plans to attack from both back entrances and have his people work their way to the falls. I will need to ease past your shield from time to time."

The sound of shuffling feet, scraping backpacks, and Maestro's growling announced everyone's readiness. Aven sighed his understanding and unfolded his arms as she focused on the group. The females wore medic backpacks. The males stood next to their stelloves, Hunter's Hearts at the ready. Maestro switched his tail back and forth. She turned to Vanqish.

"Tell your group the news." Tiel returned her attention to the group. "You will need to use your laser pistols. There will be orbs like the one that materialized in our caves to kill Orton. The kidnappers will be ready if we interfere." There were a few grunts, but all stood firm. "The worst part is that these kidnappers will be youth, around their fifteenth octave. If all the general's ideas are correct, the kidnappers are previous victims themselves, and are getting instructions from the leader through their minds."

Tiel gave the hunters time to digest this information. Everyone hung their heads, and Shaine spoke. "This is not a glorious hunt you have us on."

"No, but a rather pressing one," she agreed. "Let's make sure that those in danger do not end up as victims." Tiel started down towards the cobblestone pavements. "Let's get going. It will start within a quarter of an arm." Aven bounded to her side as the other hunters followed.

THE CHILD'S father stood in the doorway, his dirty shirt hanging out over his pants. His maicalla hung over one shoulder with the clasp missing. He held his liquor bottle in the air as he cursed at the group in front of him. His wife screamed as she pulled her daughter away from hooded kidnappers smaller than her. Aven picked up the two intruders and knocked their heads together, letting them slump to the ground which allowed the woman to pull her daughter into her arms. Another man clobbered two attackers and threw his son into the arms of his crying wife.

Tiel shook her head at the drunken man as she knocked out another kidnapper by thumping him over the head. She didn't doubt that these were children themselves. They were small, lightweight, and easily defeated with simple tactics. The angry grunts from the Dark Sentinels echoed Tiel's disgust for this battle.

They had saved two other neighborhoods in the last half of an arm. Despite the noise of the fighting, the neighbors kept to themselves, and the

Peace Enforcers did not appear. In addition, few of the parents could fight back due to inebriation or dream chem sleep.

A high whine raced towards the back of Tiel's head. She fell prone on the street just as the whine passed over her. The father who had been fighting screamed in agony. Tiel glanced over at the man. He clutched at an orb attached to his chest through his orange shirt. A small red cylinder gleamed beneath a picture of a badoe. The man tried to tear the orb off as he jerked around.

"Don't move! Don't move!" Tiel yelled at him. The man gawked at her with eyes that appeared bigger than the orb attached to his chest. "There is a bomb on the orb." The man looked down at his chest and stopped. "Pulling on it may cause it to blow up."

"Is that the same thing that killed Orton?" Anised yelled from behind as he knocked out another three kidnappers in a row.

"Yes, but this bomb is small." Tiel walked over to the man. "It will only take out a small circle rather than a whole section of a town."

The man fell to the ground, and his wife screamed in terror. Blood dripped down the man's chest, staining his yellow maicalla. Tiel knelt next to him and examined the orb. The man's heavy breathing grew weaker as dark purple patches spread under his eyes. The orb had metal spindles that penetrated the man's chest. She touched the metal with her forefinger and watched the velvety surface bend, almost like Sarje's body metal. Another whine came from Tiel's right and stopped as Aven appeared next to her.

Tiel drew out her Hunter's Heart and placed the knife under the orb. A bolt of energy knocked her flat. The orb sailed across the street and into another three orbs racing towards her. The bomb exploded knocking everyone to the ground.

"Good aim." Aven coughed out the compliment.

"It wasn't me." Tiel rose and grabbed her knife which had fallen to the ground, blood dripping from its edge. "It was almost as if they repelled each other." She shrugged at her explanation.

"A small one huh?" Anised teased her.

"Compared to the one strapped to Orton's chest." Tiel got up as Anised observed the neighborhood. Shaine appeared behind him with a pack and administered to the man. The wife used her maicalla to stop the blood flowing from the four holes in his chest and a cut caused by Tiel's Hunter's Heart.

"I am sorry. I didn't mean to hurt him." Tiel put her hand on the woman's shoulder.

"You saved him, no need to apologize," the wife blurted out.

Tiel pushed through Aven's shield with her telepathy and searched the rest of Daton. Two more neighborhoods were under attack. Another party of hunters had already rescued a third. Tiel informed her group of the news and dispatched them to the neighborhood closest to them.

"Will you two be okay here?" Anised nodded his affirmation to Tiel. "Watch for more orbs."

Tiel ran as she telepathically called for Maestro. The area she chose was the farthest away. Green lawns, colored flora, and yellow bamboodii streaked by as she sped towards the neighborhood. Aven's shield drew further away. *"It'll come back when he catches up,"* she told herself.

Screams erupted from the direction which she was traveling, and she willed herself forward even faster. Maestro had chased down kidnappers from another neighborhood. She called out again hoping he would answer. His roar echoed through the streets in answer to her plea. She smiled as she realized he had gotten there first.

More high-pitched whines sounded behind her. She ducked to her right and saw five orbs speed past her ear. Aven dove in after her. His shield surrounded her once more. Screams sounded again just around a left corner which they ducked into as the orbs once again missed on their adjusted approach.

"Where are these coming from?" she questioned as she threw herself into two tall kidnappers. Aven let four attack him. He took them on one by one, pounding each on the head with his fist and knocking them out. All slumped to the ground, unmoving. Maestro bounded within sight as he threw another kidnapper from his mouth behind the fence of the yard.

"Incoming!" Tiel yelled as the high-pitched whine sounded once again. Maestro turned and bellowed out a cone of flame as Tiel and Aven ducked. The whine stopped as liquid metal fell to her left and dissolved into the ground. Screams from women brought Tiel's attention back to the scene and she realized that the kidnapper that Maestro had thrown into the neighbor's yard was missing.

Three mothers raced in opposite directions screaming their children's names. Maestro sniffed the ground. Tiel searched the area telepathically and detected two kidnappers running into alleyways. Maestro had just caught the scent as Tiel ran forward.

"More are coming. I'll stay here and guard your backs," Aven yelled as she left. A few paces up, Maestro jumped in front of her.

"The trail splits here. I'll take the right," Maestro announced and sped off in that direction without waiting for a reply. Tiel went left and sprinted again. She ran for only a few moments before she heard someone's labored breathing. A tall man all in black appeared as Tiel rounded a corner. Two crying children cowered behind him.

"Orb!" the kidnapper called out, his young voice rasped into the warm night air. "Orb!" He called out again and gasped. He slumped as Tiel approached at a methodical speed. She smiled at the children who only stared back.

"We have destroyed them," Tiel called out. The kidnapper hung his head as he braced himself on his knees.

"You do not know who you anger," the young kidnapper rasped out.

"I do not care. Your boss is a dung heap who doesn't have the nerve to do the job himself," Tiel snarled at the youngster in distress. She hoped the old man was listening. "He nurses his bloated ego by sitting on his fat rear-end scarfing down delicacies. All the while he soils his zahule by watching children perform his crimes."

"He? What do you mean he?" the youngster rasped as his head jerked up again.

"Why? Is it she or they?" Tiel moved forward, keeping calm in the face of her mistake. She had let this one know too much. "What does it matter?"

"You know. How do you know?"

Tiel quickened her pace.

"Wait, if you are one of the lost loves..."

She knocked him out with a sure punch to the face. The children whimpered to her right as she cursed herself for her mistake. Now she hoped that the old man wasn't listening. A whistle sounded as shouts came from the opposite end of the alley. Within a few moments, a squad of gray-uniformed Peace Enforcers came into view.

"Cadets. What is the general thinking?" She observed the young recruits trotting to the commands of an old, gray-haired sergeant. "They are late, and they brought in cadets." Tiel shook her head, and the enforcers came closer. The children hid their faces against the wooden fence. The enforcers stopped a few moments later.

"We will take it from here, Huntress," the Sargent sneered.

"Sure you will, now that we did the work. You're a worthless piece of dung heap." Tiel snarled back. She picked up the children and held them close to her. "I'll make sure these children get back to where they belong. And that one over there is sure to be a previous kidnap victim." She jerked her head in the fallen kidnapper's direction. "Just get him to ManCane. It is a simple task that even you can handle."

With that, she left the alley and searched the area telepathically. The orbs had taken out two Dark Sentinels. Tiel stopped and sighed. The children hid their faces under her neck.

TIEL'S BOOTS rang on the cobblestone courtyard of Daton's village square. The octave star's purple night glow illuminated the empty tables and closed merchant abodes. She could see the silhouette of a janitor cleaning the council chambers in a lighted window. The stars above twinkled as a warm breeze carried the songs of several night birds. Maestro sat behind her, pausing from washing himself to growl every few minutes.

"Cadets?" Tiel questioned aloud. "ManCane knows he can trust me. Why cadets?"

"I do not remember the general," Aven said sitting on the edge of a table. "Would he usually be this apathetic?"

"No. It is not impossible to think the old man has eyes and ears inside the Peace Enforcers," Tiel acknowledged shaking her finger. "This would undermine the hunter's trust in the general. We have also lost at least five hunters due to the orbs. Vanqish is quiet, which is disconcerting."

"Yes, that darkens our paths. Luckily you were far enough away when they died."

"I was also blessed with your shield." Tiel smiled at him

The scraping sound of boots coming from the southeast walkway diverted Tiel's attention. She spun around as Maestro growled again. Six figures progressed swiftly and quietly. Anised lead the group, carrying Shaine, his face solemn. Behind him, two other hunters carried a male hunter.

"Shaine! Vanqish!" Tiel rushed forward only to have Aven grab her shoulders, stopping her.

Tiel groaned as Anised gently lay his stellove on a table. Dark blood coated her shirt, and her eyes were vacant. Anised caressed his stellove's face as the other hunters laid Vanqish on the ground. His stellove collapsed at his side. She clutched Vanqish's shirt and wept.

"It wasn't long after you left when an orb came out from hiding." Anised touched his forehead to Shaine's. "I missed hitting it with my laser."

Tiel opened her mouth to speak but nothing came out.

"Maestro, what is the problem?" Aven's question brought Tiel's attention back to Maestro. He paced back and forth jerking his head then used both paws to swipe at his muzzle frantically. He growled and paced once more.

"Maestro?" Tiel whispered as she lowered herself to a squatting position while reaching for her friend. He moved away as the night birds silenced themselves as if by a sudden command. A shimmer of energy pulsated through Tiel's frame.

"Cover your dead," Maestro sounded as he jerked his head once more while his lower jaw shifted back and forth.

"What?" Tiel squinted her eyes at him leaving her hand outstretched.

"Cover the dead, with your bodies if you have to." Maestro pawed at his face again and shook his head.

"I will not desecrate my stellove's body," Anised said as he continued to caress Shaine's face.

"Do it now or lose her body!" Maestro roared. His body shook as he waved his head and then he collapsed.

A green mist hissed from the ground, obstructing Tiel's view of Maestro. The wave of energy pulsated faster, sabotaging her heart's natural rhythm. Tiel clutched at her lower chest, hoping to shield her heart from the intruding wave. Vanqish's stellove covered his body with hers. The vapor grew thicker as a mocking wind surged inside her mind. Tiel looked at Aven who was also clutching at his chest. He shook his head at her.

A cracking sound echoed from the north. Tiel searched for the sound's origin as the wave pulsated faster and the cracking grew louder. She covered her ears to stop the mocking wind. It overwhelmed her senses as she fell to the ground on her knees. Aven soon followed.

The cracking split the surrounding air, and she finally identified the cause. A thin line ran down the octave star's tail. The tail pulsated with the increasing speed of the energy wave until it erupted, releasing a final wave which emitted a high-pitched screech. Tiel felt Aven grab her. He toppled a table over and placed them behind it when the wave hit. The table failed as a shield and the wave surged through it. Aven screamed as his shield around her ripped apart, leaving Tiel vulnerable to the wave which obliterated the hope within her. Tiel shrieked, barely recognizing the tinkling of the jagged shards around her.

Silence reigned on the square as the wave passed them. Tiel's heart slowed to a steady rhythm. She looked around to find the other hunters hidden behind tables except for Vanqish's stellove. She sobbed on top of his body, her blood seeping through her clothes from the several shards that impaled her back. Tiel leaned forward to assess the huntress's condition. She stopped as her frame vibrated for a few moments and a hollow moan filled the square.

Once again, silence ensued except for the sobs from the grieving hunters. Tiel stood and observed the swirling green haze that now hung like a thick fog, rotating in various directions. It crept into every bodily orifice. She could smell and taste the synthetic furniture around her; the fruit on the trees, the hard stone of the bamboodii huts, the fresh scent of the grass, flora, trees and everything else around her. The flavors and aromas mixed into a vile, overpowering experience, clinging to her tongue and throat causing her to retch out the residue. After retching failed to work, Tiel calmed herself down by forcing herself to breathe slowly as she rubbed her arms and body to sweep away the vapor's clinging cold. It leisurely curled in and out for a moment, then reached back and clung to her once again.

Just as Tiel decided that getting rid of the nuisance was hopeless, a shrill, shrieking laugh pierced the air followed by a long, low moan which silenced the grief-stricken sobs. The sounds penetrated her soul, shackling her heart with anger, fear, and hopelessness and cementing them with deep despair. A green shaft of light erupted from the forest on the other side of Daton. The shrill laugh and moaning grew louder as the light soared into the sky.

Aven's labored breathing mirrored her scorching breaths as she watched the light soar, arch, and then plummet to the ground. The subsequent tremors caused the remaining chairs and the tables in the square to over-turn, crashing into each other.

Tiel felt her body give under the suffocating weight of the darkest deso-lation and she hit the ground, scratching her arms on the cobblestone.

"We are free, brother, finally free!" a female voice screeched with laughter as sounds of crashing objects rang out from the merchant abodes. "Free once again. Even the Gods couldn't hold us forever." As the laughter sounded again, a low moan pierced through it.

"There is no freedom, sister, only endless torture." A male voice dashed the laughter as Tiel's eyes once again adjusted to the dark.

"Why do you always have to spoil my fun with your complaints?"

Tiel searched around and found two dark-green shadows facing each other. The fog now coalesced around them, swirling in and out, giving the translucent bodies slight features. Tiel perceived a female specter towering over a male specter huddled on the ground.

"I only want to go drown for an eternity in the torments of the murkiest parts of the Arasteit." Mist churned out of the male's mouth as his moans pierced into Tiel's soul. Deep despair and agony filled her, draining her remaining strength as torrents of tears gushed from her eyes.

"Why are you in a rush? You'll get there soon enough." The female's shrill voice filled Tiel with hate, loathing, and anger. Her arms trembled as she fought to control a sudden surge of energy that would enable her to slay anyone she desired with her Hunter's Heart.

"But look at this. Here is some fun right here, brother." The female glided over to the group. "Two fresh deadens for us to take and cover ourselves with." The specter moved closer, and Tiel felt the cells in her body recoil away from her. The female inched closer, her fingers reaching out towards Shaine.

A burst of blue flame blasted over Tiel's head. The floating menace fell back screaming as a white paw landed between Tiel and Aven.

"Keidera, you will get no satisfaction today," Maestro's voice boomed, causing the phantom to gnash her teeth.

"Prince Adrian," the male apparition moaned, "oh, if only I could allow you to destroy this wretched form."

"I will do just that, no matter what you want, Kehir," Maestro moved in front of Tiel and growled at Keidera. "But first, I must take care of your twin."

"Me?" Keidera laughed and twirled with glee. Tiel felt herself relax as the invading emotions faded and Maestro moved closer to the specters. "Why, I am honored, Prince Adrian." Keidera's countenance darkened as she bowed to Maestro and spat out the name.

"Hunters and huntresses, stay where you are!" Maestro commanded. He opened his mouth and sent out a volley of fire. Keidera flew back and snarled at Maestro.

"Please, please, My Prince." Kehir inched forward mimicking a subservient crawl.

"I am no prince to you," Maestro growled at Kehir.

"Yes, yes, I know. But she has important business to attend to."

Maestro roared, and Kehir buried his face in the ground.

"Prince to slave, prince to slave." Keidera's outline darted around in a taunting dance with a green cloud trailing after her. "Prince to slave, prince to slave." Tiel observed Maestro positioning himself between the swirling vaporous abominations and the hunter party. His tail swung to a separate controlled beat, far different from Keidera's erratic dance.

"Prince Adrian, or rather, Slave Maestro," Keidera snarled and turned in his direction, "hiding behind a facade, are we?" She twirled around while Maestro stood still, his tail twitching. "A little scared of the truth, are we?" Her head rotated as a wispy, hollow smile split across her face.

Maestro stood there, tail switching. Kehir stayed close to the ground watching the spectacle.

"I could give you a purpose once again." Keidera floated towards Maestro. "It would be better than sleeping away your anguish."

Maestro sent another volley of fire toward Keidera. The fog glowed with blue flashes as Keidera's screams echoed in Tiel's head, causing her to cover her ears.

Maestro growled, and another flash of blue erupted from his mouth.

"NO!" Kehir pounced, his corporal body swirling around Maestro and enveloping him an opaque cloud. Maestro coughed and leaped into the air. The miasma moved with him. Keidera bolted to Shaine's body. Tiel shrank back, keeping her eyes on the apparition. Anised whimpered and backed away as Keidera opened her hand and gathered in the green haze around her, all the while keeping her eyes on Maestro and Kehir.

Maestro fell and rolled on his back, forcing Kehir to sink into the ground, giving Maestro the chance to return to his feet. Kehir charged from the ground, and Maestro fired at him, Kehir screamed as blue flames danced around him.

Tiel heard Aven and the others moaning as her stomach churned. She willed herself to keep her eyes on the scene before her. Maestro roared and fired as Kehir raced backward. Kehir attacked once more and curled around Maestro.

Keidera continued to gather in the green fog as she floated closer to Shaine's body. She spread the compact cloud over it and watched the body seize and bubble. Shaine's clothes melded into each other creating a flowing dress. The top transformed into a low-cut top with straps that held onto the sleeves. Her skin melted, followed by the organs and bones. Every part of her rapidly coalesced into a pool of gray sludge.

Tiel watched as Keidera placed her right hand inside the sludge. The sludge crept up her figure and solidified into a human hand. Keidera chuckled a little as she used that hand to spread the rest of the sludge over her body. The apparition started with her left hand, then progressed to her arms and worked up the shoulders, neck, face, and bald scalp. The sludge dripped, hardened, and formed smooth, ivory skin. Keidera moved next to bathing her body. The fog moved and placed the new outfit around her as the skin on her torso hardened and became real. Tiel forced air past her throat and opened her mouth.

"Maestro!" Tiel croaked out, the effort tearing at her throat. "Maestro!" Keidera stared at Tiel which caused feelings of anger, despair, and fear to twist through her spine. The pain froze her body in place. Tiel wished every cell would incinerate at that moment.

"Keidera!" A roar sounded as a volley of fire swirled in the table's direction. Keidera laughed as her legs and feet finished hardening. She danced to the side, twirling the newly formed, green, wispy dress.

"Too late! Stay groveling to these hunters of dung!"

Maestro blasted fire in her direction. Keidera laughed again.

"Miserable creature, did sleep erase your memories? I am covered. You now need the power of your mate." Keidera danced around as long, blond hair formed down her back. "Where is she? Are you not powerful enough for her?"

Maestro leaped, catching Keidera by the right arm. She screamed, beating at his face as his teeth sank into her arm. Keidera's screams no longer sliced through Tiel's soul, though they still caused a headache. Maestro tore at Keidera's right leg with his back claws. She jerked free, and Maestro swiped at her with his front claws gouging her right cheek.

Keidera wiped her hands across the bloodless wounds. She laughed once more as they closed. Maestro spit something out of his mouth.

"See, you can do nothing," she taunted.

"Are you sure?" Maestro asked.

Keidera examined the gashes. They remained closed momentarily. Then a yellow goo oozed out of each one.

"NOOO!" Keidera shrieked, jumping backward, "The curse was supposed to be gone. You wretched monstrosity. I will make sure you never regain your position as a prince."

Maestro turned away and retched from deep within.

"It is time to go, sister." Kehir hovered above his sister, his moans once again immobilizing Tiel with deep despair.

"Come here before the mist dissipates and take your covering," Keidera ordered. "It's my turn to dance with His Majesty, the Prince!" she hissed in Maestro's direction.

"No!"

Maestro raised his head in surprise at Kehir's answer, still gagging. Keidera stopped her fussing to look at her brother.

"What, you will stay in that form?"

"If that is what the Gods desire, yes."

"Your remorse is touching, brother," Keidera looked at her wounds again and screamed once more. "You let that inferior beast do this!" she rasped.

"Yes."

"Why, you little heap of dung, you don't deserve to have your body back."

"My body is long gone. Stealing another soul's body will not help," Kehir moaned.

"My odor will seep out among everything soon." Keidera stomped around. "I don't care about your wicked remorse. I wanted a beautiful body. How am I supposed to get my knife with this defective covering?"

"You have what you need."

Keidera leaped at her brother, who flew backward.

"But wait, this huntress may know where my knife is at." Keidera inched towards Tiel. Maestro roared as he pounced again. Keidera dashed back, barely escaping another mauling. Maestro again retched out the contents of his stomach.

"A little sick, are we?" Keidera stepped towards Maestro only to stop at the call of a large bird. Tiel looked past Keidera and saw a robed woman moving among the tables. A large, gray-streaked, wild dog walked by her side. A falcon balanced on her shoulder.

Keidera turned as the falcon sounded its steady call again. She paused and studied the figure as it moved closer. Her arms crossed in front of her as she backed away toward her brother who bowed to the woman.

The woman adjusted her course to make her way toward the twins. Kehir's moan rattled the tables and seeped through the cobblestone to reach Tiel's insides. This time, Tiel just lay still, letting the emotions wash over her and settle. Her body shook with anguish and her eyes burned, no longer able to produce tears. Kehir rose in the air, then turned and flew away, his moans growing weaker as he disappeared into the distance.

Keidera hissed and clawed at the air. The woman, however, just moved closer. Keidera backed up, hissed once more, and fled.

The pain slowly dissipated after the twins disappeared. A pleasing absence of emotions freed her soul. She closed her eyes for a few moments and then opened them again. Maestro's face was hovering over her own.

"Calling out was foolish, you know."

"Sorry, Maestro," Tiel rasped out, "or is that *Prince Adrian?*"

Maestro glanced at the hooded figure before he crumpled on the ground next to Tiel.

"You know me as Maestro," the feline managed through hoarse whispers, his harsh breath coming in spurts. "I will be… unconscious… for a while… so take… me home please."

Tiel saw Aven's hand rise and wave in acknowledgment to Maestro's plea. With that, Maestro slumped into unconsciousness. Tiel watched the hooded figure bend over Maestro and stroke his fur before everything went black.

CHAPTER 16

PENITENCE

*C*adune's mistake was that he didn't push for more information from The Bounty Huntress. The day after the children's rescue had seemed strange. Fallon Hanover had suggested he was considering postponing writing the story for a few days; giving Cadune time to work out his thoughts and feelings. However, Cadune felt that Fallon's memories of the events concerning the children's rescue were *patchy,* even changed.

He had considered speaking to The Bounty Huntress about Fallon's memory problem on their journey home, but she had been growling during the entire trek back to the village. He often thought it peculiar she could growl like a feline. Cadune suddenly realized why he hadn't approached her. It was common knowledge that no one approached a wounded animal, and The Bounty Huntress had behaved as a powerful, wounded animal during the trek home.

Cadune was reaping the rewards of his cowardice. Fallon had posted fragments of the story. One portion he included was Cadune's bungling heroics in saving the party from the queen. That was the reason he was now in Sarom's Grand Council chambers. The capital city's inner chambers were as chaotic and suffocating as the stone city. The chamber's noise was as deafening as the multitude of hovercrafts' engines and horns that crowded the paved streets outside. Cadune forced himself to look at the commotion in front of him as he concentrated on his breathing. His citizen maicalla hung open about his neck.

Rows of long, wooden, curved tables lined the oval chamber with ornate diamond chandeliers that hung above. Grand chairs carved with ornamental representations of the various regions of Ecalardia complete with plush, colored cushions stood behind the tables. Some were empty. Others had three or four council members around them. Those same council members were speaking forcibly to each other; their faces scrunched in anger and their hands danced wildly in the air, sometimes balled into fists. Their open, council maicallas hung at their chests.

Unlike citizen maicallas, each maicalla was of one color, representing the member's region of authority. Various hues of blue symbolized those who lived by the seas. Greens meant that the council member lived in a forested area. Yellows designated light desert areas whereas browns indicated deep desert regions with the clay caverns. Mixed shades of colors represented stretches between the main regions. A silver maicalla signified the sixteen junior high-council members. A gold maicalla implied that the member was one of the eight high-council members.

The room's western wall held a raised platform with a long, curved, wooden podium. Beautiful flora decorated the top, and carvings on the front showed images of men and women in a calm agreement which was in stark contrast to the events before him. The council had asked him only one question. When he couldn't answer it, the quarreling had started about whether they should 'force' him to become emperor.

Images of the wedded gods, Coulliou and his beloved, watched over the participants with erroneous joy. On the wall behind the podium hung a broken octave star. Like every other octave star Cadune had seen today, it had a shattered tail. The emperor problem had eclipsed the octave star mystery, for now.

Lady Lavonne was the only council member sitting in one of the eight intricately carved seats lining the stage. Cadune searched her countenance for any hint of forgiveness or understanding. Lady Lavonne twisted her golden maicalla in her hands. Her glazed stare focused on the historical paintings that filled the walls and domed ceilings.

Attached to the wood molding behind the council members was an elongated piece of silver metal that stretched the length of the room and over the two sets of double wood doors. A white screen of light protruded from a thin slit in the top. That screen displayed the multitude outside, arguing over politics and promoting enacting 'the vote' or crowning Cadune as Emperor. Cadune hung his head, languishing over what appeared to be inevitable.

His head in his hands, he studied the floor. The white marble floor was bare except for the space between the tables and podium. Laid in gold marble was an image of Shea, the sun. Her rays stretched out, attempting to reach the arguing council members. The rays symbolized the truth that would light the council members' minds to the right path. He had hoped for some wisdom and insight to his dilemma. Instead, Cadune decided that the whole floor was dull and needed a good polishing.

A scream erupted from the screen, and Cadune gazed upward. The Watosh dominated the screen as a brown, diamondback acodoe slithered along a path at a good pace. It paused for a moment to look at a foreign, thick gray stick before moving on. Then lightning flashed from the stick and another place across from it. The blue sheets of lightning pierced through the acodoe's side causing the innocent life form to spasm, its mouth gaped open in agony. A collective gasp exploded from the floor as the acodoe convulsed, falling to the ground. It failed to move as the camera, capturing the horrific act, zoomed in on a green triangular gem placed in the back of its head. After a few moments, the scene started over again.

The council members stood still as the scene played two more times. Cadune heard the quiet swoosh of a door behind him. He looked towards the podium and found a swinging door and Lady Lavonne absent. The video continued to loop, replaying the revolting spasms of the acodoe's final screams of pain.

"Fellow council members!" Cadune jumped at the sudden sound of Lady Lavonne's croaking voice. He turned to see her dark complexion pale and her lips trembling. "I am afraid this horrendous scene is being displayed all over Ecalardia," Lady Lavonne shook as she played with her maicalla around her neck. Her cinnamon complexion was a ghastly white. "Someone has stolen the global feed. The Peace Enforcers are doing everything...."

A strong, baritone, male voice boomed from the screen. Cadune jerked as he stood up from his seat, grabbing at the back of the ornate chair in which he had just been sitting.

"Ecalardia, I welcome you to your destiny," as the unknown voice drowned out the acodoe's screams.

"These guardians of the Acodoe Clan have long kept our destiny from us. I bring you good news. No longer will they hide our fate. The green emerald you see on the back of this traitor is one key to restoring Ecalardia. Whoever has this crystal will deliver it to Peace Enforcer Headquarters. Yes, you will be taken prisoner, but I shall free you. After, you will thank your master and become my right-hand adviser as I am crowned emperor."

Several gasps filled the chambers as Cadune did a sharp intake of air. The voice continued. "Yes, I am the only one fit for the crown. The crippled fool who should claim it now sits as a coward, crippled not only in body, but soul and heart, while the council members sit, arguing, and drowning their already foul zahule with their own soil. Did not even your heroic Bounty Huntress claim the council was corrupt? Did she not witness the murderous cowardice act of the acodoe queen when The Bounty Huntress tried to save her unborn? Cadune and the queen are not worthy of the thrones they now hold in their hands. I will take these thrones and offer you the grand destiny that the council and the acodoe have denied you. Bring me the crystal and march with me, past the Gods' guardians and onto a new life filled with pleasure and riches."

The video began again in the now silent chamber. Cadune jumped as a trembling hand squeezed his shoulder. He turned to look at Lady Lavonne.

"We need to talk in private," her voice whispered between trembling lips.

"HOLO SCREEN OFF," Aven commanded. He could only stand seeing an innocent creature slaughtered for so long before it curdled his stomach. Tiel had stopped watching the broadcast long ago. She was across from him, jerking his leg as she tied his boot.

Jainu rushed in from a back entrance of the cave to Aven's left. He carried dirty towels in a pail of water into a hallway on Aven's right. Plain, brown, wood furniture filled the inn's room. Two chairs stood opposite the couch he sat on with a small table in between them. Small crystals hung from the ceiling, and a long silver holo tube lined the small wall to his left. Jainu reappeared' This time he carried clean towels and a steaming pail of water. He rushed past the couch and turned into the hallway on his left which led to the outside. Light from the fireplace to Aven's right danced on the cave walls, illuminating the tops of the rough edges while leaving shadows in the crevices.

"I'm happy that Emiline is giving Jainu his punishment," Aven mumbled as Tiel jerked his leg. Tiel claimed he liked his boots tight.

"Emiline is just happy to have a captive to help her," Tiel chuckled.

"Make that two captives," Emery interrupted as he rushed past, following the same path as Jainu. "Maestro is burning up the walls in the alcove. He's one sick cat, has it coming out of both ends."

"I'll come and help later, as soon as Aven dresses himself," Tiel chuckled again.

She hadn't meant it to be cruel, but the reply struck him hard due to his own questions that were tormenting him. Dressing one's self was a child's skill, he mused. He didn't remember his childhood. How much was really lost? Sure, he could remember how to fight, along with the hunter codes and higher laws. At least that was his present thinking until someone proved him wrong. But how much of a danger was he to other people? Was he trustworthy during a hunt?

He noticed that Tiel had stopped tying his boot and was studying him with her head tilted. "What is it?" he questioned.

"I think I learned a little about that shield of yours." Tiel did a slight smile and straightened her head. "Some of its strength depends on your confidence. You fear you can't even handle the simple tasks of a child. Your shield is cracking and letting some intense soul currents through."

He sunk into the couch. His heartbeat raced. What kind of thoughts was she getting? Were they painful to her? Would he be able to protect her from other thoughts now? She smiled at him. His leg thumped as it hit the floor. She kneeled in front of him.

"Aven, it's fine. You protected and helped me when I was weak," she stopped and brushed his right cheek with her finger following the long scar that was there. "The question is; do you love me enough to let me return the favor? Are you going to let me help you heal?" She raised her eyebrows as she asked the question. "You protected me well last night. Your shield during the hunt was powerful. We both took a hit when those…" She thought a moment, her face changing into a sneer. "… well, when those ghosts appeared. Together we can heal if you'll let it happen."

"You know," Aven let his worries dissipate, "I told the queen you were more mature than girls older than you." He chuckled as they put their heads together. "I didn't realize how right I was."

"I like this new scar from your fight with the Golden Plant," she kissed his nose as her thumb rubbed his cheek. "It is a reminder of how blessed I am to have you in my life."

Aven averted his eyes and contained his emotions before he said, "Let's change the subject. I prefer to be strong at this moment."

She chuckled but leaned back. "Don't you think it is peculiar that every octave star in the caverns has a broken tail just like Cong's Octave Star in Daton?"

"Yes," Aven mumbled. "I will search the repository. I am more worried about how Anised is coping with Shaine's death."

"Yes, I am sure he is stumbling around on Shea's paths right now."

"General ManCane is here to see you, Bounty Huntress." A small, soot-covered, squat face peered around the entrance across from Aven. "Plus, the Laisen called for an emergency meeting. It is two arms from now. Inform the Drakners they are invited. I have already made arrangements to have someone in here to watch Emiline's patients."

"You better get going." Aven pulled her up as he stood. "Do you want me to go with you?"

"No, you need to eat."

"What's eating?"

"Do you remember the queen saying it would take patience and repetition to help your memories heal?"

"Yes, why?"

"Because I have explained that twice. I have already informed Ma of your situation." Tiel smiled as she left. "She'll make sure you get enough to eat. I'm eager to see ManCane concerning his part in last night's debacle."

Tiel disappeared through the entrance. Aven collapsed back on the couch, weak from frustration. "Probably another skill of a child," he mumbled to himself.

———◄◄══── ──══►►———

THE CHAMBERMAID POURED two cups of tea. One for Lady Lavonne and the other for Warrior Cadune. Upon finishing her task, she left, the door making no sound as it closed.

The teacup stood on a simple black desk in a small room. Lady Lavonne laid down her maicalla and sat back. Her hand shook as she raised the teacup to her lips. Cadune tried to smile at Lady Lavonne, but he failed at the attempt. He stared at the bookshelves behind her instead. They held a collection of antique statuettes, lamps, maps, and chests along with several tomes. Cadune laid his crutches on the side of his simple chair which matched the desk.

"Angela, I didn't mean to lie to you." Angela waved her hand and shook her head.

"I am not mad at you, Cadune." She tried to pick up her teacup again but decided against it when she couldn't hold it steady. "Cadune, acodoe will be murdered in the name of a crown."

"You think it's my fault?"

"No! No!" She pounded the desk with her hands. "But what is wrong with teaching people from the inside?"

"Because people grow lazy once someone gives them what they want." Cadune stared at the floor. It needed a whitening technique applied to it. "Because people need to choose for themselves."

"What if they don't want that, how do you plan to force it on them?"

"By not becoming emperor!" He laughed and stretched out his arms. "If they don't have an emperor, they must choose something else. More people want the vote, anyway."

"But, this person may even kill to get the crown." Lady Lavonne leaned forward. "Cadune, *someone* is giving them another choice."

"No, no, that will not happen." Cadune caressed her hand. "People are basically good. They will not go with that murderer."

"So, another acodoe will die?!" Angela pulled her hands away. "How many innocent lives have to be sacrificed for your principles?"

"There must always be sacrifices for high ideals."

"You're not the one giving the sacrifice!" Angela raised her voice as she pounded her fist on the table. "You're not the one *dying* for your ideals! You're not the one suffering for your beliefs!"

Cadune sat and stared at her. Angela's eyes glared at him.

"So, are the secret lovers fighting?" Cadune turned to see a teapot of a man standing in the doorway. His round body filled the width of the frame while his height barely covered half the height of the door. His golden maicalla hung around his neck over his purple robe with a golden square clasp halfway up his chest.

"Lord Sobaigh, this is a private meeting." Angela put her maicalla over her robe and adjusted her golden square clasp to match Lord Sobaigh's.

"My dear Lady Lavonne...," Lord Sobaigh wheezed as he wobbled into the room. He lifted Angela's teacup and took a drink before finishing his sentence. "... when you two talk about where you want to go for last meal, that is a private meeting. When you discuss the merits of this cripple becoming emperor that is a public meeting." Lord Sobaigh coughed and wheezed as he wobbled to a corner chair underneath an octave star and wedged himself in between the arms.

"So, this one is broken too," he mumbled. "Every octave star I have seen has the tail broken. Someone could claim it is part of a prophecy if the council doesn't relieve itself of this wasted emperor business and pay attention to more important matters."

Cadune just stared at the fat man struggling to keep his robe from sliding him right out of the chair.

"Continue your conversation. I will intervene when necessary," Lord Sobaigh waved his ring-laden hand at the couple and sat back. Cadune looked out to the stark-white hallways where maids and council enforcers hustled to their various destinations. The arguing pulsated from the chambers as a low rumble. Cadune let air whoosh out of his lungs.

"Cadune." Angela's voice was soft again. "Even if the vote is preferred, Ecalardians still have a choice. They can choose to stay with the present system or to ask this new candidate to be the emperor. He has no qualm about taking advantage of the situation and using it to demand the crown." Lady Lavonne scrunched her forehead for a moment then asked herself silently. *"Who is the man behind the voice? How did he know about the acodoe's gems and what would he want with them?"*

Cadune rubbed his forehead. "Who would give away their right of choice?" he said, returning Angela's attention to the previous conversation.

"Plenty of people," Angela replied.

"Ecalardians don't want to choose," Lord Sobaigh's voice wheezed.

"Ecalardians want to go about their daily lives, not worrying about how their lives are affected. They want us to decide, so that they can take care of themselves."

"No, they want a voice. That is why the crowds in front of the council chambers are trying to change the minds of their leaders."

"You are so blind and dumb. Your crippled condition has crippled your mind, Warrior Cadune." Lord Sobaigh squeaked out a laugh. "There are small crowds that stand in front of the council chambers. But they only infuriate all the rest who push through to get their business completed."

Lord Sobaigh shook his head and continued, "Angela, I have never seen this light-zahuled creature stand out in the crowds for his ideals. What makes you think because he can crawl in front of a hissing serpent he can stand as the emperor? That is what scares him. Look what he would have to do as an emperor. Why, he would have to strengthen his zahule, to stand up to his ideals, to put effort into his flowering words."

"Lord Sobaigh..." Angela tried to hush him.

"No, no, my dear. Listen for once. Let us rule the dim wits like this. Let them have their moment of fame before falling back on Shea's paths. Then we will implement what's best for Ecalardia," Lord Sobaigh squeaked in laughter once more. "Just, the thought alone that he thinks there is more support for his idea... there is no way to establish who wants to vote until there is a vote." Lord Sobaigh grabbed his belly as he laughed harder, ending in a fit of coughing and wheezing which turned his face red and bulging with veins.

"Let's give them a reason to vote!" Cadune straightened up. His stomach fluttered, and he felt his spirit soar with enthusiasm.

"What?!" Lord Sobaigh squeaked. Cadune watched Lord Sobaigh jerk up. The movement caused him to slip in the chair, his legs wiggling to hold himself in.

"What do you mean, Cadune?" Angela questioned.

"Let them choose." Cadune turned back to Angela. "Let them vote to have me as the emperor. Pick a date for the Ecalardians to go to their council chambers and put in a vote. This way they will experience, and therefore see, how precious voting can be."

"Yes! Yes!" Angela jumped up and down and then sat again. "What if the majority wants an emperor?"

Cadune's spirit suddenly plummeted to the ground as he looked at Angela, her face serious and her eyes sullen. He already knew the only possible answer. "I will do the will of the people," Cadune whispered. "But I will endeavor to seek their will in matters, to get them used to voting."

"What?!!" Lord Sobaigh's shrill screech barely reached Cadune's ears.

"Is your zahule white concerning this matter?" Angela leaned towards him.

"Yes, my zahule is the whitest of whites," Cadune whispered. "I will keep my promise."

TIEL TROTTED back to the main cave entrance. A hunter stood in front of the guest meeting rooms and pointed Tiel in the right direction. When she entered, two other hunters stood on either side of the entrance, arms folded, staring towards the general. ManCane was wrapping his maicalla around his fist so tight that his knuckles were turning white.

"Leave us!" Tiel waved them off as she secured her telepathy into a firm rutzix. They bowed to her and left. "At least they are not leaving you in the cold," Tiel pointed to the fire.

"It isn't helping." ManCane tugged at his maicalla from both ends. "I feel the cold spirit within me. I have ever since I heard the news of the Hunter Clan's loss. Their bones may rise on my paths for octaves to come."

"What happened, Jack?" Tiel asked the general, his usual calm facial features scrunched into a fury that made his face redder than the stain of The Block. His eyes flared with the image of the fire.

"Ingrin's office changed my orders."

"The High General Ingrin?" Tiel stepped forward as ManCane nodded his head.

"It is not the first time it has happened." ManCane tugged at his maicalla once again. "I am not the only general whose orders he has changed. I used to scoff at the others complaining about his office changing their orders, making them irrelevant and worthless."

"That happened to yours?"

"Look!" He pointed to a table with a long holo screen tube. Tiel touched it, and a white screen showed above it.

"The first set of orders are mine."

"Yes, you put the most experienced warriors in Lower Daton. The outskirts had less experienced warriors, but no cadets." ManCane leaned against the wall and let Tiel study the orders.

"What is Ingrin's office doing?" Tiel studied the screen. "The experienced warriors were two villages away to… keep the 'undesirables from coming out of their holes'?" Tiel read the orders and searched ManCane's face for answers.

"The other generals and I will look into this and hold him to an enforcer council." ManCane picked up his tube. "However, we will need a lot of evidence. Even if he isn't the one doing this, he is responsible for those under him. Tell the hunters not to trust the enforcers."

"After last night, that won't be a problem."

"I understand." ManCane hung his maicalla around his neck without cinching up his clasp. "It is better if you keep what happened last night to yourself. Also, the kidnappers are dead. You should know the hunters are getting blamed."

"They were unconscious, not dead."

"There were the same holes in their chest as was in Orton's." ManCane raised his eyebrows and stared at her.

"Orbs were flying around last night, but we destroyed all we encountered. You heard nothing else?"

"I won't ask what you mean. Anyone I am close to will be in danger while I am involved in this investigation. I am even keeping my family out of town."

"I understand." Tiel got up. "Hopefully Shea will light your paths, and may there be few stumbling stones to slow your travels."

"I wish the same to you." ManCane held her shoulder for a moment, smiled, then turned and walked out.

"Radames."

He heard the voice. It just didn't register as he flipped through the files on the holo screen. "This isn't it either, where are those files?" he asked himself as someone shook his arm.

"Radames!" He looked up to find Lidena looking down and felt himself shrink away as he rubbed his face.

"Sorry, Lidena." He turned away from the screen and smiled. "I haven't heard my name in a long time."

"Would you prefer I call you by your title, Master Laisen?" Lidena asked through a half-hearted smile.

"Why sure, Mistress Laisen." Lidena chuckled and shook her head at his teasing. She smelled of fresh bath salts and light musk, just like she did three arms ago when they had begun the search. However, he dismissed his thoughts. She would be furious with him in a few minutes.

"I, too, miss someone calling me by my name." She sat across the table from him. They were both at a center table in the repository sitting under the exact center of the octave star in the ceiling. "I couldn't find any written form of the previous Laisens' notes."

"They could be hidden. Perhaps they suspected Sethrich as we do." Radames looked around the repository which was a library of sorts. There were two levels of shelves, stacked with books and the older, hefty tomes. Some information had been scanned into the hunter's digital information system, but not nearly enough.

"Is there something you want to say?" Lidena leaned her head to one side. "Your feet are tapping again."

"So, that's what that sound is," Radames mumbled as he held his feet still. "When are you going to go in front of the Winged Court?"

Lidena slouched in her chair and pursed her lips. She looked the other way. "That is my business," she said, her voice tense as she folded her arms.

"No, it is the clan's business. You have three more days, Huntress." Lidena sat up straight with her mouth hanging open. Radames held up his finger. "Or, I will bring your attempt at stealing someone's stellove before the whole clan, not just the Winged Court."

"What?"

"Or do you not believe our zahule to be sacred as you claimed in the last larquetz?" Radames sat back. "You already asked me to cover for you. You are now the queen's servant, her link to us. The clan needs to decide your future role concerning this."

Lidena glared at him while setting her face in a grim pout.

"Plus, if someone else brings this up before I do; I will not back you up."

Radames raised his finger in front of her face and stared her down. "I will, however, *if* you bring it up yourself." He let his voice soften.

"Ooh!" She pursed her lips again, stood, grumbled out of clenched teeth, and then left.

"Yeah, she won't be speaking to you for a while, Radames." He watched her storm out of the room, fists tight and her dress moving with the timing of her steps. Ignoring Lidena's temper, he returned to a stack of books next to him.

"Master Laisen, may we have a word with you?" a voice interrupted from behind him. He forgot the books and turned around. Jilandro and a young huntress from the Winged Court peered at him.

"Jilandro, Gunny, what is it?" Radames asked in a quiet tone, and with a wave of his finger, signaled a figure from the back to come forward. "Make it quick. I have research to do." A tall man in Dark Sentinel attire came forward. He stared down the two young hunters with his arms folded across his chest.

"A new Dark Sentinel?" Gunny asked.

"Yes, we are always training recruits, Huntress."

"You have found out about my telepathic intrusions." Jilandro looked away.

"Yes, I have suspected for some time," Radames admitted. "I know you are not trustworthy." He looked at the youth. The bruising under Jilandro's left eye and cheek were healing, the yellow splotches disappearing beneath his skin.

"Please, Master Laisen," Gunny pleaded. "Jilandro did not do as the Elder Hunter asked. He was supposed to pry into your brain, make you mindless. But, he didn't even try. He only caused you to be sleepy to appease the Elder Hunter."

"I see." Radames put down his books and turned to the two. "How can I help?"

"We have noticed that you are watching us." Gunny's light-brown hair swayed as she scanned the repository. "We hope that is because you know of our dilemma with the Elder Hunter."

"The heads of the repositories have stopped answering our questions, and they won't allow us to search the restricted areas of the repository." Jilandro explained.

"Sit, sit." Radames motioned to the chairs next to him. "By us, you mean the new initiates of the Winged Court I presume?"

"Yes, the Elder Hunter has not let us study in here," Jilandro answered.

"Ask your questions," Radames said as he sat back, "then perhaps you can help me with my research."

"Why are the tomes crumbling, old, and decaying?" Gunny queried in a quiet voice. Jilandro watched behind her."

"These repositories are from the days of Cong himself," Radames explained. "During those days, Shea had lighted paths of great knowledge for all of Ecalardia. We don't know why, but a world war ensued and destroyed all but a few thousand people at the end of Cong's reign. Their knowledge became a curse to those who survived the war. They buried the repositories and in time forgot that the repositories even existed until two hundred octaves ago when the first repository was unearthed."

"By who?" Jilandro asked.

"Our founding fathers and their step-mother excavated the caves and established the Hunter Clan. Another clan who claimed to be remnants of Cong's Elite Guard discovered another repository and became the Peace Enforcers. Both groups tried to introduce this newfound knowledge, but the fears of the past still lingered. The larger part of civilization, which you know as villages, refused to become part of this new way of life.

"Therefore, we introduced new pieces of information through those who would learn them. We now know them as master scientists, kerlars, and such. The Peace Enforcers built Sarom around their repository. It is the only one larger than our repository. Most of Ecalardia doesn't even know we have one."

"It is said Cong's wife, the Empress Jaiden, caused the war by slaughtering the acodoe only to satisfy her bloodlust," Gunny stated.

"The enforcers and acodoe warriors have spread that idea. Yet, there is no proof," Radames replied.

"So, we have all of this lost knowledge and still don't know what caused Cong's world war?" Gunny searched Radames face for an answer; her furrowed brows creating wrinkles on her otherwise smooth face.

"The repositories may be large, but the larger part of their tomes are delicate due to their age. They disintegrate when brought out into the air, or even just touched," Radames answered. "The ones that don't disintegrate are painted with a resin that protects the coverings and pages. Part of your training is how to care for the tomes and which ones are searchable. There are numerous gaps in this new knowledge. It leaves mysteries for people to solve.

"Tomes are opened with the greatest of care and treated as quickly as possible. Only a fifth of our repository is cataloged. The Peace Enforcers have only cataloged an eighth of theirs, thanks to Emery Drakner and his research on ancient languages and recording methods. We have just begun collaborating with the Peace Enforcers so that we might combine what knowledge we have."

"We are trying to study, so we can know how to judge, can you help?" Jilandro asked, barely looking at Radames.

"May I ask you some questions first?"

"Of course, you have been so helpful, Master Laisen. How can we help?" Gunny's bright, gray eyes eased Radames tension.

"Did the Elder Hunter introduce either of you to the repository?" Both shook their heads.

"If you were not introduced to the repository, how did you become a member of the Winged Court?" Radames queried.

"One member died on a hunt. The Elder Hunter asked me to join," Gunny answered. Jilandro shrugged his shoulders and nodded in agreement.

"There was no court? No test of your skills and knowledge of the laws?"

"No," her voice wavered, "the Elder Hunter told me he selected the recruits and that it was part of my training. He said he would educate me on the laws."

Radames moaned as he turned away.

"You were introduced to the repository?" the huntress repositioned herself so he could see her face.

"Yes," Radames answered. "My mentor introduced me during the time of the previous Elder Hunter and Laisens. The previous Elder Hunter was my mentor for my Pre-Ritualed studies. Sethrich, the current Elder Hunter, was only a junior mentor. I used my time in the repository for many pursuits, especially in learning the laws. We are suspicious that Sethrich is creating his own laws, which is surprising since his interpretation of the laws promote such a strict adherence that it is disturbing."

The huntress shifted in her chair, took a deep breath, and spoke, "The Elder Hunter is searching The Bounty Huntress's and de Menzaile's paths for something to bring in front of the Winged Court."

Radames held up his hand. "This I already know. I have let him think he is helping so I have time to investigate him. Now, you have just given me a lot of information. Would you and others be willing to testify in a larquetz?"

"I would," Jilandro answered emphatically.

"As would I," Gunny answered. "We can't speak for the others. But we could ask them."

"Why?" Radames asked, doubting their eager willingness. "Why are you so willing to turn on Sethrich?"

"We are tired of the abuse," Jilandro answered, looking straight at Radames, his bruising becoming more pronounced as he turned toward the light.

"Also, we are tired of being prisoners to his wishes," Gunny added. "All he does is drone on about the golden era of the Hunter Clan. We don't think he even searches for lighted paths anymore. He just stumbles in his self-made murkiness. I have grown tired of it."

"I have someone who can help you with that," Radames offered. "Come back after the clan meeting. Then you will get your help. Meanwhile, please find out what the others will do."

The two hunters bowed and left the room. Jilandro's posture seemed to be more erect as he walked away.

"What do you think?" Radames asked the Dark Sentinel behind him.

"Your snag jus' started unravlin'," the hunter laughed. "I'll take care of them little runts."

"No problem." Radames shoved the pile of books away and left to have another debate with Lidena.

THE VILLAGERS out on the village square surmised that everything was sad. The animals lay on the ground, tails still and ears down, their eyes glazed over. Passers-by would trip or walk over them without receiving so much as a simple bark, growl, or meow in protest. Birds in the trees often flopped to the ground and died where they landed. Rainwater from the previous night bled from the open wound of the octave star's tail.

The watosh past the stone fence in the nearby forest seemed to droop with boughs sagging downward. The air brought in a scent that caused their stomachs to churn and others to gag where they lay or sat. Regardless, the villagers refused to move. Some were laying on the ground, others were hunched over the tables, and a few slouched where they stood.

Sound was absent except for a moaning coming from inside the Watosh Forest. It would drift in and out, sometimes close, sometimes far away. No matter what, it filled the living with a despair that shackled their will, drowned out hope, love, and energy. This kind of despair caused their bones to cry out in pain for release from the heavy burden of the Arasteit. It also caused their hearts to plead for permission to stop beating.

A watosh bent and then snapped back. The moaning drew closer, causing some villagers to fall to the ground. A shrill, shrieking laughter rang out, followed by the foulest of cursing that assailed their ears. Still, the villagers didn't move. As another watosh snapped, something else hissed and shrieked. More watosh snapped, this time cracking and crashing into each other with their top boughs flailing. A thick, dark shadow moved through the forest accompanied by more shrieking laughter and cursing. A long black tail, with yellow ooze dripping out, swung out from the forest, crashing into the stone wall and knocked a hole into it. Next, the tail snapped back hitting a watosh, causing it to shudder and split at its base. The cracking sound reverberated through the square. Still, the villagers did not move. Instead, they stared at the watosh as it collided with the fence. The smell of dirt and stone caked their nostrils, causing some to cough. The tail disappeared back into the forest. The shrieking, moaning, and hissing faded away.

The villagers breathed freely as they sat there. Their bones ached less. Their hearts pleaded less for relief. As they looked at the fallen watosh with a dried patch of black skin and yellow ooze dripping off it, the villagers let exhaustion overtake them; and then everything turned black.

CHAPTER 17

THE PETITION

*D*oes it feel okay?" Tiel watched Aven shrug his shoulders underneath the black robe.

"How is it supposed to feel?" Aven pulled at the neckline, grimaced, and then peered down at the flowing piece of material. "Somehow, I don't think it was ever comfortable."

"You always commented that it felt *heavy*," Anised's voice was flat as he leaned against the stone wall with his arms crossed. He only wore the basic black clothes of the Dark Sentinels. No paint or emblem adorned his cheek.

"Shaine always drew your emblem," Tiel whispered as she picked up her robe from off the wooden table. Several wooden tables stood in the east alcove above the pit. Initiates carried off mugs that the other members of the Winged Court had left. She put on her robe and buttoned up the front.

Hunter's filled in the tiers of the pit as the shop lights in the caverns dimmed. Chief Del, the Drakners, Jainu, and some hunter initiates stood behind the railing that lined the top of the pit.

"And I always drew hers." Anised shifted. "But that doesn't matter now." Tiel watched him tighten his jaw. "How are the voices this day, Huntress?"

"That is not something we talk about, Anised," Aven interrupted. "I would appreciate it if you kept your voice down."

"If I go out of the caves, I will hear the old man rant and rave," Tiel offered as she walked towards Anised.

Anised grunted rubbing his chin. "About what?"

"Everything that went wrong in his world." Tiel smiled. Aven opened his mouth to say something.

"It's okay, Aven," Tiel caressed his arm, "Anised wants to keep his mind busy."

"I am sorry, brother." Aven went over to him. "How are your travels on Shea's paths this day?"

"Filled with a murky green fog that seeps into my soul," Anised choked through clenched jaws. "Vanqish's stellove died this morning. Her heart just stopped."

"Oh no," Tiel whispered. Loud bell tones rang through the caverns.

"It is time to get to our positions, hunters," the Elder Hunter said as he raced past them.

"We were just waiting for you," Aven responded to the man. "Where were you?"

"Acting like the Elder Hunter already, are we?" The Elder Hunter taunted. Tiel saw currents of jealousy seep from the man. The man's fake smile creased the corners of his mouth.

"I told you, Elder, I don't want the position."

"I know, just teasing." The Elder Hunter walked out of the alcove as Tiel searched the few thoughts that swirled from his mind. "I had business to take care of."

"He's hiding from me." Tiel positioned herself behind Aven. "He rushed past us, so I couldn't follow his currents."

"Somehow, I expected that," Aven sighed.

"Let's get on with life." Anised straightened up and strode towards the east stair of the pit.

"Give yourself some time to grieve, Anised" Aven suggested. Anised kept silent.

"His soul is full of turmoil." Tiel took Aven's hand and changed the subject. "Do you remember being in the Winged Court?"

"Yes! I just forgot that there were two clan leaders instead of one. I also forgot how to dress."

"Let's see what this meeting is about," Tiel chuckled as she exited the alcove. Aven pulled her back.

"How's my shield?" His eyes filled with an intense determination.

"Your shield is adequate." She smiled as his intensity switched to confusion. "Let's experiment though. You know there is danger from stray currents. Focus on defending me. See what happens. I will test your shield and put my telepathy into my rutzix if needed." He considered her suggestion for a moment, then agreed.

They walked into the pit and took their seats on the far right. The Laisens stood in the center behind The Block, as usual. Two couples of the Dark Sentinels stood behind, and Anised sat alone on the first tier. Master Laisen held his Hunter's Heart high above his head. Everyone silenced themselves.

"Hunters and huntresses, the Queen of the Acodoe requests an audience." Tiel's eyes blinked for a few moments before she realized that she had stopped breathing. The breathless sounds of awe told her that others had done the same thing. The question 'why' resonated through the pit. "She will tell us when she arrives."

More rumblings filled the pit. Some hunters asked how. Others questioned, 'How will she fit in? Is she small enough?' The Winged Court sat in silence. Tiel dismissed putting her telepathy into a rutzix since Aven's shield was more than adequate. To her left, the Elder Hunter stood, and everyone fell silent.

"We should ask Aven if he knows why the queen has commanded an audience." The Elder Hunter asserted. All eyes turned towards Aven.

"Elder Hunter, Master Laisen said she requested an audience. She did not speak with me," Aven answered as he sat up straight.

Master Laisen threw his knife on The Block, and the pit fell silent once more.

"The queen promises that she will not come unless we accept her request. She has proved that she is a good soul by healing one of our own when she could have left him to die. She politely requests an audience and assures us she will answer any questions."

Everyone kept still as Master Laisen stared into the crowd. Mistress Laisen kept her head lowered. The Elder stayed standing and waited.

"Elder Hunter, do you have another question?" Master Laisen asked.

"How did you get the message? How will she know if we accept or reject her request?" The Elder raised his finger, "And how long will it be before she gets here?"

"She sent a message through Chief Del and requested that he attend the meeting." The mistress shuffled her feet at this. "Chief Del explained that she would know and would appear within a few minutes. I ask one last time. Are we going to allow her an audience as she has requested?" Master Laisen glared at the Elder Hunter. The Elder Hunter bowed and sat down. "Good! Everyone cast your votes. Winged Court count your hunters' votes. If the majority says yes, stand, if not sit."

Tiel turned back and counted the hunters with raised hands behind her. Out of the twenty-five tiers they used as seats, sixteen were full. Some clan members were too far away to come, but the tiers had never been full as far as anyone could remember. Fourteen raised their hands. She decided her vote would make it fifteen as she stood and faced the center. Only three of the Winged Court members were sitting showing that most hunters in their rows had declined the queen's invitation.

"The Hunter Clan accepts the request." Master Laisen bowed. "Now, all we have to do is wait for her entrance. Winged Court, please sit." The second row did, and the hunters became silent as everyone scanned the pit and listened for any unusual sound.

The crystal lights flickered as the pit floor vibrated. Mistress Laisen's gasp caused Tiel and the others to turn. A thick, white line begun underneath the tiers at the south end of the pit, traveled through the center of the floor's octave star and stopped at the north end just before the double doors. The Block, which always stood in the center, now traveled along that line to the double doors. Radames grabbed Lidena directing her towards the center stone stairs as the vibration increased. The Dark Sentinels followed them.

Just as The Block ended its travels at the north end, the south end of the star's circle slid open. Tiel covered her ears as a high-pitched grating of rock upon rock jarred her teeth. The floor segmented itself into triangular pieces, the previous piece sliding underneath the next piece. Small rocks pinged as they bounced against the walls of a deep, circular cavern hidden underneath the disappearing floor.

The last segment of floor disappeared beneath the stairs as the bottom tier vibrated. Tiel watched Anised's hair swing in a side-to-side motion as the tier disappeared beneath him. He finally decided to run to the top of the higher tiers. The first tier grated as it slid under the vibrating second tier. The Winged Court took less time than Anised to vacate their seats.

A scratching noise began as the second tier stopped just beyond the third tier and lined up with the alcove walls. It left just enough room for the hunters' feet on the third tier. Everyone, including Tiel, looked down into the pit as the scratching became louder until a serpent's head burst out of the west side of the floor segment. The acodoe circled the pit, her jade, diamond-backed body pushing into the circle. Her neck rose above her massive body at the south end and continued to circle, forming coil upon coil, rising higher and higher until eight coils filled the immense cavern. After her tail emerged, muffled grating sounds reached Tiel's ears, and the floor vibrated once more. She surmised that the cave floor was closing. The queen flicked her tongue and opened her hood. Everyone gasped at the sight as the queen seemed to smile.

"It is said that the Hunter Clan values great entrances," she hissed and kept her gaze on the now stunned hunters. Silence ensued until a few laughed which eased the tension. Soon, the hunters stamped their feet in delight.

"May I take the honor of being one of the few who forced the mighty and honored Winged Court to frantically evacuate their seats?"

Tiel blushed as the queen waved both sides of her hood and hissed. The hunters now stamped and roared with laughter. After a few moments, Tiel saw the Elder Hunter raise his hand and bow. She followed as did the rest of the Winged Court. More cheers sounded from the crowd, and the queen bowed in return.

"Hunters, huntresses, and honored guests, may I please assure you I am only here under the most peaceful of circumstances," the queen began. Her jaded coils looped one on top of the other with her two red belly lines staying in perfect symmetrical alignment as she did so. "So, it is with great gratitude that I thank you for accepting my humble plea.

The Winged Court took their seats above everyone else. Anised leaned against the top banister that lined the pit. Tiel settled down by snuggling into Aven's left side, at which he wrapped his arm around her and laid his head on hers.

"My ancestors have taught many stories through our generations. One such story tells us that during the time of Cong, a Hunter Clan was our most favored ally, friends. We even considered this clan of man our kin. We only know that due to some dark traitorous act of a rival clan, my ancestors ended this alliance. So, imagine my ancestors' surprise when another Hunter Clan formed over a millennium later with the same eight ideologies and prime code, especially since man had forgotten a clan such as this even existed. It is also told that my ancestors were even more amazed when that clan picked the same caves to live in."

The queen stopped for a moment and studied her audience. Tiel realized that the queen was letting this information sink into their minds. After a few moments, she continued.

"As heir to the leadership, my mother taught me, just as her mother taught her and so forth. One thing shown to me was the entrances to these caves. This sanctuary used to be a great university of learning, the knowledge now long lost. I fear most that my ancestors were to blame for this. As I studied the reactions of my elders before I came of age, I sensed that there were things… some knowledge so painful… that they tried to obliterate it from the memories of my clan.

"I fear it may have succeeded too well, for their pride and fears may have infected us, namely my Jonaxx. It is because of him I came to ask for your help."

"Is he your son?" a voice called out.

"No, he is my mate. Please let me explain. When we were young and just mated, we had picked a watosh-filled spot to lie down for a while. While we acodoe sleep, we are very still, so still that many humans consider us dead watosh logs. My body often looks like a moss-covered log. A young huntress passed by and wanted to collect moss for medicinal purposes. When her hand touched me, it tickled. My laughter startled her, and she withdrew what you call her Hunter's Heart. She was about to stab me when my beloved Jonaxx slid over me and allowed the blade to nick him behind his right hood. What she thought to be deep, as The Bounty Huntress has recently learned, was a mere scratch on someone as big as us."

The queen smiled as more chuckles sounded. Tiel laughed along amused at how relaxed the hunters were. This was good considering that the queen could swallow a third of the assembly with only a few gulps. She stayed in her circle, her coils never moving, and her head in the same place. The queen continued after the laughter settled down.

"However, as often happens, things are not always what they seem. We let the young huntress go, which she did despite her trembling body. She withdrew from the clan not long after that incident." The queen's face grew solemn as her eyes glazed over, searching for memories. Her voice cracked as she continued the story. "That mere scratch refused to heal and produced a thick, odorous, yellow slime. We tried everything the elders suggested, and nothing good happened. A few months later, it became clear he heard voices. He would bang his head against the watosh trees. One day he scratched his body while doing this very thing. The new wound refused to heal until it too produced the same odorous ooze. Now, his skin itches most of the time. He is always scraping himself on the watosh, leaving layers of rotting skin filled with maggots. His mind is crowded with the sounds of voices, but sometimes he is sane. We were discussing some important events last night during one of his saner moments when he shuddered. A single tear streamed down his snout, something he had not done in ages. Then, he repeated words from the voices in his mind, a condition I am quite used to."

The queen stopped for a moment, her coils seemed to shake, and the two red stripes bulged. "The words were *We are free brother, finally free. Free once again. Even the Gods couldn't hold us forever.'* Jonaxx forgot me and left. I fear he is pursuing the sadistic entities that have been torturing him all these long octaves. I am uncertain what damage he will cause; nor how sane he will be. I need the clan's help to find him and find out *what is free.*"

Tiel heard the murmurings as her stomach tightened, the memory of the night before forced her to stay still so she would not vomit. She glanced at Aven whose eyes were brimming with tears. His thoughts collided with her mind like roaring waves. He remembered his torment in the caves, the old man's voice they often fought off together along with the fear, uncertainty, and anger at wondering if the insanity of it all would take him.

"Aven, your feelings are too strong. Please!" Tiel pleaded.

His posture became rigid, and he regarded her with concern. "My shield isn't strong enough?"

"It is perfect... from everyone else's currents. I didn't use my rutzix tonight. It leaves me open to your soul currents." He closed his eyes, and soon his currents subsided into something gentle.

"My experience has given me some insight into Jonaxx's trials," Aven said to Tiel as he returned his gaze to the queen whose coils were now slumped. "Think, stellove. You were without me for a few days. How did it affect you? Can you say you are as noble as this creature who has stuck by her beloved's side, even though she may have lost him to a tortured mind?"

Tiel tapped his chest. "No, I cannot." She watched the queen. The acodoe's hood sagged downward as she studied the assembly. "And my sojourn without you was too painful to bear without chems. I cannot imagine what her travels on Shea's paths have been like."

"We tell her?" Aven asked Tiel.

"We tell her. Except, I do not think it wise to mention *Prince Adrian* to this assembly."

"Agreed!" Aven squeezed her hand, and they stood. Aven raised his hand holding his Hunter's Heart. Hushed tones swelled throughout the assembly and the queen adjusted herself to look at him.

"Your Majesty, we may already have news to share with you," Aven stated, and the pit fell silent once more except for the scuffing of the queen's coils as she moved. "The Dark Sentinel Clan also shares in this news but may find it too hard to relate."

"I will follow your lead and relate what I can." Anised stood and nodded. The other Dark Sentinels backed off shaking their heads, showing they had no desire to relate their experiences.

"Please don't judge them yet," Tiel pleaded with the queen as the Dark Sentinels retreated. "Listen to our story first and then decide if they are too weak."

"I thank you for your charity. Continue as you see fit." The queen laid her snout on her top coil and flicked her tongue. Tiel looked at Aven and then related the events concerning Keidera and Kehir. Aven and Anised told their versions. As they told the story, tears flowed. At times their frames trembled, and other times their voices ceased working, especially describing the feelings the specters had used to invade their souls. Anised, following their example, never mentioned Prince Adrian.

When they finished their tale, the pit bore an intense silence. Not one hunter would look at Tiel or the others. Most hunters hung their heads. Tiel saw Emery, Emiline, and Jainu cling to each other. Even the queen herself hid her snout halfway behind the first coil, hood folded against her skin, with her eyes shifting back and forth between the three.

After a few moments of silence, the queen flicked out her tongue and lifted her snout. Some in the room whispered. All kept their eyes averted.

"That is quite the tale and should be taken as an omen of worse to come." She flicked her tongue and studied the threesome. "There is only one word that describes these specters. My ancestors whispered the name. You use this same word to describe someone who you ostracize from your clan. However, from the stories I have studied, this name means several things." The queen turned to look at her full audience.

"This name describes someone who steals a soul's will. It is one who forces depravities into their victim's innermost heart. It is someone described as taking another's form. I never learned why my ancestors spoke of this name in hushed tones. I just knew to speak the name was forbidden. The name I speak of is *Luhitzu*." There were a few intakes of air, but Tiel kept her gaze on the queen. "I fear that my ancestors are to blame for the lost knowledge of Cong's age. However, as Jonaxx related last night, there may be one who knows where this lost knowledge is... if they do not possess it. The knowledge may help heal my Jonaxx and allow us to identify who these specters are."

"Can this knowledge help us?" Anised's voice boomed across the pit. "Can it help my Shaine, my beloved, in her torment?"

Murmurs once again rolled across the pit. Tiel watched Anised's neck bulge as he clamped his jaw. The knuckles on his fist turned pure white as they clenched into balls.

"I thought you said she died," the queen leaned forward in his direction.

"I... I... think so." He relaxed as he stared past her, "I don't know, I..." Anised's chest heaved in and out as he sputtered. His throat rasped as he clenched his chest, his agony screwing his face into a tight grimace.

"Anised, out with it!" Tiel jerked as Aven's voice boomed past her ears.

"I heard her! She cried out in terror! I don't know how, for as far as I could tell, she was dead. But when that *thing* took her body, I heard her scream." Aven let go of Tiel and dashed toward Anised. The hunter's sobs reverberated through the pit. Tiel gathered her strength and followed Aven who had already made it over to the grief-stricken hunter. Anguished voices filled the pit with gasps and sobs. The queen leaned back. Her hood pulsated as she hissed.

"I heard her wail in terror and I could do nothing but shrink back and whimper." Anised stared into his memories. "*I did nothing!*"

"Yes, you did! You lived!" Aven seized the hunter and stared into his face. "If even her spirit knows of this, you need to help free her. She is still waiting for you to help." Anised shook his head, the grimace contorting his face into undistinguishable features. "Brother! None of us could move! Let's find out how to help her now!"

Tiel watched the two men. Anised stared at Aven before slumping into his friend's chest. He nodded his head in agreement as he took in large gulps of air.

The queen hissed and spoke to the hunters, "Let's proceed so all can heal. The same tomes that may heal my Jonaxx may help your stellove, brave hunter."

She searched and spotted the Elder Hunter and the Laisens in the middle back. She addressed them. "Tell me, Elders of the Hunter Clan, this person I mentioned earlier, the one that may know where these tomes are… what if I told you that person was of your clan? And the knowledge they access is dark and vile? Would you judge them and put their hearts on The Block?"

"That would depend," said Master Laisen as he stood, "we ostracize only the most severe cases like murder. Most hunters receive lighter punishments to atone for their wrongdoings."

"If what you say is true, however," the Elder Hunter continued, "this hunter would be capable of horrible cruelties and must be dealt with."

The queen hissed and lowered her head. "I am not even sure this hunter understands what they do. How can your judgments be so harsh?"

"If they do not understand," Master Laisen answered, "we judge them as innocent. They must have a full understanding of the seriousness of the offense when they commit it. If they do not, we give them something to atone for what they did and help them learn a different path for their actions."

"Hum." The queen leaned forward. "What if I ask this hunter privately, so they do not implicate themselves and come under a great embarrassment?"

Tiel shook her head and cried *no* aloud with most hunters around her. The master continued, "We believe as a group it is better to conquer that which ails us, Great Queen. If you are right, this hunter needs the support and understanding of the clan, their family. It is this that keeps our paths straight. We need to answer to each other. We do not put someone on The Block without a trial and the consent of the clan. If there is any proof that this hunter did not understand what they did, the clan will help them choose the right path."

"All of you believe this? That I should question this hunter now?"

Tiel yelled *yes* along with everyone else.

"Let it happen, Great Queen." Mistress Laisen pleaded. "Besides, we need the information this hunter may have to fight these Luhitzu."

The queen studied the crowd, and then, for the first time that evening, she moved forward. Her skin rustled as her coils rotated once more, allowing her to stretch to the back of the cavern. Hunters and huntresses parted to let her through. She stopped in front of Anised, Aven, and Tiel. Tiel fell back against the railings as the queen's breath, still reeked of the freshness of the blood rain, mixed in with a hint of decaying meat.

"All three of you voiced your affirmation to my question. So, do you all agree I should conduct my interview now?" Tiel gulped as she nodded. Her body felt as if it wanted to crash to the floor.

"I do this with the deepest apologies, Bounty Huntress." The queen's hiss pierced Tiel's ears, and her tongue flicked in her direction.

"By Shea's light!" Tiel murmured as she dropped to the cold, hard stones underneath.

Aven moved in front of her and helped her to stand. She stood looking at the queen, willing her stomach to settle, and swallowing the bitter vile that forced itself up into her throat.

The queen flicked her tongue. "Last night, Jonaxx, and I were conversing about the day when you and your beloved came to rescue our young. After you left, I sent my brother and his mate to watch over you. Last night, Jonaxx admitted he also followed, for he was also grateful for the help you two had rendered. When you camped in the clearing named Jaiden's Wash, you used what my ancestors termed in whispered tones as an *ungift* on the one called Fallon Hanover?"

"Yes, yes," Tiel answered. "We call it a Mind-Over-Lay, I use it only in the direst of circumstances."

"Hmmm, yes. I know you more than likely assumed you were in *dire circumstances*. But there is some knowledge that should not be used. According to my ancestors, back in the days of the old Hunter Clan, a revival clan came into power. At first, the two clans lived peaceably together. Both attended the university here and other places of learning. The ancient men and women learned from and added to the great abundance of knowledge that Coulliou blessed them with. However, the rival clan sought knowledge that was dark, and they wrote it down in eight volumes. Our stories tell that the final members of the ancient Hunter Clan captured these volumes in a great struggle and buried them.

"My ancestors taught us some names from the tomes, so we would recognize if someone discovered these volumes. One was a metal, called biometal, that grafts into muscle and bones, giving the recipient great strength. This biometal exists today and is called by that name. Another is the Orbeath. These are small metal orbs that, when attached to the chest, drain the victim's blood but keeps them alive until the very last moment. But the most insidious of all were the *ungifts*. I will not name them all, but one, known as The Soul Mask, is what you call Mind-Over-Lay.

The burial place of these volumes is unknown to us. However, there is evidence from your actions and from other events that these volumes have been discovered. The specter you met called Keidera often drove Jonaxx mad with her desires to find these volumes.

"When Jonaxx saw you use the *ungift*, he wanted to come and educate you on the dangers. He was also happy that he found someone who might know how to free him. My brother and his mate misunderstood Jonaxx's intentions and tried to stop him. A great fight ensued between the three and my brother's mate died. Jonaxx lost his focus, I believe due to his guilt, and disappeared. We worry you do not realize the damage you can cause. When and where did you study from these volumes?"

Tiel replied, "I did not study from any of those volumes, not directly at least. I was possibly taught from one volume."

Hushed whispers resonated throughout the chamber. "Explain," the queen hissed and moved her coils once more.

"After the Drakners rescued me from the merchant's caves, there was a Peace Enforcer Kerlar, other than Emiline Drakner, which oversaw the measuring of my telepathic abilities. At first, she would just have me sense soul currents or talk to her through our consciousness. When I mastered those lessons, she brought out an old brown tome. That is when she taught me how to read people's minds, to erase people's memories, or control what they thought for a moment. By using the tome, she taught me how to change everything about what they were thinking and feeling."

"Did you ever read this tome?"

"No, however, I saw the script." Tiel wrung her hands on her robe and thought a moment. "Now that I think about it, it looked like the same script that Emery Drakner is always deciphering from ancient storyboards. The kerlar could read it. When she did, she always talked in a foreign language."

"Do you know what happened to this tome?"

"No, after the Drakners removed me from the enforcer program, I never saw the kerlar or that tome again, or anything even like it."

"Did she teach others?" the queen asked as she moved back.

"I know of four others. One was Vanqish, who died last night." Tiel kept her attention on the queen. "I believe the other three are dead."

"Did you tell anybody about this?"

"Quite a few hunters know about the Mind-Over-Lay, as we call it." Tiel shrugged her shoulders. "Everyone thought it was just something that a telepath could do. I am just known as a stronger telepath."

"The Soul Mask is a way of stealing someone's will. According to our customs, it often leaves the victim bereft of any protection while trying to peel off the mask. They are susceptible to suggestions of any kind and travel paths that Shea does not light."

"What happens if someone takes it off?" Anised asked.

"No one can take off a Soul Mask," Tiel answered. "I learned it was a lie that the kerlar taught us. I was the only one who didn't believe it. A telepath forces themselves into the mind and crawls under the…," Tiel said glancing at the queen, "the Soul Mask, sees the memory and then comes out and pastes their version of the memory over the Soul Mask."

"So, now this victim has two masks to peel." The queen tilted her head in Anised's direction, flicking her tongue. "Why do you ask, hunter?"

"Because I had the now-deceased telepath of my inner clan do exactly that to this same person," Anised bowed his head.

"You also assumed that this was just something a telepath could do?"

Anised nodded his head without looking at the queen.

"He needs help until he heals. He will cause himself much damage until this happens."

"We all thought it was just a part of a telepath's power," Master Laisen exclaimed. "We will find Fallon Hanover and bring him here for safety. Will that suffice as a start?"

"A fantastic start!" The queen nodded her head and repositioned herself on top of her coils. Tiel breathed once more as she leaned into Aven.

"If Mistress Laisen and the Elder Hunter will come with me, we will have assignments for a few of you within an arm." The master left with the mistress and the Elder Hunter following him.

"Well, so much for admitting my crimes in private before I go to the clan," Tiel whispered to Aven as they walked out of the pit. Anised followed.

"Bounty Huntress, de Menzaile, and Anised!" Everyone turned back to look at the queen. "I thank you for your help, especially for you two in helping to protect my young."

"Don't be too grateful," Tiel's voice rang out, "this kerlar who taught me from the tome loved to have us torture innocent people. I dreaded her lessons because of this. Tyne Baritone, the one responsible for harming your young in the first place, was one of her favorite torture subjects."

The queen shifted her coils allowing the elders to pass through the alcove doors. "Being taught to use depravities is not your burden to bear, Bounty Huntress. As I said, I thank you for your help. Your spirit testifies to the fact that you are not the child this kerlar was trying to mold you into."

CHAPTER 18

S ethrich," **Radames talked** slowly to keep his temper under control. "This is not the time for punishments. The Hunter Clan protects the innocent. Many innocent lives are in danger, and this is the reason the forefathers formed the clan."

"Yet, you may have one, if not two, hunters with soiled zahules to the degree that the stench will spoil the Hunter Clan itself." Sethrich's voice rose in pitch. "Plus, those same hunters, including your Dark Sentinels, may be incapacitated due to last night's hunt. Psychologically, they may not be trustworthy."

"The Dark Sentinels are our responsibility," Lidena voiced from the other side of the room. They were in the meeting room. The table now held ale as the clan leaders debated the next course of action.

"Too true, but I need your and Radames' permission to claim my rights as an inner clan leader."

"Your rights?" Radames questioned. "Our laws state that you cannot claim your rights until you have fulfilled your responsibilities."

"Our laws also state that fulfilling your responsibilities means giving your hunters a chance to prove themselves," Lidena added.

"Are you sure you have enough zahule to stand in this inner circle?"

Sethrich glared at Lidena. "I seem to remember a certain meeting with Nender. You didn't even say hello as you ran past me to follow him."

"That will be decided in the next larquetz," Lidena croaked out while she grabbed at the back of the chair. "I have already made my petition."

"Until that larquetz, according to the law, she is still the Mistress." Radames slammed his drink on the table which caused Sethrich to jump. "That was a cowardly move to get your way, Sethrich. Do you or do you not respect the laws of this clan?"

Sethrich thought for a few moments. "My mistake, Radames, Lidena. It was rude of me. I should have asked about your intentions before we began this conversation." He bowed to Lidena. "And perhaps I was too ambitious. I concur that Aven should be given a second chance to see if he can handle hunter life and thrive. My main concern is with Tiel. You cannot dismiss her ill-timed use of the Mind-Over-Lay and what the condition of her heart is."

"I never dismiss the use of the Soul Mask," Radames replied as he took a drink of his ale, "no matter who uses it or commands others to use it. So, if you will sequester Tiel for her use of the Soul Mask, I shall demand you sequester Jilandro and yourself for the attempted use of the Soul Mask... on me."

"Radames," Sethrich whispered, "I never would do that. I only asked Jilandro to search your thoughts. But the Mind-Over-Lay?"

"I could bring it up in the next larquetz." Radames leaned forward. "I have been considering it."

"That is not necessary. Jilandro should have his chance to prove himself according to the law," Sethrich said. Radames raised his eyebrows to which Sethrich raised his hands in resignation. "As should Tiel. However, I move I be given both of your consents to investigate the events from the time that Tiel and Aven left to rescue the delegate's children to now."

"Some things need our attention here," Lidena said as she held her glass of ale.

"There are always things that need attention here." Sethrich dismissed Lidena's concerns. "You two are more than capable of handling those concerns. Discovering what happened to these two hunters may give us a clue on how to help the queen. And we need an independent third party to discern the truth. Plus, if Tiel will harm someone for her interests, I may find proof of her intentions. Otherwise, I should be able to uncover proof of her innocence. Is that acceptable?"

"It is acceptable. We will take care of things here." Radames raised his mug. Sethrich drank the last of his ale and then left.

"Do you trust the Elder Hunter in this?" Lidena asked.

"No, I do not," Radames answered. "But I trust Tiel. She has a good heart with a clean zahule. He won't find anything, and it will get him out of our way. This will give us the time to finish our investigation."

"Now we need to question the kerlar that taught Tiel about her telepathic abilities," Lidena stated.

"My aunt Emiline has already taken care of that," Radames smiled. "She is the kerlar in charge of Tiel's wayward kerlar. This kerlar is a patient in Sarom's Mental Barracks."

A high beeping noise sounded, and a Dark Sentinel appeared. "There is news from the Peace Enforcers," he announced.

"Let us see it," Radames ordered.

Soon a holo imager was brought in and turned on. An image of a throng of councilmen and councilwomen crowded in front of some the news probes, their maicallas all hung open around their necks. Radames recognized Cadune leaning on his crutches in the middle next to Lady Lavonne. Hegert did not appear among the leaders standing in front of the stone structure of the Main Planetary Council Chambers. A human teapot that he knew to be High Councilman Lord Sobaigh waddled up to the front of the gathering, his golden maicalla swinging back and forth. He squeaked out a welcome with an apathetic flat tone.

"Warrior Cadune would like to make an announcement. It is the opinion of the Ecalardian Council that all should listen. There is an unanimous consensus in what he proposes. Warrior Cadune." Lord Sobaigh turned and stood in front of everyone else with his head down. Cadune moved up to the front, his crutches clicking against the sidewalk.

"My fellow Ecalardians, if you know me at all, you know I am a staunch supporter of 'the vote.' I believe our voices rather than someone's birthright should represent us. However, my latest actions have brought a division among us. Some want an emperor. Others want a voice. There is no official count of either side." He gazed at the pulpit for a few moments. His shoulders rose with a large intake of air before he lifted his head.

"However, I cannot stand by while someone tries to claim a crown through murder. This type of leader would not hesitate slaying those who oppose him. So, I propose that we have the first vote of this age. The acodoe warriors have agreed to set up places in each village council chamber where all Ecalardians may come in three months and vote for the system they desire."

Murmurs sounded from behind the probes. Lady Lavonne beamed with pride. Lord Sobaigh frowned while rubbing his forehead.

"My hope is that Ecalardians will see the advantage of having a voice in their government. Therefore, they will want 'the vote' and will vote that way. However, if the majority votes for an emperor, I will accept the position. I guarantee that my zahule is white in this matter. I will not shrink from the responsibility."

Cadune smiled and nodded at the now emerging reporters who rushed towards him. An enforcer entered the frame and whispered something into Lady Lavonne's ear while handing her a piece of paper. Lady Lavonne listened and nodded before stepping forward and touching Cadune on the shoulder.

"Questions will have to wait for later. Now there is other news from the village Quri." Her voice faltered as she took a few minutes to study the paper in her hands. "It is grave news, and the council will be busy taking care of the fatalities there. Some village inhabitants have died from a deep depression caused by a... mysterious *moaner?*" Lady Lavonne looked at the straight-back enforcer. He just shrugged his shoulders. She returned to the paper and continued. "Although it cannot be confirmed, there seems to be a large black acodoe on the scene, as its tail erupted from the forest, knocked over a full-grown watosh which damaged the perimeter stone fence. However, this caused no casualties. The village Pax has also reported hearing the moaner and some hissing, but also reported no casualties."

Lady Lavonne looked back at the council. They bowed and dispersed.

"The council will check into this and report its findings as soon as possible." The screen went white again.

"At least we have an idea where Jonaxx and the Luhitzu are at," Mistress Laisen broke the silence.

"Yes, we do. I believe we have the perfect situation to help Aven, Tiel and the Dark Sentinels. They have encountered these apparitions, now let's see if they can overcome last night's attack."

IT HAD BEEN easy to slip past the sleeping woman in the front room of the caverns. Now, Diandra watched the crowd from where she sat. The tables around here were empty. Every person was watching the huge, coiled acodoe. The ones she saw sitting on the stone stairs looked like hunters. She even thought she saw The Bounty Huntress although Maestro was missing. Diandra rubbed her arms feeling the minuscule little bumps. The serpent continued talking amid some laughter.

"Awake, report, here, awake." All her inward petitions only made her forehead throb without an answer to calm her nerves. She felt herself swallow, the large lump almost sticking in her throat.

Lady had often tested her little cards by pretending to disown them. Later, Lady would reveal that The Master sent them to watch the world and report back. They were welcomed back as Honorary Elites even though no Honorary Elites lived longer than two months.

Nevertheless, according to the master, these beloved elites avoided living eternally in the dismal Arasteit. The master always taught that it was a region of dark and cold penetrating one's soul forever, only remembering guilt, always knowing one could have done better. Only the master could get someone across the Arasteit when the Day of Renewal approached. Above all else, Diandra wanted to avoid the Arasteit. She wanted to be a chosen one who followed the master to an eternity of bliss and rest.

The crowd dispersed, and Diandra controlled her nerves by using her fists to hit her legs. She discovered no useful information until she spotted the boy, the master's lost love standing between two old people. Diandra leaned closer squinting her eyes.

"It is the masters lost love!" she squealed. She had reported him when he had followed her allowing Lady to capture him. "Why is he here?" she wondered. "He should be with the master by now."

Then she realized it didn't matter. Her stomach fluttered, she took in large slow deep breaths as her spirit seemed to soar with joy. That was why she was here. To find this group of people. To lead the master to more lost loves so he could keep more from the Arasteit. That was why she was still alive. The *Master* chose her to be an Honorary Elite!

Diandra stood testing her balance. The thick, blue gown she was wearing swayed with her efforts. After steadying herself, she walked the rough, brown halls back to the rooms she had slept in.

It took only a little time to get back to the inn. However, she often had to retrieve a blue slipper that fell off every so often. She soon found herself back at the inn inside the dark caverns. Potted shrubs stood under bright-yellow crystal lights on both sides of an arched entrance with a bamboodii door. The small entrance had a few crystal lights anchored to the walls. A stone counter fashioned out of the rock inside stood in the center. Openings in the wall on either side of the counter led to a maze of halls and rooms.

She entered the suite she woke up in and after searching around, she decided that the suite was empty and ordered the holo screen to turn on. A small door opened under the octave star in the stone wall. A silver rod moved out, and a screen slid out. Several colors of squares materialized, and Diandra pushed the sequence of colors that led to other squares and so forth until she got the combination that would ring into Lady's office.

As she waited for the answer, she tried to scratch at an itch in her right ear but was stopped by a bandage and fresh pain as she touched it. She smoothed out her hair instead. A beep erupted from the screen, and Diandra stood still. Distant laughter echoed through the caverns letting her know the hunters still held their meeting. A second beep sounded, and Diandra brought her full attention to performing her duty.

The snow disappeared, and Lady's form dominated the screen. Diandra paid little attention to Lady's large purple bruises that covered the left side of her face and the swollen left eye. She barely noticed the cuts and bruises on Lady's shoulder. Those emblems proved that Lady had just been through one of her purification rites.

"What is your report?" Lady rasped between swollen and cracked lips.

"This is Diandra. I have done what you sent me to do."

"Diandra? What? Who?" Lady was often confused after a purification rite, so Diandra stood still and waited. It was all part of the process of ridding herself of the world's influence she had to visit. A trainer bent down and whispered in her ear. Lady nodded and waved him away.

"Diandra, doing your part to become an Honorable Elite, I see. We shall see if your actions warrant such a title. Give me your report."

Voices outside became chaotic, so Diandra kept the report small but concise. Lady was smiling at the end.

"You have blessed my purification this day, so it may renew me," Lady's announcement filled Diandra with pride. She smiled in response.

"Thank you for the honor, Lady. However, those of the unpurified will soon join me. What is the master's desire?"

"To wait there until you receive further instructions. Keep watch and do what they say. Tell no one you called or talked to me." The screen went white, and Diandra turned it off. She investigated the table with food and decided she had earned many free meals. She would take advantage of their kindness while she waited. That was the unpurified's fate, to wait on the purified. They just didn't acknowledge it.

Diandra picked up a sweet, morning cake. She breathed in the aroma. Spices tickled her nose and made her mouth water. She squished the top and felt the firm sponginess inside give way watching with pleasure as it sprang back once she released it. She breathed in deep again and bit down. The firm, moist cake filled her mouth with a most delightful flavor. She let out her breath and closed her eyes. When she opened them again, the master's lost love and an elderly gentleman were standing in front of her.

CHIEF DEL STOOD in front of a small abode waiting for its occupant to answer the door. He knew she was here. Because of her disease, she didn't leave her home. His wife checked on her daily and brought supplies and food.

He studied the yard as he did on his visits. The trees needed pruning where they were encroaching on the properties of others, and the grass needed trimming. The yard was always clean, just not in a pristine state like most abode owners. Del made a mental note to get his nephews working in the yard once more.

"Chief Del," said a tall, gangly woman standing at the door, "why am I blessed with your company today?"

"Is it a good day?" Del inquired.

"Physically, a great day. I do not carry around that awful stench," the woman motioned for him to enter. Chief Del noticed that her abode was, as usual, cluttered. Books, papers, and clothes were piled high on every surface. The shards of her octave star's broken tail still gleamed in and around a box filled with papers, the only thing left on the clean floors. Del located the broom and swept up the crystal shards.

"Did the pain just leave? You have not had time to clean up after your star broke," Del finished by using papers from the box to gather the shards.

"I did not see that," she waited while he put the shards into a trash box and put the broom away. Del returned to find her sitting on the edge of a black couch in her first room. The wrinkles of her green shirt and purple pants matched the wrinkled state of the pile of clothes behind her. "Mentally, it is a very confusing day."

"Do you hear the voices today?" Del probed further while sitting down on the edge of a cluttered chair across from her. He leaned back and ignored the small table filled with clutter.

"One voice now, the male moaner." The woman scratched her head under the short, thin, brown hair. Her eyes shifted in her head, keeping her from focusing on one object. Her reddish-tan hollow face was in his direction though. "Why do you ask?"

"I always ask, Quartney." Both laughed. Del patted her hands. "However, there is a special reason today. Tell me, did the voices talk about being freed last night?"

Quartney jerked her head up and gawked at Del for a moment. "How did you know? Yes, the wretched female voice, she did. She has been laughing, taunting, and cursing all day. But now, she is distant."

"I have just been to a meeting with the Hunter Clan and Sendenia, Queen of the Acodoe. They were discussing some very intriguing people, possibly the people that are in your mind. There is proof they have escaped a prison and are hunted by an acodoe."

"Oh, I see, but how can I help?"

"Where is your old Hunter's Heart?"

"I threw it back in the bin after I released myself from the Hunter Clan." Quartney rubbed her gnarled hands over her bony arms and shivered. "I wanted nothing to do with that abomination. It gave me a curse."

"Something tells me that your Hunter's Heart is a 'special weapon.'" Del eyed Quartney who seemed confused. "Just a hunch. The female voice, she calls herself Keidera, right?"

Quartney sucked in the air showing her ribs. Her whole body trembled.

"What is wrong?" Del asked.

"I have told none of your generation the names of the voices. It makes it so real now." She averted her gaze. "Sometimes in the middle of the night, the voices screamed at someone called Jonaxx. Many times I have fought the urge to end my life. Other times I can ignore the voices and travel Shea's lighted paths."

"The male's name is Kehir, and Jonaxx is the name of the acodoe chasing Keidera." Del nudged her arm with his hand. Quartney burst into sobs. He moved over and put his arms around her, letting her fall into his chest. She sobbed for well over a quarter of an arm before she stopped.

"For over a hundred and fifty octaves, those two dung heaps have tortured me. Moments of peace were rare." Del said nothing as Quartney confessed her fears. "I learned that to mention their names brought their attention to me. I can't remember when I decided not to tell anyone their names." Quartney turned to him. "But, why ask about the knife?"

"The knife may be a key to both you and Jonaxx."

"What makes you think my old Hunter's Heart is key to this dilemma?" Quartney wiped her face dry.

"First, it is what caused your and Jonaxx's wounds, not to mention the voices in your heads." Del's look made Quartney laugh, and she showed with a wave of her hand she knew he was right. He explained parts of what happened with Tiel's party the night before.

"You are telling me that when that cat mauled Keidera, those same wounds looked like this?" Quartney lifted her shirt to show a red welt with a green-yellow goo oozing out, some of it hardened.

"That is what was explained during the meeting," Del answered and moved the shirt to cover up the wound. "What did the knife look like?"

"It doesn't matter, just look for a huntress with wounds like I have. That is the one with the knife."

"The clan separates the knives into male and female knives?" Del inquired

"Oh, no, it is just that females seem to pick this knife." Quartney pushed back her hair while Del felt his brows furrow in confusion.

"When I left the clan, I searched for others that may have owned the knife. I found two," she related, holding up two fingers for emphasis. "They knew of others before them, all were female, and all had the oozing wounds I am now plagued with."

"You knew of others that had the disease?" Del paused for effect and watched Quartney's eyes move back and forth. "And you all threw the knife back, knowing it could affect another hunter with this same disease?"

Del stayed quiet and let Quartney think. Almost ten minutes passed before she spoke again.

"It sounds selfish, but it seemed the right thing to do." Quartney shrugged her shoulders. "Late at night, sometimes, I believe my thoughts are not my thoughts. When it is quietest, it is the most dangerous. The craziest ideas come. However, some seem good. I remember standing out in the front hunter caverns making that decision, to throw the knife back into the bin late one night when Dommo's light was full. This happened before the voices were clear. I often wonder about my actions. That is why I stay inside now."

Del took in this information. "Listen to my voice now. The Hunter Clan needs your knowledge. You can help. Keidera is looking for that knife."

Quartney nodded and stood. "Yes, I will go with you." She ran to the back of her hut. Del had never seen her move so quickly.

"I HOPE Emery can take care of Diandra," Tiel commented as she paced back and forth in the front caverns. Shea's paths had become a little gray for her since Master Laisen had sent word for her to conduct this interview. "Plus, I wonder when Maestro or Adrian will wake up."

Emiline stood close to her and kept watch on the outside. She let out a heavy sigh in answer to Tiel's comment. The problem with keeping her telepathy in a rutzix was that she could only guess at what people's emotions were. However, Emiline's scowl and silence meant anger. "Look, I realize you're mad at me..."

"Mad? At you? Why in the name of Ecalardia would I be mad at you?" Emiline's face shone with shocked disbelief.

"Well, I can think of a few reasons."

"Oh, give it up child. I am mad at me for not getting you out of there sooner. I knew that woman was up to something. I just didn't think it was that horrendous. And yes, Emery can handle Diandra, she will be asleep soon. I hope Maestro wakes soon too. I am not in the mood to meet Adrian."

Silence seeped into the hallway. Tiel banged her leg for a moment and then let out a huge sigh. "That may not have been your idea," she announced.

"What? Getting you out of the enforcers? No, it wasn't my idea. It was Emery's. I'm just the one that hurried things along is all. Wait, what do you mean it wasn't my idea?"

Tiel fumbled for the words to say, finding herself pursing her lips and waving her left hand in the air. She was wondering if perhaps the static would be preferable.

"Out with it, child. I believe you were about to confess something. And don't you dare use one of your forsaken curses!"

"Well, do you remember how I said the kerlar liked to use us to torture others?" Tiel tried to rub away the sudden manifestation of tension in her neck.

"Yes, I do. But, I don't remember you torturing me."

"That's because I didn't, nor did anyone else. I know because when I telepathically convinced you to take me out of Enforcer's Headquarters, your mind was clean."

"What?!"

"The kerlar was merciless. I couldn't stand her victims' screams, their anguish any longer." Tiel rushed with her words, trying to get everything out at once. "I could feel everything, especially their gradual loss of hope. That was the worst of all, so I did one final 'Soul Mask' as the acodoe call it and convinced you to get me out of there."

Tiel lowered her eyes, her arms folded in front of her.

"Did you do that to Emery?"

Tiel shook her head.

"Did you do anything to my mind after that?"

Tiel shook her head again.

"Is your zahule white in this matter?" Emiline's voice was soft as she peered at Tiel.

"Brilliantly white," Tiel promised as Emiline sighed in relief. "It surprised me that you didn't throw me out after the Soul Mask dissipated. You shouldn't have loved me as you did, those feelings I put in there would have faded."

Emiline laughed.

"What?" Tiel backed up at Emiline's sudden show of mirth.

"You really do think you are all-powerful, don't you?" Tiel gulped at Emiline's question. She continued. "You may have been able to change the victims the kerlar had you torture, but, my dear child, I suspect that was while several of you were wearing them down at once.

"Both Emery and I loved you from the moment we saw you in the mud deserts. The only reason you stayed at Enforcer Headquarters was so that the adoption process would go quicker. You made it move faster than scheduled. When the Mask dissipated, the real love never left."

Tiel wiped tears away from her eyes and sniffled. Emiline was quiet for a few more moments.

"I am confident this kerlar trained you children to think you were all-powerful. However, that was just to keep her deluded dreams alive. I suspect the reason the Soul Mask leaves one unprotected is that the feelings you put into your victims aren't real. Their memories don't match what they feel. It causes a deep anguish they need to find a cause for. And in that case, they will do what is necessary to get to the root of the problem."

A Green Medic Transport glided into the caverns. One attendant, dressed in a dark-green, plain outfit got out. The back part of the transport slid open, and Tiel realized she was holding her breath.

The medic escorted a tall, white woman out of the transport. Her black hair was tied in a ponytail, her yellow cheeks sank in defining thin bones, and her eyes had purple bags underneath.

"Kerlar Xenchen," Emiline said smiling, "may I welcome you to the Hunters' Caverns?" She turned to the Medic. "You darkened the windows during the ride?"

"Yes," the young woman answered.

"Good," Emiline took Xenchen's hand and led her to an empty guest cave with a crackling fire. Xenchen took in the surrounding scenery, finally resting her gaze on Tiel.

"Tiel?" the kerlar whispered as Emiline sat her down in a chair. Tiel saw a glimmer in her eyes as a faint smile formed. "Have all our goals come to fruition? I am sorry I could not help you study."

"Where are the tomes you used to teach me, Xenchen?" Tiel sat down next to the woman, letting her soul current flow. She hoped it would be easy. Emiline closed the bamboodii straw door and sat in a corner chair. She paid attention to her fingernails while listening.

"The tomes?" the kerlar whispered, looking Tiel up and down. "You want to learn more. I can see if I can teach you if Kerlar Drakner allows. But it will take time to get the tomes again."

"Where are the tomes?"

"I don't know. It has been so long," Xenchen's soul currents flowed around Tiel. But the currents were unclear.

"Think, what did you do with the tomes?"

"I returned them to their owner," Xenchen's currents became clearer. Tiel saw only a floor with two brownish tomes stacked upon it. Dark black boots stood behind those tomes. A deep voice conveyed disapproval of a younger Xenchen's failures. Tears dropped onto the tomes as Xenchen kneeled and begged to no avail. The streams of thought burst as the same voice echoed inside her and Xenchen's minds.

"GET THE MASTER! THE BOUNTY HUNTRESS IS QUESTIONING THIS OLD CARD."

"Why are you interested in the tomes? Their knowledge is ancient. You were to be taught from them. But first, have you kept up your weekly rituals with Vanqish?" Xenchen's questions brought Tiel back from the voices in her mind. "You wouldn't be interested in the tomes if you were."

"What rituals?" Emiline's voice broke Tiel's concentration. She signaled the older woman to be quiet with a wave of her hand.

"There was another huntress several octaves back asking about the tomes. She was worried about her Hunter's Heart of all things." Xenchen continued.

Another image of an older woman swirled around Tiel. She was standing in a white room with a steel table and chairs. The woman was of medium height, brown hair with auburn streaks, with a chunky frame.

"Are you in league with her?" Xenchen leaned towards Tiel. "Why aren't you burrowing into my mind? You have grown too gentle, my little girl." Tiel leaned back as Xenchen reached up with her hand. "I should be screaming in pain while you tear the information out of me. Be the god you are meant to be!"

"MASTER, THIS CARD IS TELLING THE BOUNTY HUNTRESS A LOT, I THINK."

"SEND IN AN ORB. SHE'S BEEN A WASTE ON MY WATCH FOR FAR TOO LONG," the old man commanded.

"RIGHT AWAY, MASTER."

Tiel grabbed Xenchen by the wrists. "Who is the master, the one speaking in your mind?"

"What? You shouldn't hear that. You haven't been paying attention to your rituals!"

"Who is the master? Quickly, Xenchen!"

"No, that's sacred."

"Tiel!" Tiel looked back at the sharp voice, Emiline stood behind her. "Let her go!" Tiel released the squirming woman and returned her soul current back into the rutzix. She opened the door and pushed Emiline out of the room.

"What are you doing, child?"

"Saving you from experiencing a terrible horror."

"What?! Let me go this instant!"

Xenchen's screams pierced the air as Tiel moved Emiline along the hallway.

"What are you doing?" Emiline tried to push Tiel aside. Tiel held her place. Xenchen's screams continued, yet Tiel breathed easy. She heard nothing in her mind. The rutzix was strong. Emiline stopped pushing and tried to move around her. "Get out of my way! What are you doing?"

"Nothing, I am doing nothing!" Tiel explained while holding Emiline by the shoulders once again. "It's an orbeath. The old man sent an orbeath!" Emiline backed away, shaking. "There was nothing I could do. I don't know how to stop those things. It could blow up the caverns."

Xenchen's screaming stopped. "Send for the medics," Tiel instructed Emiline. "They will have to carry out her body."

Emiline ran down the hall, calling for the medics. Tiel walked towards the room and opened the door. Xenchen's body lay face up on the table, looking like Orton did when he died. Except her face had a tight grimace of terror.

"THE ORB IS BACK, MASTER, THIS DUNG HEAP CARD IS BURNED."

"TURN THAT CONTRAPTION OFF. IT IS TAKING UP TOO MUCH ENERGY. I NEED MY POWER SOURCES FOR SOMETHING ELSE. COME TO THE MEETING ROOM. I HAVE FANTASTIC NEWS."

JAINU WANTED to tell Diandra to get up, stand in the corner, and keep turning around, just to watch her do it. It was only common decency that kept him from doing what he wished. She made his skin crawl and hair stand up on end.

She did exactly what someone told her. Or, she wouldn't do anything until someone commanded. Emiline already had to bathe Diandra twice today. It was Emery who commanded Diandra to use the water closet every arm. He was now sitting across from Diandra scrutinizing her. Jainu waited to see what happened. Emery had a mischievous gleam in his eye.

"You got in contact with someone," Emery voiced his suspicion to Diandra. Her eyes grew wide. However, she sat on the couch, posture rigid and still. Her hair swirled around the white bandage covering her right ear. Her hands played with the thick, yellow pajamas that she wore.

"I am sure we will find out. More than likely it was Lady Twibett," Diandra jerked at his guess but kept quiet. "I see I am right. Well, I know she told you to obey our commands. An interesting dilemma since you ate food before we got back. That means she gave you permission. Or, you have taken chances to make your own decisions before, most likely when you believed no one was watching."

Emery stopped and studied the girl. She twitched in her seat and scanned the room but still said nothing. Distant laughter sounded, and Jainu looked to find the cause but heard nothing. He turned back when he heard Emery speak again.

"Follow this command. You are not to believe anything Lady Twibett or any of her associates taught you. In fact, you are to tell Emiline everything they taught you."

Diandra gasped, her breathing came in spurts, and her body shook.

"I thought as much. But there it is. You are to question everything anybody has ever told you. Plus, if you don't take care of yourself, in other words, eat, relieve yourself, and so forth. There will be consequences. I will tell Emiline of my decision."

"EMERY IS SMART, JAINU, MY LOST LOVE," more laughter sounded, this time Jainu realized where it was coming from, and his body trembled. "I REALIZED EMERY DRAKNER TOOK IN STRAYS. I DIDN'T THINK HE WOULD TAKE ON A WORTHLESS CARD SUCH AS THAT. ARE YOU AS WORTHLESS AS SHE IS, OR WILL YOU COME HOME?"

Jainu lurched, knocking a glass candle on the stone floor. He hit his head with his fists and cried out. The old man's voice sighed.

"WHY IS IT ALWAYS SO HARD TO GET YOU LOST LOVES TO COME HOME? I ONLY WANT TO GET YOU ACROSS THE ARASTEIT. I ONLY WANT WHAT IS BEST FOR YOU. BUT, IF YOU WILL NOT LISTEN," the old man sighed, and his voice filled with deep malice, "I CAN SEE AND HEAR EVERYTHING YOU CAN. I WILL FIND ALL YOU LOVE AND PUNISH THEM UNTIL YOU ARE HOME. AND, IF YOU DON'T COME SOON ENOUGH, I WILL CONTINUE TO PUNISH THEM WITH YOU WATCHING. IT IS ONLY FOR YOUR OWN GOOD, MY LITTLE CARD."

Jainu wailed again, and Emery jumped out of his chair. "EMERY WILL BE THE FIRST." Emery reached out as Jainu backed away.

"No! No! Don't touch me! Don't touch me!" He ran out the door, wailing.

"YES! YES! TAKE ME EVERYWHERE! LET ME SEE EVERYONE!"

Jainu stopped a moment and closed his eyes. He continued to run, colliding with objects, searching for a way to get rid of the old man's taunting and laughter.

CHAPTER 19

PRISONERS

*M*aestro jerked his head up at the sound of wailing and immediately wished he hadn't. Searing pain erupted in his head and caused his mouth to water. He swallowed and then grimaced as the lump of spit caused more pain, and he let out a groan. A thick, disgusting film coated his mouth and his stomach burned.

"Jainu, wait! Come back!" Emery's voice called out in desperation. Maestro decided it was time to get up. His legs wobbled, and he lay back down for a few more moments trying to figure out where he was.

The dark stone walls around him showed he was inside the Hunter's Caverns. The black soot all over the rock walls revealed he had been very ill. Emiline would have been in charge. He shook his head as he let his voice rumble inside him. *Emiline Drakner is one very courageous woman,* he mused to himself.

The fight in lower Daton was his last clear memory. He remembered a green vapor, Tiel and Aven talking, and dead bodies in the village square. Other than that, everything was hazy. The emptiness pounded in his brain.

A small shuffle from the front reached Maestro. He tried his legs, and they worked this time. A few moments of pacing got his equilibrium working then he walked in the door. A hallway with two sets of bamboodii doors on either side stretched before him. The hall ended at an open room in which a young girl leaned out of an open doorway. He stepped forward and watched her as she leaned farther out, her head cocked to the right.

The bedrooms smelled like their current occupants. He raised his muzzle towards the first room and determined that the girl's scent lingered there. The crackling hearth fire and dancing shadows on the walls made his eyes itch. He moved silently into the first room and stopped, keeping a distance between him and the girl.

"What are you doing?" Maestro heard his voice bounce in his head and let out a low rumble as the girl faced him. He recognized her at once as Diandra. She smiled as her eyes twinkled at him. He decided he didn't like the look.

"How about answering my question?" Maestro asked, his voice causing the headache to intensify.

The girl shuffled her feet and tried to scratch at her bandaged right ear. She gazed around the room with the same smile and just shrugged her shoulders.

"I am not in a mood for this," he rumbled. He lowered himself and slunk forward. It worked. A wide-eyed fear replaced the twinkle in her eyes. She danced backward and waved her hands in front of her.

"Okay, okay," she wailed as she closed her eyes. Maestro kept his stance but stopped moving towards her. "I was just watching the master bring in a lost love."

"What?"

"Jainu, he's a lost love. The master can now connect and talk to him. It is a great honor which will bring him safely home."

"Girl, they have brainwashed you." Maestro softened his voice as he sat washing his paws. When he looked up, Diandra was staring at him, her hands still in front of her for protection.

"You believe the same as the unpurified called Emery believes?" She squinted her eyes at Maestro and leaned a little forward. Maestro laughed, a move that only now caused a slight headache, but kept washing his paws. He had learned long ago that this ritual calmed humans.

"What does Emery believe?" Maestro purred out.

"That I shouldn't believe anything that the purified have taught me."

"So, that is what they call your brainwashing." Maestro put down his paw and watched her eyes. They wouldn't dilate, a condition caused by sleep chems. Her body swayed. "Why would he tell you that?"

"Because he realized that Lady had instructed me to do everything anybody told me, so he said I had to question anything she had taught me."

"And what will happen if the master found out you disobeyed your orders?" Maestro cocked his head at her. The sharp, pungent scent of fear now enveloped Diandra, and her eyes shifted in her head.

"But, I can't act like the unpurified. I will become one myself."

"Then you will disobey the master," Maestro calmly reminded her. Diandra's body trembled, and she brought her arms in close.

"Tell me, what are lost loves?"

A shrug of the shoulders gave Maestro the information he needed. Someone had brainwashed Diandra into believing everything without questioning. "It seems Emery is wise." Maestro watched Diandra as her body slumped and head drooped.

"Come, you are sleepy," Maestro would let sleep anchor reality into Diandra's consciousness. He cradled her hand in his mouth and led her back to her room. "Open the door." Diandra did, and Maestro led her in. He let her go while keeping his body between her and the door. He pressed his head to her back, guided her around the bed, grabbed the covers with his teeth and pulled them back.

Diandra climbed into bed and pulled up the covers herself. After she had settled down, Maestro laid his body across her midsection. Diandra stirred and looked up at him. Maestro purred, and she closed her eyes. He had often helped Tiel fall asleep like this when she was younger. It had comforted her after nightmares. It worked on Diandra too. She was in a deep sleep within just a few minutes.

Maestro stayed to keep the girl comfortable and used the time to reflect on the previous day, realizing he was right. There was a part of last night he couldn't remember and trying to remember brought on another headache.

"The old man has at least two of the tomes," Tiel explained as she entered the cavern's first room. Maestro purred louder to keep the voices from reaching Diandra. Footsteps moved towards the door just before Tiel peered around the corner.

"Your little guest has been causing trouble," Maestro whispered, at which point Emiline passed Tiel and entered the room.

"I have just one question for you." Tiel inched into the room, her eyes narrowing as she studied him. "What is your name?"

Maestro jerked back at the question and Diandra moved in her sleep. He waited until she settled down again, then spoke. "When I heard you speak about the old man with this child here, I concluded you were too stressed to think. Now, I know you are befuddled since you asked me that question. However, there is no time to debate. I do not remember some of last night, my name is Maestro, and the old man is talking to Jainu." Both women cried out at the last piece of information, only stopping when Diandra moved again. "Apparently causing a lot of stress as I awoke to him wailing outside the inn and Emery chasing after him." Tiel ran out of the room. A cabinet door closed before she rushed out of the apartment.

"She will soon be comfortable enough that I can move. Will you please fill me in on my lost memories from last night?" Maestro asked Emiline.

Emiline smiled and cocked her eyebrow. "Only if you're good and tell me what Diandra told you." She nodded her head and left the room. Maestro rumbled with frustration.

"Tiel decided I needed to help the disabled to keep my mind off my troubles," Anised's voice from behind made Aven jump. He let a low hiss seethe from between his teeth as Anised moved aside the backpacks that Aven was filling with supplies. He placed two plates on the wood table. They held large pieces of cooked fowl, vegetables, and a cream pie made from a gourd. Aven looked at Anised again. "Time for you to eat again, brother."

"Oh, that." Aven put down a rock cylinder he made. "Is it really that important?"

"You normally consume at least two full plates four or five times a day. Food gives you the energy to bash a few things. Eating is the act of putting the food in your mouth, chewing, and swallowing. Your body does the rest."

"Tiel says I'll die without eating."

"As usual brother, Tiel is a brilliant woman," Anised choked as tears formed. "Shaine and I told you that as well when we encountered you outside Sendenia's cave."

"Sorry," Aven whispered and dragged a plate toward him. He picked up the fowl and sniffed at it. "Are both plates for me?"

"No." Anised pulled the other plate over to him and sat down. He picked up the roasted fowl, broke a piece off, and put it into his mouth.

Aven relaxed and followed Anised's example only to have the fowl bounce off his chin and hit his plate. He looked at the meat and felt his face grow hot.

"Do you remember how to drive?"

"What's that?"

"Something you shouldn't do until you get your hand to mouth coordination back," Anised laughed as Aven tried the fowl once again. This time he got it into his mouth and chewed.

"Chew slowly. Enjoy the flavor."

Aven followed the suggestion. The moist, woodsy flavor seeped through with a slight tang of herbs and peppers. He put another piece into his mouth and enjoyed his food.

"Since when do the Dark Sentinels enter the Winged Court's Alcove?" A harsh voice rang out behind them.

"Since he is part of the party hunting the Luhitzu, Elder Hunter," Aven replied without turning around. He picked up a small orange vegetable when Anised cleared his throat. He peered over at him to find Anised holding a little wooden tool with four thin prongs.

"Since when do you eat without utensils, Hunter?" The Elder Hunter slapped Aven's back and kept his hand there.

"Where have you been, Elder Hunter?" Aven inquired, putting down the food.

"Oh, just taking care of business. Can't seem to stop being the Elder Hunter, can we?" The man glared at Aven. "You need to pay attention to your duties instead of interrogating your elders."

"It is my duty to help keep our elders in line and their zahule clean," Aven answered as he straightened his back. "Why are you so defensive? You taught me that principle yourself."

"I didn't realize I was teaching someone who would take it literally," the Elder Hunter patted his back again. "Besides, shouldn't you be keeping your eye on your stellove? This last week has shown she's loose with her oaths…"

Aven stood and stared down the Elder Hunter, who backed away with his hands raised. "See, it is best not to get into anyone else's business. I am just tending to my business, lad, which has been approved by the Laisen." The Elder Hunter turned and passed the pit walking towards the shops in the caverns.

"He says that way too much," Aven murmured, sitting down again, and finding the same utensil Anised had shown him.

"What?" Anised kept his gaze on the back of the Elder Hunter.

"That he is going about his own business." Aven figured out the utensil and speared his vegetables with it. He managed to get the pronged utensil into his mouth and out again. "He taught me that someone who is always about his own business with no explanation is aiming to soil the clan's zahule."

A child's wail echoed through the halls followed by an adult voice yelling. Both hunters jumped up and searched for the source of the commotion. The wail echoed once more as other hunters stopped to look around.

"Jainu, be careful!" Aven recognized Emery's voice and followed the noise from where it originated. The wail sounded again as hunters moved from a circle of tables. Jainu rushed into the side of one and screamed in pain as he hit it. The boy's hands were covering his ears as he limped past the table. Emery was close behind trying to steer Jainu, but the boy batted at Emery's hands with his elbows. He ran again falling over a chair onto his face, never putting his arms out to protect himself. Aven rushed over and picked Jainu up. Blood gushed from his nose, and purple bruises showed on several places. Jainu squeezed his eyes shut. A white cloth appeared in front of Aven, which he took and put it over Jainu's nose.

"Who are you? But no name!" Jainu yelled. "No names, don't say any names."

Aven looked at Emery who just shook his head. Jainu wailed again and fought to get out of Aven's grasp. He held Jainu tight and rocked him, humming a tune he often used to sooth the boy. After a few moments, Jainu settled down and wept.

"He's talking to me. He said my name, and he's talking to me."

"Who is?" Aven slumped into a seat fearing the answer.

"The old man. He knows who I am. He says he can hear everything I can and see everything I can," Jainu clung to Aven and shook his head. "No, no you can't. I won't let you."

"Don't answer him," Aven directed while holding the boy.

"Make him stop. He's laughing. Make him stop."

Aven looked up to see Tiel rushing forward with a crystal test tube. "How does it feel now?" Aven asked as he rocked Jainu.

"He's disappearing," Jainu answered as his breathing calmed down. "He's angry about it too, telling the other voices to turn up the volume."

Tiel bent down and held the tube by Jainu. His breathing slowed, and his weeping shook his body as he finally let his arms drop to his sides.

"He's gone. He's all gone," Jainu sputtered in between gulps of air.

"De Menzaile, Bounty Huntress, Anised." Aven raised his head to find one of the other male Dark Sentinels calling to them. Upon seeing he had the party's attention, the Dark Sentinel continued. "The Laisens are calling a meeting. Chief Del brought in a source that has more information."

"Give us some time," Anised called out as Aven rocked the boy. The Dark Sentinel turned and left.

"Emery," Aven spoke to the man standing above him, "I'll help get Jainu to bed. Just remember, keep that cylinder next to him at all costs."

Emery nodded as Aven picked up Jainu.

MAESTRO DIDN'T KNOW how to describe the sensation in his mouth. He simply didn't know a word that could even compare with what was coating his tongue, cheeks, and every other surface in his mouth. Plus, anything he ate absorbed the wretched flavor. It was like eating some vile creature that bathed in everything at once. He pawed at his muzzle and growled. Emiline placed a large bowl of green tea in front of him.

"I'm sorry, Maestro, that has to be the worst... something," Aven said as he and Tiel leaned over Jainu's sleeping form.

"About the only way to describe it," Maestro laughed. "Tell Adrian no more Luhitzu snacks since he doesn't have enough zahule to stay around to experience the consequences."

"Deal. We can go now. He seems to be sleeping peacefully."

Maestro watched the sleeping boy. Diandra's cylinder lay on the bedside table.

Aven stopped humming to Jainu, and everyone relaxed. Jainu's body had gashes and bruising all over. His nose was twice the average size, but a quick med check revealed it wasn't broken. Everyone slipped out of the room.

"You didn't even try the tea," Tiel commented when they were in the first room.

"That is the fifth bowl," Maestro choked out. "If the other four didn't work, I am sure this one won't help."

"How about trying to burn it out?" Aven suggested. "I had Anised bring something over that may interest you." He left the room and came back with a cylinder made from white rock and cement. It was half as thick as Aven's leg, and the height reached over his knee. A dark, iron handle protruded from the top with an oval-shaped rock attached to one side, which left an opening in the cylinder.

Maestro sniffed at the container. He detected the eye-watering scent of kerosene-soaked rags and jumped back.

"It is an experiment I was working on," Aven explained as Maestro set his gaze on him. "I am building five other cylinders like this one, and they should be valuable after last night. You can melt stone, but it takes arms to do so. So, I made a canister that could hold your fire. I also made sturdy arrows that have stone tips soaked in oil. We could use them against the Luhitzu if you know what I mean."

"Let's do this in the open," Maestro ran out into the caverns. Aven and Tiel kept up with him, and soon Maestro let out a cyclone of fire into the canister.

As tongues of blue flame crackled and leaped out of the canister, Aven produced a thick, cloth glove from a backpack that Tiel had carried with her. He put it on his right hand. Over that, he put on a gray metal gauntlet with more cloth attached to the inside. He twisted the canister's handle, which lowered the oval-shaped stone into place and closed the canister.

Maestro felt the heat from the canister as Aven jumped back and slapped at a smoking part of his pants.

"Looks like you must take more precautions," Tiel observed.

"Are you sure this 'Adrian' didn't tell you anything?" Maestro probed as he licked his chops. His mouth felt better now that there was less slime. But he still didn't like it, not the slime and not this 'Adrian' character. Both caused him to gag, threatening to vomit the fire liquid from inside.

Aven and Tiel nodded their heads.

"I will try to burn it out." Maestro turned from his friends and trotted outside. His mind raced faster than he was trotting. He didn't like Adrian's self-hatred that burned too hot to ignore.

"I DIDN'T LIKE that knife at all," Quartney commented while sitting at the table in the guest caverns. Tiel and Aven sat across from her and Chief Del. Anised and the Laisens sat in chairs lining the walls.

"A lot of hunters aren't happy with their choice of knives," Tiel smirked.

"That is true. How a Hunter's Heart is chosen doesn't help," Quartney smirked herself. "I seemed to recall putting my hand into the Heart Stone and thinking the knife had jumped into it."

"Not me," Tiel reminisced, "I seemed the Heart I went for kept moving away."

"Each has their own stories," Quartney sighed. "However, I know this sounds unrealistic, but I could swear my knife liked to bite me. I could swear it preferred the taste of blood."

Tiel just gaped at the older woman.

"Do you have medics?" Quartney asked Tiel.

"Yes."

"Do you think they can also see about healing this?" Quartney pulled up her shirt to show three wounds, yellow ooze bubbling out of each. A white powder lay on top and around each wound. The antiseptic scent barely masked the ooze's foul order.

"Where did you get that, Elder?" Mistress Laisen inquired.

"From the knife. These are just some of the places where it bit me." Quartney kept her eyes on Tiel. "It was as if it came alive after I nicked myself for the first time. After that, I heard faint voices sometimes. The male is always moaning. The female is hateful. She always taunted someone named Jonaxx." Quartney put her shirt down and stared into the fireplace. The canister with Maestro's fire sat in the middle, the heat warming the room. The rocks dripped a dirty white-gray liquid.

"Is that how you found out about the tomes? Keidera taunted Jonaxx about them?" Tiel questioned.

"Yes," Quartney said relaxing, "she let it slip several times that the tomes held the design for that knife."

"Are you sure she did not intend to let that information 'slip'?" Chief Del probed. Quartney thought for a moment, then just shrugged her shoulders while letting out a sigh.

"How did you know Kerlar Xenchen had the tomes?"

"By accident, I assure you." Quartney rapped her fingers on the table. The lack of rhythm echoed in the room. "After I left the clan, I went to learn a trade. Your dear kerlar was a teacher at the school. She carried the tomes with her. The female Luhitzu got excited and loud every time the kerlar came around with those tomes." Quartney hugged herself and shivered. "I don't think she could see through my eyes, but it was like she could. She never got so passionate before or since the kerlar and her tomes disappeared."

"Did Keidera ever say why she wanted the knife?" Aven leaned forward and touched the woman's elbow.

"Only that she wanted her 'lover's gift' back," Quartney replied shivering, "although I don't know what kind of lover she would have. Wouldn't want to meet him. For a while, I thought it could be the male moaner. But, after what I learned, I've dismissed that idea."

"Quartney, do you remember what your departed Hunter's Heart looks like?" Tiel asked.

"Yes, but all anyone would have to do is follow their nose," she answered. "The wounds' odor is of decayed flesh, and it's eye-watering at times. Any huntress who has that knife will have an awful stench. That is why I know no one in here owns it."

"Will you help us look for it?" Master Laisen's voice broke in.

"If someone handles the knives, you bet I will." Quartney shivered and gazed into the fireplace. "I don't know how it will help, but if it can, I am all for it."

CHAPTER 20

THE MAD KING

*T*he soil on the sides of the long, curved furrow wouldn't budge under the pressure of Tiel's Hunter's Heart. The length was short, and Anised had spotted another furrow like it a few yards away. Aven put down the rock cylinder which held Maestro's flame and backed away. He now wore a gray, insulated jumper suit which still smoked from the heat. The four Dark Sentinels had steel bows and arrows strapped to their backs. Maestro paced behind the group, growling as the group covered their noses to keep out the overpowering stench from masses of rotting black skin on the surrounding branches.

"Track is fresh, but he's backtracked before. It looks like Keidera doesn't leave tracks." Tiel looked back at Maestro who kept growling to himself. "Maestro, you acted that way last night in Daton's town square. What's wrong?"

"I do not know. It is hard to stay 'conscious,'" Maestro growled as he pawed at his nose.

"More than likely His Majesty Prince Adrian wants to make an appearance. You may have no choice but to let him come," she suggested.

"What if he is untrustworthy?" Maestro's voice resonated around the forest.

"I would rather find out sooner than later," Aven called back. Tiel nodded her head in agreement. Maestro let out a sigh, jerked his head and chewed on the side of his mouth and then collapsed.

"I can't sense Jonaxx or the twins," Tiel exhaled as she watched Maestro's form breathe steadily, "and I hear nothing." She used her arm to wipe the remnants of soil from her blade. The handle sloshed with a replenished supply of clear poison. The teeth crushed the dirt as she ran the knife along her arm in both directions without nicking herself. She laughed at her unsubstantiated fears.

"I'm surprised you took that long to check it out," one huntress called across the clearing. "Since I heard Quartney's story, I have already checked my Hunter's Heart twice." As the group chuckled, the other huntress raised three fingers in the air.

"I waited as long as I could. It was driving me crazy even though I had no problems with unhealed wounds," Tiel admitted.

"Put that knife away before the twins arrive," Maestro's voice boomed from behind her. "It will cause more problems than you're ready to deal with."

Tiel looked to find the cat standing at attention, his ears straight up, tail switching.

"Prince Adrian, I presume."

"Yes, but that does not matter now. The twins and Jonaxx are close."

"I can't hear anything..." A hunter said just as a shrill scream and cursing filled the air east of the group. There was quiet for a few moments until a loud hiss mingled with moans resonated through the trees.

"Put that thing away, hurry!" Adrian nosed Tiel's hand. Aven touched her arm and nodded. Tiel shrugged her shoulders and sheathed her Hunter's Heart as louder moans filled the air, causing an ache in her soul.

"It's interesting that I can't sense them." Tiel searched the surrounding forest. Crashing noises became amplified. Trees and bushes swayed as if a great weight passed near. Moaning and cursing broke through the ruckus at irregular intervals. She searched telepathically but could see no soul currents.

"Their minds are stronger than yours. You won't be able to sense anything until they're next to you. I don't understand why you think engaging these two is a good idea. But I'll deal with what you have given me," Adrian said. He moved his head around as if considering the forest's interior.

"We are trying to save people from Jonaxx's rampage," Anised called out as he joined the now assembling group. The forest's lower plant life, a few paces away, trembled as Tiel thought she spied a long black cylindrical object move among the trees.

"So, what is the plan?" Adrian asked as the screaming voice wretched out desperate chords. Tiel saw him position himself between them and the sounds that came closer. A watosh shuddered in the distance, and a sharp hiss cried out.

"To talk some sense into him, after getting his attention," Tiel muttered.

"I can help with the twins," Adrian replied, "but Jonaxx is The Sacred Guardian of Coulliou. I will not hurt him."

Suddenly, Keidera burst out of the tall hedge to Tiel's left and cursed obscenities at the forest. Tiel refused to breathe as a fetid smell assailed her nose. The woman's once sheer green dress was now muddy and tattered. Jagged, open lesions with the putrid, yellow ooze stretched at her skin. Her yellow hair lay in strings around her face.

Strong, black, soul currents, surged through the air from Keidera, pushing on Tiel, causing her to stumble. Their edges spilled out, leaving traces of mists that seeped out the Luhitzu's emotions.

"Her soul currents are dark and more like rivers," Tiel whispered to Aven. He glanced at her out of the corner of his eye. "They combine into cords. Some are stronger and thicker than others, they all connect to something beyond the bushes."

Keidera spun around at the sound of Tiel's voice and sneered at the company, showing broken teeth. A purple bruise covered the right upper quarter of her face. "Move!!!!" She commanded, and the group parted. The cords coming from Keidera tightened, their edges almost disappearing as she ran past the group. The cords relaxed as a broad shadow appeared over Tiel. A black snake's head arched, its hood outstretched around it. Cylindrical body segments flecked with open infected wounds flew by. The stench subdued Tiel, and she dropped to one knee. Pieces of infected skin fell around her, and white maggots squirmed on the edges emphasizing the retching sounds from the other hunters.

"Move!!!" Adrian's voice roared just before Aven's body landed on her, throwing her to the ground. Seconds later Jonaxx's arched body plummeted to the ground, zigzagging aimlessly. Tiel's body jumped with the subsequent tremors. Her failed, hysterical attempts to grab at something left her bereft of any anchor, and she bounced uncontrollably, Sharp jabs of pain exploded in her body each time she hit the ground.

"Nice save, Adrian. Thanks," Aven coughed. Tiel searched around herself as she lay on the ground taking an inventory of her body parts.

"Anybody want to go home," Tiel whispered to herself. Aven's hand appeared in front of her face. She took it and used his strength to rise to her feet.

"Everyone, get a hold of yourselves. This is all part of the hunt," Aven coughed out as the last of Jonaxx's tail disappeared into the forest. "Where is everybody?"

One huntress came from behind a watosh and pointed towards the forest. The entrails of a body lay smeared across the forest floor. Blood pooled in Jonaxx's track. Another huntress along with a hunter appeared from behind a different watosh.

"Anised, where are you?" Tiel called out, forcing her stomach to stay calm as her tears flowed. Aven staggered over to the rolling rock cylinder that held the white fire. Anised stood up, having examined the body of the lost Dark Sentinel. He wiped his mouth with his sleeve and nodded. The other hunter grabbed the now collapsing huntress and carried her out of the clearing with the last huntress following.

Adrian rumbled a little as a vapor form rolled into the clearing. Despair leaked out, and Tiel had to take slow, deep breaths to control the sudden onslaught of emotion. A dark, tenuous, ethereal cord flexed between tense and lax as he floated forward.

A tunnel of blue flame encircled the vapor, and Kehir screamed in pain. The despair disappeared. "Let me live! Let me live until I achieve my desire!" he screamed out his pleas.

"What do you desire?" Tiel called out as she waved for Adrian to stop.

"Move on my other side, Kehir," Adrian moved around, and Kehir floated to the opposite edge of the clearing.

"Yes, My Most Honorable Prince," Kehir sneered as he bowed. Adrian growled back, showing his teeth.

"In Coulliou's name, stop it both of you," Tiel's voice rose as she watched the shape of Jonaxx's head dart among the forest trees. She no longer sensed the previous cords. "We don't have time."

"You do things in Coulliou's name and curse it at the same time," Kehir snarled at her.

"Speaking something such as that when you do not understand is not wise." Adrian agreed with Kehir, a snarl also appearing on his face.

Tiel jerked her head towards the cat and then let the remark go unanswered. "What do you desire, Kehir?"

"The complete destruction of my sister. It is my only reason to exist."

"But you are doing nothing, just floating along," Aven retorted, walking up to the form while staying behind Adrian.

"I can do nothing at this point. Coulliou connected my life energy to my sister's, just as I connected it to her through my deeds in life. I cannot escape her."

"So how are you able to see to her destruction?" Tiel questioned Kehir.

"If I convinced someone to plunge her lover's Heart into Jonaxx's first wound to heal him, it would be a start. However, so far I have not found the right group to take care of my business." Kehir turned and regarded the hunters. "Yet, maybe I have. This is our second meeting, right?"

Another of Keidera's screams pierced the air as her body flew across the clearing and hit a watosh. She stayed suspended for a moment as breath escaped her lips, then she fell facing the ground. The telepathic cords around her went limp and dropped to the ground. Their forms thinned allowing Tiel to see several beads of thoughts that zipped back and forth along the chords.

Jonaxx darted into the clearing once again, his head switching back and forth with the curves of his body. Keidera's telepathic chords melded into his head, and a blur of beads rushed in. He hissed at the group and lunged towards Tiel. His large snout moved in as his tongue flickered in and out. Tiel dashed to the right just as Aven's rock cylinder arched into the air towards Jonaxx.

"No!!" Adrian roared and leaped past the oncoming snake towards Aven, his claws and teeth bared. Tiel grabbed the cat's two back feet as he passed over her, and she lunged to the right, which altered his arch. Aven ducked, and Adrian fell on his side. The canister hit Jonaxx behind his outstretched hood. Blue flame leaped up Jonaxx's side, and he squirmed in agony as the black cords grew thinner.

"Does that help to clear your mind, dear King?" Aven called out as Adrian rose again.

"Look what you did! That welt will soon turn," Adrian protested.

"It does not matter," a hissing voice sounded above, "I'll get more wounds just from scratching myself. It is part of the curse and does not matter where they come from anymore."

"What were you doing?" Tiel slugged Adrian on the shoulder. The cat jumped back while looking away. "When you're with the hunters, you are working with them."

"Stay where you are, Anised!!" Tiel looked to where Adrian focused. His roar had stopped the hunter in his tracks. Anised turned, his Hunter's Heart in his hand.

"I kill her. I save Shaine." He turned back. "Now is the time to strike."

"You will only wake her, and your Shaine will still be a prisoner," Adrian's soft rumble penetrated the forest. Tiel watched Anised slow. His hand went limp and hung motionless. "In time, when I have what I need, I will free your Shaine."

"Maestro keeps his promises," Anised eyeballed the cat, his eyes narrowed. "Yet, Prince Adrian attacks his comrades behind their backs and lets them die." The cat lowered his head.

"This Luhitzu has slept long," Jonaxx hissed back. "He is wallowing in confusion and self-hate, preferring hiding instead of *living*." Jonaxx's tongue stretched out before him as he hissed the last word with emphasis. "He no longer has any allegiances except to his pain."

"What do you mean? *That* is Luhitzu," Tiel waved pointing to Kehir and Keidera.

"What, my Prince," the fog rolled out of the Kehir's mouth as he laughed, "you have not told them everything?"

"Keep it up, and I will make sure I consume you."

"Just so you can keep your secrets, a good choice."

Adrian roared, and Jonaxx shook his head as a loud hiss erupted. "Please, too much pain. Keidera is sleeping. Let my mind be free while it can. It will only last a few moments."

All eyes turned to Jonaxx. His body relaxed, and he allowed his head to

slump a little. Tiel studied the ethereal cords around him. Their hazy forms
swirled with currents and thought beads that bounced back and forth
between Keidera and Jonaxx. One cord was compact and perfectly round. It
traveled from Keidera's torso and into Kehir's torso. No thought beads
passed through those currents.

"The quiet is precious," Jonaxx explained to the group. "Why are you
here? There is a reason you have come."

"Your chase of the twins has caused great harm. We were hoping we
could talk you into leaving the chase, maybe go sleep somewhere." Tiel
pleaded as she stepped next to Jonaxx's large snout.

Jonaxx turned away as he contemplated Tiel's plea.

"That is not wise. If I am chasing Keidera, it will keep her from doing
more harm. But I see your point. Her voice drives me mad, and I cannot
control myself." Tiel moved a soul current close to the cords. She sensed
anger, hate, despair, and a faint glimmer of hope. She gasped in shock as she
realized the hope came from Jonaxx.

"Keidera. You're not after Kehir?" Anised asked, his hand clutched his
Hunter's Heart.

"No, Kehir follows."

"*Stellove, I might be able to help Jonaxx,*" Tiel telepathically called to Aven.

"*How?*" He answered immediately.

"Why do you follow?" Tiel voiced to the apparition. Aven nodded his
understanding that she wanted to keep track of the group's discussion.

"Perhaps you would like to share in my agony," Kehir raised his hand, a
black current issued forth from him. "My emotions are powerful." Blue fire
enveloped the vapor as arrows shot through. Kehir's screams vanished as
the fire subsided. Tiel turned to see Aven with an empty bow. He kicked the
almost indistinguishable rock cylinder to the front.

"*The cords I mentioned earlier are attached to Jonaxx. I can possibly sever some
of the weakest. But...*" Tiel continued her telepathic conversation with Aven.
She also listened to the discussion in the clearing.

"Aven's invention, no matter how crude, is working, Kehir," Adrian
rumbled. "Think how horrible it will be if we both attack."

"*But what?*" Aven did nothing to hide the frustration coming through his
thoughts.

"Kehir," Jonaxx hissed, "cooperate. It can be the start of your redemption."

"But it would be painful. Her emotions are strong, even while asleep. Maybe if I can sever some of the weakest cords, it can help lessen her hold on Jonaxx. Do you think it's worth it?" Tiel peered at Aven. His focus was on the ground as he rubbed his chin with his forefinger. Tiel waited patiently and listened to the discussion.

"I am bound to my sister," Kehir bowed toward the group as he flowed backward.

"No, Coulliou bound you to each other," Jonaxx corrected. Kehir considered the snake's words. After a few moments, he nodded his head in agreement.

"Yes, we are bound together. We cannot be apart too great a distance, or there is great pain." Kehir's shoulders slumped. "I follow because I can do no more. I follow and dream of the pain I could bring my sister for her treachery towards me…"

"Do it but be careful. It may give Jonaxx the needed strength of mind to keep these two in the Watosh. That will help keep Ecalardia safe while we search for the mysterious knife," Aven consented, though Tiel felt a wave of unease pulsate towards her.

"Enough, your sister will not sleep long." Jonaxx interrupted the discussion. "You can keep her in one place, yes?"

"The pain would be too great."

"Let me remind you of real pain," Adrian growled as Anised tightened his bowstring and lowered his arrow towards the canister.

"No, no. My existence keeps my sister bound."

Tiel released herself from Aven's mind to protect him. She took her telepathic current and wrapped it up into a thick cord, like the ones connecting Jonaxx, Kehir, and Keidera. Yet, her current was nowhere near the size nor strength of their cords.

"You are just following your sister," Aven scowled at Kehir. "You are doing nothing to keep her bound. People have died when your group has strayed to the forest's edge. Some have died from your moaning and despair."

"Do you not crave redemption?" Jonaxx asked again.

"Redemption? Coulliou will redeem these two?" Tiel thought to herself as she thinned out the end of her current, so that it resembled a blade. *"Oh well, even the smallest knife can cut and injure if used properly."* She reasoned while inching her current towards the black cords, piercing Aven's shield first. She looked at him. He stood straight up, paying attention to the discussion. He showed nothing that would give away what she intended on the telepathic plane.

"More than likely I have given up on redemption," Kehir moaned his answer to Jonaxx. "When will you use Keidera's Lover's Heart to heal Jonaxx? It is not prudent for us to die until that happens." He explained to the hunters.

"We are planning on destroying that knife to keep it from Keidera," Aven replied as he shook his head.

Kehir laughed. Jonaxx coiled his body and hung his head over the side.

"Keidera wants the knife so she can heal herself from time to time. If you destroy it, it will anger her to know she cannot live in a beautiful body. However, soon she would own Jonaxx's mind, and we would no longer just 'stray to the forest's edge.'"

"Great," Tiel voiced as she moved her current slowly closer. She checked on Aven whose face had become a queasy shade of gray. She heard Anised suck in his breath.

Tiel attempted a smile but failed. Her current was getting closer allowing her to sense Keidera's emotions.

"You have not yet found the knife," Kehir laughed. "If you destroy it, there will be no reason for me to help you."

"Kehir," Adrian growled.

Jonaxx relaxed further, the black cords thinned out even more. The beads of emotion and thought slowed their movements. Tiel moved her current closer to what seemed to be the weakest cord. She watched Aven. He crossed his arms in front of him, but he stayed quiet. She turned back and sliced the chosen chord as beads of anger traveled towards her. She sliced quickly before they could connect with her mind.

"Leave him be, Prince." Jonaxx interrupted the discussion. "You have no right to make demands." His coil shifted to show a large smear of fresh blood. "I ask you, Luhitzu, which do you think is worse for me? The pain I already suffer, or the knowledge I have killed someone. Next time, use your

helping Aven up. "The poison and the healing are in the knife's programming," Tiel watched Kehir turn as his sister stirred. "Find where the Empress placed her storyboards." Kehir floated towards his sister as she rose.

"What? She died over three centuries ago," Anised objected.

"The knowledge you need is recorded on them. You'll find it at Jaiden's Wash where she and her maids used to bathe."

Tiel watched as Keidera rose. Her bruise was gone, and her skin appeared fresher, except for the infected wounds. Keidera glared at the group, and air seethed between her teeth.

"Stop!!! I can't," Anised yelled holding his head, letting his Hunter's Heart drop to the ground. Jonaxx hit Keidera with his tail. Her body flew far into the forest, out of view. The leftover cords became rigid. Jonaxx hissed and darted after her. Kehir moaned as his cord tightened. His form jerked from the strain as he turned to Tiel.

"Get the storyboard," he screamed as the cord pulled his form backward. "Go to Jaiden's Wash," Kehir screamed once again as Tiel doubled over with pain that had erupted in her midsection.

"Did you sever any of the cords?" Aven hissed between his teeth.

"Yes, three or four. I was trying to go for a stronger one." Aven tilted his head at her answer. "I should have quit or not even tried. There's no way to know if I helped." Tiel shed tears as she realized how much strain she could have put on their relationship, how she hurt Aven.

"Well, now we know it will affect both of us," Aven's voice grew softer even though his teeth were still clenched as he held his torso with one arm.

"Yes, but Kehir is right. I don't know enough about these situations to make much of a difference," Tiel admitted. "Kehir's hold was strong. I don't know if I can handle anything like that again."

Aven took a deep breath. "Anything may help. But we should be careful. The good news is that you and Maestro know where Jaiden's Wash is at," Aven croaked out.

"What?" Tiel looked at him as she rubbed her midsection, raw emotions still ebbed inside her. She decided she didn't like it. It wasn't like her to take such chances.

"Didn't Queen Sendenia say you stayed the night at a place called Jaiden's Wash, along with the Delegate's children we rescued?"

"Great," Both Tiel and Adrian said. Tiel averted her face from Aven's furrowed brows.

"If I remember right, taking on Emiline is Maestro's job," Adrian yawned and sunk into unconsciousness.

"What?" Tiel yelled at the sleeping form. "I have questions I want answered."

"Anised, are you all right?" Aven held out his hand to the Dark Sentinel doubled over on the ground as Tiel half-heartedly kicked the sleeping cat.

"I heard Shaine weeping, pleading for my help," Anised's voice choked. "It was deep down in my soul. She hates what is being done to her body. She wouldn't stop wailing."

"I am sorry," Tiel said forgetting Maestro and watched Aven help Anised to his feet. "Is it over with now?"

"For now," Anised nodded and shook his body. Sweat stains covered his black outfit.

"What did you mean by great?" Aven questioned her. She opened her mouth to answer only to be interrupted by the call of a wild bird.

"That sounded like the same hawk from last night," Anised announced. "I'll investigate."

"Can I get an answer?" Tiel turned back at the sound of Aven's voice.

"Yes, Maestro and I are in trouble with Ma," Aven raised his eyebrows at her answer. "We possibly found and dug out the storyboards already." A smirk appeared on Aven's upper right lip. "What makes it worse is Pa could have already been studying them, possibly even have the answer."

"Hey, someone just happened to leave a large cart that can carry Maestro back to our transports," Anised's voice called out.

"Gee, that's fortunate," Tiel mocked as she walked out of the clearing.

CHAPTER 21

HOPE AND DESPAIR

The little mirror hid more than it showed. Sure, she could apply her lipstick with no problem, but she preferred to see the overall picture. After all, Fallon was a tough customer. She needed to look her best. Jenn searched down the stairs and on the walls. Lizard was gone. She smirked into the mirror before putting it away into the handbag that matched her yellow and black dress and thin black sandals. She fanned her neck and took a whiff. *"Not too heavy or too light. It'll do."*

"The more time you spend primping, the less time you'll have for our little story," a weak grating voice echoed from below.

"Fallon?" Jenn started down the stairs, all made of cement mixed with stone. A warm burst of air hit her as she arrived at the bottom. She peered in and paused. Pieces of furniture lay strewn all over the floor, pages of books littered the area. Lizard's sliding string was split in half. Both parts were a wispy string fluttering in the breeze from the heating ducts.

"Careful where you step, especially if you're in heels." The grating voice came from her right. She saw Fallon's head over the back of his chair. His desk was whole, but the holo screen on the wall was shredded. She searched again for Lizard and decided that it was safe. Her foot hung in midair, turning until she used her toe to push debris out of the way.

"You could clear a path, especially since you invited me." Fallon ignored her reasoning through silence. "I just may turn around and come back when it's safer."

She stopped as a hissing echoed behind her and she looked back to find Lizard sticking her snout out of a small hole in the wall.

"Lizard will not come out." Fallon's voice grated with heavy breaths. "I terrify her."

"Why?" Jenn questioned. "Fallon, are you okay? Hurting her is so unlike you."

"I have not hurt her."

"Fallon, did the Dark... people return?" The question added weight to the surroundings. "Did you upset them?"

"The Dark Sentinels, de Menzaile, The Bounty Huntress. Their images have all made appearances along with the 'Golden Plant,'" he chuckled. "The worst is when an acodoe hisses at me from my screen over the desk."

"What?" Jenn only now realized that his breath came in labored gasps. His head lolled on the back of the chair.

"It's ironic. You're the only person I can trust." Fallon's shoulders shook as he sobbed, only stopping when he gasped for air.

"Fallon!" Jenn walked to him and rotated the chair around only to scream. His misshapen face showed severe bruising, and his chest inflated between grimaces. His tattered clothes revealed more bruising and swelling. His left arm, broken, protruded at an unnatural angle.

"We need to get you to the medics!" Jenn twirled around looking for a holo screen and stamped her foot when she remembered Fallon destroyed it. "How did you get a hold of me?"

"Listen," he said. Jenn ignored Fallon as she searched the basement. "Listen," he pleaded again, grabbing her arm. She stumbled in his direction, almost twisting an ankle as his dead weight pulled on her arm. "The Dark Sentinels fix made my mind worse. I need your help with a story. The citizens of Ecalardia need to know... things."

She put his face into her hands, and he let his arm fall into his lap. "You said I was the only one you could trust. Now trust me." Fallon's subsequent sobs were short bursts interrupted by a low moaning as Jenn reasoned with him. "I'll let you tell me everything while we wait for the medic transport, all right?"

Fallon nodded his head in agreement.

A DEEP-SLEEP RUMBLE sounded from the back where Tiel watched Maestro's form inflate and deflate. Aven watched the holo screen image on the windshield. Sarje was on auto drive, so Tiel was free to move and gaze out the windows.

The barren, brown landscape streaked by while the points of the red Watosh Mountain Range crept towards them. The mountain's main body grew to where she could now see the dense Watosh Forest adorning its side. Somewhere amid that mountain range were the Hunters' Caverns.

"Have those emotions disappeared yet?" Tiel asked Aven. His features were soft again. His muscular body shifted every so often as he fought to get comfortable.

"Yes, finally," Aven answered. "What emotion did Kehir use on you?

Tiel shifted her gaze to the window again as voices from the screen failed to fill the emptiness inside Sarje. "You don't want to know."

"I already do. It filled me also," Aven replied. "Those weren't our emotions."

"I agree. It was just too easy for Kehir to change them." Tiel turned back to him. "I hated doing that to others, and it hurt me. It was so easy for him to do it."

"Let's change the subject," Aven suggested.

"All right. You're frustrated that you don't remember how to drive." Tiel watched his face as he chuckled a little and peered sideways at her. "Your shield is cracking again. It's pathetic and cute when that happens."

"Enraged is more like it." Aven shifted once more as he drummed his fingers on his leg. "I remember driving. I remember that it quieted the voices in my head, permitting my mind to work on problems."

"Is that a male thing?" Tiel questioned. Aven just shrugged his shoulders. The ground continued to race by as scattered shrubbery came into view every so often.

"I'm sorry, stellove. Everything is different." Aven sighed and leaned back in the seat. "It's bad enough when you don't remember something. It's like living in a dream, and I kept telling myself, 'this part of me will soon wake up.' However, knowing I was supposed to do something and not remembering how just made the whole situation *tangible, real...*" He pronounced the last two words between clenched teeth.

"I want to help you," Tiel whispered as she grabbed his hand lying by her side. "I wish I could fix everything."

"Stellove, just accepting comforts me." He squeezed her hand. "Now, why don't you tell me what is really bothering you?"

"Well, it's not the old man. He has been strangely quiet. There's not even a background buzz."

"So, what is it?" Aven prodded.

"It's the prophecies. We possibly just met the Mad King."

"Possibly?" Aven laughed, "When are you going to admit what is happening?"

"I loathe being part of something I had decided was a fantasy," Tiel said as she laughed along with Aven.

"I know you believe in Coulliou."

"Yeah, I do. I just thought no one knew his mind." Tiel shrugged her shoulders. "None of the prophecies ever harmonized with each other. So, how could they be true?"

"I always thought they were all part of a whole." Aven leaned on his fist while his elbow rested on the door. "Coulliou wanted to give something to keep us from being bored. So, he created a mystery."

"Yeah, now we are in the middle of that mystery."

"Great place to be. We've got something to do."

"Maybe not so great, when the prophecies come true," Tiel countered.

"With the prophecies, there will come answers. We already have one key packed in the trunk of this vehicle."

"Humm." Tiel gazed out the window once again. "Now all we have to do is find Quartney's old knife."

"That will give us a lot of excitement." Aven leaned forward and gave her a small kiss. Tiel ruffled his hair and returned it.

"This is Master News Anchor Rand Belfast coming to you with a developing story. My source behind the news orbs is with Fallon Hanover outside his home." A man with short, clipped, black hair and a slight suntan appeared on the screen. "Let's turn to our informant, Jenn Ondin."

"Thank you, Rand. Today, General Jack ManCane of the Peace Enforcers will walk a very thorny path. His favorite darling, The Bounty Huntress, has soiled his zahule beyond recognition." Tiel gasped as Jenn's voice carried through Sarje's cab. A swollen and bruised Fallon was being carried from his home on a stretcher behind her. A corner of a green medic transport showed on the screen. "In an act of sedition, The Bounty Huntress used her telepathy to alter the truth about events surrounding the rescue of the delegate's children."

"Sedition? That is a strong word." Rand's voice overrode Jenn's voice.

"The Bounty Huntress used a telepathic technique called a 'Mind-Over-Lay' to alter Fallon Hanover's memory of the events, possibly to hide that de Menzaile is not her rival, but her lover." Jenn waited a moment to let this information sink in. Aven's exasperated breath echoed in Tiel's ear. She realized that her trembling hand was over her mouth. "She also wanted to hide the truth about the acodoe queen's attack of de Menzaile. One will have to ask if Councilwoman Hegert has been right all along about The Bounty Huntress' temper and her soiled zahule."

"What? Are you sure?" Rand's voice faltered a little.

"I am not only sure of it; I witnessed an event a few days ago, where some bounty hunters, called the Dark Sentinels, came to fix this 'Mind-Over-Lay.' It failed as you can see. He is now seeing images of de Menzaile, The Bounty Huntress, and acodoe attacking him. He thinks he's defending himself, but he only harms himself. The results are disastrous. He has several injuries including a broken arm. Plus, there are concerns about lung damage.

"What does de Menzaile say about this? Was he there when The Bounty Huntress performed the 'Mind-Over-Lay'?" Rand inquired.

"No, he was not there. However, he is protecting her," Jenn answered. "He and the entire Hunter Clan are protecting her and refusing to turn her into the authorities. Not only that, but they are in league with the queen concerning the renegade acodoe attacking our villages."

"What?" The holo screen's image turned fuzzy for a moment as Tiel's head swam and her stomach churned.

"Those medics… they are hunters." Aven pointed at the screen.

Tiel looked at the spot his finger touched. "Yes, the Crimson Twins."

"Fallon will be in our care. But it may not be a good thing."

"No, it will bring the clan a lot of trouble."

"Yes. It will." Aven pointed his finger at her. "It will also increase the public's distrust of you and me." She watched Aven's eyes wander for a moment. "Aren't the Crimson Twins part of the Elder Hunter's inner circle?"

"Yes," Tiel answered, "in fact, they are up for the next two empty slots in the Winged Court. Why?"

"This obstacle on Shea's paths reeks of the Elder Hunter." Aven stared out the window. "He was absent after the meeting with the acodoe queen which means he's planning something. I don't like to wait for someone to strike."

"Neither do I," Tiel agreed. "But I'm afraid we must wait to find which fate we meet on Shea's path." Tiel threw her hands up in resignation.

"He'll end up hurting others." Aven continued, "You are at the top of his list. Why?"

"Possibly because I turned him down."

"What? When?" Aven bumped his head on the roof and winced as he rubbed it.

"When I was fifteen. The Elder Hunter approached me and offered to train me for the Winged Court. My trainer had always taught me to take responsibility for my education. So, I talked with the older, experienced initiates instead and learned how to apply for the Winged Court. I studied and applied for the position in front of the Laisens.

"The Elder Hunter had kept up his 'invitations' for lack of a better word." Aven interjected a grunt, stopping Tiel. He waved his hand signaling her to go on. She continued. "He was always more interested in my telepathy than I liked. When it became obvious I would gain entrance into the Winged Court legally; he became irate. He's been shadowing my paths ever since."

"I think it got worse when we became united," Aven suggested. "Remember when he tried to hack into Sarje's programming?"

"You remember that?" Tiel laughed. Soon Aven joined in until Tiel's laughter stopped.

"Kehir said the poison and antidote were part of the knife's *programming*," Tiel murmured as she thought.

Aven's eyes opened wide at her implication. "Do you think the knife is programmed, as in computer programming?" he asked.

"It's possible," she replied shrugging her shoulders. "Hopefully the story-boards will enlighten our paths."

"Breaking news from the Peace Enforcers," Rand Belfast's voice disturbed the calm that their conversation had created. Tiel and Aven paid attention. "General Jack ManCane has an announcement concerning the allegations against The Bounty Huntress. We take you to the news orbs on-site at Peace Enforcer Headquarters."

A crowd of news masters stood in front of a large, white-granite podium in a lush garden. The Peace Enforcers' Headquarters, constructed of the same white granite, towered in the back. Three men and four women dressed in the uniforms of a general stood around the podium. General ManCane stood in front, a frown dominating his features and creasing his forehead with fury.

"I am here about the allegations against The Bounty Huntress..." General ManCane addressed the crowd. His voice resonated with authority, dispelling all hopes of questions being answered. "... along with Fallon Hanover's condition, the same victim who generated these allegations. We of the Generals High Court find it necessary to examine these allegations against The Bounty Huntress."

General ManCane's eyes seared through the news orbs as his voice surged with disappointment. "I, myself, have vouched many times for the character of The Bounty Huntress and the Hunter Clan. I trusted that my travels with them on Shea's paths was brilliantly illuminated and would only whiten my zahule." General ManCane returned to the crowd. "We will perform a thorough inquiry concerning this, and we will take appropriate measures to rectify this tragedy." The general turned, parted the line of his peers, and walked out of the garden.

"HOW ARE YOU DOING, TIEL?" Emiline's voice echoed through the front entrance of the caverns as she and Emery greeted the trio entering Jacquard's. The bar echoed with emptiness. Maestro moaned as he wobbled behind. "What has happened to Maestro?"

"He's waking up. We had another audience with Prince Adrian," Aven answered, stopping Emiline in her tracks. "And no, she is not doing well."

"There is nothing that the Generals High Council can do after the chastisement from Jack," Tiel exclaimed stopping a short distance from the Drakners.

"I know it hurts, but he left room for an explanation." Emery smiled as he stood behind Emiline.

"Let's hope he is willing to travel along Shea's path with the Hunter Clan long enough to see that path clearly." Aven placed his hand on Emiline's shoulder. "However, Tiel is in no mood to receive another lashing. Please listen to her story."

Half an arm later, all eight pieces of the storyboard lay on a plastic table in the Winged Court's Alcove. Each piece of stone had painted pictures etched into them. The colors were muted but still easily seen. The same tall and elegant dark woman was painted onto each stone with different pictures swirling around her. A hawk rested on her lax fist while a wild dog stood at her left side, its hind end disappearing behind her.

Emiline had kept quiet while helping her excited husband gather up what he needed to clean the stones. Tiel had watched Emery stir the cleansing agents together in a small bowl, observing the swirl as the agents combined. After the concoction had turned a bright yellow, he used the thick painter's brush he had ordered and had covered the stones with the fluid. Maestro had stayed out of the way by lounging near the pit, the lapse of time growing between each yawn.

Tiel stood next to Aven on the other side of the table and followed his gaze. He appeared to be studying the top of the storyboards. Two thin, steel rods lined the top of the stone lengthwise, with some gaps in between the rods.

"What is it?" Tiel leaned over and whispered to Aven.

"Well," Aven said as he kept his eyes on the storyboards, "at first, I wondered whether the rods were destroyed. But they all have the same pattern. The top rods have the same three gaps while the bottom rods have five gaps." Aven shifted his weight and scrutinized the tablets for a few more moments. "But see, on the right end of the top rods there are notches, but the fourth tablet's rod has one notch. The end over there has four notches." Aven straightened up and moved his head side to side while waving his finger. "There is an order to these storyboards." Aven wasted no time showing Emery his discovery.

"Good work. None of the other storyboards I have examined have been in this good of condition. Most do not even have a rod. Now we need to find out if there is another reason besides organization for those rods," Emery said nodding his head in agreement while Aven just stared at the pieces of stone, his mind somewhere else.

"Bounty Huntress," Mistress Laisen interrupted. "General ManCane is in a guest cavern with a lower general. Master Laisen is with him now. We require your presence but will stay while he performs your inquisition." The woman's eyes were stern.

"Why don't you bring the general back here. Seeing all this and hearing the full story may bring comfort during his travels on Shea's paths," Emiline raised her eyebrows at the young ladies while Emery resumed his work on the stones.

"That may be a good idea," Aven agreed.

"We will talk to Master Laisen and see if he agrees," the mistress replied.

"I knew I had seen that somewhere before," Aven exclaimed which caused everyone to jump. "It's a good thing I have worked on the furniture." He bounded down the stairs of the pit and examined The Block. "Anised, get a larger bowl and let's mix up more of Emery's cleaning agent. We will need it, along with gentle pressure from a water pipe."

Aven lifted open the slits just under the top of The Block. Tiel shrugged her shoulders. "He's lost now. Once he gets involved with a project, there's no disturbing him."

"Yes, I know," Mistress Laisen whispered as she gazed at Aven. Her lips trembled, and she turned towards the front of the caverns. Tiel gave the mistress time to collect herself before following at a distance.

The pace would have been quicker if Quartney hadn't stopped them. The hunter medics had given her some salve which held back the stench of her condition. However, Tiel did not make even the slightest movement that would have disclosed her preference to be far from Quartney. The woman was sacrificing her comfort to help. The last thing she needed was to be shunned. Tiel noticed that Mistress Laisen acted just as calm.

"I am sorry, ladies. I have only been through half of the Heart Stone and still haven't found the knife." Quartney's eyes turned moist as she witnessed other hunters altering course upon approaching her. "I don't believe others can stand the stench. It may not be a good idea to have me here much longer."

"You are one of our honored elders," Mistress Laisen assured her as she touched Quartney's shoulder. "I will send a message to the other hunters. You are giving much to help us."

"Perhaps she would like to see what we are doing. Kehir did say we have the answer to the knife on the storyboard."

Mistress Laisen nodded at Tiel's suggestion. "You may have insights, Quartney. You need a break. Get something to eat. I am sure Kerlar Drakner would love to see you and help all she can." Mistress Laisen pointed Quartney in the right direction and then continued towards the front caverns.

Master Laisen stood at the entrance talking with General ManCane. Upon seeing Tiel, the general straightened up, his face falling into an immediate frown.

"Please, general, your previous chastisement has already produced many cruel and cutting thorns for my travels on Shea's paths. I assure you, I am more than willing to cleanse my zahule with the same blood those thorns have released. I will answer all questions you and the council seek to ask." Tiel felt the wet sting of tears rolling down her cheek as she reminded herself to stand up straight. But, she preferred to look elsewhere besides the general's eyes.

Her adverted gaze brought Tiel's attention to an albino woman standing behind the general. Her red hair was twisted in a tight knot. She wore the same uniform as ManCane, but her bright blue eyes vacantly glared at Tiel.

"What makes you think I planted those thorns you talk about? All I did was cut off the armor wrappings, made with denials and excuses, around your feet so you could feel the thorns you planted yourself. However, it is good to see you are ready to clear your path," ManCane said.

"We are here to help her clear those thorns. She only did what she thought was right." Master Laisen interjected.

"I am also here to help. Do not think for one moment that I do not care for The Bounty Huntress," ManCane replied. Master Laisen eyes widened at the general's straightforward comment. "She has put all of us on dark paths with her choices. The only reason I was able to prevent a blockade of your caverns was because of an impending inquisition concerning the High General. I am sure as the leader of this clan you are not naïve to this problem."

"Yes, I know of that," Master Laisen responded. "Yet, you and your peers complain when we do something that inconveniences your plans. However, you did not see fit to provide for us adequately the night our hunters were there to thwart abductions in Daton. *You* solicited our help. Then you mysteriously disappear until you feel you must correct one of our own, which is the same huntress who lighted our path to your problems."

"It was not his fault, Master Laisen," Tiel interjected. "The High General Ingrin, or his office, has been changing orders. They changed ManCane's orders the other night. That is why Ingrin's office is going through a general inquisition. General ManCane requested that he not be briefed on recent developments. He thought it would keep the Hunter Clan safe."

"I see," Master Laisen acknowledged. "Your paths *are* dark and clouded this day. The knowledge you keep yourself from may help light your paths."

The general thought a moment, released his frown and sighed in agreement.

"What has happened to Fallon Hanover?" he asked the three hunters.

"He is with the medics at this moment," Mistress Laisen answered. "It was our telepaths that injured him. We only seek to repair the damage they caused."

"That may not be good. Many people are already clamoring for Tiel and Aven's arrests. They think Fallon is in a peace enforcer's medic center. This may bring more trouble to your clan."

"We know that," Master Laisen answered. "Before the newscast, we sent hunters to find Fallon. However, they did not stop to think of the consequences during the broadcast."

General ManCane sighed. "I am familiar with the problems subordinates can cause. Let's take this one step at a time." The general addressed the woman behind him. "Junior general, go to the medics and assess Hanover's condition. Wait there until I return."

"But The Bounty Huntress's inquisition…," the general objected, not taking her eyes off Tiel. Tiel let her currents surround the junior general. A voice from the junior general's mind drifted over to Tiel. She recognized it as the old man's voice, with no static behind it.

"That is why my mind has been quiet," Tiel mused to herself. *"The old man is busy with another."*

"The Bounty Huntress and any other hunter responsible for Hanover's condition will face a proper inquisition so that all may know what has happened. Do I need to remind you that you are only an aide, and I am doing what the council and I have deemed fit?"

The junior general shook her head.

"Follow me, please." Mistress Laisen led the company to the other side of the caverns. A room filled with beds lay empty except for the one in which Fallon slept.

"Junior general, here you may stay. The medics will make sure that your needs are met." The junior general entered the room, looked at her boss, and hung her head. She headed over to Fallon's bed. A huntress dressed all in green met her.

"She will need to be watched," Tiel said once they left the room. "She is following a voice inside her head."

THE CLEAR CRYSTAL tube dangled between Jainu's fingers by a small string wrapped around the lip of the tube. The smoke inside curled in lazy waves that bobbed against each other, failing to obscure the glimmer from the thin copper wire that hung from the middle of the cork.

"What are you?" Jainu whispered as if his voice would break it.

"Awake, answer. Awake, answer." Diandra's voice resounded from the first room. She would repeat those words every so often for a while, quit amid sobs and start over again. Her footsteps were soft, but the changing distance of her voice let Jainu know she was pacing.

"I bet Diandra misses you," Jainu whispered again. He listened to her sobs once more and slumped down on the bed. He was dressed like Aven except for the boots. His bandaged feet wouldn't fit into them, so he had opted for some plain, brown leather slippers. "Wonder what information she'll trade just to hold you again," Jainu put the tube in a leg pocket on his pants and gingerly walked out the door of his room.

"Awake, answer. Awake, answer." Diandra's voice was louder as Jainu entered the hallway. He could see her shadow growing smaller on the wall as she paced towards the water closet at the other end.

He walked around the corner on the right. Diandra was dressed in plain, blue pants and a loose shirt. Her hair covered her bandaged ear, and she held her fingers up to her temples. Tracks of tears reflected the orange firelight of the fireplace. A basket of various fruits stood on the small table in front of the couch.

"It doesn't matter how much you talk, nothing will happen," Jainu called out to her. Diandra just turned and repeated the same phrase.

"I have something you want." Jainu raised his voice. Diandra failed even to notice him. He squared his shoulders and moved a little quicker to block the troubled girl only to jump as pain flared up his right leg when Diandra stepped on his foot. Jainu limped for a minute. His breath imitated a shrill scream escaping between pursed lips.

"Diandra!" Jainu screamed as he threw a red fruit at her. It hit her arm, and Diandra spun around. Recognition flashed across her face, and she closed her mouth. The tears ceased, and she stood at attention, gazing at him.

"What do you want?" she asked in a flat tone, looking him up and down.

"For you to be quiet," Jainu replied. Jainu sat down and rubbed his foot. It only caused more pain, so he put it down and relaxed.

The girl just stood, waiting for instructions.

"Why do you keep saying those words?" Her face gave no noticeable expressions. "Awake, answer, over and over again."

"You understand the master's sacred language?" Diandra asked trembling.

"What sacred language? It is the same language that everybody speaks," Jainu laughed. "They really messed with your brain."

"No, it is not! The purified have a sacred language they speak." Her eyes lit up in a way that made Jainu's stomach turn. "You've accepted the master. Now my mistress, Lady Twibett, will allow me back."

"No, you are brainwashed." Jainu pulled the tube out of his pocket and dangled it in front of Diandra. "Are you missing this?"

"That does not belong to me!" Diandra walked a little closer. "What's that string inside it?"

"You're the one who's supposed to know." Jainu watched her shrug her shoulders at his announcement. "It came out of your ear. Everybody thinks it's why Lady Twibett could communicate with you in your mind."

"LIAR!" Diandra screamed. "LIAR! The purified have always used their sacred language. Don't talk and don't listen. I am speaking in the sacred language, so go away. Leave me alone!!" Diandra paced once more, fingers on her temples, once again repeating the same words.

Jainu watched her for a few moments before covering his face with a couch pillow. He heard the word "help" enter the string of words that Diandra was muttering.

CHAPTER 22

ANCIENT WISDOM

*M*aestro's roar resounded through the caverns as the group approached. He paced around the edge of the pit with a lazy gait and head hung low. His tail didn't even switch back and forth. It dropped and bounced along the ground.

Emery and Emiline were busy cleaning up the last of the storyboard tablets. Aven and Anised were in the pit. One side of The Block was open as they worked with the gears on the inside.

"That thing opens?" Mistress Laisen called out, her voice barely a scratch over the crowded noise of the other hunters moving through the caverns.

"Apparently so, Mistress," Anised called out as a clang rang out from the pit. Aven grumbled and picked up a long, steel object.

"You're supposed to face that tool the other way," Anised whispered to Aven even though his voice still carried to the top tiers.

"This appears to be technology we did not know of," Anised once again addressed his sister. "I will make my report as soon as I get definite answers."

"Are you sleepy again?" Tiel asked Maestro as he paced near her.

"No," Maestro growled as he passed her.

"Are your paths clouded today?" ManCane called after him.

Maestro turned and stood firm, his gaze taking in the general. "I have been obscuring my paths, losing myself to a sadistic demon within."

"Excuse me?"

"It has come to our attention," Emiline interrupted looking up from Emery's work, "that Maestro is suffering from a rather basic split-personality problem."

"Basic?" Maestro glowered at Emiline. "What's basic about this? I can't even remember what Adrian does when he's in control."

"That is natural," Emiline countered. "When he 'disappears' he takes his memories with him."

"Does this 'Adrian' know how to use his fire?" The general's posture was straight as the side of a stone building, his face as white.

"Yes, but he only uses it on Luhitzu when he thinks it's convenient," Maestro answered over his shoulder.

"The first thing you need to do is stop referring to Adrian as a separate entity," Emiline called out. "Everything you do is because you decide to. Recognize that, and your personalities will combine. Plus, according to Jonaxx, you're also Luhitzu." Maestro roared at her logic.

"Catch me up while everybody finishes their projects," ManCane requested and turned to Tiel, "please."

"I bet that is the last time you ask me to keep you out of the loop," Tiel chuckled as the general ran his fingers through his hair. Two arms later, he was sitting down in a chair, slumped over a table, his head in his hands. A blank stare dominated his features as Tiel finished the tale. Maestro had lain down once again by the now-closed Block while Aven and Anised transported the clean storyboards to a table next to it. Emery and Emiline chatted excitedly as they cleaned up the last of the chemicals and made their way down the stairs.

"So, do you want to see what we discovered?" Tiel smiled at the general. "It'll be a newsworthy first."

The general straightened up and looked at the pit. "No, I want to run and hide. But to live, I need to see what waits on my path. So down I go." He stood, steadied himself, and made his way down to the middle tiers and sat on the stone benches. "I'll stay here," he announced and folded his hands between his legs, shoulders slumped.

Tiel walked down, squeezed his shoulders at which the general harrumphed. She smiled at the man before she located her seat on the lower tiers of the pit close to Aven.

"Will you tell us your idea now, Aven?" Master Laisen called from the top tier of the pit. Mistress Laisen sat beside him, playing with her fingers.

"Yes, I was hoping the Elder Hunter would join us; but he is probably on some personal business again." Aven picked up a stone from the storyboard. "I have worked on the lights for The Block several times and recognized the same patterns on the rods inside as on the storyboard pieces."

"Interesting," Mistress Laisen reacted with whispered awe.

Aven picked up a storyboard and pointed to the right side of the rods. "This has one notch on the rod, so I believe it is the first. Let's see what happens." He inserted the stone through the opening. A click sounded at the same time a mechanical whirring began, and the stone slid inside. The pit vibrated as the stone doors beyond the alcove shut, erasing the line between them. The crystals around the pit dimmed.

"You hunters have great masters in your ranks," General ManCane acknowledged.

"Agreed," Master Laisen answered. "Through the ages, our hunters have been studying to get everything working that was uncovered in these caves."

"Aven is one of our masters," Tiel said smiling at the general.

He cocked an eyebrow in her direction. "Surprising, as many times as he's dropped the tools. According to Anised, he was using them the wrong way."

Tiel nodded and watched Aven. He was too engrossed in his work to hear anything else. "There is a reason. I'll explain later. Keep that observation quiet."

A bright, robust image appeared on the doors as the crystals shut off. The muted colors on the storyboard were brilliant on the alcove doors. A tall woman in the middle had black skin and stood straight and tall, looking up to her right at the dual eyes representing Coulliou and his beloved. Her face was bright, and her eyes were wide with a tinge of excitement. A forest of large dark brown trees on her right held different sizes of yellow blinking eyes.

Tiel leaned in and studied the scene on the left. It was of a far-off bustling city. The buildings were taller than any she had seen before in her life. They were of a silver material, and windows glistened in Shea's light. Great highways encircled the city with many vehicles traveling on them. Large farms pregnant with various produce flourished in front of the city.

"There is no written language that I can see," Emery muttered.

"Let's see what the second storyboard shows us." Aven picked up another piece. "There is room for all eight," he added as he stuck the storyboard into the slot. The engine whirred, screeched, and stopped.

"What the...," Aven murmured only to have the storyboard burst out of the slot. He barely caught it in his arms and plopped the stone on the table while The Block whirred louder. The first stone flew out of the slot and Aven intercepted it before it hit the ground.

"Well, master hunter," ManCane chuckled, "that was quite a show. Almost ended it all."

Aven glared at ManCane then returned to the problem at hand.

"What about putting the storyboards in backward?" Tiel suggested. He looked at her and then rummaged through the storyboards and picked one.

"This is number eight," he put in the storyboard and braced himself for an ejection. The Block whirred, the storyboard disappeared, and the noise stopped. Nothing showed on the alcove doors.

"Number seven," he announced as he put another storyboard into The Block. The whirring noise sounded once more and stopped. Nothing showed on the doors. After a few moments, Aven put in the next storyboard with the same result. He continued with putting in the tablets until he got to the first one.

"Here we go," he announced and put in the last storyboard. After it disappeared inside, the light inside came on once again and a soft humming came from The Block. The image once again appeared before them, but this time it had a third dimension so that the characters appeared full and real.

Animals, including acodoe, moved in and out of the forest. Vehicles raced along the highways. Shea's light glistened in the windows. The wheat from the farm and forest trees swayed in a breeze. The woman went from smiling and laughing at the forest and its animals to frowning and crying when looking at the distant city. Then the whole scene would start over again.

"Well, that's interesting," Tiel said aloud as ancient symbols rolled across the screen.

"This will take time to study," Emery explained with a grin. "Why don't you all get some food."

"Well," General ManCane said getting up from his seat. "I need to check on Fallon."

Tiel just shook her head. Emery's eyes were twinkling. "How much time do you need?" she asked.

"Give me four or five arms. I've been studying this language all my life," he stepped forward, his grin spreading across his face. "However, there are new symbols I have not seen. Plus, I have to learn this new technology." He turned to her. "But there is a story, I guarantee it."

Tiel laughed as she went looking for food.

JONAXX'S BREATH stirred everything around him. Kehir watched it work as the great pits on either side of the serpent's snout widened and flattened in a calm rhythm. His breath moved Keidera's hair, making it swirl around her broken and battered face. The long, oily strands caught on cuts in her lips. She didn't stir. She would stay still for quite a while. Jonaxx kept her unconscious by pummeling her with his tail whenever she woke up.

Kehir stayed still hovering over the two and laughed to himself. *"She figured it out. The one called The Bounty Huntress figured out the connection."* A fox skirted the edge of the clearing and Kehir floated toward it. He inspected his hand. Clouds of fog swam around it. Through it, the fox's frozen stare never changed. Kehir inched forward, and the fox bent close to the ground, its eyes growing wide.

"There is a way to calm it, how is it done?" He thought for a moment while floating closer with his hands outstretched. The fox just laid its ears back and leaned towards the bushes. Kehir put his hand down, cupping it on the fox's head only to find that his hand glided through the animal. The fox shivered, snarled, and bit through his misty hand before darting out of the clearing. If he were mortal, there would be a deep wound. But the fox's teeth had passed right through. This body had form, just not a solid form that could interact with the mortal plane.

His sister moaned in her sleep, and Kehir turned back. Coulliou's punishment had been perfect. When he was mortal, he had used his faculties to commit heinous crimes, all in the name of a mere mortal he had foolishly made into a god. Now he could do nothing. He couldn't taste, hear, smell, touch, or experience the world around him. Thousands of octaves filled with anguish had erased his mortal appetites.

To make his paths even darker, his one dream that had kept him alive died. He had worked hard to put his sister in prison. When they were mortal, she had lied. She convinced him that what he was doing was right and prodded him on to commit his depravities. After their release, all he had wanted was to see her banished into the Arasteit. But, ever since his meeting with the hunters, he dared to hope for some small redemption. That hope was pushing him to keep his sister bound to this clearing.

He didn't know how it worked, but their imprisonment together had bound them somehow. When she roamed too far, it was like being torn at the most basic level. That would drain his energy, causing this world to melt away in hazy increments. During the most painful times of keeping his sister here, he actually saw into the Arasteit. He had seen its smoking tendrils reach out to him. Their influence recalled all the horrors he caused.

"No, it didn't just bring it back to my mind. I could experience it once more." He shuttered at the thought of living in a place where he relived his greatest atrocities repeatedly, always knowing he had the chance to make something different of his life and losing that opportunity. The experience had caused his soul to wail like never before, draining his new found hope out of him.

Once, he had even wished for the Arasteit, thinking it would be a respite from his torment. Now he shrank from it, preferring to hover, doing nothing. But the futility of it all increased his grief a hundred-fold. Since the huntress had severed some of Keidera's influence; Jonaxx's mind had become clear enough to realize their challenge. He had knocked out Keidera and kept her unconscious, giving himself and Kehir time to rest.

When her Lover's Heart awoke though, there would be nothing Jonaxx could do. Keidera would sense it, and it would empower her will. The mortals could no longer feel her hate, but she would have almost complete control over Jonaxx.

"Silly Mortals. Always so worried, using too much energy to get answers when the answer is right before them. Probably won't even figure things out before the knife wakes up." He chuckled to himself with empty delight. At least he

thought it was empty. Even his feelings, except for his despair, were foreign to him now.

Now, he hung there. With the Arasteit gone again, his energy was replenishing. He could not sleep, run away, or anything. Kehir let out a wail that made the trees around him shake, their leaves already drooping from his presence. Dead birds fell out of the branches. He watched others try to fly away only to drop dead in mid-flight.

"Keep quiet, do not wake your sister," Jonaxx hissed with his eyes still closed.

"I wish to sleep, to do *something*," Kehir wailed, but stopped when Jonaxx hissed in pain.

"Practice focusing that energy of yours on a single target."

"What?" Kehir asked Jonaxx.

"Do you think all you have to do is keep your sister here until her knife awakens?" Jonaxx opened one eye and stared him down. "You will need to extricate your will from your sister's. You must protect the hunters from her and me. Possibly sacrifice your hopes, no matter how small or frail, for the good of others. You may have to abandon yourself to the Arasteit."

Kehir shuttered once again. "No! I wished for it once, but no more. I now hope for redemption.

"I said you *may have to*," Jonaxx emphasized his previous statement. "However, in some way, you must show you can care for others more than your own hunger. Trapping The Bounty Huntress like you did made your task even more difficult."

"She needed to know what could happen after the others are released."

"Didn't you tempt her to take the chance and sever my cords?"

"Perhaps," Kehir eyed Jonaxx. "You knew what she was doing. You let her."

"Yes, I did. But you entrapped her."

"To teach her. Honestly, the others wouldn't have let her go, even with Adrian's flames. They would have held on, letting those flames engulf her mind. It would have made her their prisoner, combining their telepathic powers, using her..."

"Can and would your sister do that?" Jonaxx interrupted.

"She would enjoy it."

"Perhaps your heart is purer than even you understand. Practice

focusing your energy. Decide now if you will give up everything for others."
Jonaxx closed his eye again. "But now, I am enjoying my solitude. Stay still
and keep vigilant. Soon you will get your release... and your judgment."

"My judgment," Kehir sneered. "Easy for you to say, oh righteous one."

"Your sarcastic tone was perfect for that taunt," Jonaxx lifted his head
and flicked his tongue at Kehir. "You know what I did when I was under
your and Keidera's influence."

"Keidera was the one who could see through your eyes," Kehir
whispered.

"Then let me enlighten you," Jonaxx scoffed. "I would wait at the forest's
edge for wandering villagers and then eat them. Often, I would eat whole
groups of people. I swallowed my own kind, claiming it was a burial. I am
called the black death, by those who believe in the acodoe. Yes, Ecalardians
dread me, weep because of me, and I know it is my fault.

"I am the one who listened to the elders instead of the prophets. I agreed
that man didn't need the truth because of something that happened three
millennia in the past. I even kept the truth from my beloved Queen. Now I
am cursed, and I have felt the pull of the Arasteit many times because of you
and your sister. But I still fight, because I still want hope.

"I know what needs to be done, and I gave you a solution to your problems, even after you drove me mad. It is the same exact thing I must do.
Take my advice, don't take my advice. You are the master of your fate. You
will choose whether to abandon yourself to the Arasteit or whether to give
yourself hope.

"I DON'T SEE why I should go," Diandra pouted as Tiel watched the holo
screen. Ecalardians postings on the web stream concerned her. They had
discovered that Fallon didn't check in at Sarom's medic center.

Jen Odin stayed busy, fanning the flames of hatred towards her, Aven,
and the clan. She interviewed Hegert and played with the idea of the Hunter
Clan murdering Fallon and scattering his body throughout The Watosh in
some fabled ritual. This was leading to calls for her and Aven's death, and
now there was talk about a march on the caverns. Tiel groaned as she shut
off the holo screen.

"Why should I go? I want to stay here." Diandra brought Tiel's attention back to the caverns.

"Because Emiline is tired of feeding you dream chems," Tiel answered. "Either you go, or I carry you!" Tiel threatened when the girl stomped around. Diandra looked at her and then walked out the door.

Jainu giggled as he ran outside. It took more time than Tiel wanted since Diandra's pace was slow, but they finally made it to the pit. Jainu was limping along the walkway while munching on the last piece of fruit he had at lunch. Diandra had eaten only a little, but at least she was eating. Tiel knew the little stick-thing she guided would fatten up when Emiline took over.

"Aven!" Jainu called out and waved. Aven turned and waved back smiling.

"It's true! You are friends with de Menzaile." Diandra's face fell, making her sallow cheeks sink in even more.

"We're not only friends, we're stelloves." Tiel patted Diandra's head. Diandra looked up with a bewildered look. "We're married." At this, Diandra's eyes grew wide. Her arms went limp, and her pace slowed far more than Tiel thought possible.

"Why? Marriage only makes you drown in sorrow when oaths are broken. I have seen many married people break their oaths."

"And I have seen many married people keep their oaths becoming the best of friends and lovers."

"Give me one couple."

"Well, the Drakners live in Daton where you work. Have either of them come into Lady Twibett's Party Zones?"

"No," Diandra shook her head and stopped moving.

"Oh, by Coulliou, keep walking and please realize that things aren't the way you have been brainwashed to think they are." Diandra moved with Tiel's command. When they arrived, she sat Diandra down on one of the tier seats around the pits and commanded her to stay. Diandra obeyed. She sat there like an emancipated, plastic doll.

Tiel turned and saw Aven walking towards her. "How is Emery doing? It's been at least two-and-a-half arms."

"He's got possibly an eighth of it figured out," he whispered back. Tiel leaned in as his arm wrapped around her and they both stood watching

Emery. His eyes never came off the screen. His lips moved nonstop as the symbols rolled across the alcove doors.

"There are other problems on Shea's path today," Tiel whispered to Aven.

"If you're talking about the web streams, the Laisens already know."

"And you need to address those problems," Radames' voice interrupted Aven. "Bounty Huntress come with me. You too, de Menzaile."

"Stay with Diandra," Tiel commanded Jainu. "Be nice," she instructed while squeezing his shoulder. He pushed her hand away, and Tiel heard him mumble something, but she didn't stay to listen.

Radames led them into another cavern. There were several holo screens attached to cavern walls. Four hunters sat in chairs speaking into microphones. The screens continually switched images. He pointed to the second screen on the right.

"You know the talk about a possible march on our caverns?" Radames asked. "They aren't rumors."

"Shea's light," Tiel whispered.

"They are gathering because they think we are 'in league with the acodoe.' Somehow they received information about our meeting with Sendenia."

"The Elder Hunter," Aven grumbled.

"I agree," Radames said. "In this section," he continued as he pointed to another screen, showing crowds inside a parking lot, "they are ready to advance. I believe I don't have to tell you how out of control the web gossips have become. Whatever the Elder Hunter is doing, it is working." Tiel watched the images. Some Ecalardians were holding signs, none of them presented a positive vision of her or Aven.

"What happened with Jonaxx?" Radames asked.

"Do you want the truth, cousin?" Radames nodded to Tiel's question. "Well, we spoke with him after Aven set him on fire." Master Laisen grumbled at this news but let Tiel continue. "He and Kehir will do their best to keep Keidera inside the Watosh."

"Kehir?" Radames chuckled a little as he turned to face her and Aven. "Kehir? What happened out there?" He stood with his arms folded, a disbelieving smile crossed his face.

"Would you like the whole story or just a compressed version?" Tiel ventured.

Radames stared, his smile fading, his eyes shifting between them. When he decided they were serious, his eyes grew wide. He grabbed a chair, positioned it where he wanted and sat down.

"Cousin, you were always good for entertainment," he chuckled at Tiel. "Don't stop now. Sit, sit. Enthrall the Arasteit right out of me." He pointed to a row of chairs and Tiel sat next to Aven.

"Redemption!?" Radames bellowed out in disbelief after their report. "Jonaxx is trying to help Kehir get redemption? What did he do to get imprisoned by Coulliou?" He stopped and stuttered for a moment before asking the next question. "There are other prisoners?"

"That's what he said," Aven confirmed.

"Why didn't you tell me about *Prince Adrian* before this?" he grilled.

"We didn't think it prudent to say anything in front of the whole clan." Radames face grew red at Aven's answer. "And, I am glad we didn't. Imagine the damage the Elder Hunter could have done with that information."

Radames eyes wandered in thought.

"You know, now I feel like going into a corner, rolling myself up into a ball, and waiting for the Day of Renewal to swallow me up," he laughed. "But, let's take things one at a time." Radames raised his forefinger. "First, you two will record a message that our hunters here can run as an answer to the gossips' newscast. Second, find that knife and heal Jonaxx. Third, well… then I'll consider the plan about rolling up into a ball. Questions?"

Aven and Tiel shook their heads at Radames determined countenance.

"Good, let the people know we have Fallon Hanover in our care and why. Next, let them know of Jonaxx's condition, without giving away too much. Even I am tempted to consider your tales as fantasy. Let's not give Ecalardia that option."

Aven and Tiel agreed.

"Good. Get to work. I'll find our lovely mistress and sit with her on the tiers waiting for Emery to figure out the storyboards." Radames stood up, stared at them once more, then left.

"What shall we say?" Aven asked.

"Follow my lead," Tiel answered and walked to the holo screens. "Ready?"

"Let's go."

During the broadcast, both hunters provided evidence that Fallon was in their care. Tiel stressed that because Fallon's condition was due to Tiel's actions, they considered it their responsibility to care for Fallon.

Aven expressed his apologies as well and implored the citizens of Ecalardia to think about what they would do if they were in Tiel's position. He explained that her act was an act of love. Both clarified that Sendenia had solicited the Hunter Clan for help with her mate Jonaxx. They tried to explain Jonaxx's illness without revealing too much.

They had to start and stop the recording several times to get the message right. After it was all done, they left the cavern. Tiel felt drained in every inch of her body and Aven admitted to her he felt the same. They both plopped down on the stone tiers in the pit.

Hunters were entering the pit, and the Laisens sat at the top with General ManCane. Emery was in front, still trying to figure out the ancient writings. Emiline was next to him, jotting down notes on paper as he instructed. Jainu was sitting one tier above Diandra who, Tiel believed, had never moved. Maestro was gone. Tiel assumed that he was out hunting.

"Bounty Huntress." Tiel turned to find Quartney coming down the stairs. "Would you mind helping me find the knife? It has proven to be a long process."

"I will if I can, but I have a thought," Tiel answered. "You said sometimes you don't know when your thoughts are your own. So, did you really put the knife back?" Quartney nodded as she sat next to Tiel. Tiel breathed easy even though the nauseating stench was filtering through the powders that Quartney used. "Please, Elder, think. Are there things you have done to soften the voices unconsciously?"

"Of course, there is, but not that," Quartney shrieked, "that I remember clearly. Besides, I am not married. Didn't Jonaxx's prophecy speak of stelloves?"

"How do you know?"

"Master Laisen sent a message to all the hunters explaining things."

"I see," Tiel mused as Aven rubbed his eyes. "Yes, Jonaxx mentioned stelloves in his version of the prophecy. But how much of the prophecies can you believe? That part may not come to fruition."

"Really?" Aven smirked in her direction. "Still in denial?"

"No, you got that one wrong," Jainu's voice interrupted the conversation.

Tiel spun around. Jainu was smiling at Diandra who was facing him. "I saw your lips move just like Emery's. I could tell what you were saying."

"No, I got nothing wrong. I am a master of the sacred language." Diandra retorted.

"Hey, I know the sacred language, so just how mystical can it be?" Tiel opened her mouth to end Jainu's taunting, only to have Aven hold her back by putting his fingers to her lips.

"There is nothing 'mystical' about it," Diandra sneered at Jainu. "It is sacred, and I can read it and get it right."

"Prove it! Nobody else can understand what you're saying, so what does it matter?"

"I don't have to prove anything to you." Diandra turned around and curled up in a ball, her arms wrapped around her legs.

"Yes, you do. That was a command, and you must do what you're commanded, remember?" Diandra jerked back towards Jainu, her eyes wide. "Or I'll tell the master next time he talks to me." Jainu smiled again and leaned back, propped by the tier above him. "So, read it out loud. Prove that I don't know what I am saying."

Diandra set her face in defiance. "All right, if you command it. However, since you and I are the only ones that speak the sacred language, I'll give you a warning. If the master finds out you interpret what I say to the unpurified, you will wish he *only* tortures your mind." Diandra nodded and stood. Emery was pushing a few buttons on The Block.

"Tell me when it is at the beginning," he instructed her.

"Jilandro, listen to me carefully." Jilandro listened to the Elder Hunter's voice on a holo screen just outside Jacquard's. "I have uncovered evidence that will prove The Bounty Huntress is a murder suspect."

"You did?" Jilandro said this quietly in the right subservient tone; avoiding suspicion.

"Yes, you need to instruct my other pupils. Instruct them to listen and agree with me. That is all you need to know. The evidence is sure, sound beyond debate. There will be a short trial immediately."

"What sentence will be handed down?" Jilandro waved off a person to his right. The older man backed up and waited.

"There is no way I can get her deemed a Luhitzu, much less put her heart on The Block, especially with the way the Laisens are running things. No, we will recommend her for retraining. We will also recommend that Aven be put on trial as an accomplice. That trial will begin later."

"What kind of retraining will we recommend, my Elder?" Jilandro tried to sound as humble as possible. He felt his shoulders hunch over and straightened them immediately. That question was almost more than he dared to ask. It could reveal that he was thinking rather than just obeying. He tried to sound as pathetic as possible and relaxed when the Elder Hunter took this moment to teach.

"I must train her to accept her responsibilities as my other pupils have. Tiel and Aven became united without the blessings of their inner clan leader, me. That means that when one of them is found guilty of a heinous crime, like murder, I can declare the marriage void."

"Oh, I see," Jilandro whispered and watched the man lean against the wall. He folded his arms, and his eyes gazed into some thoughts that Jilandro couldn't penetrate. This man's will was stronger than any he had ever encountered... something that Master Laisen had warned him about, something about him being a shield.

"Do you see, my pupil?" the Elder Hunter's condescending voice brought him back to the conversation. "We need The Bounty Huntress. Her telepathic powers are stronger than yours, and she can... no, she will help with controlling the Hunter Clan. You have failed many times in that attempt. She can teach you, and she can help us retrain the whole clan. It is necessary."

"Sorry, I spoke too soon, my Elder." Jilandro bowed to the screen. "I now understand that I am only beginning to see the goodness of your councils."

"That is better. The other pupils are there?"

"Yes, my Elder."

"Then tell them."

"Yes, my Elder." The holo screen went blank before Jilandro finished his sentence. He turned to the man next to him. He was tall and thick with the supple muscles of those who lived only thirty octaves. Yet, his dense hair and beard had a liberal amount of gray. His bronzed face sported crinkled eyes and a wrinkled brow. His hazel eyes held the wisdom of at least fifty if not sixty octaves.

"You can help with this, Mr. Lambrie?" Jilandro whispered.

"Stand up straight, judge! What do you think?" Jilandro obeyed. Not because he feared the man, but because the man was full of optimism and exuded love for others. Therefore, in their short time together, Jilandro had already developed a deep respect for him. He was straightforward, gruff even, but his countenance showed confidence and gentleness at the same time. "'Course I'll help. I never quit the Winged Court."

"You have the same last name as Tiel, The Bounty Huntress, Mr. Lambrie, sir," Jilandro noted.

"Huh," the man grunted, "the girl took my name when I trained her. I gotta talk to her. The little snot's gotten herself into trouble agin. Call me Dawg."

"Yes, Dawg, sir." Jilandro walked behind him as Dawg moved out of the cavern.

"And leave off the sir, you're a judge," Dawg instructed Jilandro.

"Yes, you keep telling me that."

"Then act like it. Did you contact everyone?"

"Yes, sir… Dawg, all are here, even the older judges." Jilandro answered. "I just don't know if we can help. The Elder Hunter is cunning…"

"Why are you acting like a scared little toad now? You're no one's dung pot." Dawg's firm hand seemed to infuse courage into Jilandro's being. He stood straighter just by being in this man's presence. "You're a man! Now be a man! Let's move and get it done!"

Jilandro smiled for the first time. He was about to give Dawg his thanks when Dawg raised his finger and moved to the entrance. His brown outfit stayed loose on his body, and his boots were quiet as he walked.

"Hey, kitty kat, nice to see ya."

Jilandro ran to the entrance to find Maestro staring back. The panther stood, his muscles bunched as if he was ready to run the other way.

"Welcome back, kitty boy. Have you decided to live yet? Or are you still licking that self-pity of yours?" Maestro's eyes turned away and Dawg grunted. "What ya hear?"

"Everything Dawg."

"Are you going to do the right thing or disappear?"

Maestro said nothing, his face just twitched, and his tail laid on the ground, not moving.

"I need to knock sense into you, kitten boy."

Maestro regarded Dawg for a moment before trotting away. Jilandro watched Dawg's eyes squint with tears brimming at the edges.

CHAPTER 23

JAIDEN'S SINS

*E*mery was still fiddling with the buttons on The Block when Maestro appeared at Tiel's side and bumped his head against her chest.

"What is that for?" Tiel patted his head.

"I feel you need it, especially with Adrian acting the way he is," Maestro grumbled, "and…" He took a deep breath. "I think he made another appearance."

"Why do you say that?"

"I was coming back after hunting, then it was almost an arm later, and I was inside the Hunter's Caverns. Dawg was behind me as I was walking away."

"Dawg?" Aven asked. "Dawg Lambrie?"

"Yes," Maestro answered.

Tiel almost jumped out of her seat with pure excitement.

"He's a legend in the Winged Court," Aven mused.

"Yes, and my trainer. He never resigned his position at the Laisens' request. Because of him, I wanted to join the Winged Court."

"Want to go find him?" Aven chuckled.

"No, when he's ready, he'll come find me." Tiel kept her attention on the pit. "Besides, I want to see what is on the storyboard."

"As for Adrian," Tiel said giving Maestro a hug, "you'll win. Thanks for telling me." She squeezed him harder and enjoyed the soft rumble of his purr.

"There, that's the beginning," Diandra called out.

"How can she think she is speaking two languages?" Aven wondered.

"She's brainwashed. That's all there is to it. It will take Ma a long time to get her mind straight," Tiel answered.

"All right, young lady, you may begin," Emery called out. The subjects in the picture moved as the symbols rolled across the door's surface.

"I am the Empress Jaiden," Diandra read," and this is my confession. How I led Ecalardia into a dark, ignorant age. I do this hoping that my language has survived. I will also assume that whoever reads this knows the basics of the prophecies, the Arasteit, and the entrance to the Arasteit."

Tiel snuggled into Aven, getting comfortable while she rubbed Maestro's head. A deep purr rumbled out of him as he lay down next to her. There was some movement above as a fully robed Winged Court took their seats on the second tier. Tiel noticed that the older members were in attendance along with Dawg. She brought her attention back to the presentation as Diandra continued.

"Already, I am a witness to the destruction of many of my beloved libraries and universities. My people fear knowledge because of my decisions. They loathe it and often won't use the knowledge and skills they possess. In the past, they led themselves to starvation, sickness, and immense poverty. They were without homes and wandered the land looking for shelter and fought to gain essential commodities. It was all because they wanted nothing to do with the knowledge that they felt caused so many atrocities.

"I help where I can, but trust isn't given freely. Everyone is divided into clans which war amongst themselves. They carry on the bloodshed that my husband, Emperor Cong, taught their parents so long ago. The parents infuse the hate, fear, and distrust into their children. It will take many octaves before they eradicate these evils from their lives.

"But I digress. My story began when I was just a young girl thirsting to learn the knowledge available to us. The leaders of Ecalardia stayed locked up in their mansions, fearing a revolt from the people they had enslaved.

Their fear was real. The uprising was on the horizon as most people worked long days just to afford the necessities of life.

"However, the elite learned and practiced all the great arts. Science, history, math, language, religion, philosophy, engineering, and many other arts of knowledge filled great libraries and universities. Almost every child yearned to learn and study from these noble institutions. I dreamt of the day when my discoveries would be sung on the lips of every Ecalardian.

"I, myself, came from a humble family. Therefore, I struggled to earn the funds needed to support my studies. Nor was there a Lord or Lady which felt I deserved a higher education, hence; I could not get a letter of recommendation.

"Not to be deterred, I made my services available only to the great masters of these universities for a fraction of an average wage. It worked even though I scrounged and often begged for food and a place to sleep. These masters appeased my appetite for knowledge while I listened at their feet, often questioning them, and getting answers I would research further.

"It was during this time that I was recruited by a great kerlar of the eastern shores. His empathy and compassion knew no bounds. This kerlar's love for the least of Ecalardians conquered my heart so thoroughly that I became a kerlar myself. I stayed at his side, researching his questions, observing his every move. Soon, he allowed me to perform menial everyday medical tasks. Then I graduated to performing minor procedures. As my knowledge grew, he allowed me to assist him in the medical clinic performing experimental procedures until he admitted that I had surpassed his ability to teach. He wrote a letter of recommendation to the Abyss University, aptly named, for its mission was to teach the student to construct bridges of knowledge for all to travel upon.

"I was now in a better position to support my studies. It also thrilled me to study under the Acodoe Clan themselves. These gentle creatures' long lives enabled them to gain much knowledge, and I endeared myself to them. In time, I became a Junior Master Kerlar and traveled with my peers. We would go to the small villages and heal the sick and infirm.

"It was during one of those visits that I met a young, handsome, but very conceited, young man. His complexion and eyes were almost as black as the coal he mined. His muscles contoured his body in such a beautiful way I forgot my work and sat staring at him, along with my other female peers. I even stopped to listen to his stunning, rich voice that boomed through the village when he boasted of his accomplishments.

"It was after a visit to an elder's abode when I noticed him following me. After introducing himself as Cong, he bragged about his exploits, some of which I knew were lies. Never once did he ask about me, and I didn't offer. Instead, I found myself carried away by his voice and I didn't notice when I had arrived back at my quarters.

"Knowing I could never unite myself with him, I left before Shea showed her first rays the next morning. I tripled my efforts in my studies and traveled far and wide to other villages.

"During this time, my fame had blossomed, and my instructors introduced me to Their Majesties the King and Queen of the Acodoe. They were pleased with my accomplishments and invited me to study under their daughter. This acodoe was the top authority on medicine, and her underlings were the most sought-after kerlars.

"I accepted the invitation, and soon after, my teacher and I developed a great friendship. She was the founder of a successful Hunter Clan which I joined. It kept me close to her, and I often enjoyed her company. She detested the trappings of sovereign societies and demanded that her students learn to be self-reliant. So, I learned the arts of hunting, planting, harvesting, and cooking.

"By now, I was a Master Kerlar and had students studying under me. Whispers of awe would follow when we entered the villages. We always stayed long enough to do the work and then would disappear. Many times, my team would be busy with their daily work only to find that my master had followed us to observe. This I considered irritating but a necessity for gaining the knowledge I sought.

"I remember the day well when I heard of Cong's Sacrifice, as it is called when he had outwitted an acodoe to save his friend's life. He had not come out of this ordeal without injuries, and my master assigned my team to his care. I understood this to be the opportunity I sought to start studies of my own. My master couldn't make it to Cong's village, which allowed me to work without fear of intrusion.

"When I saw his body, I couldn't control my dismay. His beautiful muscles were in a state of atrophy and his voice squeaked out answers. His eyes would roll back into his head when one of his many seizures overtook him. The serpent's fangs had gouged two holes in his body, and the poison was devouring him.

"We went to work at once. After a few weeks, his sunken cheeks filled, and his seizures lessened. I had to thank my two most intelligent students for their work. Keidera would often sit up with Cong when my body would become overpowered with sleep. Her twin brother Kehir often searched the forest for herbs and food. It was a long process that took more than an octave. But slowly, his muscles worked, and the pitch of his voice became lower.

"He became better while the humble Ecalardians came out into open revolt. It took only a few months, but the elite were slain or banished to the outer desert rim, leaving an opening for leadership. Cong's sacrifice was not forgotten, and many wanted him crowned as Emperor. So Ecalardia waited to see if Cong would heal.

"While I was watching him one night, Cong inquired why I had left the village last time without saying goodbye. I just smiled and said something nonchalant. He thought for a moment and then asked how he had hurt me. I tried to provide a general answer, but he kept begging me to tell him the truth. Finally, I told him that his ego had irritated me. 'I will tell you how beautiful you are every day' he promised. He then fell asleep and left me to my thoughts.

"Afterwards, he shamelessly courted me, and his attentions were so genuine that I forgot my earlier impressions. After he healed, we were united in marriage and Cong accepted an offer to become Emperor. The citizens established a lower form of courts under him and gifted a fine mansion to my husband with wings renovated for the use of the lower courts.

"I left the Hunter Clan and my studies. Faithful Keidera and Kehir followed me into palace life. There, I made part of the mansion into a university and accepted students. Here my appetite became an addiction. I studied whatever came within reach. I implored my students to do the same. I was content to let my students explore with no boundaries or supervision.

"I used my position to persuade others to donate to many causes, and we eradicated some diseases. My husband was now back to full health, even in better health than before if that were possible and returned to his regular duties. It was during this time we learned that the acodoe who he had outwitted sought revenge. It now had an appetite for human flesh.

"My husband did his best to repair the relationship between him and this acodoe. But it did not work. One day the acodoe tried to attack him again, and my husband barely escaped. To protect him, I gave my husband access to my team. Kehir invented some weapons. Two sticks, when used together, would create streams of electricity, or several lightning bolts. When something large, like an acodoe, would pass between a pair of these sticks, several bolts of lightning would erupt. The shock was strong enough to kill an acodoe.

"Cong convinced me he knew where this acodoe hunted and that the king and queen were on his side. He would use himself as bait, and when the acodoe was dead, he would bring the weapons back. His plan worked. However, my husband didn't realize that other acodoe now hunted him for the death of their comrade.

"Cong had to regrettably use the weapons again to protect the surrounding villages of the Watosh Forest. He and his warriors tried to be careful, yet as so often happens, there was an accident. The Acodoe King got caught between a pair of these lightning sticks and died.

"It was then that the acodoe retreated into the forest and attacked anyone who strayed too far into its domains. The villagers fought back, and tensions rose to where my husband had to gather warriors to protect both sides. He asked Keidera and Kehir to create more weapons.

"It was a long five octaves. I stayed in my wing of the palace and taught my students, hoping that by staying focused I could somehow help. However, bad news kept coming from the battlefield until one day, to my great astonishment, my old master sent me a summons. Refusing to let this chance slip by to help ease tensions, I left telling no one, even my husband.

"I entered the cave under guard from the now defamed Hunter Clan who my husband had labeled as terrorists. All my old master would say was 'follow me.' She led me through her cave and out a different entrance. We walked up to the top of a hill which looked down into a valley.

"I do not know if I can adequately explain the scene which my eyes beheld. Thousands of people lay dead, only three acodoe were among the bodies. I looked for a sign of life, but all I could see was a mound of arms and legs, some not even attached to their bodies. I tried to run down, but my master's voice stopped me. 'The kill is fresh. It takes a little while.'

"I stared at her, for her blunt honesty was disturbing. These were people, not animals to be slaughtered for mere delight. Despite this she kept watch, and so I watched the battlefield with her. Slowly, first just three, then maybe ten, then many more humans stood. Blood smeared their bodies, but they wiped it off or ignored it as if it was only a nuisance. As they casually walked over the dead, I saw their skin slide off and a gleaming metallic structure lay underneath.

"'Behold, the real destroyers. Your claim to fame.' I immediately denied anything to do with this atrocity, but my teacher was quick to point out that these things were wearing my husband's uniforms. She bade me once again to follow her, which I did, stumbling past horrific scenes of death. We approached a village where the roar of war reverberated through the air. Here, there was no acodoe, but my husband's warriors fighting the villagers.

"'But why?' I asked.

My master shook her head. 'Your Keidera has caught many of our hunters, members of your old clan. The few who escaped reported many things. One is that Keidera likes to record everything she does. She claims these writings will be a testament to her greatness. If you have any idea where she keeps these writings, I would search there for your answers.'

"My teacher left me alone to ponder. Soon the Hunter Clan escorted me back to a point where I could get to the palace safely. Upon arriving, I discovered that my husband and most of my team had left for the northern borders and would return in a few months. It was night, so I consigned myself to searching in the morning.

"It surprised me how little searching I had to do. I knew Keidera loved to journal, but I didn't realize how detailed she was. One would think she would hide such incriminatory evidence of her deeds. The crimes she boasted of were so deplorable that I couldn't stomach the tales except in spurts.

"I also learned that Cong and Keidera had carried on an affair behind my back before Cong and I were wed. He had only married me because Keidera didn't want to be Empress. She had alluded to my husband's journals, and I vowed to find them. The search took a week, but I uncovered a hidden panel in one of our sitting rooms. In the corners, there were several rows of his journals. I opened one and learned how much of a monster he really was.

"In it, he admitted to concocting the story of his outwitting an acodoe. He and his friend had searched out the Golden Plant for their lovers; my husband's being Keidera. It seemed they wanted the sample to make their lovers special knives that would use nature and science to keep their appearance young. My husband admitted to killing his friend during the search. When he found the Golden Plant, it attacked him, but he escaped with the help of an acodoe.

"Cong blamed the acodoe for his misfortunes. Using my team's inventions, he hunted the poor creature and murdered it. As I compared the two set of journals, I realized that Cong and Keidera were so obsessed with their self-worth they thought themselves to be above everyone else. They became fixated on finding the entrance to The Abyss and felt that Coulliou wanted to keep them from a more deserving life. They convinced themselves that a better world lay beyond the opening and would do anything to open the entrance, even kill innocent Ecalardians.

"I decided the time had come for me share this knowledge with the courts. I left my wing and entered the judges' wing. Finding that all the judges were either dismissed or killed, I entered the councils' arena and found the same situation. My husband had made himself sole ruler of Ecalardia.

"I had one course left. I summoned the prophet to my palace. It was Ecalardia law that he could judge crimes of the leadership when no one else was available. He took weeks to come. Until then, I busied myself cataloging the journals. It was a quick briefing with the prophet, but he said nothing until I finished. Then he asked, 'What do they do with the bodies of the dead?' I did not understand what he was talking about and relayed this to him. He repeated the question and suggested there had to be somebody in the palace who knew.

"Kehir had not left with the others, so I summoned him. When he saw the prophet and the journals, he stood straight and stiff and never took his eyes off the prophet. When the situation was explained, he bowed and waved for us to follow him.

"He took us downstairs to the basement and his lab. In it, the bodies of the dead were being dissolved with a chemical mixture. Kehir explained that this was his crowning invention. He could use the chemical mixture to dissolve the skin, restructure it and mold it over the mechanical bodies of robots. They, in turn, would slaughter any who opposed Emperor Cong, for he would get us to a more vibrant world that the gods were hiding. His eyes were wide with excitement and anticipation. His smile was fanatical.

"When I shook my head and told him what he was doing was wrong; he shook his head, informing me that everything had been done by my command. I denied this accusation. He repeated my words that my team 'was to help my husband in all his endeavors.'

"I remember screaming. I defended myself by saying I thought my husband was a good man, interested in only the welfare of Ecalardia, and that I would never agree to such atrocities. The prophet held me for some time and let me cry on his shoulder. He told me that Coulliou had already judged my husband and those who were his allies. I learned that they had already tried to breach the entrance and had harmed Ecalardia. They were now trapped in the entrance and had become Luhitzu. Only one had escaped, Keidera. She was roaming Ecalardia. The prophet did not know what she was doing. I turned to Kehir who, by this time, had lost all color in his face and slumped in his chair. The prophet warned that our next actions would influence our judgments. He would be back the next day.

"After he left, I took a moment to comprehend my predicament. I still do not understand it hundreds of octaves later. But, I had to convince a stammering and shaking Kehir that we still had a chance. I asked him why the metal warriors still fought. He told me they were obeying commands that he programmed into a computer east of his lab.

"Kehir called the monsters back. When all had arrived, Kehir shut them off and destroyed the lab; thus, ending the war, but not the terror. The prophet gave us our judgments the following morning. Coulliou would imprison Kehir with his sister; they would inhabit the first lock. The Prophet related that Kehir's invention would keep their ethereal bodies in suspension. Coulliou would release them when the Day of Renewal was near. However, Kehir would not be imprisoned until he helped incarcerate his sister. Only then could he hope for redemption.

"My curse is to live until the Day of Renewal. I shall never have the privilege of crossing the abyss in that blessed day. I do not expect to have children of my own. We have not found Keidera. She is cunning and lives off the land.

"I have learned many more things about my husband from Kehir. He uses my ears for his confessions. Cong had been successful in getting a sample of the Golden Plant. He made Keidera's precious knife, and she calls it her Lover's Heart. In it is a solution that keeps her young, but there is a considerable price.

"Half of the elixir is made from the chemicals that dissolve tissue, and the other half is made from blood. At first, she cut herself and injected the elixir into her body. The solution worked for a few octaves, then it slowly infected and destroyed her body. Her body produced a yellow substance that stunk and caused her skin to rot.

"It took some time, but she figured out that if she used the knife to kill someone, their blood will mix with the solution inside. Now, after committing murder, she uses the knife to remove her rotting skin. The potion will enter her skin as the knife cuts, healing her malady. As far as we know, she is in remission for a few octaves. When the disease resurfaces, it is stronger than before. I am not ashamed to say I have no desire to find a cure for her condition.

"As for Ecalardia, they have embraced some basic knowledge. Perhaps one day I'll start another Hunter Clan with the same ideologies. Until then, I am to witness the effects of my actions. I have Luhitzu from the abyss to help and guide me.

"My crime? The prophet told me it was being overzealous and not using my skills to enlighten my students to the true path. I could have left my comfortable wing in the palace and become more involved in the life of my subjects. But I just wanted to get knowledge and fill my appetite for adoration by giving my gifts to those who misused them. I never learned that getting real knowledge meant interacting and learning from others. If I had only left the palace just once, would it have mattered?"

The crystal lights of the pit flickered on. Emery stood looking at the characters running across the screen.

"So, Jaiden is still alive?" Anised broke the silence from his seat at the bottom.

"By her account, she should be," Emery answered. "Now, according to what Diandra just read, there are two types of Luhitzu. The words are very similar…"

"WAIT!" Diandra shrieked aloud. "How do you know about the sacred symbols?"

"I have been studying them all my life. You filled in the pieces."

"Wha… wha… what?" Diandra's body collapsed. "I spoke the sacred language. You couldn't understand. You're unpurified." Her lips trembled, and her voice slowly dissipated with each word.

"You were speaking common Ecalardian!" Jainu yelled. "Get it into your brain! They've lied to you."

"That will be enough, young man," Emiline scolded Jainu. He closed his mouth and sulked. "She doesn't understand this. Now both of you come up to the top." Jainu rose and walked up the stairs. Emiline helped Diandra stand and steered her towards the stairs. Heavy sobs came from the girl as her feet missed every step. Emiline carried her up the stairs without even the slightest grunt.

"Go on Emery. I'll hear you up here," Emiline ordered. Emery began again. "If you look at the two words for Luhitzu… yes, here it is." Emery pointed to two words. Both appeared to be the same. Now that Tiel studied them, they weren't too dissimilar from the letters presently used. Except for these letters were more rigid. Emery pointed to the middle of the last Luhitzu where a small wavy line underscored the three middle letters.

"This would imply a difference. Very interesting. Every other mark I have encountered has been above the letters, not below them."

"So, is there information about the knife?" Tiel asked.

"I believe there is another file." Emery pushed the buttons on The Block. The moving pictures disappeared, and rows of ancient words appeared next. "Well, this is another report from Jaiden. I can read this, especially after hearing Diandra read the last." Emery readjusted his seating position and began.

"I have done damage once again. I should have researched to find a cure for the solution in Keidera's knife. Now, over a thousand octaves later, we have found Keidera. Kehir went to his prison at the abyss entrance. I do not miss his negativity, but I do miss his companionship. He knows the project I am working on and has helped me form these stones.

"Yet, Keidera did not have her knife. She buried it somewhere in the western expanse, and many have her disease. I do not know if it spreads like a virus, or if the knife has wounded that many people.

"I do not know what the knife looks like. Neither did Kehir. After living so long, he doesn't remember. I look for it daily and have had no success. However, Kehir instructed me on the inner workings of this knife. I record this in case someone discovers it. Maybe some master or student can reverse the infection it delivers.

"Inside is a thin strand of what Kehir called a biothread. Twisted along this thread are two streams of the Golden Plant somehow integrated with the particles of his chemical. One strand comes from the male particles of the plant, the other, the female particles. When a male hand touches the knife, it activates the female particles and vice versa. It has a mechanical program inside which senses blood. It will vibrate and cut whoever is holding it, mostly females since the male molecules are highly activated from being stimulated so long by Keidera's life force. Be careful. The knife thirsts for human blood and getting a cut from this knife will start the infection that plagued Keidera. The chemical solution is made from..."

A clunking sound from The Block stopped Emery's translation. Black smoke poured out of the slits while The Block jumped around. Emery retreated to the other side of the pit.

Aven ran to help amid murmurs and exclamations from the hunters. He flinched and covered his face when sparks shot out of the slits.

When the commotion died down, Aven inched forward and opened a slit.

"It's on fire," he announced as he retreated. "This is what happens when we misuse ancient technology. The fluids from the knives have ruined the wiring inside."

Aven peered inside again. Black smoke poured into the air. The smoke from below tickled Tiel's nose, and she sneezed along with other hunters. "We must find another Block or wires, plus the tome that will instruct us on how to use this." The clink of the slit door closing echoed. "This is the end of the show."

"My dear de Menzaile," the Elder Hunter said, his soft voice overtaking the noise, "the real show has just begun."

CHAPTER 24

*E*veryone **faced Sethrich**, the Elder Hunter. "You both have disgraced the Hunter Clan for the last time."

"I am taking care of the Peace Enforcers," General ManCane interrupted. His jacket was off, his shirt rumpled, and his pants wrinkled. Yet he stood with a dignity that belied his exhaustion.

"I have seen how you plan to handle it. There is a troop of Peace Enforcers on their way."

"I have not sent for any troops," the general declared, his hands now balled up into fists.

"Maybe you are not in command." Sethrich stepped towards ManCane. "A message originated from these caves. It informed the High Council that Fallon Hanover is a prisoner here."

"The Junior General," ManCane hissed among shouts and yells from the hunters.

"It does not matter. You are not part of this clan. Therefore, you have no voice here."

"That is enough, Elder Hunter!" Radames' voice quelled the commotion. "Who speaks is not up to you."

"*Stay close,*" she called to Aven with her telepathy, "*these are intense emotions.*"

"Why do you think I'm here?" Aven's soft squeeze on her shoulders calmed Tiel, and she watched the proceedings.

Sethrich glared at Radames. "The citizens demand that de Menzaile and The Bounty Huntress be brought before the council. They are following the oncoming enforcer troops to make sure that happens," Sethrich explained. His eyes held a malicious twinkle. His lips were pressed together in defiance.

"Why? Aven had nothing to do with Fallon Hanover!" Lidena called out as she scurried to the steps.

"He protects The Bounty Huntress," Sethrich responded. "Anything she does, he will defend. He is guilty by association and is not trustworthy." Sethrich focused on Tiel. "Bounty Huntress, I command, as your Inner Clan Leader, that you relinquish your Hunter's Heart. I have called for a court, and they will put you on trial!" Tiel growled and shook her head.

"You call the trial now?" Radames advanced towards Sethrich.

"Yes, I am the head of the Winged Court. And as Tiel is a member of that court, it is my responsibility to call a larquetz."

"A larquetz?" Lidena asked.

"And since you petitioned to make a plea for yourself in the next larquetz, that means you relinquish your rights as a leader," Sethrich smirked at Lidena, and the hunters murmured amongst themselves.

"Lidena, should you be stepping down, child?" Dawg's voice stopped all murmurings. Sethrich stumbled down a few steps before he regained his balance.

"What are you d-d-doing here?" he stammered.

"Master Laisen asked for my help." Dawg raised his voice. "It seems that was a good idea."

"I will step down," Lidena whispered, and she sank onto the seat.

"I will take the empty spot," Dawg offered, "with a consenting vote from the clan."

"All stand who will accept our previous Elder Hunter, Dawg Lambrie, as a full member of the Winged Court with all privileges," Radames cried out.

Every hunter in the pit stood firm and screamed their acceptance.

Dawg raised his Hunter's Heart. Silence filled the pit.

"See what comes from real respect, Sethrich?" Dawg advanced closer never losing contact with Sethrich's eyes. "Master Laisen, let's get this done. Let him call his court."

"Agreed. Tiel, Aven, down to the pit." Tiel watched as Radames grabbed Lidena's elbow and led her down to the lower tiers. He placed her next to Quartney before positioning himself in the center. The hunters stamped and screamed their approval. General ManCane cupped his hands over his ears. Maestro moved to the pit floor and lay outside the star circle.

The smoke from The Block had subsided. Aven and Tiel placed themselves in front of Radames while the Winged Court stood behind him. Dawg and Sethrich placed themselves across from Aven and Tiel.

Radames raised his Hunter's Heart, and the commotion stopped.

"Are we not going to throw our knives into The Block?" Sethrich questioned.

"No," Radames stated between his clamped teeth. "Aven, do you prefer to be here with Tiel?"

"Yes!" Tiel smiled at Aven's firm answer.

"Anised, please stay nearby, in case there is trouble." Anised stood and placed himself behind Aven.

"Sethrich is too involved," Dawg commented. "Replace him with Jilandro."

"I agree." Radames turned to the judges. "Jilandro, will you accept the task of spokesperson?" Jilandro stepped forward and bowed his head in agreement.

"Good, we are deciding if there should be a trial and when. Does the Winged Court understand this?"

The dark robed figures nodded.

"Good. Now, Elder Hunter, what are your charges against The Bounty Huntress?"

"The Bounty Huntress is guilty of murder..." A cry rose from the pit, and Tiel stared at her accuser, daring him to look at her. "... and attempted murder." Tiel stumbled back as he faced her, his eyes boring into hers.

"Never!" Aven raised his voice to a fevered pitch moving toward Sethrich. The hunters stamped their feet and yelled out their support for one side or the other.

"You weren't there, dear boy," Sethrich informed him, "at least not for the murder. I am sure you let the attempted murder pass without a single thought."

Radames raised his knife, and the hunters quieted down. "Clarify your accusations," Radames demanded.

"If I may, I will allow The Bounty Huntress herself to clarify my accusations," Sethrich snarled at Aven. "If her great protector will allow me one question."

"De Menzaile, step aside," Radames ordered among some boos from the hunters. Aven's shoulders heaved with his breath. "De Menzaile, step aside, or I'll have Anised remove you," Radames ordered again.

"She's a ritualed hunter, boy," Dawg interrupted. "She will take what comes to her."

"Brother, please," Anised's hand appeared to Tiel's left and landed on Aven's shoulder. Aven shifted to the left and Sethrich sneered at Tiel. The pit quieted down to a low murmur. Tiel could feel that Aven was close enough to keep his shield around her.

"Be quick with your question, Elder Hunter," Radames ordered.

"Where is Tyne Baritone?" Sethrich smiled, and Tiel's stomach became as heavy as a rock.

"Tyne?"

"Yes, Bounty Huntress. Tyne Baritone. The one you rescued the children from. The one you captured. You have not mentioned him, and he has disappeared. Where is Tyne Baritone?"

"I...I... I do not know," Tiel stuttered, her tongue felt thick and unwilling to move as more boos sounded but then quieted down.

"A renowned huntress such as yourself does not know?" Sethrich questioned, glee underlined his tone.

"He disappeared during the commotion Jonaxx caused with the queen's brother. I tied him to a tree. After the commotion, we found he had disappeared."

"And you didn't go after him? Did you even think about him? Or was his life worthless?"

"Enough," Radames ordered.

"Wait!" Dawg demanded. "You said 'we.' Tell the whole story girl!"

"There was a fight between Jonaxx and Sendenia's guards. Sendenia told us that."

"You're stalling, girl. Who found him?" Dawg insisted.

"Maestro. I sent Maestro when things quieted down."

"He came back?" Dawg questioned.

"No, I had to search for him. He was there, and the cords broken. I figured…"

"You assumed, didn't ask. Got it!" Dawg interrupted. "Go on, Sethrich." The hunters stayed quiet, and Sethrich stooped just a little.

"You h-h-have not once c-c-called me by my t-t-title," Sethrich stammered.

"I don't use titles on sniveling brats," Dawg snarled. Laughter mixed with oohs came from the hunters' seats. "Continue, Sethrich."

"She injured a man during the fight in Daton," Sethrich leaned back from Dawg's stare.

"Several people were hurt during that hunt," Anised spoke up among some rumblings. "My Dark Sentinels also fought many people that night."

"This man claimed Tiel did it while helping him," Sethrich said. "She used her Hunter's Heart to remove an object from his chest. The poison from her knife entered his system. Now he suffers in the medical clinic."

"I didn't try to poison him," Tiel defended herself. Incoherent rumblings rang throughout the pit.

"Where is your proof she intended to poison the witness?" Jilandro asked. Sethrich turned to him, his face contorted in anger for a moment. Then he relaxed and answered Jilandro's question.

"That will be provided during the larquetz."

"According to our laws, you must provide enough proof before demanding a larquetz," Jilandro's voice shook, but he kept his posture firm. Sethrich stayed silent and stared at his pupil. "With no proof, you cannot ask for a larquetz for the attempted murder charge," Jilandro stated, not taking his eyes off his master. The hunters hooted their approval.

*"They **have** been studying,"* Tiel called to Aven.

"Yes, and Jilandro is doing a grand job of standing up to Sethrich," Aven responded.

"Agreed."

"Then I have enough proof of the murder charge," Sethrich reversed his stance, still glaring at Jilandro. "*My* Winged Court is ready and prepared to conduct the trial."

"That is *the* Winged Courts' decision," Radames rebutted.

"Wait! There is another witness," Dawg interrupted.

"What? Who?" Sethrich asked.

"Adrian."

"Who's Adrian?" Sethrich asked.

"A fat-bellied coward afraid to live. Likes to lick his wounds." Tiel watched Dawg move over to Maestro. "Let's get the truth, kitty cat." Dawg jumped onto Maestro's back. The lower tiers emptied as Maestro leaped up onto his hind legs roaring. Dawg put his arms around Maestro's front legs and held onto the cat's neck with his hands, pushing it down. The hunters screamed and stomped at the new spectacle before them.

"Time to come back, kitty boy," Dawg grunted while Maestro struggled.

"Is he insane?" Sethrich yelled out. Maestro was now jumping backward, trying to throw Dawg off his back. "This is who you solicited for help?"

"Yes, and he may just be the genius we need," Radames chuckled aloud.

"Wake up, you lazy house cat!" Dawg yelled in Maestro's ear. Maestro jumped back once more and fell on top of Dawg. Dawg bellowed and used his leg to roll the thrashing panther over onto his stomach, landing him on top of Maestro once more. The crowd of hunters, including the Winged Court, screamed and jumped at the display. Tiel tried to run toward the commotion, but Aven held her by her shoulders.

"Not a good idea," Aven whispered in her ear. "Let Dawg handle this. Adrian hasn't been honest with you."

"I know," Tiel whispered back. "It is just so hard to watch. There has to be a better way."

"I don't believe so, stellove." He wrapped his arms around her, and she relented.

Maestro snarled, baring his teeth, and jerked his head around. He raked his claws against Dawg's arms shredding the black robes but leaving the sleeves of his brown leather outfit untouched.

"Lame, kitty boy!" Dawg yelled. "I know your tricks."

Maestro crawled forward, snarling once more, jerking his head around.

"Dawg, just what do you think you're doing?" Emiline's voice rang out above the commotion.

"Just some good old therapy," he called out as Maestro fought to get back on his feet.

"This is not good therapy." She marched down the stairs, her hands on her hips with Emery behind her.

"Sorry, little sis, no time for food and fluff," Dawg answered through a grimace as Maestro tried to roll onto his back, paws waving in the air.

"Fluff, you called my therapy fluff?" Emiline moved to intercept, but Emery pulled her back, shaking his head, laughing.

Tiel could tell Emiline was unsuccessfully arguing with Emery. He kept shaking his head while watching the show.

"Come out you lazy…"

"I'm here," Maestro's voice sounded. The hunters kept screaming. Out of the corner of her eyes, Tiel saw Radames raise his Hunter's Heart. It took some time, but the hunters quieted down.

"Did you say something, kitty boy?"

"I'm back, you moronic mutt!" the cat yelled back.

"Well, Adrian good buddy, nice to see you." Dawg laughed but refused to let go. "Now do your job, Luhitzu." The hunters gasped at this announcement. "Your bondswoman is about to be put on trial for killing Tyne Baritone."

"He's not dead," Adrian yelled out. Gasps echoed all around the pit.

"Why not?" Dawg probed.

"Because I freed him," Adrian answered.

"What?" Tiel cried out.

"He was of no danger to anyone as long as his brother wasn't torturing him," Adrian announced. "Jonaxx led him into the Watosh after that."

"You had no right to make that decision," Tiel cried out as she felt her cheeks flush with anger. Adrian collapsed on his stomach with a grunt and Dawg rolled over onto the ground.

"And you had the right to erase Fallon Hanover's memory?" Adrian questioned looking up at her. "The young kerlar taught you well, child," he snarled. The hunters turned silent.

"Enough, Luhitzu, you're supposed to help." Dawg looked Adrian straight in the eye. "You can't do it while wimping out. You failed 'cause you weren't there to help!" Dawg got up and brushed off his robes and outfit.

Adrian looked away and coughed out a few roars. Jainu raced down the steps and knelt next to him. Adrian held his ears back at first, then relaxed. Jainu put his arms around the cat's neck and buried his face into the fur. Adrian sighed and rested his head between his paws and closed his eyes.

"Master Laisen, that is enough." Dawg took a few breaths and walked to the center. "There's the proof. She's not guilty of murder."

"Agreed," Radames said with one eyebrow cocked. He directed his attention to a gawking Sethrich. "Is there anything else?"

"There is not enough proof to hold a formal larquetz," Jilandro commented as he backed away from Sethrich's stare.

"I did not want to burden the Winged Court, but now I shall have to add one more charge." Sethrich's speech was deliberate and pronounced with a sharp edge on every syllable. "I bring the charge of blackmail, which according to our laws is treason. Even more treacherous than murder." Sethrich held up his finger. "And if we find The Bounty Huntress guilty, the only punishment allowed is banishment, to become Luhitzu, the hunted."

The hunters did not make a sound. The stale air in the pit hung like a heavy weight pushing down on Tiel.

"What blackmail?" Radames demanded. "Where is your proof?"

"All over the web, Master Laisen." Sethrich's tone was deeper than normal. "Have you not heard? She demanded to be paid three times the original amount, and Councilwoman Hegert created the bounty to save a life."

The pit stayed silent, and Radames scrunched his face in confusion. "It is normal for a hunter to require more compensation for damages," Radames answered.

"But, according to our laws," Sethrich said as he smiled, "from the time our forefathers created our beloved clan, a hunter may only ask for a higher compensation after they have brought their case before the Winged Court."

The pit filled with rumblings once more as Tiel gaped at the Elder Hunter. Radames looked as shocked as she did, a member of the Winged Court was whispering to Jilandro.

"Elder Hunter, to bring that case at this time, you would have to put almost everyone here on trial. We have set a precedent meaning that law could be illegitimate."

"Unless one leader finds it and realizes the implications of not following it. And then brings it before the clan and has it reinstated. I am that leader." The pit became silent once more. "And I have the proof.

Hegert has published her complaints, the newscasters have legitimized her story." Radames wiped his face with his hand as Sethrich continued his argument.

"Hegert has used this to bring more accusations against the clan. And now... now, we have a peace enforcer troop coming here with a mob following. They threaten our existence." Sethrich's voice rose in a fevered pitch. "All because The Bounty Huntress soiled her zahule by blackmailing one of the High Council. She didn't even let me or you Radames, our Master Laisen, look at her evidence. She only showed it to Hegert and threatened her with it to get more compensation."

The room erupted with shouts of disbelief, and the hunters stamped their disapproval for Tiel.

"This is why our forefathers created the law," Sethrich yelled. "Who will hire us now? Who will trust our zahule if all Ecalardia fears that we will cheat them? The Winged Court should decide how a hunter is compensated." The hunters yelled and stamped their approval again.

Sethrich raised his hunter's heart, and the crowd calmed down. "I have demonstrated real leadership through knowledge, my clan. But our wise creators always gave our brothers and sisters a way out. All Tiel must do is turn herself in for retraining to her inner clan leader. I am gracious enough to still accept her as one of mine." Sethrich turned to Tiel. He beamed at his victory as the hunters roared even louder.

"Master Laisen," Jilandro called. Radames raised his Hunter's Heart, and the hunters fell silent. "There is a discrepancy in Sethrich's interpretation of the law."

"But the law is there," Sethrich hastily ascertained.

"According to one elder, yes," Jilandro agreed. "But the law isn't absolute. It gives guidance not specifics. The hunter or huntress may ask for a certain amount if it does not exceed a certain limit. However, we don't know what that limit is. Do you, Elder Hunter?"

"No, I don't," Sethrich admitted. "But, do I have enough proof to ask for a larquetz concerning blackmail?"

"Are you asking?" Jilandro inquired.

"Do I need to, Bounty Huntress?" Sethrich turned to Tiel. She froze in his stare. "I will accept your request for retraining, to whiten your zahule."

Aven's grip on her shoulders tighten. The room fell quiet as all eyes turned to her. The pit in her stomach dragged her hope away, but she knew the answer.

"I will take..." She gulped as Sethrich smiled with glee. "... my chance with a larquetz." Sethrich's smiled faded. "I know *exactly* what you want," Tiel growled, "and you will never get it. May your soul wander the Arasteit for an ETERNITY!" Tiel roared amid gasps and boos from the hunters. Aven held her back as she reached forward to strike her inner clan leader.

"Tiel Lambrie!" Emiline's shocked disbelief did nothing to erase the anger growing inside. "There is no reason..." her voice disappeared among the hunters' clamor.

"Girl, ya made your case worse," Dawg yelled. Tiel turned to him. "Cool ya'self, act like a clan member, I know what's goin' on." She stared at Dawg for a moment then stood still.

"Then I ask for a larquetz," Sethrich sneered. "If this child's zahule is so spoiled that she thinks she can curse me to the Arasteit, I will rid myself of her. May she be hunted and tormented the rest of her life." Sethrich turned to Jilandro. His glare and twisted grimace dared anyone to oppose him.

"Then at that larquetz, I shall be a witness and bring recorded proof of your real intentions," Jilandro warned. "You have a chance to back out, Elder Hunter."

Tiel gawked and stood still at Jilandro's announcement.

"Never!" Sethrich yelled. "My case is infallible. You know your job, do it! Jilandro, *my initiate!*" Sethrich's spit flew in Jilandro's face.

Radames raised his knife once more, and the hunters quieted. "Honored Winged Court, you need to decide if there is enough evidence for the blackmail charge," he instructed.

Aven held Tiel tight and rubbed her shoulders. She stilled her breathing and waited for the Winged Court's answer.

"We will need to debate this," Jilandro said bowing.

"What?" Sethrich raised his voice. "I brought the evidence myself."

"No one has ever denied the Winged Court their time to deliberate," Radames held Sethrich by the shoulder as the hunters stamped in fury. "Will you be the first?"

"No, of course not," Sethrich asserted.

"Wise choice, Sethrich," Dawg grunted.

Tiel looked at the Winged Court. Twenty-two of her colleagues huddled in a circle, whispering. Sethrich stood, his gaze wandering to each of the members.

"Do you need more time to debate?" Radames asked the Winged Court after a few minutes.

"No," Jilandro announced turning back to the center. "Per the laws we swore to uphold," Jilandro said, running a quivering hand through his hair, "we do not believe this is a time to hold a trial. Oncoming peace enforcer troops and a mob take precedence." Jilandro jerked at Sethrich's scowl. "Plus, per our laws, The Bounty Huntress needs time to secure legal counsel from a master lawyer."

"What?" Sethrich shouted.

"However, we concur that there is enough evidence that supports the relinquishing of her Hunter's Heart. Because of her actions concerning Councilwoman Hegert, there is enough to consider that her zahule may not be as white as she claims." Here the young man took a deep breath and folded his arms. He leaned toward Radames. "She will need to turn it over to you, Master Laisen, as Sethrich is too biased in this matter."

"Well done!" Radames nodded his approval. "Dawg, do you agree?"

"I agree," Dawg stated.

"Bounty Huntress," Radames held out his hand to her. The pit in her stomach turned sour as Tiel inched forward. She pulled her Hunter's Heart out of its skin pocket, grasped the handle, and moved the blade to lie underneath her arm next to her wrist. The handle warmed in her grasp as she fought to control her shaking arm.

"I make bare my Hunter's Heart as the proof of my innocence." The hunters clapped and cheered.

"Is there a counselor you would like us to notify?" Radames asked.

"Dawg, will you take the job?" Tiel asked her trainer.

"Of course, child," Dawg winked at her. The hunters shouted in agreement.

"Nice choice," Radames commented and stretched out his hand to accept the knife. Tiel rotated the knife's blade outward so that the teeth faced her body. Radames reached out to take the knife, but Sethrich was faster. He grabbed Tiel's arm and pulled it forward, straightened her Hunter's Heart so that its tip pointed straight at Jilandro, and forced her to shove the knife into Jilandro's belly.

"How dare you defy your master!" Sethrich yelled at Jilandro, and then he turned to Tiel. "And may all hunters know you for the murderer you are." His voice drowned out the cries of confusion coming from the other hunters. His face disappeared from her view as Aven's fist rammed into Sethrich's nose which caused Tiel to jerk, moving the knife. Jilandro's face relaxed, and his eyes rolled back in his head.

"Ma," Tiel screamed staying still, trying not to worsen Jilandro's injury. Emiline was next to her before Tiel could draw another breath.

"Let go, girl!" she ordered. Tiel released her grip and found blood flowing down her fingers. She glanced to the right. Anised and Aven were binding up Sethrich. Dawg had his Hunter's Heart pointed at Sethrich's neck. Sethrich's hands were clean, but blood flowed from his nose.

"Ouch, that knife bit me," Emiline cried out. "Emery, get me a glove."

Tiel moved aside. Mistress Laisen came up next to her with some soap and a wet cloth. Quartney screamed. Tiel spun around to see Emiline holding the bloody knife out in the open.

"Emiline, quit shaking, I can't take the knife," Emery told her, holding a towel under the knife.

"I'm not shaking. The knife is vibrating and... ouch, that's hot!" Emiline dropped the knife, and it clanged against the stairs. Quartney screamed again as the blade clinked against the stone, chasing her. Tiel came out of her shocked state and dashed after the knife. She tried to grab it, but it slipped through her bloody fingers while burning her hand. Quartney changed tactics and climbed the stairs. The knife followed and slammed into the lower tier. Tiel lunged, grabbed the knife with both hands and held on tight.

"QUIET!" Adrian's roar echoed through the caverns. Everyone stopped talking or moving. "Listen!" he commanded.

In the silence, a distant shrieking laughter sounded beneath the pit. Tiel took in a deep breath as the knife cooled down and stopped vibrating. "Keidera comes. Jonaxx and Kehir will follow. Hunters to their safe places. Now!"

"GO! GO! GO!" Radames screamed, and the pit emptied.

"You've got blood all over that knife," Adrian declared as he bounded towards her.

Tiel moved to where the mistress had left the soap with a basin of water and cloth. She washed her hands and the knife.

"It won't help. Your hands still have Jilandro's scent."

Tiel stopped as Keidera's echoing shriek sounded again.

"You didn't want me to show the knife when we were with Jonaxx." Tiel squinted her eyes. "You knew."

"No, I only knew it was a large knife," Adrian answered. "Keidera would have killed to determine if it was her knife."

"Well, at least you have some of Maestro's qualities," Aven interrupted as he came to their sides. "What do we do?"

"Hide, and not in here." Adrian ran up the stairs. "Someone must thrust that knife into Jonaxx's first wound behind his hood. I just wish we could have done it while the knife was asleep. It would have been much simpler."

"Yes, it would have. But, you prefer to sleep rather than give us information," Tiel challenged over Jonaxx's hissing and Kehir's wailing.

"Now is not the time, Tiel," Aven warned.

All three hid behind shop entryways that bordered the pit.

"It is best for us to stay in the cav..."

"Junior General, get your carcass out here!" Tiel heard ManCane yell from the front caverns. She looked to find the junior general searching the empty caverns. Her eyes were vacant, but Tiel knew the Old Man was in control of her.

"NOW, junior general!" ManCane demanded. Tiel stayed hidden as the junior general departed.

"If we can keep Jonaxx in here," Adrian called out from his hiding place, "it will be much easier to take him."

"Don't hold back the firepower!" Aven called from somewhere in the distance.

"Against Jonaxx?" Adrian's voice faltered.

"Luhitzu, do your job!" Dawg called out from somewhere on the right.

"Ow, ow, ow!" Adrian roared.

"Can you aim fire at me?" Tiel heard Emiline's voice clearly as the tiers moved back.

"No! Ow!" Adrian roared.

"I have thicker books than this to swat you with, cat. You do your job and protect the hunters even if it means hurting Jonaxx!" Tiel winced as she imagined the look of fury on Emiline's face.

"Or you know I will tell Coulliou in my prayers of your treachery." Emery's voice came out of the distance.

"Man, those two aren't scared of anything." Anised's voice made Tiel jump. Keidera's shrieks and swearing rang out into the caverns now. Kehir's moans caused the plants to wither. Jonaxx's hisses punctuated the noises from below.

"Okay, he will not hold back anything," Emiline reported.

"Good! Now get to safety," Dawg commanded.

Tiel looked at Anised and found bloodstains on his hands. She pointed at them.

"Jilandro gave us his robes. He asked those of us who stayed to rub our hands in his garments."

"What? Why?"

Anised furrowed his brows at her as if she should have expected it. "We heard what Adrian said. Now there will be more than one of us with Jilandro's scent. We all stick together, Huntress."

Tiel patted him on the shoulder; her emotions too strong to say thank you.

"I've got Keidera. If anyone hurts Shaine's body, it should be me!" Anised yelled out.

"Stupid boy!" Dawg called out. "Now is not the time for a lover's heroics."

The argument ended as soon as Keidera ran up the stairs. Her green dress, now black, was so torn that it barely covered her body. Her blond hair now held clumps of mud in its matted tresses. Bruises were disappearing as she stood, looking around.

"I smell a bunch of playmates," she cackled. "Who will win our little game? Just give me my Lover's Heart, my dollies, and I'll make your torture sweet."

Kehir moaned from the pit. Tiel expected Jonaxx to burst through. Instead, a squishy plop sounded to her right, and a now familiar stench filled her nostrils. Tiel looked up and saw Jonaxx slither along the wall behind the shops. His head shifted from side to side as his tongue flickered in the air. His body passed over, scratching the roof of the abode she and Anised were hiding in. Bright red blood sparkled, discoloring his scales. He kept flicking his tongue as he stretched his hood. A small, blue, glowing wound showed behind it.

"Keidera," he hissed, "leave this place."

"No," Keidera snickered, "you help me find my Lover's Heart." Jonaxx shook his head. "Yes, Jonaxx, help me find it. You will love what happens next, my friend. You'll be able to forget all your guilt, your pain."

"*Aven, where are you?*" Tiel called out.

"*Just two buildings away. I helped get Emery, Emiline, and the kids to safety.*"

"*Of course,*" Tiel chuckled, "*I'll keep in contact.*"

As Tiel let her rutzix disintegrate, the black ethereal cords materialized before her eyes. The weaker cords appeared first, then the thicker cords took shape. Their borders pulsated with the telepathic waves beating around them. Jonaxx pushed more thought currents across than he had last time Tiel saw him.

"Jonaxx!" Another hiss sounded from the pit. Queen Sendenia rose above the tiers.

The cords relaxed at the sound of Sendenia's voice. For once, Tiel felt love seep out. However, Keidera pushed more emotions through, almost drowning the straggling emotion from Jonaxx.

"Forget her, my pet!" Keidera attempted to persuade Jonaxx.

"Is that the wound?" Tiel questioned Aniseed as she pointed towards a glowing open wound. A moist scab covered it, ready to fall off at any moment.

"Could be."

"*Aven,*" Tiel called out.

"*Is this safe?*" Aven called back.

"*Yes, they are concentrating on each other,*" Tiel answered. "*I'm right behind Jonaxx. I can see the wound.*" Keidera tried to move closer, but Jonaxx snapped at her, hissing with his hood outstretched. She retreated and cackled once again, dancing in a circle.

"*Are you going to use the knife?*"

"*Should I?*" Tiel watched Kehir as he came closer to Keidera, the edges of his ethereal form fluttered in the air. Tiel thought his emotions felt more controlled although she couldn't be sure.

"*It's your call. I don't see what could happen.*"

"*Here it goes. May have to cut a cord or two. Let the shield go.*"

"Done." Tiel drew in her telepathic currents as Aven's shield disappeared. The air pulsated with emotions. The black cords became hazy, but she could still distinguish them.

"I'll get there when I can," Aven called back. Tiel didn't answer.

She motioned to Anised. He nodded his head in understanding. Tiel inched towards Jonaxx, keeping herself hidden behind his hood.

"It can't be this easy," she thought as she inched closer. She caught a movement out of the corner of her eye and looked to see Sendenia shaking her head. *"She's not communicating with me. It's Jonaxx she wants."* Tiel crept closer and raised her hand higher. Jonaxx hissed, and Tiel drew close, took a deep breath, and plunged her Hunter's Heart into the wound. Jonaxx screamed, and his whole body wrenched, throwing Tiel back. The knife collided into the hut next to her.

"Yes, yes. That last plunge will make you all mine," Keidera shrieked. "You can't fight me now."

The ethereal cords snapped tight and wavered. One by one, they merged. The most prominent cord grew thicker, stronger with each infusion.

"No!" Sendenia sprang forward and pummeled Keidera into the wall. Tiel's gaze returned to Jonaxx. His open wound was spraying red blood and yellow ooze with maggots down the sides of his wriggling body. Jonaxx turned to her. "Did you not listen?" he hissed at her. "I was trying to protect you. Where is your stellove?"

She backed up and grabbed the knife.

"Kill them! Kill them all!" Keidera shrieked from somewhere in the caverns. She screamed and went silent. Jonaxx's pupils shrank, the whites of his eyes focused on Tiel.

The last of the cords fused together and surrounded Jonaxx's whole head. No beads of thought issued out of Jonaxx. All emotions transmitted from Keidera.

Tiel backed up and cried out in pain as her shoulder refused to move. She kept her eyes on Jonaxx as he hissed, his head moving from side to side, tongue flickering. Her left hand hit her Hunter's Heart, and she picked it up while wishing she hadn't gotten rid of her rutzix.

"Tiel!" Aven called from the other side of Jonaxx.

Jonaxx opened his maw to swallow her. She jumped to her feet and ran towards the pit. Jonaxx followed. Tiel swerved between the tables, her right arm swinging limply at her side. She watched Jonaxx's shadow cover her and veered to the right. His body crashed down on the floor just behind her. She bounded with the vibrations as she ran.

Jonaxx hissed at her, and she thought she could feel his tongue tickling her back. She sped up as Adrian came into view, racing beside her. He gathered up his muscles and jumped, opening his mouth. Tiel ducked as a tunnel of blue flame burst over her head. She didn't stop running when she heard Jonaxx's high-pitched screams.

Something slammed into her side, and she went down, scratching her arms on the cobblestone pavement. She cried out in pain and rolled over onto her back. She looked into Keidera's empty eyes surrounded by matted hair and a maniacal face with maggot filled wrinkles that lay on top of one another.

"My knife! Give me my knife!" she screamed her mouth opened wide letting in puss filled maggots.

Tiel turned from the scene and wrestled with her, keeping the knife under her back. Anised slammed into Keidera, pushing her off Tiel. A gray, telepathic current hit Keidera in the face and threw her back. Kehir zoomed above Tiel. She peered to her left to find several hunters pointing large laser guns at the now confused Jonaxx, hood outstretched, hissing and lunging. Adrian roared to his right. Sendenia pleaded from behind.

"Get over here, girl!" Dawg pulled her up by her shoulder. She cried out in pain, but Dawg just pushed her into the top tiers of the pit. "Get down, now!" he ordered, and she obeyed.

"Well, what happened?" Dawg demanded. Jonaxx's head was swerving around, his tongue flickering.

"I stuck the knife into Jonaxx," Tiel whispered, "now my arm's out of its socket."

"Quit your whining," Dawg grabbed her shoulder. A large crack sounded in Tiel's ear as pain simultaneously radiated down her arm and up her neck. She cried out, and Jonaxx jerked his head towards her.

An oversized bush flew through the air and hit Jonaxx square on the snout. He hissed in pain, water welling out of his eyes. He surveyed the scene to find out where the plant had come from.

"Hey, you overgrown worm. Come and get me!" Aven's voice thundered over the commotion. Jonaxx slid over, more rotting skin flaking off as he did so. Two hunters did not get out of the way, and their cries ceased as Jonaxx's body glided over them. Lasers bombarded his hide. Jonaxx lunged, and two hunters went flying.

Tiel searched the scene as she moved her shoulder again. It was weak and sore, but she could use it. She found Keidera trying to get over to the pit. A bruised Anised tripped her up as Kehir let out a wail. Keidera crumbled to the ground, and Kehir smothered her with his ethereal body. She struggled and screamed, waving her arms in the air.

"About time your boy showed up, even though he's barefoot," Dawg grunted. "They're giving their lives to give you time. Now figure things out, girl." Dawg commanded.

CHAPTER 25

REDEMPTION

*T*he fireplace was lit, keeping the room warm enough. Jainu paced the room while Diandra sat at the table and sobbed. Aven had told him they would be safe here, and he believed him, even though he jumped whenever a crash sounded. And those crashes often happened, accompanied by shouts and cries from the hunters. He had heard Aven call Jonaxx a worm which meant he was trying to become the target. Jainu cringed on the inside as he thought about it. He liked it when Aven became the hero, but only if he lived afterward.

The door opened, and a tall woman wearing an enforcer general's uniform walked in. She looked at the two and smiled. The bun on her head pulled her face back smoothing some of her wrinkles.

"There you are, Jainu," she cooed as she advanced towards the boy. "The master is confused and worried. Why can't he get a hold of you?"

"He claims he has a cylinder that drowns out the master's voice." The tears glistened off Diandra's now smiling face. "He said it used to be in my ear. But I knew he was lying."

The woman stared at Diandra for a minute. She put her hand forward and caressed Diandra's cheek. "Lady Twibett will be purified for letting such a devoted child go." The woman patted the girl's head. "You stay right here."

Jainu backed up against the wall, suddenly preferring a gigantic rampaging snake to this woman.

"Now, precious," the woman said as her tone grew harsh, "give me the cylinder."

"No!" He ran to the other side of the room. Diandra's face gleamed. Jainu wanted to punch the smile off her face.

"It is time to come to the master," the woman commanded. "Give me the cylinder."

Jainu ran around the other end of the table and behind Diandra. He felt a slight bump as he passed her but ignored it.

"CAN THE BOY HEAR ME YET?" the old man's voice boomed inside Jainu's head. He reached into his empty pants pocket and gulped. Diandra wiggled the cylinder in front of him.

"Well now, that's a good girl..." The junior general stopped speaking as the Drakner's emerged through the door.

"She's with the old man! She's with the old man!" Jainu yelled. Emiline wasted no time landing a powerful punch on the woman's nose with a bandaged hand. The woman staggered back and fell, cracking her face against the wall. She stared and smiled at nothing.

"JAINU, WELCOME BACK TO THE FOLD," the old man laughed. Jainu closed his eyes and covered his ears.

"WELL, WHAT YA GOT, GIRL?" Dawg asked as Jonaxx whipped a huntress with his tail. Her body went flying a few feet and landed with a sickening crunch. She didn't move. Jonaxx's skin had several bruises from lasers that were almost drained due to the Watosh Forest's shield. A whirring sound irritated Tiel, and she looked up to see the gossips' news orbs floating above.

"Shea's light, do you gossips always have to get involved?" Tiel murmured.

"Focus, girl."

"The knife didn't work with me," she mused aloud.

"You said that. Think," Dawg demanded, "or go die with your stellove!" Tiel saw Aven connect another bush with Jonaxx's snout. Jonaxx had stopped screaming. He just hissed and attacked now, using the snake-like lunge of his species.

The fight had scattered tables and chairs across the hunters' commons. Several shop fronts lay strewn around the edges; their wares broke beyond recognition. Pieces of diseased skin dotted the chaos.

Jainu cried out from beyond the wreckage. He held his hands to his ears as he bumped into walls once more, eyes closed. Emery and Emiline followed him. Tiel let her breath hiss between clenched teeth. Diandra appeared smiling, holding something small in one hand, and leading the junior general with the other. The junior general held a cloth to her face to stop the flow of blood from her cheek.

"How can your boy handle that hot crystal he's brandishing?" Dawg asked, his voice full of amusement.

Tiel looked to find Aven holding the wrong end of a crystal lamp. Its hot edges smoked, but Aven made no move to throw it down. Instead, he gripped it harder as he aimed the lamp at Jonaxx. He connected with the snake's snout once again as Jonaxx lunged at him. Jonaxx veered back and slid out of the way.

"His hands are made from a biometal that looks like skin," Tiel answered.

"Just like Kehir's invention with the robots?" Dawg asked.

"Yes, he can handle…" Tiel gazed at her Hunter's Heart. It was cold in her hand.

"Dawg, take this knife," Tiel put the knife in his hand. The handle burned a deep red.

"What?" Dawg cried out as he dropped the knife. Tiel picked it up before it could slide away on its own again.

"It burned your hand," Tiel exclaimed as she examined his skin. It was already blistering.

"What do you think?" he yelled.

"Jonaxx's prophecy is the answer." All orbs focused their one eye on her and flew in closer.

"What?"

"Jonaxx knows the full prophecy of the Mad King," Tiel breathed out while trying to hide her face from the orbs.

"He would," Dawg grunted.

"In it, it talks about a huntress' stellove using the knife with his inward gauntleted hand. Plus, Jaiden's explanation of the knife's programming suggests that it will need to be a male that uses the knife."

"Quit explaining, just do the job!" Dawg demanded. He shook his head and left the pit, running towards Jonaxx.

"Hey, worm, over here!" he yelled. Jonaxx riveted his head in response and concentrated on Dawg. Tiel took the cue. She darted out of the pit towards Aven.

"Stellove," she called. Aven turned towards her. *"You are supposed to heal Jonaxx. Catch."* She threw her Hunter's Heart. Aven dropped the crystal lamp and stepped forward, his arm up to reach the knife. As he put his foot down, he stepped on a piece of Jonaxx's decomposed skin, he slid and lost his balance. Tiel skidded to a stop and darted after the knife as Aven hit the floor.

A black telepathic cord whipped in front of Tiel's vision and hit her in the face. She flew back into an upturned table, the edge striking the middle of her back.

The air whooshed out of her, and an electric jolt traveled her spine. She rolled over onto her side gasping for air.

"My knife!" Keidera shrieked behind her. Tiel breathed in and fought through the pain. She grabbed a broken table leg, jumped up, and swung it around. It connected with Keidera's abdomen, and Keidera tumbled over, passing out on the floor.

Anised limped up behind cradling his arm. His left eye was swollen shut and blood dripped out of his mouth.

"I'll take care of her." Anised offered as Tiel struggled to breathe. "You have only a few bruises," he observed.

"There's still time," she gasped and stumbled. She looked and found that Aven held the knife in his hand. He nodded to her and ran towards Jonaxx.

"The good news is," Anised said leaning on his knees and breathing out as Kehir floated up, "that he's learned how to aim that moaning of his. That's why I am still in one piece."

"Good job in not using your telepathy as a weapon, Huntress," Kehir's voice sounded distant, and his features were less distinct. She thought Kehir smiled.

"I had a good teacher," she said smiling back. "Good job, yourself. Are you okay?" Kehir just sighed and seemed to keep smiling. "I have other work to do." She ran in the direction in which Jainu had disappeared.

"Why are you gossips in here?" she asked the whirring noises behind her.

"We heard the commotion," several metallic voices offered at varying times.

Tiel slowed down as she passed through the front caverns out into the open clearing. Several rows of Peace Enforcers with olive-green, laser cannons lined the road. A horde of gossips and citizens roared behind them as Tiel exited the caverns. She ignored the mob trying to push beyond the cadet enforcers.

On her left, Jainu was flailing his arms. Emery was trying to hold the struggling, screaming boy and the junior general fought to pull him free. Emiline held Diandra close while the girl gripped the small crystal vial that Jainu needed.

Tiel marched forward and slapped Diandra across the face despite the sharp gasps from Emiline.

She freed the vial and held it in front of Diandra's face. "Do not take this again," Tiel ordered. Diandra glared at Tiel.

Cavern rock exploded from the entrance. Emiline lost her grip and Diandra ran away only to stop and scream at the blood-stained, black acodoe above her.

Tiel pushed Emiline to the ground and then covered her head. Different sizes of rock and boulders tumbled around her as she cringed and wriggled away from the near misses. The crowd screamed in horror, and laser cannons screeched. Tiel lifted her head as General ManCane rushed up and waved his arms as the enforcers aimed the cannons' barrels at Jonaxx. They all stopped at different angles, and the general disappeared behind one. The cadets followed him after he yelled something.

Jonaxx slithered around the clearing. Tiel could now see Aven desperately trying to climb up his back with the knife clenched between his teeth, and his feet, saturated with blood and yellow ooze, slipping on Jonaxx's scaled skin. More hunters followed along with Dawg.

Tiel looked around and found Emiline running toward Diandra whose legs had disappeared under a boulder twice her size. Her body wriggled as she tried to extricate herself.

Adrian rushed out of the opening and jumped again, his fire hitting

Jonaxx's already swollen snout. Aven climbed up the serpents back towards its head. Jonaxx dove at Adrian who barely jumped out of the way in time.

"No! No! Be quiet," Jainu's voice brought Tiel back to where Emery and Jainu had been. Emery struggled to get to his feet amid the shower of boulders around him while rubbing his head. Jainu snuck up behind Emery, aiming a rock at the back of the older man's head.

Tiel sent a current to Jainu. His mind was closed to her, but she could hear the old man's voice.

"I'm Emery, and if you don't come to me, I'll kill Aven and Tiel. I'm Emery, come to me," the old man's voice snickered.

"Hey, Old Man, leave Jainu alone!" Tiel yelled inside her head.

"What!?" The old man's stunned voice echoed in Jainu's head.

"I said, leave him alone, you dung heap of a coward!" Tiel pushed her thoughts harder and thought she heard an echo of a roar. The diversion worked. Jainu paused, and Tiel grabbed his arm and placed the biothread container in Jainu's pant pockets. Jainu shook his head as if coming out of deep sleep and dropped the rock as he burst into tears.

"It's okay. It's okay," Tiel held him close, paying attention to the combatants before her. Aven's body was swinging as Jonaxx twisted his coils trying to get to Aven. Anised burst through the opening and dove behind rocks. Blood ran down his face as Keidera came out shrieking and cussing. Kehir followed, scanned the scene, and focused his wails on the line of citizens now lined up behind the tanks. The citizens dropped to the ground. Tiel noticed, for the first time, signs demanding her arrest, death, or even both as they fluttered to the ground. The laser rifles dropped one at a time.

The telepathic cord surrounding Jonaxx's face was secure. It pulsated with thought beads coming from Keidera. Jonaxx screamed in pain once again, and Tiel looked to find Adrian's maw clamped onto the serpent's lower snout with all four claws tearing at Jonaxx's underbelly. Jainu and the Drakners retched from the stench issuing from Jonaxx.

Aven, now close to the serpent's head, swung over the opposite side of Jonaxx and disappeared.

"NO!" Keidera screamed and ran towards Jonaxx. Anised sprang at her, catching her at the waist, and both fell to the ground. She fought back, raking with her nails at his chest. He cried out, seized her hands and rammed his head into hers. Both slumped onto the ground, unconscious.

Jonaxx raised his tail and swatted at the side where Aven had disappeared. Aven groaned. Tiel released Jainu and sprinted towards Jonaxx. A glint caught her eye, and she found Anised's Hunter's Heart on the ground. She picked it up without losing her momentum. Picking an open wound, Tiel plunged the knife into it and twisted it around. Tears streamed down her eyes as Jonaxx's tortured screams were the highest since the battle begun.

A shadow crept over her, and she looked up. As Sendenia watched her mate, great teardrops rained around Tiel.

"I'm so sorry," Tiel whispered, then repeated it aloud.

"I know," Sendenia choked out. "It should be over soon."

Another shadow passed over as a brown acodoe jumped over her, straight at Jonaxx. Its snout collided with Jonaxx's face and the serpents went down.

"Tiberus!" Sendenia hissed. Tiel pulled out the knife. Tiberus rose above Jonaxx and spoke.

"Will you continue with this rampage of murder, brother?" the snake hissed in anger at the black form beneath him. "Will you, or do you relish the memory of how you strangled my beloved to death?"

Jonaxx's eyes opened wide in terror. "No! No!"

"Are you sure? Because that is the last memory I have of her. At least I can know someone will enjoy that memory."

Jonaxx twisted under Tiberus' stare. "No! No!" he asserted vehemently.

"Stay still and let them heal you. The Luhitzu is unconscious. Fight her one last time."

Jonaxx averted his gaze from the smaller acodoe. Then his scream tore through the air as his body convulsed. Tiel looked up to discover Aven hanging onto Jonaxx's hood with one hand. His other hand pushed the knife into the wound. The black cord went limp and frayed where it connected to his head. Beads of pain from Jonaxx eradicated every other thought bead on the cord. Soon the cord flattened, showing the rivers of telepathic power empty of any activity.

Tiel formed her current into a sharp edge and cut the cord. Jonaxx screams intensified, but the cord broke away, and no emotions assailed her. As the cord unraveled, it grew smaller and became opaque, allowing Tiel to see through it like all other soul currents. With one final, swift motion she severed the cord. It whipped toward her and hit her in the chest.

Tiel felt her body lift and sail over Jonaxx's convulsing body. She slammed into the ground on the other side. Her back arched and her legs trembled as pain exploded inside.

"Tiel! Aven!" Jainu's voice screamed from somewhere. Dawg appeared in front of her vision.

"You helped break the cord connecting those two," he commented as he put his hand on her mid-section. Somehow, it seemed to ease the pain, and she relaxed.

"You knew about it?" Tiel asked.

"I'm a wave-seer," Dawg said laughing. "Never thought it was important to tell you."

"That's how you knew I was using my telepathy," Tiel sputtered out.

"Of course, why do you think I took you on as an initiate," Dawg pulled out a piece of cloth, and pressed it down on Tiel's chest. "Pretty cut," he remarked smiling. "Hope that boy of yours accepts scars as war trophies."

"Where is Aven?" The pain diminished to just a sting. She scanned the clearing and saw Aven limping towards her. Beyond him, Tiberus retreated to the forest's edge.

"Aven, is Tiel okay?" Jainu screamed from across Jonaxx.

"She's fine, just got herself a pretty war trophy," Aven yelled back and kneeled in front of Tiel. Dawg backed away and let Aven apply pressure to her chest.

"How deep?" she inquired.

"Not too deep," he replied. Dawg reappeared with Mistress Laisen who carried a first aid kit. They bandaged her up after which she got up and examined her chest. A white bandage crossed her chest from her lower right abdomen to her upper left shoulder.

"Your lips are swollen," she said as she looked up into Aven's face.

"I may have bio-metal in my hands, but not my lips." Aven's tears streamed down his face. "Do you think Emiline can take care of the blisters?"

"She owes me first after her brutal attack with those books," Adrian moved his muzzle over his body. Parts of fur lay matted with slime and blood. "Maybe I'll survive this experience."

Anised groaned from somewhere beyond Jonaxx. The party moved towards him only to meet Keidera. Her arm was facing the wrong direction, and bruises covered her body from head to foot. She limped towards them, focusing on the trio out of her partially opened eye.

"Where's my Lover's Heart?" She choked out.

Aven raised his hand which held the melted handle of the crystal knife.

"I will haunt and torture you as long as..."

The shrill cry of a predatory bird sounded with the rhythmic beating of huge wings. A falcon landed on a boulder beside the cavern entrance. Its dark-brown feathers radiated a tinge of red-gold as the bird moved in Shea's light. It shifted its gaze to focus its right eye on the group.

"Fendir, what are you doing here?" Adrian asked the bird.

"Jaiden agrees that you need help. So, I am here. There is another that has taken my place." The falcon's voice was that of a young male.

"Where's my..."

"Adrian, she has fallen," the falcon whispered.

Adrian moaned and then moved toward Keidera. "Let's get this done."

"No! I will not go back!" Keidera screamed.

"You cannot go back. Your cell is destroyed," Adrian answered her. Tiel felt Aven pull her back. She searched the area and found Jainu now snuggled next to Emery. Emiline cradled Diandra in her arms. Dawg and the Laisens were bandaging up fallen hunters, each turning every so often to watch the Luhitzu. The gossips' eyes whirred around the scene.

"Now was your time to make amends. You chose not to." The falcon's voice had a tinge of anger.

"You'll have to catch me."

"Kehir faced his sister. He opened his mouth and let out a resonating mournful howl. She crumbled at his feet. Kehir's wail rose in pitch as his form disappeared, then reappeared, with his evaporating features full of pain. Keidera screamed and lay prone on the ground.

"How long have you been able to do that?" she cried out.

"It does not matter. It just matters that it worked." He answered, his form growing thin, almost melting into the air, then reappearing.

"So, you will make it to the Arasteit before me," Keidera cackled. "That is what you get for your heroics, DAMNATION!" She screeched the last word as she tried to stand."

"The falcon opened his curved beak and took in a deep breath. A tunnel of green mist shot from his mouth and encircled Keidera.

"NO! I'll change, I'll change. NO! Not me, not me!" Keidera's wails turned to inconsolable weeping as she banged at the wall of ice forming around her. After a few moments, she stood trapped inside with her face frozen in terror and her fists suspended in an attempt at a futile escape. The falcon kept the whirlwind of ice going until Keidera disappeared.

"That should be enough," he proclaimed after a few recovering breaths.

"My turn," Adrian declared with a sense of satisfaction ringing in his tone. He took a deep breath and his cone of blue fire encircled the large block of ice. Mist crept out and trailed along the ground. It twisted away from all life forms and soon disappeared into the air.

Tiel saw Anised watch as Keidera's cell grew smaller. Streams of mist rolled and disappeared into the air until the perfect, fully dressed, unbroken body of Shaine rested peacefully with a smile on her lips.

"Can I have her body to bury?" Anised cried out.

Adrian just laughed and walked forward. He nudged her shoulder with his paw and Shaine took in a deep breath. Her lungs inflated with air, and her eyes fluttered open. She looked around and smiled.

"Anised?" She sat up and spied her stellove. His bruised, bloodied, and broken body contrasted the look of utter joy that beamed from his face. "Anised!" she cried out and ran to him then kissing him as the hunter broke down into tears.

"Where is Keidera?" Tiel broke the silence.

"Where I shall go," Kehir answered, his voice barely an audible whisper as the surrounding miasma thinned then coalesced once again. His face twisted in agony with each change. "The Arasteit, or have I earned the privilege to travel The Abyss?" He implored, his figure slumped to the ground. A glint of hope dared to manifest in his features.

Adrian and Fendir just smiled and shook their heads.

"But why?" Kehir asked.

"Because you have earned a better redemption," Jonaxx's voice sounded as his eyes opened. He coiled his body, and Sendenia slithered forward, Jonaxx continued, "It is Coulliou's will, which you have promised to obey for the past millennium. Do you wish to keep your promise?"

The black acodoe rose and shook his body. A smile broke through his swollen snout. "My mind is free," he whispered reverently.

"I am sorry about the wounds," Adrian said.

"But they will heal now, old friend," Jonaxx laughed.

"Am I to stay in this form?" Tiel could swear fear dominated Kehir's voice as his ethereal body thinned even more.

"Look!" Jonaxx pointed his snout to the forest beyond Tiberus. A small whirlwind of dust and dirt emerged. Its winds whipped around, stinging Tiel's skin and pushing her hair into her face which she held back with her hand.

The whirlwind enveloped Kehir and whined for a few minutes until it dissipated. The mortal form of a young, robust, golden-haired youth in a white shirt, green pants, and a long green coat stood before them. Kehir fell to his knees and examined his body.

"I can feel, eat, do anything I desire," he cried out among bursts of laughter.

"Just make sure your desires conform to Coulliou's wishes from now on," Sendenia whispered.

"Of course, of course," Kehir laughed using his hands to assess his new body.

"And what about you, love?" Sendenia brought her attention to Jonaxx.

"I can think for myself," he cried. "My mind is free!" he hissed in glee. He twisted his coils into various positions all the while letting out a booming laugh. Then he stopped. "Thank you, little brother. I am..." He never finished his sentence. Tiberus just lowered his head and disappeared into the forest.

"You figured out the knife puzzle." Emery winced as he rose to his feet.

"Yes. I had to admit, in front of the gossips' eyes, that the prophecy of the Mad King was real." Tiel hid her face from the orbs that now surrounded her.

"Is that a bad thing?" Jonaxx questioned.

"To do it in private, no," Tiel clarified her answer. "But you had to come in, tearing up the caves, which interested the news gossips. They sent their orbs at the most inopportune time. When I had to admit out loud that a prophecy needed to be fulfilled and how to fulfill that same prophecy." Jonaxx bent down near Tiel.

"I blame you for my predicament. You know how difficult my travels will be on Shea's paths trying to stay away from the gossips now? My apparent change of heart will be all over Ecalardia for the next few weeks."

"Humm," Jonaxx uttered, smiling in return. "I am sorry for your troubles. Perhaps we have both grown from these past few days."

"Perhaps," Tiel reluctantly agreed.

"If the gossips of Ecalardia or the voices in your head become too daunting for such a great huntress as yourself," Jonaxx said winking his eye at her, "the Watosh Forest will always be a friend and a shield."

Jonaxx turned and his eyes softened as he gazed at Sendenia. Tiel saw a wave of deep admiration and love for his mate rush through the clearing. Then the former mad king followed his queen into the shelter of the Watosh Forest.

The diminishing shouts of the crowd produced no real threats and Tiel moved with Aven towards the caverns. Emery approached Emiline who cuddled the children as she tightened the bandage on her hand. Emery stopped and then looked at Tiel, his face gray and tears welling up in his eyes.

"Aven stop, please," Tiel pleaded. "Is there more antidote in the knife's handle?" She grabbed his hand with the knife. A few drops fell to the ground and Tiel pushed Aven's hand up to keep any leftover liquid inside.

"I don't know," he answered. "I focused on healing Jonaxx and pushed the release as long as I could."

"The knife bit Emiline," Tiel whispered and then an all too familiar click sounded in her mind.

"I NEED TO CONSIDER THESE LAST FEW MOMENTS, TIEL" With the old man's voice a searing pain pulsated through Tiel's head causing her to shriek in agony. "YOU ARE ONE OF MY MOST DEAR LOST LOVES. I THOUGHT I WOULD NEVER FIND YOU. BUT NOW, I EMBRACE YOUR CARD ONCE AGAIN."

His echo bounced around inside distorting her vision as the ground rushed forward to meet her. Someone called her name, and she felt a pair of arms wrap around her waist.

"OH YES, THE MIGRAINE. SORRY ABOUT THAT, IT'S NORMAL WHEN I HOLD A LOST LOVE'S CARD SO TIGHT. A HABIT OF MINE THAT COMES FROM THE JOY OF FINDING ONE SO PRECIOUS." The agony intensified at his words. Tiel grabbed the nearest thing next to her, which was Aven's shirt collar. She gulped and wavered."

"Tiel?" He whispered, his eyebrows furrowed in concern."

"He's talking to me," she croaked out. "The old man says he's found my card."

"I am not that old," the old man chuckled. "And, I am not heartless. Lovers like you need to say goodbye. I will allow that."

Tiel saw Radames come to their side. "Who's the old man?" He asked, looking between the two. Aven just gave the knife handle to Radames and pointed to Emiline. Through the haze, Tiel could see Emery rush over and carefully take the melted handle. The old man's words drowned Adrian's sudden roar full of despair.

"You don't need to tell him. But it will be your decision. Soon you will come willingly, but it will be slow. So, I will give you some time to say goodbye. If you don't come willingly, I will force you! I know how to get my cards to do what I want. Soon you will obey my commands, without even questioning me.

"Goodbye, until I talk to you again, my precious lost love. I'll come back soon, gently. There will be no more buzz, I promise. I must get you used to me, slowly. It shall be pleasant from here on out. I'll bring you home, where you belong."

EPILOGUE

TYNE'S PATH

The ground shook beneath Tyne Baritone's feet. He had tried three or four times, but he had never gotten this far. His brother, the master, had always stopped him. His brother had never tortured the information out of him though. He hadn't even suspected a thing. Now, it seemed their plan finally worked. Perhaps the news got out he was dead. It didn't matter, the master…

He stopped and searched the forest beneath the ledge he stood on. "He's no master," he declared. His tone took on a menacing feature. The ground shook again, bringing his attention back to his task. He would have to leave all negative feelings behind. The memory of his brother didn't inspire positive feelings.

He concentrated on the beauty surrounding him. The air was sweet and clean. The colors were vibrant and real. Watosh trees stood strong and majestic. The sound of rushing falls in the distance rang out clear musical chords. The yip of a dog, the call of the bird, even the buzz of the fly passing by his ear sounded magical. He breathed in and let the thump-thump of Ecalardia's heartbeat tickle his feet. There were no voices in his head but his own. The ground shaking subsided.

Shea shone brightly in the sky as Tyne scanned the interior of the cave, the entrance to the blessed Abyss. The highway across the Arasteit. He relished the fact he had finally made it to Ecalardia's heart. Something he had never thought to hope for again.

He searched the forest beyond the cave and saw no sign of anyone. The forest animals still made all of their noises. Something scampered across the clearing. He moved forward and turned back again. He breathed, his own heart threatening to jump out of his chest. Still, he saw no sign of anyone.

He pulled a large velvet black sack out from underneath his blue cloak that covered his tattered prison suit. Ecalardia's heartbeat drummed steadily through the cave as he rounded the corner. His trembling, bandaged hands fought with the knots, but he finally opened it. He put the sack down precisely at the spot he wanted and lifted the eight-sided crystal orb he had been carrying. Its rainbow prisms decorated many walls inside the cave. The atmosphere now beat with the heartbeat he had wanted to hear for many octaves.

Taking one last look, he moved forward. The gray stone of the surrounding cave sparkled from the minerals inside. Soon, even those lights faded... or rather, gave way to a stronger prism within. Ecalardia's heartbeat drummed steadily.

He heard his breathing become louder and gulped in some air. His hands sweated, and he had to wipe off the crystal orb with his cloak to keep it from dropping. He progressed farther. His heartbeat drummed in time to Ecalardia's steady rhythm as the prism before him intensified.

Finally, Tyne Baritone reached the glowing star before him. Formed out of Ecalardia's blood when Cong had sliced his way through three thousand octaves ago, its edges burned with phosphorescent light. Its arms merged into the sides of the cave, into the veins that flowed through the living planet except for the shattered tail. Its emptiness testified of the recent prison escape.

Jagged edges of dull fluid caked the inside and the broken sides of the tail. A dried-up pool of the same liquid covered the floor beneath. Mists of blue, red, orange, yellow, indigo, purple, even a milky white swirled in separate arms. But the mist in the eight-sided center was an inky jet-black.

Tyne brought up his orb, its shape fit the center perfectly. Ecalardia's heartbeat drummed steadily.

"Time for a change of guards," Tyne whispered, then cringed at the sound of his voice in this hallowed place. He felt around the middle of the star and located the exact center where it was flat. He forced his trembling hand to pull out a rectangular slat on the edge of the orb he was holding. Little by little, he drew the orb towards the center. Ecalardia's heartbeat drummed steadily.

Several times he located the center again until he had finally brought the orb's open end to the spot he wanted. As soon as the orb touched the star, a sucking noise sounded. Clear liquid flowed around the edge, sealing it. The black smoke drained into the sphere. Tyne kept a secure grip on the orb, fearing it would drop, releasing the prisoner inside. All the while Ecalardia's heartbeat drummed steadily.

To his amazement, the orb didn't release, and the smoke kept pouring in. The center of the star filled with liquid, causing tears to emerge from Tyne's eyes. Ecalardia's heartbeat quickened, Tyne's own heart followed. "Sorry, my dear Ecalardia. I didn't mean to make you bleed once more."

When it was done, the orb released, and the center of the star glowed with pure white light. Tyne giggled looking at the blackened interior of the sphere.

"We succeeded," he gloated as he inserted the door. "We succeeded." His fingers fumbled, and the door fell, clattering against the stone floor. Ecalardia's heartbeat drummed faster. "No, no, no," he cried and dropped to the ground. He placed the orb next to him, and he ran his fingers over the cold, uneven floor. The heartbeat raced, his own heart following causing a slight pain in his chest. A wisp of smoke trailed out of the orb's opened end, and Tyne hurried to find the door, moving his fingers along each ridge of the floor. The heartbeat raced faster, Tyne's breathing scratched his throat.

Another wisp escaped, and something jabbed his finger. He stopped, found the object, and breathed out a sigh of relief. Ecalardia's heartbeat slowed, the pain in Tyne's chest subsided as his heartbeat relaxed. A third wisp of smoke escaped and he quickly, but carefully, capped the orb. He used his finger to gather some liquid and rubbed it on the door. The liquid sealed the opening and the black smoke curled inside its new prison. He breathed another sigh of relief and stood, picked up the sphere, and exited the cave without looking back. Ecalardia's heartbeat drummed steadily once more.

The center star lighted his way until Shea's light once again guided his feet. He examined the orb once more before reclaiming the bag from where he placed it. He dropped the orb into the bag and used several tight knots to secure it.

Stepping outside helped his heartbeat regain its natural rhythm with only a slight tinge of discomfort. He noticed that Shea was close to beginning her third path. He giggled and skipped until he almost fell off the ledge. Deciding it was safer on the forest floor, he ran down the rock stairs carved into the ridge at his left, fits of giggles erupting every so often, until he reached the bottom where he burst into a full roar of laughter.

"We did it Jonaxx and Adrian! We succeeded. We finally succeeded!" he bellowed to the surrounding forest, raising the bag above his head. The forest grew quiet, and a small rat died at his feet. Tyne kept up his jubilant chorus never noticing the rat or a black wisp floating down the stone stairs, breezes causing it to separate. It coalesced back into a wispy shape after only a few moments, trying to reach for Tyne with a flimsy tentacle. The tentacle flung back and touched a bird in mid-flight, causing it to fall dead at the end of the stairs. Oblivious, Tyne laughed and giggled as he disappeared into the Watosh.

ACKNOWLEDGMENTS

Thank you to all who have helped me with their love and support.

Thank you to my husband Joe for believing in me, and being there no matter what happened.

Thank you to my mother for showing me how to never give up on a dream.

Thank you to my father for showing determination and how to grow to become the best he can be.

Thank you to my daughter Angel for risking her safety by taking chapters to her friends at school to read.

Thank you to my brother Alex for help with some of my fight scenes.

Thank you to my sister Raquel for editing my book at least three times and for always being the voice telling me to finish the book.

Thank you to my sister Valerie for one edit and taking such a beautiful photograph.

Thank you to my Nephew Emmanuel for being a test reader.

Thank you to my friend Katrina who suggested the glossary.

Thank you to you, the reader, for reading this book. I hope you found this world enjoyable.

ABOUT THE AUTHOR

Taunia Neilson is an emerging author in fantasy and science fiction. This is her first book and she is vigorously working on the next installment in this series and the first book in another series. Taunia loves anything that takes her to the mountains. She also loves to read ancient mythology, mysteries, fantasy, science fiction and clean romance novels. She is a wife, mother, and grandmother and presently lives in the Wasatch Mountain Region in Utah with her husband and youngest daughter.

I invite you to visit my website authortaunianeilson.com
to find news and updates about my upcoming novels.

Thank you for reading this book. I hope you enjoyed reading about the world of Ecalardia. Please remember to leave a review with your online retailer and/or Goodreads. Thank you.

May you find joy and laughter on the paths you travel during life.

Taunia

Lightning Source UK Ltd.
Milton Keynes UK
UKHW010633171218
334136UK00011B/511/P